UNICORN RAMPANT

John rode down into the haugh and on to the winding path which followed the bends of the river. The young woman heard his horse's hooves and turned to wait, smiling. And her smile was a joy.

'Janet!' he said.

'John! Or did I hear aright, back there? Should it now be Sir John?'

'Not to you.' He dismounted and stood before her, looking doubtful.

'What . . . how did it come about? This knighting? You must tell me.' She sounded eager to know.

'It was nothing. Or my part in it was. Little worth the telling. It was all a foolish mistake. At Edinburgh. They had arrested the King, and . . .'

'Arrested? The King! Surely not—that cannot be so? You cozen me . . .!'

'It is true. They did not know it was the King. A mistake, as I say. I was able to put the matter to rights. Then later I was able to do him some other small service. And when he was knighting Provost Nisbet he called me to him and knighted me also. That is all.'

She stared at him. 'I cannot believe that it was all so simple as that, John.' She had a warm, throaty voice which affected him not a little. 'You are not telling me the half of it! What really did you do?'

Unicorn Rampant

Nigel Tranter

CORONET BOOKS
Hodder and Stoughton

Copyright © 1984 by Nigel Tranter

First published in Great Britain in 1984
by Hodder and Stoughton Limited

Coronet edition 1986

British Library C.I.P.

Tranter, Nigel
   Unicorn rampant.
   I. Title
   823'.912[F]   PR6070.R34

   ISBN 0-340-38635-5

Printed and bound in Great Britain for
Hodder and Stoughton Paperbacks, a
division of Hodder and Stoughton Ltd.,
Mill Road, Dunton Green, Sevenoaks,
Kent (Editorial Office: 47 Bedford
Square, London, WC1 3DP) by
Richard Clay (The Chaucer Press) Ltd.,
Bungay, Suffolk

Principal Characters

JOHN STEWART OF METHVEN: Illegitimate son of Ludovick, Duke of Lennox, and Mary Gray.

MARY GRAY: Mother of above. Illegitimate daughter of the late Master of Gray.

MARY, COUNTESS OF MAR: Sister of the Duke of Lennox and wife of John, Earl of Mar, Lord High Treasurer of Scotland.

KING JAMES THE SIXTH AND FIRST

GEORGE VILLIERS, EARL OF BUCKINGHAM: Current favourite of James, who called him Steenie.

THOMAS HAMILTON, LORD BINNING AND BYRES: Secretary of State, Lord Advocate and Lord President of Session.

LUDOVICK STEWART, DUKE OF LENNOX: Lord High Admiral of Scotland and the King's cousin.

SIR GIDEON MURRAY OF ELIBANK: Treasurer-Depute of Scotland.

ALEXANDER SETON, LORD FYVIE: Chancellor of Scotland. Later Earl of Dunfermline.

JAMES DRUMMOND, LORD MADDERTY: Strathearn landowner.

JANET DRUMMOND: Daughter of above.

QUEEN ANNE OF DENMARK: Consort of King James.

MARGARET HAMILTON: Extra Maid-in-Waiting to the Queen.

CHARLES, PRINCE OF WALES: Later King Charles the First.

SIR WILLIAM ALEXANDER OF MENSTRIE: Master of Requests. Later Earl of Stirling.

ELIAS WOOLCOMBE: London merchant.

WILL COCKAYNE: Master of Merchant Venturers of London. Sheriff of the city and later Lord Mayor.

WILLIAM MIDDLEMAS: Deputy-Keeper of Dumbarton Castle.

WILLIAM VANDERVYK: Dutch papermaker.

ALEXANDER GRAHAM: Friend of John Stewart.
ROBERT NAPIER OF KILMAHEW: Sheriff-Depute of Dunbarton-
    shire.
JAMES PRIMROSE: Secretary to the Scots Privy Council.
JOHN OF THE DALE: A tinker.
THE LORD ERSKINE: Deputy-Keeper of Stirling Castle. Heir
    to Earl of Mar.
SIR FRANCIS BACON: Lawyer, Lord Chancellor of England,
    later Viscount St Albans.

PART ONE

1

There were crowds of people puffing and panting up that grassy hill, many seeming already to be in various stages of exhaustion. John Stewart had not realised that so many would be smitten with the same idea as himself, although perhaps he ought to have thought of it. However, he did not fear that there would be any lack of room at the top, for most of these looked as though they would never reach there, feeble townsfolk unused to employing the muscles God had given them, unlike a country-bred stalwart in his twenty-fourth year such as John Stewart of Methven. Not that he was actually making for the top of the hill himself—no point in that when the eastern shoulder above Duddingston village and loch would give the better view in the required direction.

So, at the level of the high tarn of Dunsappie, cradled darkly in a fold of the hill, he swung away from most of the crowd, right-handed, to contour along a subsidiary ridge, steep on the south, whin-grown and blazing yellow in the May sunshine.

Here there were only two or three others and no gasping chatter, so that he could hear the cuckoos calling from the Prestonfield woodland far below.

He did not have to go so far as the shoulder before he saw all that he had come for. Before him, eastwards by south, the coastal plain was a sight to behold, a rippling carpet of colour and glitter, from no more than a mile or so off to almost as far as he could see, spreading over the fair Lothian countryside like a vast army. The young man had looked for a fine and stately cavalcade; what he saw was a mighty sprawling host of thousands. Small wonder that the King was late.

The question was where *was* the King in all that multi-tude—or rather, where was his father, for it was not so much James as Ludovick Stewart whom John had come looking for. But his father would be with the King, almost certainly. Would they be at the front of this vast concourse, or in the midst? It could make a difference of almost hours as to when they would reach the gates of Edinburgh.

He waited, staring, trying to distinguish details at a distance, a good-looking young man, not handsome but with pleasant open features, regular if on the blunt side, a little above medium height with wide shoulders tapering to slender, muscular hips and long legs, plainly dressed but in good quality clothing; not one who would be apt to stand out in a crowd but who might attract a second and third glance from the discerning. His own glances still failed to distinguish where the King and his close entourage might ride in all that farflung array. Not being a warlike host there were no banners to identify the leadership. Eventually, still no wiser, he decided that the chances were that James would be at or near the front, and if so it was time that he himself got back to the city streets and his mother, if they were to gain a good viewpoint to watch the forthcoming proceedings.

So he all but ran back whence he had come and down the steep hill below the red-stone crags, to where the grass gave way to the first buildings—mainly byres, stables and pigstyes—reaching out towards Arthur's Seat from the tall tenement wynds on the south side of the Cowgate.

Now he was into more crowds, thronging the fairly narrow street, all heading westwards, like himself, and much slowing him down. Naturally all sought the middle of the cobblestoned thoroughfare, the crown of the causeway as it was called—for the sides were no more than wide gutters abrim with filth and sewage, to be avoided at all costs. So there was much jostling and pushing, much shouting and reviling, although in the main the mood was good-natured, as befitted the atmosphere of holiday. Occasionally, however, there was cursing and fist shaking as some belated great one rode up behind mounted grooms or men-at-arms with cracking whips or even the flats of swords, forcing a way through, and now and again a lumbering coach, heraldically painted, with bawling outriders and horn-blowing postillions—and then all on foot were forced into

10

the swills and stinks of the kennels in furious profanity, with even some of the ordure itself scooped up and hurled at the gleaming paintwork.

John Stewart, being nimbler and fitter than most, managed to avoid any major contact with the excrement, and pushed ahead with fair success. At what was still called the French Ambassador's House, the lodging of the present Secretary of State—known to his master and most others as Tam o' the Cowgate, Sir Thomas Hamilton—John turned off up another steep and narrow lane, little more than a stairway, called Libberton's Wynd, which brought him out on to the main spine of that extraordinary climbing city, Scotland's capital, the High Street and Canongate conjoined. Here, quite close to the new Tolbooth, were the lodgings which he and his mother rented for the occasion in the house of a decayed gentlewoman, widow of a former Perthshire laird of their acquaintance.

Hurrying upstairs he found Mary Gray at the window of their room, looking down on the teeming excitement of the High Street below.

"They come," he announced, a little breathlessly. "A great legion of them—thousands. Spreading over the land. I have never seen such a host."

"Then His Grace will be in an ill mood. He does not like large numbers in his tail—since they have to be fed and that costs siller!"

The woman turned to smile at him—and she was a joy to behold. Now in her forty-first year, she retained the figure and stance of a girl. Darkly lovely, she was of slender build, with delicate features and great lustrous eyes and an expression which seemed to combine quiet gravity with ready humour. It seemed ridiculous that she should be the mother of the well-built young man before her. Like him she was simply but well dressed and carried herself with grace and an air of unassumed assurance. John Stewart was very proud of his mother, even though her name was not his.

"We had better hurry," he said, "or we shall not be in time to get a good position with all these going."

"How near were they? The King and his close company?"

11

"I could not tell, there were so many. But the foremost were across the Figgate Burn, I could see."

"Then we have plenty of time. James never hurries, save when hunting. And they have quite some distance to ride around the city walls to reach the West Port."

"The *West* Port? But they come from the east."

"Yes. But the Chancellor and the Secretary know their sovereign-lord, Johnnie. After much travelling, James would be apt to go straight to his palace of Holyroodhouse, to eat and drink and sleep, and never enter the city at all. And so would miss all their fine welcome and speeches—which the good city fathers love and their liege loathes. So the King is to be met by Chancellor Seton and Secretary Tam and cunningly led round the south walls, to see the site where his good friend, and ours, Geordie Heriot's fine new hospital is to be built—and so, in at the West Port. Thus he has all the town to pass through before he can win back to Holyroodhouse. Endless opportunities for speeches and spectacles and mummery. Is not that clever? I am told that Tam o' the Cowgate himself devised it all—Geordie Heriot was his cousin, of course. So there is no hurry at all, at all."

Nevertheless John Stewart was impatient, and Mary Gray allowed herself to be conducted downstairs and out into the smelly street to join the crowd; she laughing, but not unkindly, at all the excitement. That woman had had long and comprehensive experience of such occasions.

They pushed and inserted their way up the High Street, past the High Kirk of St Giles, to the entrance of the Lawnmarket, having to squeeze under two decorative arches of scaffolding and painted canvas on the way. On the arches cupids and angels perched precariously, the street and close-mouths were strewn with flowers and evergreens, largely becoming sadly trampled, and tapestries and hangings draped from many of the tenement windows. Down the West Bow, they and the crowd turned and surged, and at the foot there was another and more elaborate arch over-sailing a stage, this all hung with cloth-of-gold which flapped and fluttered in the breeze, for Edinburgh is ever a windy city. The wide space of the Grassmarket beyond under the towering cliffs of the castle-rock, had been cleared of its usual clutter of booths and stalls and was now crammed with the horses and coaches, the grooms and retainers, of the rich and noble. The West Port of the city wall opened at the far end of this Grassmarket.

The approach to the great gateway was by a narrow canyon of a street beneath more high tenements, and this was so choked with humanity that there was no passage for even the most agile or aggressive. Mary Gray declared that this was of no matter, that there was no need to go further anyway, that they would see all they would want to see in the Grassmarket itself; but the young man was eager to be where the King, and therefore his father, would first halt and be welcomed. He had not seen Ludovick Stewart for almost two years and he was very much his father's son, as well as his mother's.

However, the problem was solved for them by the noisy arrival of a handsome canopied double-chair, painted black-and-white and blue-and-white, in the Erskine of Mar colours, and carried by four liveried chairmen with a body-guard of stave-wielding servitors who chanted: "Way for the Countess of Mar! Way for the Countess!" and bored through the crowds like a bull at a gate. Held up for only moments at the choked throat of the street, it was long enough for the sole occupant of the chair, peering out, to recognise Mary Gray and to halt the equipage by slapping on the front panel.

"Mary! Mary Gray, my dear—and John. I did not know that you were in town," she called. "Are you for this reception? Vicky comes?"

"Yes, praise God! He is back from France."

"We can get no further, Countess," John declared.

"Then come with me. Mary—in beside me here. There is room. John—walk between the shafts, behind. You will do very well there."

This was another Mary and another royalish Stewart at that, the Lady Mary Stewart, a daughter of the late Esmé, Duke of Lennox, first cousin of the King, and sister of the present Duke. She and Mary Gray were old friends.

"Where are you lodging, Mary?" she asked. "You should be biding with me in the Cowgate."

"We are at old Lady Tippermuir's, near the Tolbooth. She can always do with a merk or two of lodging-siller . . ."

So they were carried in fits and starts up that constricted gully of a street, through the close-peering faces and thronging bodies—but here there were fewer catcalls and shaken fists, for these were mainly gentlefolk and suitably impressed by the Countess of Mar's position. Getting through the West Port gateway itself taxed even the Mar retainers; but beyond it was blessed relief, for here, just outside the city wall, was a wide open space known as the Barras, renowned as the scene of many trials of chivalry between noble jousters, and in more humdrum necessity as a place for the country folk to wait, with their carts and garrons, bringing produce to sell on market-days, until the city gates were opened. In this wide arena today the aristocracy of Scotland and the luminaries of her capital city strolled and chattered around a great erection of planks and poles, flags and bunting, comprising a platform with steps up, backed by rising tiers of benches for the more important spectators.

To this the Countess directed her chairmen and, secure in her cousinship to the monarch as well as her husband's appointment as Keeper of Stirling Castle, the greatest fortress of the kingdom, she quite courteously ordered lofty-looking folk already seated on the lowermost but most prestigious bench to move aside for her and her companions. John was embarrassed by this unsought-for privilege and prominence; they would go and stand in some less kenspeckle place he said. But his mother, after brief comment that this was not necessary, accepted it all as quite appropriate, with her usual calm assurance, and sat down beside her friend. John could not do otherwise.

Two of the city officers came along and looked at them doubtfully, but the two ladies ignored them and they went away.

Much was going on all around, last minute adjustments, re-arrangings, even some hammering, where a purple canopy was being erected in the centre of the stage, on poles. A succession of notables came up to pay their respects to the Countess, not all of whom knew Mary Gray. It was

14

noteworthy, however, that most of those who did paid her almost as much respect as they did to the Lady Mar.

Presently a horseman came cantering from the south, shouting that His Grace was near, no further than the High Riggs area. He would be here in a few minutes, just.

Great was the excitement. The panoply of purple velvet was hastily secured against the breeze—this presumably had been kept under cover hitherto in case it rained. The city magistrates and councillors, led by the Provost, came bustling up on to the platform, to be formed up in a row by the city officers. The Lord Lyon King of Arms and his heralds placed themselves to one side, a colourful crew, and a group of Privy Councillors and Lords of Session took stance opposite. Musicians were beckoned forward to a lower, subsidiary platform nearby, and started to tune up.

The long-awaited moment arrived—fourteen years awaited, in fact, for this was 1617—and Scotland's curious absentee monarch came into view round the burgh wall, riding at a brisk trot before a multi-hued company of gentlemen which stretched away out of sight. All who sat rose to their feet, and after a false start and some uncertainty the musicians struck up with the rousing strains of Bruce's battle-hymn before Bannockburn, generally called "Hey Tutti Taitie".

To this stirring accompaniment the royal cavalcade clattered up. James Stewart, as ever, rode like a sack of corn—which was strange considering that he was one of the most enthusiastic horsemen and huntsmen in his two kingdoms. Overdressed but with most of his too-decorative clothing neither quite properly fastened together nor very clean, he wore one of his notably high-crowned hats with jewelled clasp and feather—odd choice for riding—tipped forward over his nose. As far as could be seen beneath it, he appeared to be scowling.

But neither John nor his mother were really considering their liege-lord and his little eccentricities, concentrating their gaze instead on a stocky, plain-faced man, superbly mounted but much less extravagantly dressed than was the King, who rode immediately to the right, although not nearly so close as the exquisite youth on the other side, clad in the height of London fashion, whose mount almost rubbed against that of the monarch. Behind this trio rode a solid phalanx of impressive-looking gentlemen, and following on came the endless stream of riders, led by a troop of horsed guards in the royal colours, all gleaming armour and nodding plumes.

King James and his two companions trotted up to the dais-platform and, timed to synchronise with this, a file of one hundred of the Edinburgh Town Guard marched round from either side of the stage area, all uniformed in unlikely white satin, no less, with beribboned halberds over shoulders, to form up around the monarch—who eyed them somewhat askance, especially the halberds. James did not like weapons of any sort. Thereafter a pair of scantily dressed ladies emerged from behind the solid black-velvet-clad rank of magistrates and councillors of the city, tugging between them what seemed at first sight to be a baby in long clothes but which thankfully proved to be only a life-sized doll. Uttering shrill cries, partially lost in the martial music, the ladies pulled and shook fists at each other until a gorgeously robed figure wearing a crown and carrying both a sword and a sceptre, appeared, apparently to remonstrate with the furious females, although what he said could not be heard for Bruce's battle-hymn. However, his purpose was made sufficiently clear when he raised his sword above the baby, conveniently stretched out between the claimants, obviously to cut it in half, whereupon one of the disputants let go of the doll, wringing her hands and presumably howling, whilst the other clutched it, only to have it snatched from her by the man with the sword, who gave it to the other, who presented it to her bared breast as though to give suck. The crowned individual then turned and bowed deeply to the true and modern Solomon whose unerring judgment was thus exemplified, and all three retired backwards around the Town Council.

James attempted to speak, but "Hey Tutti Taitie" was still in full swing. Glaring from large, eloquent, indeed quite beautiful Stewart eyes, the monarch, who had no ear for music anyway, took off his high hat and flapped it at the enthusiastic instrumentalists. Without the overshadowing headgear, God's Vice-Regent on Earth, as he was wont to style himself, could be seen to have somewhat shapeless features but a high forehead to suit his hat, a slack mouth from which a pink tongue was apt to protrude—for it was too large for the rest of him and consequently he dribbled fairly consistently—and a wispy beard. Now aged fifty-one, his hair was beginning to thin and grey and he had developed a paunch—scarcely an impressive figure, save for those eyes.

The musicians' leader got the message and the victorious paean ebbed away.

"God be thankit," Majesty declared thickly, and then nodded towards the stage. "Aye—och, maist appropriate and homologous. Aye, and perspicacious, perspicacious. Was it no', Vicky? Mind, yon wifie that didna get the bairn was auld enough to ken better, as you could jalouse by her paps. She was yon Jean Stewart, Lindores' lady, if I'm no' mistaken, and no' far off a grand-dame her ainsel', I'm thinking." He nodded sagely, and clapped on his hat again. "Now—what's next?"

"Let us hope no more Latin poems, Sire," the good-looking youth on the King's left announced, in the loud and clear, if clipped tones of the English ruling class. He yawned, frankly.

"Wheesht, Steenie, or they'll hear you," James said, equally audibly, and leaned over to pat the other's hand, to show that there was no real reproof intended.

The Provost stepped forward from the ranks of the magistrates, dressed like them all in black velvet for the occasion, but this enhanced by a special fur-lined cloak, very fine. The Lord Lyon King of Arms, in heraldic tabard, raised his baton and intoned:

"The Provost of Your Majesty's City of Edinburgh, Alexander Nisbet of the Dean."

"Aye, well—he has our royal permission to speak," James nodded graciously. "But no' for too long, mind."

Thus advised, the Provost bowed low and began. "Your Grace, in the name of your ancient capital and royal burgh of Edinburgh . . ."

He got no further meantime, James interrupting: "No Grace, man—Majesty. You should ken that by now. Grace

17

was the auld Scots usage, aye. But now it's for archbishops and dukes and siclike, eh, Vicky? Majesty, mind. And this Edinburgh's no' the ancient capital at all, see you, Provost —Nisbet is it? Nisbet's a right Merse name, frae the Borders, is it no'? Mainly rogues come frae the Borders, I've found, guidsakes! Ask Alicky Home. I've been biding at yon Dunglass wi' him yester-night. Aye, and the Homes are the worst o' the lot. Eh, Alicky?" And he turned in his saddle to scan the ranks behind him, where the Earl of Home quickly changed his black scowl into a smile. "Aye, well—Perth and Stirling, aye and Dunfermline and even Roxburgh, no' to mention yon Forteviot, were a' capitals in their day, before Edinburgh. *Sic transit*, you ken. So dinna get too high in your opinion o' this bit town! Proceed, Provost man—proceed."

Quite put off his stride, the chief magistrate hummed and hawed. "Majesty, I . . . I crave Your Majesty's pardon. I . . . ah, a slip o' the tongue, just. I was going to say . . . I was going to say . . ." Clearly, in his confusion he had forgotten just what he *was* going to say. Looking around him in desperation, he jettisoned his prepared speech. "I, I welcome Your Majesty on behalf of the City of Edinburgh, after your so long absence from it. To our loss, aye our great loss, to be sure. And, er, call upon the Town Clerk, Master John Hay, to make known the leal greetings of the Council and citizens."

The Town Clerk, a bustling little lawyer, thus prematurely thrust forward, produced a large swatch of papers from inside his velvet, with which he fumbled—and which James and others eyed with some alarm. However, as befitted a man of words, he fairly quickly found his place and launched forth into a flood of, if not exactly eloquence, at least verbiage.

"Your Gr . . . er, Majesty, blessed be God that our eyes are permitted once more to feed upon the royal countenance of our true Phoenix, the bright star of our northern firmament," he began, paper held close to his face the better to read.

He was corrected. "Phoenix, man, is no' a star, in this or any other firmament. It's an unchancy crittur, a sort o' fowl, wi' a habit o' burning itsel' in a bit fire every 500 years. You're no' likening your royal prince to siclike beastie?"

"No, no, Sire—no! It is but a figure, do you see. A figure of speech, just. Representing Your Grace . . ." He changed that quickly to gracious Majesty. "Aye, our sun, the powerful adamant of our wealth," he read on, "by whose removing from our hemisphere we were darkened. Deep sorrow and fear possessed our hearts, where had rested the imperishable, unconquerable by the fires of this world and the flames of tongues of evil men . . ."

"Ooh, aye—and there's plenties o' those, eh Steenie? Plenties—especially in yon England! A right incubatory and hatchery for flaming tongues! But go on, man—and be quick about it. We've been here ower long as it is."

"Yes, Sire." Master Hay had to find his place again. ". . . tongues of evil men. Aye, the very hills and groves, accustomed before to be refreshed by the clear dew of Your Majesty's presence, not putting on their wonted apparel, but with pale looks representing their misery for the departure of their royal King, a King in heart as upright as David, wise as Solomon and godly as Josias! Your Highness, formed by nature and framed by Education to be the perfection of all elegance and eloquence, we, protected under the wings of Your Majesty's sacred authority from the Beast of Rome and his Antichristian locusts . . ."

"Hech, hech, man—Beast o' Rome is sweeping, aye sweeping! And the good ambassadors o' their maist Christian and Catholic Majesties o' France and Spain—here present, mind—will no' like yon o' Antichrist and, and locusts, was it? Right enough about David and Solomon and the like—but moderation in a' things, mind. Aye, and in length too, mannie. Enough is enough."

"Yes, Your Majesty. On the very knees of our hearts, we . . ."

"Quiet, man—quiet! I said enough. If you hae knees to your heart, then you're a right wonder! Myself, I'm hungry—and it's a guid mile yet to Holyroodhouse, forby! Have done. Is that a', Mr Provost? It's usual, mind, for a bit presentation and recognisance, at such time. Secretary Tam—did you no' say . . . ?"

In his urgency the Provost actually interrupted the monarch. "To be sure, Sire—Your Majesty. Here it is. The city sword and keys, delivered to your royal keeping."

"Ooh, aye—but I wasna just meaning bits o' iron, man." Gingerly James looked at the two city officers now bearing down on him, one bearing aloft the great sword, the other the keys on a crimson cushion. The monarch was expected to signify his acceptance of these symbols by touching them and returning them to their keepers. But throughout James had remained sitting on his horse instead of dismounting and coming to sit under the fine purple velvet canopy erected for him. So that the two officers were up on the platform and, though the King was approximately on the same level, there was a sizeable gap caused by the steps up. The bearers of the capital's emblems were in a quandary. Were they to descend the steps and then hoist up their awkward burdens, or would the sovereign dismount or even climb to the platform? Actually, James, who hated and dreaded cold steel—save for the gralloching-knife of the deer hunt—waved away custodians and symbols both, looking round accusingly at Sir Thomas Hamilton, the Secretary of State, now created Lord Binning and Byres, who had come to the Figgate Burn to meet him.

That bulky but shrewd individual raised the powerful voice which had so often intimidated the Court of Session —for he had long been Lord Advocate and was now Lord President of Session as well as Secretary of State. "The cup, man!" he shouted. "The siller cup."

Provost Nisbet, whose day this seemingly was not, hastily turned to the City Treasurer who handed him a silver chalice, with which he came forward, almost at the run. Again there was the gap to contend with. He hurried down the steps and more or less thrust the cup up at the King, wordless.

James leaned to take it, and hefted it expertly in his hand, peering within. "Light," he pronounced. "Gey light." He passed it over to the plain-faced man on his right. "How much, Vicky?" he demanded, frowning. "Scanty, I'd say— aye, scanty."

The Duke of Lennox grimaced. "Now, James? Here?" He had scarcely been attending to all this performance, his gaze tending to be fixed on the persons of Mary Gray and his son, sitting there across the platform.

"Aye, now. You'd no' have us ignorant, Vicky, about so important a matter? Eh, Provost?"

"No need to count it, Sire. There is five hundred pounds there, in double-angels," Nisbet asserted.

"Five *hundred*, just?" James sniffed. "Five hundred, eh? Och, well." He turned and glowered back at the Secretary of State. "You hear that, you Tam?"

"Wait, Sire," that individual called.

"Na, na—we've been here ower long as it is. I'm awa' . . ."

"Sire—the Provost," the Duke reminded, in a penetrating whisper. "It is customary to knight the Provost of this your capital city."

"Customary, eh? Customary! Na, na, Vicky—no' for five hundred pounds, it's no'! You should ken that. Geordie Heriot wouldna have said the like. He kent what was what. See you to this Provost-mannie—I'm awa'. Come, Steenie." Majesty dug in his heels, reined his horse half-round, and headed off for the West Port archway.

Ludovick Stewart looked at the unhappy Nisbet, shrugged and dismounted. He tossed his reins to one of the Town Guard, handed the silver chalice to another, patted the cloaked provostly shoulder sympathetically, and ran up the steps on to the platform and straight over to Mary Gray, his son and his sister.

"My dear, my love, my heart!" he cried, and enfolded the dark woman in his arms, there before all. "At last! At last!"

Mary Gray hugged him, laughing between kisses. "Dear Vicky! Dear, dear Vicky! But . . . but is this wise? So many . . . to see."

"Let them see! All know, anyway. And I am a widower now, mind!"

"And growing fat on it!"

"That is French food. Too much oil!" He turned to embrace his sister—but still kept one arm around Mary Gray. Then he held out a hand to his son. "Johnnie! Johnnie—how good! Damn it—you're a better-looking man than your father!"

John Stewart was speechless.

"Where are you lodging? With the old Tippermuir dame? Then I will come to you there as soon as I can get away from James."

"Will he let you go, Vicky? He is always so demanding."

"He has this new pup, George Villiers, whom he calls Steenie. He dotes on him, even more than he did on the late and unlamented Carr. So long as he has young Steenie he maybe will scarce miss me . . ."

"Look—there seems to be some trouble at the gate," the Countess said.

There was indeed now a great milling of horsemen and guards at the West Port arch, although that was to be expected with so many to get through the narrow entry. But, by the shouting and jostling, with the white-satined Town Guard hurrying thither, there appeared to be more than mere congestion.

The Duke felt that he might be required, as so often he was by his crowned cousin—for one thing, because of James's fear of naked steel, he alone was permitted to carry a sword in the royal presence, which weapon was required more for knightings than for anything more martial, but, in the sudden crises and panics which were so apt to develop out of nothing with this Lord's Anointed, James was glad to have both sword and reliable kinsman ever near-at-hand. So now he hurried to the gateway. John went with him.

Actually there was no call for any alarm. All that had happened was that the royal interest had been caught, typically, by the three grinning malefactors' heads stuck on spikes above the West Port archway, a favoured display spot for such relics, where they would do most good. Being James, he was intrigued not only by the various expressions thereon but in the varying stages of decay and putrescence, demanding of the gate-porters to know just how long each had been there exposed and wondering why one, not the newest apparently, should be still reasonably whole and intact—save for the eyes pecked out by crows—and a later example little better than a grisly skull? Nothing would do but that all three items should be brought down for royal examination. Not only had all this delayed passage through the gateway but, it so happening that the ladder to mount to the wellhead above the arch being kept behind one of the halves of the great double-doors, this half had to be pulled out, thus part-closing the already constricted entry. Such semi-closure, with the monarch on the other side, was of course incomprehensible for much of the royal train queueing up, and there ensued, in some, a scare that some sort of attack or assault was in progress, especially amongst the English courtiers—and much of the huge cavalcade was English-born—who were prepared to believe that everything in Scotland was barbarous, hazardous and probably treasonable into the bargain. So confusion developed outside the gate, and an anatomical study inside.

By the time that Ludovick and John Stewart had pushed their way through the noisy throng, however, at some risk from horses' stamping hooves, and discovered all this, the monarch had lost interest in the relics, and, yielding to Steenie's gasping complaints about the stench, shooed the heads away and set off eastwards down the street towards the Grassmarket at a brisk pace, scattering the crowded citizenry before them like squawking poultry. They left behind major disarray and doubts, as the most illustrious of two kingdoms sought to get through into the city after their liege-lord.

The Duke, of course, found himself in the forefront but without his horse. "A plague!" he exclaimed, "James will not stop now until he gets to Holyrood! Where the devil is my horse? He'll be shouting for me, God knows!"

"He'll have to stop," John pointed out. "There are other arches and spectacles to get through, three more at least. At the West Bow and St Giles and the Tolbooth . . ."

"Lord!" his father groaned. "He'll be in direst straits then, I swear! I'll have to be after him, or he'll be yelling treason! A horse . . . ?" He looked about him and reached for the bridle of the most forward-placed mount he saw—which happened to be that of Thomas Howard, Earl of Arundel, chief of the greatest house in England, and who should have been Duke of Norfolk but for the attainder of that title by the late Queen Elizabeth. "Off!" he shouted. "Off with you—in the King's name!" And, more or less, he tugged that astonished young man out of the saddle by main force. "Sorry, Tommy—you'll find my grey somewhere. This is important," he panted. Mounting to the vacated saddle, Ludovick looked down at his son and held out his hand. "Up behind me, Johnnie—you'll know where these damned arches are. Come!"

So, mounted pillion behind the only duke in both kingdoms, and quite deserting Mary Gray and the Countess, John Stewart of Methven was carried jolting down the street and into the Grassmarket even faster than the sovereign of the United Kingdom had gone before, scattering all before them and leaving utter chaos behind.

The Duke of Lennox's alarm was not uncalled-for. They caught up with royalty at the far end of the Grassmarket, where the winding street known as the West Bow curled up to the main spine of the city, the mile-long Lawnmarket, High Street and Canongate. Unfortunately, however, here where was erected the temporary but elaborate cloth-of-gold-covered arch with figures, such royalty went unrecognised. Dean of Guild Aitkenhead and others of the city guildry and merchant company, who officiated here, were perhaps scarcely to be blamed. After all, they had looked for a monarchial figure at the head of a great and noble train, and, when only two mounted persons came clattering up, one distinctly odd-looking with a high hat aslant and clothing disarranged, the other a mere youth however pretty, they were barred from further progress and told to go whence they had come. That these good burgesses should not know James Stewart's distinctly memorable features was not so surprising either, for it was now fourteen years since he had departed from his native land, on succeeding to Elizabeth Tudor's throne in 1603, and this was his first return. Hence all the excitement. But it did mean that few there were in any position to recognise him. Moreover, when James got upset, as now, he spluttered and dribbled more profusely than ever, becoming practically unintelligible save to the initiated, and here his hot protestations that he was the King and that they were all shameful and seditious scoundrels went quite uncomprehended. As he continued to gabble and gesticulate, Master Aitkenhead assumed him to be a madman, and, being Moderator of the City Constables as well as Dean of Guild, he ordered the constables there on duty to apprehend this disturber of the King's peace, and his companion, and remove them. So Majesty was hauled down off his horse, struggling and bawling, Treason, Murder! Steenie protested too, that it *was* the King and that he was George, Earl of Buckingham; but his aristocratic English voice was scarcely more intelligible to his hearers than was his spluttering master's, and went equally disregarded.

This was the situation when Ludovick and John rode up, with the now weeping sovereign and his favourite being hustled away by the constables, and the platform-party seeking to soothe Dame Music and her choir of children and instrumentalists who were naturally agog, the lady all but in hysterics, a spectacle in herself, for she was large and pink in diaphanous robes and they had already been there for almost three hours.

In these circumstances, the arrival of two more hurrying horsemen, but only one horse, was bound to have a less than calming effect. The Duke of Lennox ought to have been recognisable, for he often returned to Scotland and indeed had acted as Viceroy. But the King's cousin would not be expected to be giving a lift to a pillion-passenger, nor to be unaccompanied either. Also Ludovick, as well as being plain-faced, dressed plainly and not in court fashion, and John was likewise. So the newcomers' shouts were ignored also, as the platform prepared to deal with more madmen.

John, who rather prided himself on being fit and agile, indeed something of a mountaineer, leapt nimbly down from the back of his father's saddle, without waiting for representations or explanations, and in three strides launched himself bodily upon the two unfortunate constables who were with difficulty manhandling the shambling, struggling monarch. One he cannoned into with sufficient force to send him reeling, and the other he lashed out at with his fist, spinning him round, whereupon the other fist, to the jawline, felled him to the ground. James, not knowing whether he was being rescued or undergoing further attack, cringed and staggered helplessly.

John, with an instinctive gesture of protection, held open his arms. And Majesty, recognising this at least for what it was, hurled himself into that embrace, gabbling.

The Duke, seeing the King in good hands, dismounted, and, ignoring poor Steenie, stormed up on to this second platform, calling out who he was. Lennox at least was a name all there knew, and it gained him a hearing. At his shouted information, utter consternation dawned and reigned in that ~ompany. Dame Music's hysterics developed uncontrolled.

Leaving them to their appalled deliberations, Ludovick ran down to James, who was still clutching John. Although seldom at a loss for words, even eloquence of a sort, however difficult at times to comprehend, now the monarch was completely incoherent, babbling of treason, *lèse majesté*, savagery, skaith, damnation and the like, but also of saviours and angels of God—presumably referring to his deliverers. Declaring that it was all a mistake, that the folk here had not known that it was the King, that it might have been in fact some move *against* the King that they were seeking to counter, the Duke sought to soothe his cousin. John kept silent, but continued to provide a sturdy pillar to which his sovereign could cling. Steenie released, ruffled but apparently none the worse, complained about the manners of the Scotch.

James was somewhat calmed when Dean of Guild Aitkenhead, supported by two of his colleagues, ventured tentatively down from the platform, dread and reluctance in every line of them. But however humbly, even servilely, they approached, the monarch saw them only as further menace, putting John between himself and them and calling on Vicky to draw his sword and run them through, the scoundrelly miscreants and treasonable dogs. In vain they pleaded, and Ludovick reassured; Majesty once aroused was not easily placated.

Fortunately it was at this difficult juncture that the first of the distinguished train turned up, somewhat puzzled by the scene—and James broke off his fulminations to cry shame on all his earls, lords and court for deserting him in his hour of need, him and Steenie both. The choursed and righteous protest, unanimous but of no avail, was proceeding when there was a diversion. The children's orchestra at the back of the platform suddenly struck up, and after three or four bars, the choir joined in also, youthful voices singing, to the effect that:

> King James returns to his own land, and all do bow before him;
> He shines his light on every hand and his folk all adore him:
> Auld Scotia's Lion brave is he, in wisdom he is peerless.
> He glads our eyes his face to see, in all our cause most fearless.

Presumably the youngsters had been instructed to start when the cavalcade drew up, and start then they did with or without Dame Music.

James, distinctly doubtful as to the appropriateness of all this youthful enthusiasm in the circumstances, began to point a minatory, quivering finger at them, when he paused, to stare upwards. They all did.

A loud cranking and clanking and squealing sound penetrated the music, apparently emanating from the top of the cloth-of-gold triumphal arch, which shook somewhat in sympathy. Then from behind the draperies slowly descended a great globe of painted glass, out of which a markedly good-looking Cupid, naked except for the wings, was lowered in turn, standing on a realistic cloud of swansdown and bearing in his hands a silver basin. Any such mechanical device, not to mention the naked youth, could be guaranteed to preoccupy James Stewart, who for the moment forgot his indignation to gaze in expectation. Cupid completed the descent safely, to musical accompaniment, achieved a flap of his wings and came forward with his basin. At the front of the platform he paused, hesitant, clearly uncertain as to who to present it to.

The King was certainly not going up those steps. He still clutched John Stewart indeed. "See what's in it, Vicky," he directed. "Hae the laddie doon." His voice quavered.

Beckoning Cupid down the steps, the Duke looked into the basin. "It's keys," he declared. "More keys."

"Keys, just? Guidsakes, is that a'? We've had their bit keys, already!" That was almost a wail.

"These are the keys of the Guildry Court and Merchants'

Hall," the Dean of Guild explained. And, greatly daring, if somewhat doubtfully, "And of all our hearts, Your Grace."

"Ooh, aye," James said, giving him a nasty look and pulling down his hat more firmly. "Keep your keys, man. Aye, and be thankfu' that you keep your head on your craig, forby! In my mercy—aye, my mercy!" He peered round for his horse. "Where's my beast? Fetch it. You, lad—heist me up." He tweaked John's sleeve. "Up wi' me." Laboriously in the saddle, he looked down. "Who are you, man, that God sent to my aid, eh? Your name?"

"John Stewart, Your Majesty."

"So! Is that a fact? I might ha' kent it would be a Stewart! Though there's a wheen o' them, mind—and no' a' o' the best repute!"

"This is my son, James—John Stewart of Methven, of whom you have heard," the Duke said.

"D'you tell me that! Hech, hech—so this is your bit by-blow by yon quean Mary Gray. I saw her sitting, back yonder. Save us—an' this size already! And as well he was—a right paladin and God-send when I was in sair need. *Hoc erat in votis*!" James was obviously feeling better when he could resort to Latin.

"I did nothing, Sire," John said.

"D'you ca' it nothing to rescue Christ God's Vice-Regent frae malevolent hands—aye, maist malevolent? And your kinsman, John Stewart, in a sort o' a way. You will ride by my side, John Stewart—find yoursel' a horse. Take Steenie's, there. You, Steenie Villiers, were nae guid to me at a', in that stramash. Nane. You did naething. Gie him your horse, for he's got mair spunk than you!" And without further ado and no single gesture towards the platform-party, their sovereign-lord rode off once more.

There was much mounting and reining-round behind him.

So a bewildered John Stewart found himself now riding up Edinburgh's West Bow on the Earl of Buckingham's fine black, on the King's left, whilst his father rode on the right, three Stewart kinsmen whatever the differences in rank and station, the brilliantly clad throng behind wondering what next? There was not a lot of sympathy for poor Steenie, who was less than popular.

They had a reasonably clear run through dense crowds up into the High Street. But there, outside the huge High Kirk of St Giles, was another barrier. The King, glowering, undoubtedly would have crashed his way through this one, decorative and flower-decked as it was, had he not perceived the magnificent figure in archiepiscopal robes and mitre, with tall crozier, standing in the forefront. Since this was Archbishop Spottiswoode of St Andrews, Primate of Scotland, and very much James's own appointment, head of the bishops whom the King had insisted on introducing into the Reformed Kirk, he could hardly ignore him. Also, as it happened, the Mercat Cross which stood nearby had been ingeniously treated to spout red wine from its cannon-like drainage-spouts, and this being instantly turned on, naturally caught the royal eye, especially when suitably disrobed bacchantes trooped forward to offer filled cups of the wine and platters of cakes to the horsemen. James, muttering that this was the first sensible thing that had happened since he reached this town, graciously partook. Meanwhile, an older lady, more comprehensively clad, announced in ringing tones that she was Dame Religion, and invited the King's Grace to step within St Giles Kirk and hear a discourse from the Archbishop. It is to be doubted whether, fond of archbishops and bishops as he was, James would have acceded to such request at this stage had it not been that the lady issued her invitation in Hebrew—and James was probably the only person present, apart from Spottiswoode himself, who understood what was said, and knew that he was so. To everyone's surprise, therefore, he dismounted, nodded familiarly to the Archbishop, and lurched with his peculiar knock-kneed stride into the church, still chewing. Perforce all must follow.

It was as well, perhaps, that the succeeding address was an episcopal one and not a sermon by one of the Kirk's more reformed divines, so that it was mercifully brief. Not that the monarch now seemed concerned, for once in his throne-like seat, with Ludovick and John standing on either side of him, he tipped forward his hat over his nose—he never took his hat off in church, nor in most other places, in case, as he would explain, bats fell from the roof into his royal hair—and promptly went to sleep. It is to be feared that few of the remainder of the entourage crowding into St Giles in loud-voiced protest, got much more out of the Archbishop's excellent Latinity.

It was the subsequent music which waked the sleeper and, unappreciative of such noise as ever, immediately he got to his feet and marched for the door—but not before he had grasped John's arm and propelled him along.

The service broke up in less certainty.

Going back to the Mercat Cross for another cup of wine, James remounted and headed determinedly down the High Street.

As they trotted after, John reminded his father that there was still another hurdle to get over, outside the new Tolbooth, before they entered the burgh of the Canongate. The Duke shook his head, wordless.

They came to this quite quickly, the most elaborate and extensive arch and platform of all—and were surprised to see Provost Nisbet and the magistrates and Council awaiting them again thereon. Presumably they had managed the move from the West Port while the church service proceeded. Sundry hearts sank at the sight and James looked almost ferocious.

"Nae mair keys!" he shouted thickly as he approached.

Whether the Provost heard or not, he prudently interposed a trio of handsome ladies between himself and the oncoming monarch. The first of these held up a hand and declared clearly and in pretty fair Greek, that she was Dame Peace. James could scarcely do other than draw up, however reluctantly, for this was another of his own illegitimate cousins, and another Lady Mary Stewart at that, sister of one of the battlers for the baby back at the West Port and widow of the late famous, or notorious, Master of Gray, Mary Gray's sire. The Scottish aristocracy was like that.

Dame Peace thereupon enunciated a dignified welcome in classical Greek, at which the multilinguist sovereign nodded approval—he claimed to be able to converse in fourteen languages—and thereafter the next lady, Dame Plenty, launched forth into a similar oration in Latin, to suitable comments in the same tongue by the recipient. The third, Dame Justice, rendered her contribution in braid Scots, also much approved, James having been brought up to speak thus by his foster-mother, the old Countess of Mar. He glanced round slyly to observe how most of his train of Englishry were taking all this, well aware that few if any would have the least notion of anything that had been said, his opinion of English education frequently enunciated.

This over, and the King nodding agreeably and preparing to ride on, his face clouded again as the Provost stepped forward once more.

"Majesty," Nisbet called, almost pleadingly, "one last token before Your Highness leaves this our burgh for that of the Canongate." And he waved up two of the satined Guard, who bore between then a large cauldron, apparently of silver.

"Sakes . . . keys . . . !" James began, when the obvious weight of the burden, on two stalwart men, struck him. "Hey—what's in it?" he demanded.

"I advise Your Majesty to go and see," a fruity voice from behind said genially—the Secretary of State again.

"Eh? Eh? Me? Na, na, Tam—*you* go, Vicky Stewart. You see."

The Duke dismounted, sighing, and climbed up once more. He looked into the cauldron, shrugged, and then lifted out first a small roasted chicken, then a small ham, a loaf of bread and a flagon of wine.

"Houts!" the monarch cried. "What's this? Comestibles, just. Guidsakes—viands and belly-cheer! Are you run clean gyte, Provost man?"

"Go on, my lord Duke—more!" Tam o' the Cowgate urged.

Handing over the provender to the Provost to hold, Ludovick delved in again and brought out a large white napkin. Then he stooped forward, peering. He plunged in his hand and brought it out dribbling gold pieces. In he dived again.

"Lord!" he exclaimed. "There's hundreds, thousands, here!"

"Eh? What's that? Thousands . . . ?" For one so ungainly, James was off his horse and up those steps with remarkable

31

alacrity. Almost running he came to plunge his own two hands into the cauldron.

"Aye—plenteous! Maist beauteous and convenient. Convenient, aye," he approved. "How many? How much, man?"

"Ten thousand, Sire—10,000 merks, in double-angels," the Provost informed, beaming now. "Yon other, the 500, was but a sweetener, as you might say!"

"Ten thousand, eh? Och, now—that's mair like it. That is duteous and right suitable. Whence comes it, man? Och—but *non olet pecunia*! Eh? Aye, well—you, Vicky, you look after this, now. See to it. Wi' the utmaist care, mind. You'll need a bit hand, see. Saddlebags will be best— saddlebags. Stow it a' in saddlebags. They can keep their poultry and that. But first—gie's your sword, Vicky. Sword, aye. Carefu' with it, now—carefu'! Dinna birl it around, that way. Now you, Provost man—on your knees. Doon wi' you." Taking the proffered sword as though it was red-hot, Majesty poked it in the general direction of the alarmed Provost. Then he paused, looking up and over. "Aye—you, lad. You here, too. Here wi' you, Johnnie Stewart. Come, man—dinna just sit there staring like some houlet! You were mair spry, afore! Come and kneel by this Provost chiel."

As in a dream, John dismounted and climbed to the platform, not believing any of it. The Provost, still clutching the chicken and the rest, was already kneeling and eyeing the flickering sword point apprehensively. John was gestured down beside him.

"Put thae comestibles doon, man—you canna be knighted wi' an armfu' o' belly-fodder! And dinna jink your head about that way, or you'll maybe get skewered like your ain chicken! Now—what's your name, again? Aye, Nisbet— William Nisbet. Well—still, noo. I hereby dub thee knight, then. So . . . and so! Arise, Sir William Nisbet—and be you guid knight until your life's end. Aye—now you, Johnnie Stewart."

John was too bemused to take avoiding action and sustained a swipe on the head as the sword came over. Fortunately he had a fine thick crop of hair and took no hurt.

Again the litany. "I dub thee knight, John Stewart. So . . . and so! You did well, back yonder—when others were less forrit! Arise, Sir John Stewart o' . . . o' Methven, is it? Aye, well—be a guid knight until thy life's end, Sir John man. Up you get . . ." James turned, without pause. "Here, Vicky—take your whinger. I've been thinking—you'd be better wi' a bit sack than the saddlebags. You'd need a wheen o' them, and some fell rogue might be off wi' one. Find you a sack, and then come on to Holyrood. I'm awa' there now—and I'll no' be stoppit this time, as God's my witness! I've had enough."

Allowing himself to catch no one's eye, James Stewart shambled down to his horse, mounted and spurred off round the archway, cleaving the crowd and heading for the Netherbow Port. After that Holyroodhouse was only some hundreds of yards, sanctuary indeed. After him streamed his court.

Father and son eyed each other, the Provost, the magistrates and Council, the ladies and the rest.

"Well, well," Ludovick said, at length. "God's will be done! Or His Anointed's, which is much the same thing! Congratulations, Sir John. Who would have thought it? And to you, to be sure, Sir William. That was a notable contrivance!"

The Provost was still too shaken to utter coherently, John still more so.

The Duke shook his head. "I am to find a sack, for this money. By royal command! Who will find me a sack, in Heaven's name? Someone—come to my aid! Johnnie—you had better get back and find your mother. Lord knows where she will be now. Tell her that I'll be up to your lodgings so soon as I may. James will want to eat and drink and sleep, after all this—so I should hope not to be very long. Off with you, and give her the news that she has got a knight for a son! I see you have lost your fine horse! Steenie Villiers won't forgive you for that! Now—this sack, of a mercy . . ."

2

It was later that evening than he hoped for before Duke Ludovick managed to make his way up from Holyroodhouse to the Lady Tippermuir's lodging in the High Street, to fall into Mary Gray's arms, John looking on with a somewhat embarrassed grin. It was a while before anything very sensible was said.

The woman it was who first recovered her composure, she being a notably composed character normally.

"You will have eaten, I suppose, by this time? I had a meal prepared."

"Aye, Murray, the Treasurer-Depute had a great banquet awaiting us—I could not escape it. James actually had me counting out all that money at the table. He appears to look on me as Geordie Heriot's successor, as man-of-business, Heaven help me—for as you know I cannot add three to five and win the same result twice! You heard about the ten thousand merks?"

"Yes. It was a strange device. It is said that Tam Hamilton—or the Lord Binning and Byres, as now we must call him—concocted it all, to ensure that the King partook in all the ploys. If he had been given all that gold at the start, we would not have seen hide nor hair of him thereafter until he had it all safe stowed away in Holyroodhouse!"

"It could be so. A dire reputation for our lord and master to have! He is a great fool, but . . ."

"But you still love him, nevertheless, Vicky?"

"I would scarce call it love, my dear! But I have an affection for him, yes. And there is much that is admirable about him, as well as the rest. His virtues outweigh his vices, I swear. Kings cannot be as other men, but James, whatever his faults, is no tyrant and has a heart. Aye, and a head too, however he looks and sounds. He is shrewd, the shrewdest man in all his court. I have little doubt . . ."

"Dear Vicky—you are ever loyal! But . . . we are not come together again, after so long, to talk about James Stewart, are we? There is so much I want to hear—and have to tell. And Johnny was as full of questions for you as an egg of meat—only this odd knighting has driven it all out of his mind, I think!"

"Not so," their son denied. "The knighthood is nothing. Or . . . not exactly nothing." He was a fairly honest young man. "It is . . . good to have. Agreeable. And could be useful, I think. I had never dreamed of this. But it, it changes nothing that is important. I am just the same. And you both are just the same. That is what is important. And, oh—I am glad to see you home, Father!"

"Well said, lad!" Ludovick nodded. "Excellent sentiments. But knighthood *is* important—or should be. James has made too many knights—and often for the wrong reasons. But it is an honourable state, a standing which should set you apart from other men in some measure. There is more to knighthood than being called Sir John Stewart!"

"Dear me, we are serious tonight," Mary complained, but smiling. "Come, sit to, my solemn duke and knight—we can at least drink a little wine to celebrate our long-delayed reunion. You were not wont to be so sober, Vicky. Of course, you are two years older . . . !"

"Aye—I am growing aged! Whereas you, my heart, grow younger each year! It is unfair, I say!"

"Well seen that you have been biding in France, to teach you such flattering speech, my lord Duke! My father used to say that they all were deceivers ever, there—and *he* should have known, the greatest deceiver of them all! Tell me, have you brought home a new Duchess from France? I am told that French women are very . . . enticing!"

"No, I have not! Think you that I would? I found them mostly painted hizzies! I look for my new Duchess a deal nearer home than that. Here, in Edinburgh, in fact—or at least, in Methven!"

"Ah, Vicky, my dear—that nonsense again! How often

have I told you, it is not possible? I thank you, with all my heart—but you must know that that is a dream, no more. It cannot be. You *must* know it . . . ?"

"I know no such thing. I am not a simple youth, any more, to do as I am told. I am a widower, of middle years, and can marry whom I will."

"You are the King's cousin—the only, male and legitimate. If you were one of the others, it might be different. You are the only duke in this United Kingdom. James would never allow it."

"I am James's cousin and friend, yes—not his slave! I serve him faithfully, but . . ."

"You are his representative and envoy, Vicky. You were Viceroy, and High Commissioner to Scotland. Think you that he would send you, as such, with Mary Gray as your wife? The bastard daughter of Patrick, Master of Gray, his enemy? Mother of your own . . ." she baulked at that word as applied to their son who stood, listening, ". . . your own offspring."

"I would not ask his permission. Think you that I care whether I am ever Viceroy or envoy again . . . ?"

"Perhaps not. But *he* cares, the King! And his word is law. He relies on you. He will not let you go. He trusts you, and almost only you. See how he sent you as his special ambassador to the King of France. Could Mary Gray have gone also? You know that I could not. In France you would associate and treat with all the great ones. Would they have accepted such as myself? So, enough of this. Tell us what you did in France, who you saw and what you achieved . . . ?"

"No—you will not change the subject so easily, Mary. I want you to marry me. I should have insisted when Jean died, five years ago. You talked me out of it then . . ."

"And must do again, my love. James would have the marriage annulled, nothing more sure. He could do. He is head of the Church of England. And up here his archbishops would leap to do his bidding. We would be wed for only days, I swear. But . . . let us have done, for now at least. Have pity on poor Johnnie, who should not have to spend his first evening as knight listening to this sad old story."

"I think that you should do as Father says, Mary." She had always asked him to call her that, not mother. "If the King did insist on the marriage being annulled, at least you would be wed in the sight of God . . ."

"We always believed that in the sight of God we *were* man and wife, anyway," she asserted. "Always we held to that, John."

"There at least we agree," the Duke declared vehemently.

"Then why all this to-do if our true union means so much to us? Another marriage would be but for show. We have each other, and John here. And our home at Methven. Is that not sufficient? Is it not what we agreed on, so long ago . . . ?"

It was indeed the arrangement made between these two away back in 1597 when they had fallen in love, she only seventeen and he already wed in an arranged child-marriage to a daughter of Scotland's Lord High Treasurer. When John was born, he had made over, in the boy's name, the fine estate of Methven in Strathearn, really for Mary, and installed there mother and child. James had insisted that his cousin accompanied him to London, to take over the throne of Elizabeth, in 1603, and to set up the United Kingdom; Mary and the boy had to be left behind. Ludovick had come back to them as often as he could, but the King was demanding and piled many duties on his cousin, declaring that there was none other whom he could trust in the same degree. There had frequently been long periods of separation. In fact, the Duke was no courtier and would much have preferred to act the country laird and family-man at Methven. But it was not to be.

"Am I to be bound, always, by what we decided when we were little more than bairns?" he demanded. "But— we will talk of this anon. I want to hear of your doings, both of you. Of what goes on at Methven. Of all that has happened . . ."

So he was told of the new stabling and other extensions being added to the castle on its shelf above the loch; of the great drainage project on Methven Moss and the Cowgask Burn; of the timber extraction in Methven Wood and the tree-planting to replace it; of the parish minister and his lengthy sermons; of the MacGregor raids on the farmers' cattle and the counter-measures; of the great heather-fire only the previous month, which had destroyed much grazing; and all the other matters of concern to a large lairdship on the verge of the Highlands. This was mainly of John's recounting. Mary told of the state and doings of their neighbours, friends and unfriends.

"When will you come to Methven, then, Vicky?" she asked. "How soon can you get away?"

"Lord knows! James plans a progress round Scotland. He talks of Linlithgow, Stirling, Dunfermline, hunting at Falkland, St Andrews, Dundee, even Aberdeen. For how much of it all he will need me, or at least demand my presence, I have no notion. But he does demand me much, as you know. I will escape when I can, but . . ."

"He surely does not need *you* all the time, Vicky? Has he not hundreds of others, all those courtiers . . . ?"

"Not hundreds, thousands! Do you know, there were over five thousand in his train by the time we won to Berwick-on-Tweed? Home nearly died a death, meeting us there, when he learned how many mouths he had to feed! The same with Winton at Seton, where we lay last night."

"Well, then."

"The trouble is that James *trusts* so few, almost none. I mean, in arranging his affairs. He affects to despise the English, says that they could scarce manage a cattle-fair! Worse, they waste his siller—the greatest sin of all! Very few will he allow to manage what concerns his person."

"But this is folly! You are not to be tied to him like some servitor, because of his childish distrust of the English. Forby, there are plenty of Scots."

"You would think so. But he must have all done his way. Would you believe it, he had me send up from London, months ago, two black velvet cloaks, one with fur-trimming, as examples for the magistrates and Town Council to copy, for this visit. An improvement on those worn by the aldermen of the City of London."

"And yet I swear that he scarcely looked at any of them today," John put in.

"He would see, nevertheless, and note, lad. Not much

eludes the royal eye, however short-of-sight. If there is aught amiss with those gowns, the new Sir William will hear about it tomorrow! James even sent up rolls of white satin for the Town Guard—and fools they looked in it, to be sure!"

"But why, Vicky? For what purpose is all this done?"

"He is eager, you see, that the English nobility, who think themselves superior to all, shall not come and consider Scotland backward or inferior in any way. They will, of course; nothing will change their belief that we are all bar-barians up here. But James keeps trying. It is all part of his policy, you see, to maintain his ascendancy. The English lords gained altogether too much power during the last years of Elizabeth, when she was an ageing and ailing woman. All along, James has been seeking to bring them down a peg or two, so that the King remains supreme. He does not chop their heads off nor maltreat them, as did Henry the Eighth, and Elizabeth too when she was younger. But he appoints Scots to high places about him to humiliate them, he scoffs at their lack of education—for they care little for learning—he chooses Scots as ambassadors. And now he would show this great horde of Englishry that Scotland compares well with anything that England can show. He does not give in easily, does James Stewart!"

"And when does this hero of yours start on his progress round the land?" Mary asked. "Do you come to Methven before or after?"

"I do not know, lass. I believe that the intention is to pass tomorrow in Edinburgh, then the next day to proceed to Linlithgow. He may not require me when we get to Falkland. I should be free, at least, for when hunting I am not needed."

"Then what do we do? Wait here another day or two, in the hope of seeing you on occasion? Or go back to Methven and await you there?"

"I think that you must wait here meantime, my dear. For almost the last thing James said to me, when I sought permission to leave his table, was to tell that son of mine, 'my saviour' as he put it, that he expected to see him at court. That he was a swack chiel and he would see more of him. I am to bring you to Holyroodhouse tomorrow, Johnnie."

"I do not think that I like the sound of that!" Mary Gray said.

Ludovick laughed "John will be well enough. He is not the sort that is in danger from James. Or, I sometimes think that it is James who is in danger from these unpleasant youths and their scheming sponsors! Usually it is these who put the creatures his way—for their own advantage. You would scarcely believe the fine names behind George Villiers!"

"Hateful! How you can bear it with all that goes on at court, Vicky, I do not know."

"There is much to enjoy, also. Bacon, who is here with us, calls it the human comedy!"

"If the Earl of Buckingham's name is George Villiers, why does the King call him Steenie?" John asked.

"Because he looks like a picture of St Stephen which James has."

"There are saints and saints!" the woman said. "You watch King James, young man . . . !"

Next forenoon, when father and son presented themselves at Holyroodhouse, it was to find the monarch gone, and long gone. James had his own attitude towards the clock, as towards most other things, indeed. He was fond of his bed and would retire to it at any time of day or night; on the other hand, he would leave it at equally odd hours, to the confusion of more conventional sleepers. Where hunting was concerned, his great joy, no hour was too early to start; and apparently this morning he had been up before sunrise for a quite unscheduled hawking in the great park, which surrounded the towering bulk of Arthur's Seat that overlooked the city of the east. None being warned of this, indeed a very different programme having been arranged, James had gone off with only a small and not very enthusiastic group, none knew just where. Now the palace was thronged with folk, many thankful to be, as it were, off-duty, others agitated, especially those in any way responsible for the day's planned itinerary.

Ludovick immediately found himself in much demand, as authority. Where was the King? When would he be back? Would the programme be re-arranged? If so, what items should be abandoned—for obviously there would not now be time for all? There was considerable competition and argument amongst the claimants, needless to say. As so often, the Duke objected that he should be the one to take the decisions—for already present were the Secretary of State, Lord Binning; the Chancellor or chief minister, the Lord Fyvie; the High Constable, the Earl of Erroll; Lyon King of Arms; and numerous members of the Privy Council, including a clutch of the monarch's illegitimate relatives. But none apparently dared to make decisions for their unpredictable liege-lord and unanimously put the onus on the Duke of Lennox.

Ludovick called for silence, admitted that he himself had no notion as to the day's programme and asked for information. He was thereupon met by such a barrage of detail and engagements, interspersed by complaints from sundry English notables as to the quality of their lodgings, that he put his hands up to his ears. Perceiving there Sir Gideon Murray of Elibank, the Treasurer-Depute, and knowing him to be a level-headed and practical man, responsible for making most of the financial arrangements for this visit, he besought him for particulars.

"His Majesty was to visit the Royal Mint, first. Then be received by the Constable of the Castle, with cannon-fire. Then to inspect the proposed site of George Heriot's Hospital. Then attend a mid-day banquet at the Council Chambers, my lord Duke. All this after examining what has been done here at the palace in preparation for his coming. Then . . ."

"Enough for a start, Sir Gideon—of a mercy! See you—the Mint will not go away. Nor will Heriot's Hospital. Nor yet the Castle. But this of cannon-fire—His Majesty would not wish to miss that, I think. He likes cannon-fire. When is he expected at the Council House?"

"By an hour after mid-day, my lord—or as near as possible."

"M'mm. It is little more than an hour to mid-day now.

41

We have not got over-long. I think that the Council will have to be warned, Sir Gideon, that there may be some slight delay. And the cannon-fire put off until the afternoon. Can you see to this? Meantime, we must find the King . . ."

"My lord Duke—I must make protest!" an authoritative English voice interrupted. "The quarters I have been given are entirely unsuitable. They are not even in this palace but in a squalid burgher's house out in the street. Where I have to share with some clerk. Named Laud, I believe—the Dean of somewhere. It is not to be borne. Some ridiculous mistake. It must be righted, forthwith!"

"I too, Lennox . . ." another indignant noble voice began, when Ludovick held up his hand.

"My lords—I beg of you. Not now. No doubt other arrangements can be made. But first things first. The King's day's business must be set to rights . . ."

"I will not be put off, Lennox," the first protester insisted. "I am Philip Herbert, Earl of Montgomerie, Lord of the Bedchamber. And I . . ."

It was Ludovick's turn to interrupt. "*Extra* Lord of the Bedchamber, my lord," he mentioned, gently enough. There were titters. It was always difficult to deal with James's former favourites, demoted. "Wait you, if you please. Much re-arranging may well be necessary. But later . . ."

"I have already waited sufficiently long. I protested to this man, last night. Told that he was responsible. And he has done nothing." He pointed to Sir Gideon Murray.

"May I speak, my lord Duke—to this lord and to others?" that harassed individual said urgently. "His Majesty sent me command to find lodging for 5,000 persons. Five *thousand*! And stabling hereabouts for 5,000 horses! Can any here turn their minds to these numbers? To finding 5,000 beds? Of *any* quality! This palace of Holyroodhouse has been empty and unused for many years—save for a servants' wing. I have had to rebuild and refurbish, put on new roofing. Even so, in its present state the palace cannot sleep more than 1,500. I do what I can, but . . ."

While this heart-felt disclaimer was proceeding, Ludovick turned to his son, still at his side, to whisper. "Go find the

King, Johnnie. You will know this park and demesne well enough. Find James and ask him what he intends. Tell him what is to do here, but chiefly of this banquet. He may know well enough, and care not. He may have forgotten. But tell him that *I* must know what is to be done. If I am to look after his interests. Save us—he has a Master of the Household whose task this should be—but Lord knows where *he* is. Probably hunting, also. Off with you now, lad . . ."

Looking doubtful indeed, but anxious to help his father, John nodded and slipped away.

So, John Stewart traversed the green slopes of Arthur's Seat for the second day running, but this time he did it mounted, as befitted a knight, for he was learning how to behave at court and had grabbed the first good-looking horse he saw tethered in the palace forecourt 'on the King's business', none gainsaying. With not the least idea where James might be by now, he was uncertain in which direction to ride. However, since it was said to be a hawking-party, the probability was that the sportsmen would be somewhere in the vicinity of water—for indeed there was little else for them to hunt these days than wildfowl. The deer which used to be so plentiful were now all gone, mainly poached by the Edinburgh citizenry but also dying out as the woodland around the skirts of the hill, which had given them cover, was gradually cut down. There were still a few hares and rabbits on the hill but Majesty was scarcely likely to go chasing these. A royal decree had come up from London some months previously declaring that, from that date, no muirfowl, partridges nor pout—meaning game-birds—were to be killed by any whatsoever on pain of £100 fine; so clearly James had his eye on such. He would not find many partridges nor muirfowl—that is red grouse or hazel-hens —on Arthur's Seat, but the three lochs were a great haunt of wild duck, wild geese and swans. So the hawking would be apt to start in the vicinity of one or other of the lochs.

The nearest was St Margaret's Loch, which lay on the low ground at this north-east side of the hill, named after the well nearby where King David the First had drunk for much-needed refreshment after he had been attacked by the wounded stag—which of course had been scared off by his chaplain waving the casket containing his mother, St Margaret's, famed Black Rood, or piece of the true Cross of Calvary, the occasion for his founding of the Abbey of the Holy Rood and the palace which developed therefrom.

John rode to St Margaret's Loch, beneath St Anthony's Chapel on its knoll, but there were no sportsmen there; and some children playing at the water's edge declared that John was the first horseman they had seen. Which left Dunsappie and Duddingston Lochs.

Dunsappie, which John had skirted the day before on his climb, was not much more than half-a-mile off, to the south, but some three hundred feet higher. It was small, really only a mountain tarn, and without the great reed-beds of Duddingston, to shelter and feed the wildfowl—so the latter was the more likely. However, Dunsappie was as it were on the way, although involving the ascent; and from the ridge above it a panoramic view of all the Duddingston, Priestfield and Craigmillar area could be seen and the hunts-men surely to be picked out.

With a horse to do the climbing for him, he was soon up to Dunsappie, scattering sheep. The place was deserted and looking desolate, so different from yesterday. He seemed to have Arthur's Seat to himself.

But from the ridge to the south he had no difficulty in spotting his quarry. Far below, on the firmer ground beyond the vast sedge-beds of Duddingston Loch, on the lands of Priestfield—now being called Prestonfield, priests being out-of-favour after the Reformation—about a dozen horse-men could be seen milling around, presumably flying their hawks. The chances of them being other than the royal party were remote.

Although not much more than another half-mile away as the crow flies, to get down to them was less simple. First of all, the slopes at this side were exceedingly steep, really a southwards extension of the great red crags which soared above Holyrood, with a peculiar pillared rock formation known as Sampson's Ribs. Then, at the bottom was the quaking sea of reeds. No horseman could descend the first nor cross the second. So John had to ride on eastwards at this high level, and in the wrong direction, to get down the more manageable slopes beyond, where their Pictish ancestors had dug cultivation-terraces out of the hillside, to reach Duddingston village itself. Then he had to work the long way round the loch and its sedgy extension westwards, although most of this he could do at the canter on fairly level ground so long as he kept well back from the shore. In this royal demesne the King could not have chosen a hawking-ground further away from his palace.

As he rode up on to the Prestonfield parkland, the mounted huntsmen were well scattered and mainly in pairs, much shouting and wagering going on and dogs barking. The sport consisted of the dogs being sent into the reeds to put up duck, geese, herons, swans or other fowl, and then the hawks to be unhooded and released from their owners' wrists to fly at selected birds. Although the sportsmen would prefer to choose each their own fowl, it was usually the sprung hawks that did so. Then the owners would wager on whose hawk would stoop on what quarry and make the kill, whilst they strove to ride as nearly beneath the aerial chase as was possible, shouting encouragements or curses—although here, much of it being over water or swamp, this was difficult. The dogs were then sent in to retrieve the plummeting game and the trained hawks called or whistled back to their owners' wrists. It was all a lively, noisy, ploutering business.

The ideal was for two hawks to aim at the same quarry, so that their owners could wager against which would make the kill, in which case the riders tended to be in pairs. But that by no means always happened and frequently, with sufficient game put up by the dogs, as here, the hawks all went after different fowl—in which case the wagering had to become more complicated. A further complication now was the reluctance of the others to wager against the King— who liked to win, and moreover kept notably good and well-trained hawks. Reigning favourites, such as Steenie Villiers, usually prudently saw to it that they flew inferior birds so that the monarch was unlikely to be offended by losing to them.

John had no difficulty in spotting James, whose extraordinary sacklike posture in the saddle was unique. He was with two others, Steenie—who presumably was forgiven for yesterday's failure—and the rubicund Bishop of Ely, who of course came from splendid wildfowl country in the Cambridgeshire fens. The young favourite looked bored.

Boredom took on an added sourness at sight of John riding up. The King spared only a glance from his hawk's assault on a great, lazily-flapping heron.

"Ha—Johnnie Stewart, come a-hawking! You're late, man—right dilatory. Long abed, nae doubt. Lying in after your knightly vigil, eh? Or after chambering and wantonness, mair like!"

"No, Sire, neither. My lord Duke sent me. We . . . he knew nothing of this hunting and hawking. He sent me for Your Majesty's instructions."

"Aye, well—no' the noo, laddie. Can you no' see I'm busy? I . . . ha—a strike! An excellent strike. Feathers! Aye, a notable stoop. Yon heron will no' survive another, I say. It'll no' survive another stoop. Ten gold nobles, Bishop, that it comes doon on the next strike."

"Taken, Your Majesty," the prelate said, if without enthusiasm.

"Aye—at him, Hippogryph! At him, my bonny bird! He's big, but nae spunk, the great muckle brute! My Hippogryph's mair'n a match for him, Bishop. Hippogryph—you catch the allusion, John Stewart, eh?" A quick look at the younger man. "The winged hero, mind! Ha—there he goes again! A kill . . . och, well, no' just. Yon was no' really a strike at a', Bishop, mind. A miss, just. No' to be counted . . ."

"But feathers, Sire! Look—see them fluttering down. That is ten gold nobles . . . !"

"Na, na—those are loose feathers frae the last strike, man. It was no' a hit, I say. Was it, Steenie?"

"I . . . ah, did not notice, Sire," the beautiful youth said.

"You should keep your bit mind on the sport, boy. Dreaming, eh? Och—maybe dreaming o' your auld gossip

46

Jamie, belike? Aye, maybe! You, John Stewart—you've got guid eyes, I warrant. *You* saw it was nae strike?"

As has been said, John was an honest young man. He coughed. "It . . . it seemed to me to hit, Your Majesty. At the base of the neck. A fair stroke. But—see! It is coming down, I think. The heron. Yes, it loses height . . . !"

James, who had turned to glare at his new knight, looked back. "Guidsake—aye, so it does, lad! It comes doon. See—there it fa's. I was right, Bishop man. Yon great waffling fowl hasna survived a second strike. Ten gold nobles . . . !"

The heron's deliberate flapping had changed to an ungainly aerial floundering, and in an untidy bundle of long wings, neck and sticklike legs it fell with a splash into the reeds. Majesty spurred in after it in triumph.

He did not get far, of course—his horse had more sense, swinging round and back as it sank up to its knees. The dogs retrieved the heron, and James began to coax down his hawk with wheedling cries.

John tried again. "Sire—the Duke of Lennox requires your instructions. There is much, much concern at the palace. Matters have been arranged for Your Majesty. For this day. Many wait, not knowing what . . ."

"Aye, lad, folk are ay arranging matters for my Majesty! No' always to my taste, see you. Whiles, I prefer my ain arranging."

"Yes, Sire. But the Duke my father requires to know Your Highness's will. In especial in this of the banquet in the City Chambers. It is due to start within the hour, I think . . ."

"Then it will hae to wait. It will do them a' good. They're ower fond o' belly-pandering, these folk." James had retrieved his hawk and hooded it, stroking its feathers gently. "Is my Hippogryph no' a bonny bird?"

"Undoubtedly, Majesty. Shall I go tell the Duke then that Your Highness will not be attending the banquet?"

"No' so fast, Sir Johnnie—no' so fast! I didna say that, did I? I said they'd hae to wait. You'll need to listen mair heedfully to my royal words if you're going to serve me, mind. Eh, Steenie? Bishop—your doited bird is after a shelduck, see. Shelduck are nae guid—you should ken that. Even you Englishry'll no' eat shelduck, I warrant!"

"It is a passage-hawk, Sire, and may have fed on them wild . . ."

"And what of the cannon-fire?" John asked, getting desperate.

"Eh? Eh—cannon-fire, did you say? What's this?" He had the royal attention now.

"The salutation, Sire. From the Castle. The Constable is to fire cannon there, in your honour."

"When? When is this, man?"

"It was to be forenoon, Sire, I think. About now . . ."

"Sakes—they'll no' fire them and me no' there, will they? This Constable man—he canna dae that!"

"I do not know. If it is but a salutation to mark Your Majesty's return to your Scots capital city, it could be fired at any time, for all would hear it . . ."

"Hech, hech—that would be a wicked waste! He'll no' hae done it? Already? Would we hear it, here?"

"Oh, I think so. With the Castle set so high. It ca nnot be more than two miles."

"Aye. Then off wi' you, John Stewart. To Edinburgh Castle. Tell yon Constable, whoever he may be, that he's no' to fire a single cannon until I come. *I'll* fire thae cannon! You have it? You go tell him."

"Now, Sire? *Before* I go back to Holyrood?"

"Aye, now. Instanter. In case the fool starts up. Nae time to lose."

"But—what of the banquet?"

"Deil tak their banquet! It can wait. Off wi' you."

"Yes, Sire. I am to tell the Constable to wait until you come? When will that be?"

"Hoo can I ken that? So soon as I can get there, man. What think you?"

"Before the banquet . . . ?"

"Guidsakes—hud your wheesht aboot this banquet! What's one banquet mair or less?"

"It is just that the Duke said I was to find out, Your Majesty. If Your Majesty wishes to go to it . . ."

"My wishes are that there is to be nae cannon-fire until

48

I come. See you to it—and nae mair havering aboot. Go, John Stewart—or you'll no' be knight for muckle longer, I promise you!"

John bowed from the saddle and reined round his borrowed horse.

He rode, fast, round the south-western flanks of Arthur's Seat, in past the hospice and hamlet of St Leonards, with the suicides' graveyard, and through the Greyfriars Port into the city. Thereafter, down Candlemaker Row, up the West Bow again, scene of yesterday's heroics, and into the Lawnmarket. Thereafter it was merely a straight canter up the causeway to the castle gatehouse and drawbridge.

Today the bridge was down and John was able to ride in unchallenged, a highly unusual state of affairs. He found the various wards and terraced-courts of the great fortress on the crest of the rock thronged with folk, mostly looking bemused and worried. None asked a single young horseman what he was about.

He rode up to the Constable's quarters in one of the topmost towers, to be dismissed briefly with the information that that luminary was not there, and whereabouts unknown. Deciding that the actual battery, where the main armament of cannon were ranged, high above the gatehouse and moat, to protect the only approach not guarded by precipices, was the likeliest place in the circumstances, he hurried thither. This great semi-circular fortification, built forty years earlier, had no fewer than fourteen cannon-ports, pointing to east, north-east and south-east, and was known as the Half Moon Battery. Here, although there were plenty of people surrounding the ranked cannon, enquiries brought him to, not the Constable but the Master of the Royal Ordnance, John, eighth Lord Borthwick, who appeared to be in charge, a cheerful, burly character in his early thirties, who was whiling away the time of waiting by eating an alfresco meal and emptying a flagon of wine. When John had explained his identity and mission, Borthwick informed that the Constable had gone down to Holyroodhouse to discover what had happened to the King. But he added that it was he who would actually order the cannon to be fired, as Hereditary Master-Gunner. He was in no hurry and no fret, he assured, prepared to wait all day—unlike that Constable, who was something of an old wife. He suggested that Methven—John was bashful about informing others that he was now *Sir* John—join him in refreshments.

The pressure being thus eased, the visitor was in three minds whether to return to the King, go back to his father at the palace, or to remain where he was. However, he decided that the monarch might be anywhere by now, on his way here, or returned to Holyrood first; so the best course was probably to wait.

It was as well that he did, for Lord Borthwick, who seemed glad of his company, was showing him the various pieces of artillery, rhapsodising over the mighty Mons Meg, its virtues and vices and odd name, when there sounded a great clattering of hooves from the approach-causeway below. Hurrying to the parapet, they peered over. About a dozen horsemen were pounding up fast, strung out; but well to the fore was a rider whose jouncing, sacklike seat and high hat were unmistakeable.

"It's the King!" John cried. "He has come right away. 't is James himself."

"You say so? Then—the guns should be firing. Quick . . . !"

"No, no—do not fire. He said that *he* would fire them. None to be fired until he came. He was strong on that . . ."

"James? Fire them himself? The King . . . ?"

"Yes. My father says that he likes cannonading."

Borthwick shrugged. "He could blow himself up! Like James Second, at Roxburgh yon time!" He shouted to the gun-teams at each of the nine cannon in use, to stand to and await orders.

James came beating up, swaying in the saddle, hat askew, horse foaming, hooves striking sparks from the cobblestones. John ran to help the monarch down.

"You were in time, Johnnie man," Majesty gasped. "As well, mind. Whae's this? The Constable, is it—or Keeper, or whatever he ca's himsel'?"

"I am the Lord Borthwick, Sire—Your Majesty's Master of the Ordnance."

"You tell me that? Och, I kent your faither, then. A right lecherous auld rogue, too! But leal enough. Noo—whaur do we start? You got plenty powder and shot?"

"Plenty of powder, yes. We'll not need shot, Sire. Or we could be killing folk and bringing down chimneys!"

"Och, there's surely some bit open space where we could aim withoot hurting folk? Just a ball or two. Firing a cannon withoot a ball's like trying to mow a woman lacking the same gear, eh?"

"It is dangerous, Majesty. If the ball falls short . . ."

"If you're a guid cannoneer it *shouldna* fa' short, man. That's the art o' it—you, my Maister Gunner, should ken that. Yon bit ayont the High Riggs, where Geordie Heriot's new hospital's to be—yon's fine and open. A ball there'd dae nae harm. Noo—this muckle great brute's auld Mons Meg—I ken her fine. We'll start wi' her. Is she a' primed and loaded?"

"Primed, Highness—not loaded. None are loaded. Meg throws a seventy-pound ball over two thousand of paces . . ."

"What of it? We'll gie her a bit bang, anyway. You'll hae some wool, man?"

"Wool? No, I never use it, Sire. Some of the gunners have it . . ."

James peered at the master-gunner beside Mons Meg, saw the white lamb's wool plug stopping his ear, tweaked it out and put it in his own ear. He dodged round behind the man to extract the other one. "Noo—gie's your bit lucifer, laddie." Taking the flaring match-rope, he went to the cannon, bent to gaze along the line of the huge barrel, clucking his tongue at the fact that it was lined up on nothing in particular, and applied the flame to the touch-hole.

The explosion was shattering, tremendous, shaking the surrounding buildings, however substantial—as well it might, for the charge contained no less than seventy pounds of gunpowder. John put hands to ears, head seeming to split open. Everywhere people gasped and reeled. A ball of smoke rolled out from the muzzle towards the Lawnmarket.

James actually clapped his hands in delight, sparks flying from the flapping match-rope. Then he ran to the next cannon, a basilisk this one, and lit the primer.

Again the mind-cleaving detonation, a little less powerful than the first but sufficient to bludgeon the senses. Not the King's, however. Gleefully he sped to the neighbouring basilisk, and then the next, bellowing his enthusiasm.

There were only four pieces on either side of Mons Meg, some of the ports being empty; so their liege-lord had to go shambling back, to start on the other four. The echoes and re-echoes reverberated from all Edinburgh's hills in thunderous rivalry.

The royal cannoneer was so expeditious about it that he was back at Mons Meg well before it was fully re-primed, dancing his impatience.

"Quicker, dolts!" he shouted, but slapped the back of the master-gunner nevertheless. "You are fell slow! Hae them all primed, man Borthwick, so that I can keep them whanging withoot pause. A right batteration! Haste you—all o' you!"

So the deafening din recommenced and continued, and if there were any brief interludes, the echoes filled them and there was no respite. Those without ear-plugs clutched their heads, or covered them with clothing—or better, fled for cover indoors, Steenie, the Bishop and the other hawkers amongst the first. Borthwick seemed impervious, presumably inured; but John was dazed, all but paralysed. Surely never, even in time of war and siege had Edinburgh heard so much gunfire and in such quick succession.

Presently, of course, the powder ran out, raggedly. James was dismayed, indignant. There must be more, he declared. A great fortress the size of Edinburgh must have more powder than that. Besides, he had not yet fired his cannon-ball.

Borthwick admitted that there was more powder in the cellars. James could not hear him, of course, until he removed his ear-plugs.

"Then get it, man. Have it up. It's no' every day you'd get a chance to breenge it off this way! *Fulmen brutum*, eh?"

Whilst the Master of the Ordnance went to obey the royal

command, his sovereign polished off the remains of his outdoor meal with evident appreciation.

John would have made good his escape; but James, finding the rest of his party bolted, turned on the young man, to read him a lecture on the different kinds of cannon and demi-cannon, culverins, sakers, falcons, falconets, basilisks and so on, their merits and demerits, weights, ranges and powder-requirements, all sounding most expert, the more so as interspersed with approximately apposite Latin tags. He was still at it when Lord Borthwick arrived back, leading a file of men bearing on their shoulders more kegs of gunpowder.

Nothing would do but that a ball must be fired at Geordie Heriot's site. James chose the second basilisk from the right, declaring that he liked the feel of this one and informing that the feel of a cannon was as important as that of a woman, with sundry similarities pointed out. For a man so interested in pretty youths, he was very knowledgeable about the opposite sex—His most catholic Majesty, as the Duke of Lennox was apt to put it.

Loaded, primed and aimed, he was about to apply the match when Borthwick, nervous for that cheerful character, intervened hurriedly. The aim, he suggested, was a little off, only a little perhaps, but enough to put the ball into Greyfriars Churchyard.

The King denied that, indignantly, and would not hear of the other adjusting the lay. However he did edge the barrel just slightly to the right, unobtrusively, before igniting the charge.

The bang on this occasion had a more muffled sound to it, the smoke-cloud being different too. A black fountain of earth and rubble rose satisfactorily at the very edge of the open ground above and behind the Grassmarket, and within only yards of the kirkyard wall.

"Bonny! Bonny!" James admired. "A notable shot! Did I no' tell the aim was fine and guid, man Borthwick?" And before there could be any other view expressed, he added, "Come, then—let's get on wi' the whanging. In wi' the powder . . ."

The bombardment of the ears recommenced.

In the midst of this the Duke, the Secretary of State and others arrived, having come hot-foot up from Holyrood when the first cannonade started. They came to all but plead that the monarch should now come down to the City Chambers where the banquet was still being held preserved, in some state, and ambassadors, churchmen and the illustrious of two nations had been waiting for hours.

James, with the second lot of powder all but exhausted, was prepared to consider this—but not to be hurried. The newcomers were not to get away without an exposition and demonstration of the cannon and its delights and quirks, before at last they could escort their master down into the city.

Edinburgh uncovered its ears thankfully.

Equally grateful to be forgotten in all this excitement, John Stewart went to return his borrowed horse to Holyrood and then hastened back to his mother's lodging.

3

It was early rising for them all next morning—despite the fact that the Duke did not win back to Mary's bed until the small hours, being unable to get away from his royal cousin at what had become a hard-drinking party at the Secretary of State's house in the Cowgate. The evening's arranged programme had been dinner with a select few, hosted by Lord Tam; but since the city banquet, so delayed in its start, did not finish until early evening, the guests, full of food, merely moved down Libberton's Wynd to the former French Ambassador's House and, dispensing with the actual meal, started on the liquor. This, fortunately or otherwise, was in plentiful supply, and James in high spirits. Hence Ludovick's belated return.

As indicated, the King paid little attention to clocks, and this early start was necessary if the royal cavalcade was to reach Linlithgow, eighteen miles away, for the mid-day meal to be provided there, with suitable elaborations. It transpired that John, whom the monarch now appeared to look upon as something of a mascot and help-in-trouble, was expected to go along. And since they were all making for Stirling after that, which was on her way back to Methven, Mary Gray took the chance of Ludovick's company at least as far as this, and went along too.

So they had to be up betimes, despite the Duke's sore head, packed up, mounted and down to Holyrood all too soon after cock-crow. There they found the usual chaos, compounded by the fact that Steenie was nowhere to be discovered. He had left Tam o' the Cowgate's party early, having as yet only a moderate head for liquor, James advising his bed. Apparently he had not been seen since, and his couch in the royal chamber had not been occupied. Great was the upset, the King refusing to set off without his youthful gossip.

With another day's arrangements looking like being dis-organised, the handsome Chancellor, Lord Fyvie, backed by the Secretary of State and others, was trying to persuade James to make a move; assuring him that the Earl of Buckingham would have come to no harm in the capital city, that he had no doubt gone to ground in one of the many ale-houses between the Cowgate and Holyrood, and would appear in due course and come along after them. Such large cavalcade could move only slowly, as they all knew, so Steenie would no doubt catch them up quite soon.

James was not convinced, fearing a variety of disasters, and threatening himself to go searching for his lost lamb, when his strangely lustrous eye fell on John Stewart, standing listening beside his father and mother. The royal expression lightened somewhat and he pointed at his humble kinsman, whom he obviously considered to be Edinburgh's answer to most problems.

"You, Johnnie Stewart, knight—God be thankit! *You'll* find Steenie Villiers for me. You'll ken where to look in this ill toun! Belike some wicked rogues and scoundrels ha' taken hold o' him . . ."

"I think that highly unlikely, James," Ludovick said. He sounded a little sour this morning. "The entire city has been waiting to welcome you. All sturdy beggars, sorners and wastrels have been driven out, by your own express orders. All remaining seek to pleasure you. None would mistake George Villiers for anything but one of your company! None could be more safe in Edinburgh today."

"I agree, Sire," the Secretary of State said.

"I'm no' sae sure. There's ay ill folk aboot, seeking whom they may devour. I blame mysel', mind. The puir laddie was no' right when he left your house last night, Tam Hamilton. I shouldna hae let him go alone. Neither should you. I should hae seen him to his bit bed, the innocent loon!"

The Duke somehow managed to disguise his choke as a cough. "That would have been ridiculous, James! He is not a child, God knows! He will be sleeping it off somewhere.

We should be on our way. They await us at Linlithgow and then at Stirling. Johnnie Mar will have all ready for you . . ."

"Easy for you to talk, Vicky! You'll find him for me, Johnnie Stewart? You're a guid lad. Aye, and wi' mair gumption than your faither! Bring him safe after us. And quickly, mind."

"I will do my best, Sire."

"Aye, you will! Tak a troop o' the Guard, if you need them."

"I would not think that to be necessary, Your Majesty." John bowed and hurried to his horse, before he got any further extravagant instructions.

Trotting away from the crowded palace-forecourt, he pondered his problem. Probably the suggestion that Villiers would have found his way into one of the innumerable taverns and ale-houses was the most likely answer. The trouble was where to start looking. If he was in an inebriated state when he left Hamilton's house, or feeling sick as he might well be, he might not get far. So it would be sensible to start at the top end.

John rode up the Cowgate, the street and its offshooting wynds all but deserted at this hour, save for scavenging dogs and rooting pigs and poultry—and noted gloomily that none of the numerous hostelries and dens appeared to be open yet. It was the best part of a mile to the French Ambassador's House.

There he dismounted, after riding into the courtyard, hitched his horse to a post and went to rap on the door. Since the owner was with the King at Holyrood, presumably his servants had long been up and about. John was not so well acquainted with Edinburgh's amenities as his liege-lord assumed.

The serving-wench who answered thereafter produced the establishment's major-domo whom, in the King's name, John promptly enlisted in the project, assuming that he would be likely to be more knowledgeable as to the Cowgate than himself. This worthy, at first doubtful, warmed to the quest when he learned that the monarch's favourite was involved. He was able to recollect a young man leaving the house considerably before the others, and indicated, without actually saying so, that he had been considerably the worse for liquor but had brushed aside suggestions of an escort. Further enquiry from the night-porter at the courtyard-gate—who had to be roused from his bed to answer—revealed that the illustrious young reveller had in fact turned left-handed, westwards, on issuing from the gate, instead of right, in other words *up* Cowgate not down towards Holyrood—presumably too drunk to know the difference.

This information put a different complexion on the matter—unless of course Buckingham had presently discovered his mistake and turned back. For it was not far from the Hamilton house to the head of the Cowgate, and according to the major-domo there was only the one ale-house in between. John insisted that he come along with him to enquire there.

After considerable banging at the door of a low-browed den in the basement of a tall tenement decorated with a handsome coat-of-arms and godly motto, a slatternly old wife, wrapped in a tartan shawl, eventually opened up, screeching abuse. She toned down at the sight of the major-domo however, whom she obviously knew; but assured that she had no young men sleeping within, no man of any sort, hers being a respectable house—as Mr Purves knew well. When Mr Purves looked sceptical at that, she added that, if it was *that* sort of house they were looking for, they need not go further than round the corner into Candlemaker Row where there were no fewer than three stews for their inspection.

Cowgatehead, in a mere fifty yards, opened on to the Grassmarket, with the West Bow ascending on the right and Candlemaker Row on the left. Where to look in all these? The Grassmarket was full of ale-houses and taverns, as became a major marketplace. But where to start?

John had an idea. Villiers, with the rest of the royal party, had apparently come down Libberton's Wynd from the City Chambers, in the first place. If he was in something of a drunken stupor when he left the Hamilton house alone, then he might be vaguely looking for a narrow street climbing up on the left, Libberton's Wynd. Candlemaker

Row did that, on this other side. He might well have turned up there by mistake.

Mr Purves admitted the possibility, shaking his head censoriously. No doubt it ill became such as himself, the Secretary of State's chief servitor, to go rapping on the doors of houses of ill-fame at this or any other hour of the day—and apparently all the hostelries in Candlemaker Row approximated to that description. But John was adamant—and this was on the King's business.

So they went to knock at the first door, semi-subterranean, steps down from street-level. It took much thumping before they got any answer, when a bleary-eyed creature, very obviously female however unappetising, came, part-covered by a dirty blanket, to demand their business. Snores from within, on a blast of hot and foul air, indicated at least one male presence; but the lady denied with cackles the custom of any young English gentry. They were entertaining some lords' men-at-arms, but did not aspire to their masters.

Taking her at her word, they went further up and across the street to a slightly better-looking establishment known apparently as Lucky Broun's. Here the door was opened quite promptly and by a much more trim, indeed buxom woman, adequately dressed, who greeted Purves like an old friend, calling him Dand and urging him and his young gentleman inside for a sup of ale. The major-domo, embarrassed somewhat, hastened to point out that this was an ale-house and Mistress Broun a most respectable matron. John cut all this short, to ask the necessary question.

Mistress Broun eyed him warily. "A young gentry Englishman, is it?" she repeated. "Now, I wonder? Mind, they come and go, sir. English, you say? And young . . . ?"

John produced a silver merk.

"Ooh aye, now. It is coming to my mind, sir. Up the stairs, there and the bit door facing you. It's maybe no' your friend, mind . . ."

"Mr Purves—you have that sup of ale with Mistress Broun. I pay." John started to climb the steep stair.

There were four doors up there, three closed. Knocking on the one facing the stairhead, and getting no response, he opened it—and his eyes widened to an unusual sight. Six breasts very much met his gaze, directly opposite. The two in the middle were very feeble masculine ones on a white, hairless and not notably brawny chest. But no such criticism could be levelled at the pairs on either side, all large, round and satisfying, bulging over the rumpled blanket, one with brown aureolas, the other pink. The three tousled heads above, two fair and one dark, had shut eyes.

John considered—and it was a prospect worth considering. This was interesting. He had rather assumed that Steenie's tastes would be otherwise. The vision before him, in consequence, far from shocking him, rather enhanced the favourite in his eyes. They all looked so peacefully replete—it was a pity to disturb them. But a royal command was just that. He coughed loudly.

This producing no results, he went forward to lean over the bed and shake Buckingham's bare shoulder. The young woman directly below him—they were both youthful, obviously—opened her eyes, yawned and smiled up at him, making no attempt to cover herself.

"My lord," he said. "Rouse yourself."

The other girl awoke and reacted differently, starting to giggle and make a great to-do of wrapping the blanket round her exposed upper parts—which had the effect of dragging it right off the female at the opposite side, revealing all her plump nakedness—which sent both off into fits of laughter.

This at last woke Steenie, who peered about him owlishly.

The uncovered lady indicated cheerfully that there was just room for John on the bed alongside her, it being, like herself, of generous dimensions. Expressing his appreciation but regrets, he concentrated on the central figure, who was now sitting up and frowning.

"You, Stewart!" the Earl said. "What is this? How . . . how dare you . . . ?"

"His Majesty's express command, my lord. To find you and bring you after him, with all speed."

"This is not to be borne! I am not some scullion, to be ordered thus—and by such as you! Leave me, sir!"

"I fear not, my lord. I must obey the King's commands,

not yours. He was entirely specific. I am to bring you after him to Linlithgow. He and his train have already started out. He is much concerned for you . . ."

"You say that they have already set off? For this place? What hour is it?"

"Late enough if we are to win to Linlithgow by mid-day."

"A plague on it—and on you! This is insupportable!" The other looked around him. "Where are we?"

"In a Mistress Broun's house-of-convenience in the Candlemaker Row. See you, my lord—I will leave you and your, h'm, friends, whilst you dress. Come down at your earliest and we shall return to Holyrood."

"I'll thank you to watch how you speak me, Stewart. I am the Earl of Buckingham and will not be used so—and by some bastard of Lennox's. I . . ."

John turned on his heel for the door, slammed it behind him and stamped down the stairs.

He sent the major-domo to fetch his horse from the Cowgate house.

Actually George Villiers was down, dressed and scowling, sooner than might have been expected in the circumstances. What arrangements he had made with the ladies John did not enquire—although Mistress Broun indicated that two silver merks would be appropriate payment for entertainment provided. The humiliated and sore-headed client had to admit that he had no money on his person meantime and so must borrow from Stewart.

His humiliation was further emphasised when presently Purves turned up with John's horse, and the Earl found that he had to mount and ride pillion behind his escort—that, or else walk alongside all the way back to Holyrood, which in the present state of his head was contra-indicated. So, in a heavy silence, the two young men trotted down the Cowgate to the palace.

There was considerable delay thereafter, Villiers taking an unconscionable time—no doubt deliberately—about his preparations for the journey, John fretting, although telling himself that it was all no real concern of his. It was almost mid-forenoon before they finally set off westwards.

Linlithgow lay half-way to Stirling, in the rolling West Lothian country-side. Villiers rode fast now, on his magnificent grey—although, not knowing the roads, he was dependent on John for frequent directions. They went by the Waters of Leith and Almond to Kirkliston and Niddry Seton. There was no great sign of horse-droppings on the roadways and tracks, as there would have been had a large cavalcade passed that way, so presumably the royal party had followed another route, probably by Dalmeny and the Queen's Ferry and Abercorn. They went in the main without conversation, neither finding the other's company to his taste.

That is, until the smoke of Linlithgow town appeared rising before them out of its green hollow cradling the loch. Then, slackening pace somewhat, Buckingham allowed the other to draw alongside on the crest of the grassy ridge.

"No need to tell His Majesty, Stewart, of my circumstances. This morning. He would scarce . . . understand."

"Perhaps not."

"It was but a, a mischance. Last night. I do not recollect just how it came about. I was making for Holyrood, you understand, when those wenches accosted me. They, they dragged me inside. I was not, ah, myself."

"To be sure, my lord. It might happen to anyone! Say no more."

"So long as His Majesty is not troubled with it . . ."

The grey town in the hollow, strung round the south shore of the loch, was buzzing like a beehive disturbed when they clattered down into its long and narrow single street. The King and his entourage were already up at the palace apparently and their retainers and men-at-arms were making the most of Linlithgow's amenities.

The two young men trotted uphill to the handsome brown-stone palace on its green mound above the waterside, birthplace of James's ill-fated and beautiful mother Mary. They learned that the meal provided by the magistrates was already proceeding in the great banqueting-hall. Some sort of recitation, from an extraordinary figure in the centre of the hall, was going on as they entered.

Recitation or none, James greeted his Steenie like a ewe-lamb rescued from the slaughter, positively drooling over him and calling on all to rejoice with him. Pushing aside the Provost of Linlithgow, sitting on his right, he made a place there for the prodigal. John Stewart was ignored, and went to seek a modest place at the foot of the hall. However, Mary Gray signalled for him to come and sit beside her and the Countess of Mar, the Duke being placed up at the King's left-hand, as usual.

"You found his estray, then," his mother said. "And small thanks you get! Our liege-lord has been like a mother bereft. We might as well have been riding to a burial!"

"Now perhaps James will be able to pay some heed to this oddity," the Countess observed, referring to the teetering figure enclosed in the plaster-cast of a ramping lion, clutching a paper in one paw and most apparently uncertain whether to proceed or to retire, whilst the monarch fed his favourite with titbits from his own platter.

John consumed the viands brought him, in more hum-drum fashion.

Presently the reciter tried again, at a sign from the Provost, with the King now sitting back, although still with an arm round Buckingham's shoulder, and straightening his high hat:

> "Thrice Royal Sir, here I do you beseech,
>   Who art a Lion, to hear a Lion's speech,"

came forth from the red-painted jaws in a distinctly high-pitched and squeaky voice.

> "A miracle—for since the days of Aesop
>   No Lion till these times his voice dared raise up;
> To such a Majesty, thou King of men
>   The King of Beasts speaks thee from his den,
> Though he now enclosed be in plaster,
>   When he was free was Lithgow's wise Schoolmaster."

A somewhat falsetto roar ended this peroration and for a moment or two there was an agonised silence. Then James nodded his head and waved his wine-cup at the perpetrator.

"Aye. Felicitous. Maist callidatious," he approved. "*Ars celare artem*, as we might say. *Curiosa felicitas*—eh, Steenie?

Mind, yon Aesop, or mair correctly Aesopus, wasna the true begettor o' the Lion fabulosity—yon was an Egyptian by name o' Lokman, centuries before. You, a schoolmaister, should ha' kent that, man. But och, we'll owerlook it. Guid kens I've heard worse harangs in my day! Your name, schoolmaister?"

"Wiseman, Sire—James Wiseman."

"Ha—is that a fact? James the Wiseman—then we hae something in common, eh?" Majesty hooted laughter, and looked round for approval. Everybody dutifully applauded.

As Master Wiseman sought to bow himself out, backwards, a difficult manoeuvre for an upright plaster lion, the King abruptly shouted for him to halt, declaring that he desired to see how the creature was fabricated. Getting to his feet, and pulling up Steenie with him, although he was by no means finished eating, he used the youth's shoulder as a support to totter round the top-table and down the hall to examine the plasterwork. At this uprising of the monarch, of course, everyone else had to stand also, whatever the state of their platters.

A cursory inspection of the lion, with some acid comments on the workmanship and, as so often, James suddenly had had enough. Turning, he beckoned the Provost, told him that he had to get to Stirling, near-on twenty more miles and he had no more time to waste. He thereupon stumped for the door to the courtyard.

Great was the disarray behind him.

It seemed to take a long time to reach Stirling. For a couple of hours, indeed, the magnificent bulk of its castle, the strongest fortress in all Scotland, rose dramatically out of the littoral plain before them, seeming to get little nearer. Horses and riders were tired now, of course, over thirty miles from Edinburgh; and the midday feasting, although welcomed, had not been conducive to hard riding thereafter. Of all the great company the King himself was one of the most spry, for however odd-looking an equestrian, he greatly enjoyed horsemanship and could ride all day without tiring of it. Not all his court felt likewise.

Passing the pows or pools of Forth at Bannockburn,

64

those forward enough to hear were treated to a royal lecture on that great battle, the strategy and tactics and the consequent entire eclipse of the English; also the speaker's step–by–step descent from the victorious Bruce, the hero-king. When England's Lord Chamberlain, the Earl of Pembroke, feeling his years perhaps, had the temerity to point out that his liege must also be descended from the loser, Edward the Second, or he would not be sitting on the English throne, he was left in no doubt that such comments were uncalled for, and that, besides, any unfortunate Plantagenet blood had been well and truly affused and diluted in the more wholesome fluid of Stewart, Douglas, Drummond, Guise, even a droppie of Tudor—although that was in fact the good Welsh name of Theodore, let none forget. Having made this clear, the monarch set off at his fastest the remaining two miles to Stirling.

So it was a distinctly strung–out and straggling company which entered Scotland's most significant town, and arguably its true capital, at the first crossing of Forth, in the centre of the land, where Highlands and Lowlands met, where more royal events had taken place, more parliaments been held and more blood spilled than anywhere else in the kingdom. Cannon-fire from the castle greeted their arrival, to groans from many, James himself in two minds whether to approve of Johnny Mar's enthusiasm or to deplore his foster-brother's waste of good powder before he himself could expend it.

Stirling's streets climbed even more steeply and consistently than Edinburgh's, although there were not so many of them. There were no triumphal arches and spectacles here, for this was only a necessary halt in passage, as it were, dictated by the crossing of Forth and James's dislike of salt-water travel. The main visit to Stirling would be on their return journey. This had been devised in order to allow the Earl of Mar, who had travelled north with the King and who was hereditary keeper here, time to organise special and suitable reception and entertainment. After all, this was where James had been brought up, in the Mar household.

So here, to everyone's relief, the Provost and magistrates

contented themselves with presenting an ode of welcome in Latin. James glanced at it, pointed out an error in construction in the second line, declared ominously that he would peruse the rest at his leisure, thrust it at Ludovick and spurred off up the cobblestoned hill for the castle, to the cheers of the citizenry.

Stirling Castle, although superficially so like that of Edinburgh, was in fact very different. Crowning a similar mighty rock it was smaller in area but an even stronger place, all but impregnable. Where Edinburgh's was a citadel, almost a town in itself on its hilltop, with palace, mansions, halls, a chapel, barracks, armourers', blacksmiths' and other workshops, even its own alehouses, Stirling's was much fined down to essentials. There was a small palace, where James was headed, but it would not hold many of his entourage. It had been all that he knew of home, for most of his childhood—save when he had been captured by this ambitious lord or that and held hostage in their various strongholds.

In these circumstances the Countess of Mar had to act hostess to many of the company. The Earls of Mar had their own private mansion, almost a palace indeed, not in the castle itself but halfway up the hill thereto, a much finer house than the royal one, known as Mar's Wark. Here some of the more illustrious guests were installed. Although Mary Gray and her son were scarcely to be so described, the Countess invited them into her own personal apartments, where it was hoped that her brother would join them presently. The rest of the company had to find what lodging they could in the town, with the usual outcry.

Ludovick arrived quite soon, explaining that James, feeling disinclined for more feasting, was settling down to another night's hard drinking, with Johnny Mar, who was a notable toper, and a few other cronies. Not being able to face two consecutive doses of this, the Duke had managed to make his escape. It had been like this all the way north from London, he revealed. James had a phenomenal capacity for liquor, although no one could remember ever having seen him drunk. But tonight it would not be wines or ale that they were drinking but spirits, the potent Scots *uisge-beatha*,

66

the water of life. Heaven alone knew what would be the effect on those unused to it—Steenie Villiers, for instance.

Buckingham was, of course, a subject for discussion, and all were eager to hear John's account of his finding and restoration to his master's embrace. That young man was uneasy about telling all, even to these three, in view of Villiers' charge not to inform the King as to details; but his elders assured that it would go no further than themselves—and, besides, James undoubtedly would piece together the story for himself, sooner or later, for he was an expert interrogator, having, as it were, served his apprenticeship in the witch-trials, first in Scotland then in England. So all was revealed to his father, mother and aunt.

In the consequent mirth and jollity, John was surprised to find himself actually defending George Villiers, after a fashion. He declared that it was scarcely to be wondered at if he broke out occasionally from his wretched role of royal lap-dog; and at least this had shown that he was sufficiently masculine and normal at heart—if heart was the correct location. The women, with their instinctive hatred of cata-mites, would have none of this, asserting that if so this all made Villiers' shameless behaviour with James the more reprehensible, a young man deliberately corrupting himself for royal favour, power and influence. It was getting to the stage where, like the late and unlamented Carr, Earl of Somerset, almost all office and privilege had to be sought through the favour of this infamous youth. He was no better than a disaster, and a sickening one.

The Duke took a somewhat different view. While dis-liking the favourite and all he stood for, he claimed that he was not necessarily a disaster—as admittedly Carr had been. He was more intelligent, for one thing, and less vain, and so far had not been responsible for any very grievous devel-opments. He was, to be sure, being manipulated by the powerful and ambitious men who had groomed him and brought him to James's notice; but it would be a mistake to underestimate the King's own part in the matter. Almost everyone consistently failed to recognise James's shrewd-ness. He looked a fool and sounded a fool—and was not. Deliberately he set out to be underestimated, the better to work his will. This habit of dealing through favourites was a device, a premeditated policy. It fell in with his peculiar tastes and fondnesses; but he used those, as he used all else, to further his own purposes as ruler. All was planned. James ruled alone, all but an absolute monarch. Parliament—the English Parliament—was hostile and kept him permanently short of money, refusing to impose his taxation. He had suffered, in Scotland, from over-powerful lords and factions; and when he went to England he found the same there, for during Elizabeth's later years she had allowed the Cecils and the Howards to usurp almost all the powers of government. James had been changing all that. It was extraordinary what he had achieved against entrenched privilege and influence. His policy had been to work through middlemen and nonentities, not the great nobles—hence the Cokes and Egertons, the Cranfields and Mostons and the rest. And this of deliberately using favourites through which such could be brought to him and, as it were, strained and filtered for consideration, was all part of the plan. The great lords would not so demean themselves. James had worked out various ways of keeping them down, without resort to armed might as had done previous kings. This was one. Also, of the bribes and payments which Steenie and his like collected for their favours, some substantial proportion found its way into the royal pocket, kept empty by parliament. Those who judged James Stewart witless were themselves the fools.

The ladies were not wholly convinced but John grew the more intrigued by their peculiar liege-lord. He asked many questions. When the talk veered to more personal matters, especially about certain affairs at Methven, he it was who sought more than once to bring it back to King James. But his aunt was incurably romantic and persisted with her hints and allusions. When at length she lost patience with John's parrying, she came out with it bluntly.

"What of Janet Drummond?" she demanded.

Her nephew feigned surprise. "You mean Madderty's daughter? I have not been to Innerpeffray for some time, so do not know. Is she a friend of yours?"

"Her mother and I are acquainted. She tells me of Janet."

"Then you are probably better informed as to her health than am I, Countess." That was almost curt.

The Duke looked from one to the other, head aslant. "Do I detect something here that I perhaps should know?" he wondered.

"No," his son said briefly.

"Johnnie is keeping his cards close to his chest!" Lady Mar said. "Perhaps it is his new knighthood?"

"Damn the knighthood!"

Mary Gray came to her son's rescue. "It is no great matter," she said lightly. "John has been seeing something of Janet Drummond—amongst other young women, to be sure. She is grown uncommon attractive. John is not the only one who has noticed it, for she has half the young men of Strathearn agog, even young Perth himself. That is all."

"Ah. Well, something of the sort had to happen, sooner or later. Do I take it that you are scarcely a front-runner, lad?"

"The knighthood might help, you know," the Countess suggested.

"The matter is of no moment and I would prefer not to discuss it," the young man declared. "What, sir, are the arrangements for tomorrow?"

Ludovick grinned, nodding. "Very well, so. Tomorrow our liege starts the day with gunfire! Then we cross the bridge and proceed along Forthside eastwards to Culross, where Bruce receives us at the abbey, with unspecified delights. Then on to Dunfermline for the night, at Fyvie the Chancellor's charges. The next day to Falkland for the hunting—where pray God we can break loose and come to Methven."

"We? So John goes too?" Mary asked.

"Oh, yes. James will expect it. John is for the moment part of the court, and none can leave court without permission."

"Well, I can! I am not part of his circus, Heaven be praised! I shall make for Methven tomorrow. I can expect you there, then, in three days or four?"

"I would hope so, yes. But James is ever unpredictable."

"Oh, for the day when you are no longer dependent on the whims of that so clever crowned clown!"

"Let us just be thankful that James is not very interested in women, my dear," the Countess said. "So we are not thus hobbled! Myself, I shall bide here until they all come back—and my royal cousin will never notice."

"Be not so sure," her brother said. "Not much escapes those great hart's eyes."

Stirling was rudely awakened early next morning to the incessant crash of cannon-fire, which seemed to come from directly above, like a thunderstorm, so steeply under the castle-rock crouched the town. Presumably, if any ball was fired, on this occasion, it fell into the pools and marshes of Forth. To this din they breakfasted and all too quickly, when it ceased, had to take hurried leave of the ladies to join the royal retinue which came jingling down the hill on the way to Stirling Bridge. No crowds saw them off at this unsuitable hour—with two-thirds of the entourage missing besides.

Across the ancient bridge and on to the causeway through the wetlands beyond, the King drew rein and treated the early-morning company to a lengthy exposition on William Wallace's famous battle fought here and the grievous English failures which brought about their defeat. However unwelcome to most there, this at least enabled the late-risers and stragglers to catch up. Thereafter, at Causewayhead they turned eastwards to head past Cambuskenneth to the north shore of the quickly-widening estuary.

It was some eleven miles, by Alloa, Clackmannan and Kincardine-on-Forth, to Culross, a small whitewashed, red-roofed town and harbour, where the venerable St Serf had established his Celtic abbey at the end of the sixth century—which abbey, Romanised to the Cistercian Order, had passed to the Bruce family at the Reformation. Now Sir George Bruce, with many West Fife gentlemen, met them at the approaches to the town, a round, bustling little man of middle years, genial and laughter-loving, far from typical of the Scots aristocracy. Indeed, he was exceptional in more than manner and appearance; for he was one of the greatest traders and merchant-venturers in the land—and would have been roundly despised and shunned by the gentry, in consequence, had it not been for his undeniable descent from kin of the hero-king Robert. He had taken over, as a going concern, the extensive coal-mines and salt-pans of the monks of Culross and had, with a lively business-sense and no nonsense about the unsuitability of making money from trade, developed and amplified these industries to a notable degree, as well as adding new ones, so that now he was one of the richest men in Scotland. He had built up a vast overseas traffic in coal and salt, in ironware and salted-herring and other items, to the extent that as many as 170 vessels at a time had been counted in and lying off Culross harbour. Even this May noonday there were fully fifty ships there.

James, always preoccupied with money, the lack of which had haunted him all his days, was much concerned to discover how Bruce seemed to be able more or less to coin it; and at the same time to seek to devise means by which he might be separated from some substantial part of his gains. The crowded shipping impressed him, although he did not fail to point out that he misliked and distrusted sea-going vessels; and the unsightly heaps of slag from the mines drew the shrewd comment that, though they looked like the Devil's ordure, if all this waste material was to be dumped out in the shallower waters of the estuary there, in the form of artificial reefs, then the area within could be drained and reclaimed, to provide new land for salt-pans, abstracted from the evil sea—a triumph for God and man against Satanicus, as he put it. Sir George, blinking, promised to consider this. But meantime would His Majesty care to honour his poor house at the abbey for a light repast? They could examine the possibilities of the mines and salt-pans later perhaps?

Majesty graciously agreed—but first elected to inform the company that it was fell suitable that this small bit atomy of his ancient kingdom should flourish as a hot-bed and *fons et origo* of industry and indefatigation—*perfervidum ingenium*. For was it not from here that the excellent St Serf—more properly St Servanus, mind—had sent forth the laddie Kentigernus or Mungo, with a bit cart drawn by two wild bulls, unchancy brutes, to found the city of Glasgow on the Clyde, whose industriosity thereafter was an ensample to all. *Forti et fidele nihil difficile!* Mind, Glasgow's fair operoseness was the more commendacious in that the place was over near to the territories of the deplorable Hamiltons. Having delivered himself of this profound observation, the monarch, with a glance around to see if any Hamiltons, in especial the Secretary of State, were within hearing, set off for the proffered refreshment at the Abbey House.

Bruce had called the provision light but it proved to be in fact the most substantial and ambitious spread yet provided in Scotland, with liquid accompaniment in keeping; with the inevitable result that when, at length, the King declared himself satisfied and eager to discover the secrets of profit-making, precious few of the company were of a mind or in a state to accompany him. Which entirely suited James, who had no desire to share his findings, if any, with a multitude, especially with Sir George pointing out that mine-workings, like salt-pans and stores, were scarcely places for crowds.

Only about a dozen, therefore, accompanied their host and sovereign down the hill again to the narrow and busy coastal flats, the Duke and John amongst them. James elected to inspect a mine first.

Almost straight away there was difficulty. For, although the entry to the chosen pit probed unexceptionably into the hillside, away from the shore, and led gently enough down through a tunnel, lit by lamps carried by specially-washed minions, after a mere hundred yards or so they came to a gaping shaft in the floor, surmounted by an erection of timber scaffolding with pulley-wheels and ropes. The King eyed this contraption suspiciously, especially when the wheels began to turn and squeal, declaring it obviously to be a device of the Devil. His alarm was only enhanced when up out of the depths came a wooden platform hoisted by the ropes, with a miner, naked to the waist and streaky black, standing thereupon. A blast of hot air and a curious smell seemed to come up with this vision—which had James pointing out how right he had been about Satanicus and the Nether Regions, as this Devil's Acolyte and the hellish stink demonstrated. Bruce explained that this was merely the hoist-man, Dod Durie by name, who worked the ropes and would take them down. He gestured forward. When the monarch realised that he was expected actually to stand on this precarious platform and descend into the black depths on it the expedition all but ended there and then in loud protests and accusations. Their host soothingly pointed out that it was entirely safe, that hundreds of men, women and children went up and down in it every day, and if His Majesty wanted to see the mine, as intimated, this was the only way. Looking round him in major distress, the King's eye fell on the useful John, and lightened a little. Steenie was not present.

"You—aye you, Sir Johnnie. *You* go. Aye, you go doon there. See if it is to be trusted wi' our royal person. Try out this ill contrive and see what's what. You have spunk enough. Come back and tell me—if you can! Mind, if you dinna come back, I'm oot o' here like a wheasel! You be quiet, George Bruce!"

Swallowing a grin, John stepped on to the platform and Bruce signed to the hoist-man to lower away.

To a loud creaking and clanking the platform descended into darkness.

"Yon's a right feartie!" the man Durie shouted, above the din. "Whae is he, at a'?"

"That's the King."

"Him . . . !" The rest was left unsaid.

"He is none so ill." John found himself defending his sovereign. "Some things he fears excessively—plots and cold steel and deviltry and witchcraft, they say. It is believed because his mother the Queen Mary's secretary, Rizzio, was stabbed to death in front of her eyes just before James was born. He is courageous enough in other ways . . ."

His unseen companion sniffed but said nothing.

It was getting hotter all the time in that black shaft. Presently a faint glimmer of light began to show through the cracks in the boarding beneath their feet and this developed into the yellow flame of a lamp hanging from a gleaming ebony roof where the platform clanked to a halt. John peered out. They seemed to be in something like a great cavern, dimly lit, walls and ceiling of chipped jet, with various

73

openings off, some man-height, some only half that. Even as he looked a completely naked, black-streaked figure came crawling up on hands and knees out of one of the lower cavities, dragging a wicker basket filled with lumps of coal. This, when risen upright, the figure hoisted up staggeringly, to tip it into a large wooden trolley standing there, with others, in a black cloud of dust, before crouching down and entering the hole again, with the basket, like an animal into its burrow.

"Saints above!" John exclaimed. "That . . . that was a child. A girl, I saw, I saw . . . !"

"Aye, the lassies are right guid for hauling up yon braes," Durie explained. "They're ower low for grown folk."

"But . . . but . . . down there! Below this . . . ?"

"Och, aye—the workings are further doon. The galleries where the hewers work, just. The men cut, the weemen drag the coal frae the face and the bairns draw it up the braes."

John was silent.

"Up, then?" the man asked, and at a nod started to pull on the ropes.

Emerged again into the half-light of the upper entry, James cried out at sight of them.

"You survived, man—God be praised! Is it secure and unjeopardous? Nae pitfalls?" He was relieved enough to chuckle. "Pitfalls, eh—right apt!"

"None, Sire. Only strangeness and, and the unnatural. There are children down there."

"Is that a fact? Och, then it should be safe enough." James allowed himself to be assisted on to the platform.

There followed the problem of who was to accompany the monarch down, for the hoist would take only seven or eight at a time, and with John, whom he clutched tightly for safety, Sir George and the hoist-man, there was room only for three more, for James would by no means have the thing overloaded. He solved the matter by beckoning Ludovick on, then selecting the two lightest-looking men there, Chancellor Fyvie and Sir Gideon Murray, the Treasurer-Depute, rejecting Tam Hamilton as too large and the Earl of Southampton as having too gross a belly. Huddled together, this company descended, to loud instructions to Durie-man to go canny and to John to keep close, exclamations at the wicked darkness, the satanic heat and the noxious stench. John could feel the royal body pressed against his own, trembling.

At the bottom, escaped out of the shaft, Bruce explained that this had been the first level of mining, but that as this seam of coal was worked out, they had had to probe down lower and lower, so that now they were working three seams at least two hundred feet further down, reached by these adits or braes. Unfortunately His Majesty could scarcely proceed down there since they would have to go on hands and knees. But further along this main gallery there was a new and shallow working where they could observe coal being won . . .

Whilst this was being announced, Sir George's voice began to be overborne by the rumbling and creaking as one of the large trolleys emerged from the main tunnel, pushed from behind. When this halted, the pushers appeared round the sides and proved to be two women, both naked from the waist up, ragged skirts kilted high and tucked into rope belts, thighs bare also. Covered with coal-dust and sweat they made no lovely sight.

"Guidsakes—those are women!" James gasped, peering in the dim light. "See their paps! Shameless hussies and maist undecorous!"

"It gets very hot down here, Sire—as you may feel. And they have a long way to push these carts before . . ."

Bruce was interrupted. "Mercy on us—look at that!" The King was pointing to another of the low-browed apertures, where a child and his basket had appeared, a boy this, all grinning white teeth in a black face, wholly unclothed and looking no more than perhaps eight years. "An imp of Satanicus himsel'!"

The boy, rising from his knobbly knees, had difficulty in hoisting up his heavy-laden basket to empty into one of the trolleys and John went to aid him, blackening his hands in the process. The lad, staring open-mouthed at the gentlemen, looked shocked and guilty at this unsuitable assistance, and bolted for his hole, still more like a rabbit.

"Save us—what's he at?" James demanded. "Did you see that, Vicky? Did you ever ken the like?"

Whilst Bruce was explaining the children's part in the mining process, the women set off with a loaded trolley, the one in front putting on a sort of harness consisting of a double chain attached to a broad leather band which she placed round her forehead and so bent to the task, whilst her companion pushed from the rear. They had to strain hard to get the laden cart moving and once again John went to help overcome the initial inertia—to the rear woman's skirl and Sir George's chuckle that he would employ this young man any day. Embarrassed by this reaction, John left off pushing—but remained embarrassed as the elegant party strolled on along the main gallery behind the straining women.

It seemed that they had quite a long way to go, along this jet-black corridor lit by only occasional lamps—although Bruce now carried a lamp himself to ensure if possible that the distinctly shambling royal feet did not trip on the uneven floor.

There was a hold-up presently when a second pair of women, one quite elderly by her figure, returning with another truck, had to pass the first in a space just wide enough and no more. Bruce tut-tutting, declared that they had better get past or they would be all day reaching their destination. So they squeezed by, the King taking the opportunity to pinch one of the female behinds in passing by way of acknowledgement.

They passed many low-set side-alleys, some seeming to keep the same level, others sloping steeply downwards. One or two disgorged children. In time they came to a higher entry, almost man-height and Bruce led the way in, stooping. James promptly knocked his high hat off, muttering indignantly—and John had his first glimpse of his prince hatless. He was alleged to wear headgear even in his bed.

They slanted down this narrow passage in single file, it getting steeper and hotter. At one stage they paused, having to press against the black wall to allow a convoy of a woman and three children, all on hands and knees hauling filled baskets, to get past. James, gasping a little for breath now in the heat, observed that the place was fair crawling with the creatures, like an ant-hill, whereat Sir George informed that he employed nearly three hundred in this pit alone, men, women and bairns. It was what he called a family pit, where an entire family could work together. Was not that an excellent arrangement?

His hearers may have seemed only moderately enthusiastic.

Soon they were hearing the clink and thud of picks and hammers, and rounding a bend there was light ahead. Here, illuminated by three lamps, was a scene which might have come out of Dante's Inferno, with the damned working out their grim destiny. Two men, entirely unclothed, hacked and battered at the coal-face, whilst two others crouched, heads down, recovering nearby. Three half-naked women stooped behind, scooping the hewn coal back and into baskets, with wooden shovels and bare hands; and a group of children waited for the filled baskets, all panting in the heat.

The visitors considered this scene for a while, unspeaking. Then James said, "Here, I say, is work for felons, skellums and gaol-limmers, no' for honest subjects o' mine. Man Bruce, you sell dear-won coals!"

Astonished, Sir George protested. "Why, Sire, they are paid good siller. All are glad of the work. As I say, all the families can work together. None go hungry."

"Aye. Let us be out o' here. I mislike it."

Crestfallen, Bruce led the way back.

Up at the main gallery again, James was for turning left-handed whence they had come. But their host led them to the right, saying that there was still something to see.

They went on for a considerable distance further, passing numerous trolleys and entries, and James, who was no walker, was soon complaining, with Bruce assuring him that they would have further to go if they turned back. The monarch was becoming disenchanted.

In the event, he hailed another hoist almost with relief—only almost, because this one was more than twice as large as the first and so capable of being twice as dangerous. As they waited, the platform came down, to disgorge two women and an empty trolley—James declaring that they were the same pair they had first encountered, he recognised them by their mammilla he added, their faces being no more distinguishable than were black Moors.

Gingerly entrusting himself to this platform, which was of a size to take the entire company, the King remarked on the lowering temperature as they rose, contriving a parable out of this, in Latin, for the edification of at least the Scots present—only English priests and siklike apparently being taught Latin, he revealed.

This enlightenment ended abruptly, as they emerged into daylight, bright daylight, indeed sunlight, and sunlight reflected on water. James gasped, choked, and made a grab at John Stewart.

"Treason! Treason!" he yelled. "Wae's me—all's undone! Treason! The sea—the fell sea!"

Sure enough, they had come up a shaft, extended with notable skill to rise from the bed of the estuary and to finish as a sort of isolated jetty or wharf, almost a mile out from the shore. The King—whose dread of the sea probably dated from his return, with his bride, from Denmark, when a storm off North Berwick and the Bass Rock, engineered by witches, had much distressed him—was appalled, instantly terror-stricken, imploring the aid of Heaven, the saints and all true and honest men, clinging to John. In vain Sir George explained that this was a device for loading coal directly on to ships, without them having to crowd the limited space of the harbour; that it was perfectly safe and in use every day. The monarch was convinced that it was all a dastardly plot. Torn between a desire to hurry back whence they had come and escape all this terrifying water, and fear of the long, black passage below to be walked, he wailed and clutched and refused to be reassured.

The Duke pointed out that there was a handsome pinnace moored to the timbers directly below, but James cried that it was to be approached only by a more deplorable ladder down which he would by no means descend. Bruce was at a loss, declaring that this was the only way down and that there were only a dozen or so rungs anyway; but Majesty would have none of it. He was not a Barbary ape, he asserted, to swing from branches and pendicles.

It appeared to be stalemate, with progress neither backwards nor forwards to be considered. John ventured a suggestion.

"If I was to take Your Highness on my back, pickapack . . . ?"

"Eh? Eh?"

"If you clung to me, and I carried you down, all would be well, Sire. I am much used to ladders. At Methven . . ."

James stared. It is probable that he would never for a moment have considered it; but he had come to look upon John as something like a saviour; moreover, no other solution offered itself. He bit trembling lip.

John turned, offering his sturdy back. The Duke urged James on, indeed assisted him up.

So, arms round John's neck, all but throttling him in fact, knees dug in at the waist with a horseman's grip—being better on a horse than on his feet no doubt helped—the sovereign of two kingdoms was brought to the ladder-head and lowered step by step, hat askew and babbling incoherent instructions. John was a fairly muscular young man and very fit, and did not feel the royal burden too sorely, although he could have done with less of the strangling. They reached the pinnace to paeans of thankfulness.

The others descended with no comparable difficulties and oarsmen soon had the boat heading shorewards. Bruce endeavoured to efface unfortunate impressions, and to distract the royal passenger from contemplating now death from drowning, by holding forth on the mutual advantages of coal and salt production, the coal being used to heat the great shallow pans of seawater which, evaporated, left the salt. The salt was used to preserve the fishermen's catch, which was then barrelled and exported to Muscovy and the Low Countries. The coal and salt were shipped in bulk also, of course. Moreover there were potteries using local fireclay and an iron foundry smelting local ironstone . . .

But James was not to be diverted from his contemplation of the dire dangers and potential perils he had just been in—and still was—and from which only Almighty God and Johnnie Stewart had rescued him. Sir George was much discountenanced.

Once safely ashore, the King would not hear of any further inspections, entertainments or refreshment. He was for Dunfermline, that was what, a decent godly place with no devilments and hazards. Alec Seton would conduct him there.

The Chancellor declared that he would rejoice to do so, even though somewhat earlier than anticipated. He was building a new palace there, in which His Majesty would be most comfortable, even though it was not yet completed. It was only another eight miles or so.

Sir George Bruce was left, dejected and with scant thanks, to send on the bulk of the entourage, still presumably roistering in the Abbey House, to follow their lord eastwards.

Dunfermline, quite a large and thriving town, the capital of Fothrif or West Fife, stood on rising ground well back from the Forth estuary, dominated by its great royal abbey, the first Romish one in Scotland, built by St Margaret, Malcolm Canmore's famous Queen. Here she was buried, along with her husband's reinterred remains and those of her sons, and successive Kings of Scots, down to and including Robert the Bruce. James expounded on this theme, as they drew near; but, when Chancellor Seton suggested a call to inspect the royal graves, the monarch made it quickly clear that he had had enough inspecting for one day and had been near enough to death's door without examining his predecessors' sepulchres. All he desired was some decent peace and quietude. Seton, Lord Fyvie, a discreet, sensitive and able man, a poet indeed and architect, knew his royal master well enough promptly to cancel the programme of welcome and display devised by the town, and led them straight to the palace.

Here James forgot his preoccupations sufficiently to exclaim over the great changes since he had been here last, in 1603. Malcolm Canmore's simple old stronghold had been replaced by a vastly finer and larger establishment, of graceful lines and excellent taste, designed by Seton himself. The situation was peculiar, in that, although it was still a royal palace, Fyvie was using his own money to rebuild it. He had been granted the abbey-lands of Dunfermline, very rich, *in commendam*, succeeding the Master of Gray, Mary's father, who had also acted Chancellor. A brother of the wealthy Lord Seton, he had already erected a splendid new castle at Fyvie in Aberdeenshire and had just finished another at Pinkie in Lothian. Here, at Dunfermline, the backward Prince Charles, now Prince of Wales since his brother Henry's death, had been put in Seton's care, as a child, and largely reared.

James exclaimed at all that was being done and what it all must be costing, remarking that being Chancellor of Scotland must be almost as effective a way of minting siller as was digging coals. He would have to see about this.

The magnificent interiors further impressed, but the King was glad enough to show them off to the English lords, with their proud Tudor·mansions, as example of what the Scots could do in architectural excellence.

But, in the midst of all this admiration, James suddenly announced that he was going to his bed—wherever that might be in this supervacaneous house. His belly was upset —no doubt as a result of bad air in yon devilish pit and then tossing on the sea in the bit boat. Aye, and descending ladders. It had been a dire day and he had had sufficient of it. And tomorrow he was for Falkland and the hunting, nigh on twenty-five miles. All who had listened to James's nostalgic tales, in London, about Falkland's legendary and superlative sporting facilities were well aware that this was meant to be the real highlight and pinnacle of the monarch's return to his native land. It would be appalling, and all would suffer, if James was too unwell to hunt.

Alexander Seton was much concerned. He had arranged a notable banquet and entertainment, and the Dunfermline folk had even composed a special grace-before-meat which would be sung by the boys of the abbey choir. James suggested that he gave the feast to the choirboys and let them come and sing their bit grace below the window of his bedchamber. He would hear it fine from there.

So presently, whilst the rest of the company waited for their repast, all were treated to the clear young voices in glad refrain—Seton hastening to point out that it was not his own composition:

> O Thou our God who does provide for all Thy servants' need
>   And sends King James to be our guide, on him our minds to feed.
> Our eyes to glad, our hearts to warm, our bellies full to fill,
>   We thank Thee for his gracious form, who keeps us from all ill.
>
> King James returns to his own land and all do bow before him,
>   He shines his light on every hand, his ain folk do adore him.
> Auld Scotland's Lion brave is he, in wisdom he is peerless,
>   He glads our eyes his face to see, in all our cause most fearless.

"Lord save us," Ludovick Stewart murmured to John, "I scarce recognise our Cousin James! This ought to gladden *his* heart, too. Let us hope that it works suitably on his belly also, so that he is fully recovered by the morrow. For if he is sick and cannot go hunting, I fear that we will never get to Methven."

4

Ludovick drew rein where he always did when approaching Methven after an absence of any time, where the drove-road up Strathearn from Perth, having crossed the north flank of the waste of Tippermuir, rounded a hillock above the moss. Abruptly the wide and lovely mid-strath lay spread before them, and none of it fairer than the immediate foreground where the land dropped away gently to a green hollow, fertile after the brown moorland, embosoming a little loch. Behind this the ground rose again quite steeply to a tall, green ridge, from which soared dramatically the red-brown towers of Methven Castle. Serene and assured, it seemed to contemplate the rich and sylvan vale under the blue regard of the Highland mountains, a place to dream over.

"Why in God's good name do I continue to exist in that wretched court in London when I could and should be living here, with those I love?" he demanded.

John did not answer. He had heard that question asked too many times.

They rode on round the shore of Methven Loch and up the steep bank, by a zig-zagging track, with the cuckoos calling from the scattered hawthorn trees, and on to the terraced ridge on which the castle sat amongst its gardens and orchards. It was a lofty square building of four storeys and an attic, with crowstepped gables and a round tower at each of the four angles, all rising a storey higher and capped by graceful ogee-roofs of slate, the walls provided with shot-holes, but more mansion than fortalice. It had been there a long time, in some form and in Stewart hands, although much of its present appearance was Ludovick's own work.

They found Mary working in the orchard, in old clothes, hair windblown, but a picture of loveliness for all that.

She greeted them with surprise and delight, welcoming Ludovick to his true home and saying that she had not expected them so soon.

"We feared that ourselves," the Duke agreed. "Especially when James claimed to be sick, at Dunfermline. But he merely feigned it, I think, to avoid further engagements and undertakings, and was up with the dawn again yesterday morning. So we reached Falkland by noon, and he was a changed man, leading not led, off after the deer within the hour. Last night he was full of plans for driving the West Lomond and Bishop's Hills today. For that he by no means needed me—or even Johnnie! When I said that we required to visit Methven, he cared nothing. God bless the harts and hinds, I say! We left at sunrise—and here we are."

"Good, good. How long have you?"

"That depends on James. He did not say when he wanted me back. At Falkland he lives only for each day, caring for nothing else than the chase. But he knows where I am and will send for me, I have no doubt, when he decides to move on. It is less than thirty miles."

"Where does he go from Falkland?"

"St Andrews and Kinnaird. Then Dundee, even Aberdeen, before returning by Perth to Stirling and Edinburgh. He is due back at the Palace of Dalkeith, Morton's house, early in June, and will hold a parliament in Edinburgh in mid-month . . ."

"But this is only the twentieth day of May. So if he leaves you here until he returns by Perth, as would be the obvious course, then we could have two whole weeks together!"

"One can never look for the obvious with Jamie Stewart! But we can hope, my dear . . ."

"There is so much to do and see," John said. "I have been telling him."

"Just to be together," his mother amended.

Both were right, of course. For Mary and Ludovick it was enough to have each other's company, in the simple daily round and peace of home life. But for son and father it was otherwise, with a host of activities to essay, places to visit, improvements to inspect, projects to discuss and people to meet. Methven was a large and important estate and barony of over ten thousand acres, and, set on the verge of the Highlands, provided a great mixture of opportunities and problems—agricultural, stock-rearing, sporting and timber-producing; and of course of human employment and relationships. John had been running the property, with the help of an old steward, for years now, for he was Laird and Baron of Methven; it had all been put in his name from the first. And he was making an excellent job of it. But he did not fail to recognise that all really was the Duke's and that he was in duty bound to render account always to his father, to seek his guidance and naturally also to demonstrate his successes. So there was something of a tug-of-war for Ludovick's time and attention.

John had two main preoccupations at this time—the felling, sawing up and selling of timber, from Methven Wood in especial, but also from other parts; and the drainage of much of Methven Moss and part of Tippermuir, for agricultural purposes. The one helped to pay for the other. For drainage was a costly process, requiring much labour; and unfortunately the advantages which would accrue could be looked for only years hence. Meanwhile the profits from the timber were disappearing into endless miles of ditches, drains and culverts. But John had seen what could be done elsewhere, especially in Monteith and the upper valley of Forth, and was determined that Methven should hereafter blossom, and burgeon, with much prime grain-growing land, providing winter-feed for all their Highlands neighbours'—and their own—cattle. This in turn would mean that a vastly greater number of beasts could be kept, especially in breeding-stock, over the long winter when the hills produced no pasture, instead of having to be sent off in droves and sold in the South, or else killed off, as at present. So the Highland economy of Strathearn, utterly dependent on cattle, would flourish, as well as the milling trade in grain. But it did mean that, meantime, rather less money was available to forward for the Duke's expenses in London.

Ludovick, listening, and inspecting the far-flung drainage-works and lines of busy diggers, declared that *he* was not complaining. After all, he did have other sources of revenue!

John was grateful for that—but revealed that there were others who did complain. Unfortunately or otherwise, both Methven Wood and Methven Moss were notable haunts of deer and wildfowl, all but sanctuaries for the game, the greatest in mid-Strathearn. Neighbouring lairds and major tenants or tacksmen, who put their sport before agricultural improvement, were displeased, claiming that he was destroying their hunting and hawking. They could not stop him, to be sure, as he held the baronial rights; but they could and did object that both the chase and the falconry, which was all that some of them appeared to live for, was being spoiled and would be more so as time went on. This troubled him—but he was determined to continue.

The Duke sympathised—and marvelled not a little that he should have produced such a son so concerned with well-doing and improvement. At his age, so far as he could recollect, his own attentions had been wholly taken up with very different matters—such as winning the favour of Mary Gray and seeking at her behest to circumvent the machinations of her father, the Master of Gray; not that he had been very successful at this last. So far as he knew, none of his forebears had demonstrated any great love for soil and people, here or in France, at Aubigny where lay their great estates. So it all must come from Mary and the Grays—although he could not imagine the late Patrick mightily concerning himself with making two grains of corn grow where only one had grown before.

"I think that the King had better not come to Methven, John!" he said, smiling. "He would be torn in two—whether to approve of your efforts to make the land flourish and so make more of his beloved siller; or to frown on your spoiling of his equally esteemed hunting. We will pray that he comes no nearer than Perth!"

"But you—what do *you* say?" his son demanded.

"I say all success to you, lad. You are laird here. If this is what you want to do, then do it. Make your wilderness flourish. Never heed the complainers—in reason, that is. You will not destroy *all* the hunting hereabouts, I swear. There is enough game in these Highlands hillskirts of ours to provide all the sport required . . ."

"But that is just the point, do you not see? There are plenty of deer and wildfowl in the foothills and lochans, yes, on the Highland side of the strath, to the north, our side. But on the south side, beyond the Moss, where are most of these others' lands, there is a deal less. The high ground beasts do not come down there, save in snow. So Methven Wood, in especial, is the main refuge for the low ground deer. I tell them, those who complain, that the game will find other places to lurk and breed, at Gask and Dollerie and the like—but they will not heed me, scoff at me as too young to know." He hesitated. "Would you, would *you* speak with them? Or some of them? You they would respect, the Duke of Lennox, the King's cousin. Tell them of the need for grain-lands and winter feed, and the wealth it could bring to all the strath. And that there would be plenty of waste and moss and woodland left all along the valley, for the deer and the fowl."

"I cannot go round Strathearn preaching your gospel, Johnnie! It would look devilish odd. Besides, I do not know the half of it. Now that you are a knight, especially honoured by the King, probably they will heed you better."

"Not Lord Madderty. He considers himself a great man. And he is the principal objector . . ."

"Ha—James Drummond! Is he your problem?"

"Yes—and the other Drummonds follow his lead. His lands of Madderty, Inchaffray and Innerpeffray flank ours to the south. He . . . disapproves of me. Always has done."

"For more than Methven Wood?"

"Yes."

"Because of your birth, lad?"

"Yes."

"I see. Then yes, perhaps I had better have a word with my Lord Madderty." He glanced sidelong at his son. "And, of course, he is father to the fair Janet Drummond we spoke of, is he not? Which could make it . . . awkward?"

John did not rise to that.

"Well, we shall go see the Drummonds. I used to know him well enough, before he was Madderty. Perhaps your mother will come with us."

87

"I think not. Lady Madderty gives herself airs."

"Indeed? Then the more fool her. Anyone who gives themselves airs in the presence of Mary Gray lacks wits as well as manners . . . !"

It was two days later that father and son presented themselves at Innerpeffray. Strathearn, one of the finest broad vales in all Scotland, was some thirty miles long, averaging from eight to ten miles in width, the River Earn, flowing out of Loch Earn, running down the midst, with the Highland mountains crowding the north side. The ancient semi-royal earldom of Strathearn, one of the seven original mormaordoms of Alba, the Celtic Scotland, had been long defunct; but the Stewarts, to some extent the successors, had clung to much of the mid-strath, mainly on the north side, centred on Methven, whilst Holy Church and the house of Drummond shared most of the south side between them. At the Reformation the Drummonds, who had provided two queens for Scotland and several royal mistresses, found themselves in a strong position to grasp the Church lands; and the fourth Lord Drummond became first Earl of Perth. His uncle, James of Madderty, got the Abbey of Inchaffray here, and in 1609 was created Lord Madderty. He began to build a fine new mansion for himself at a sheltered bend of the Earn some four miles west of the abbey precincts, using much of the abbey masonry, near the chapelry of Innerpeffray—itself safe from demolition because it was the Drummond burial-place. Innerpeffray Castle was tall, plain and commodious, without architectural flourish, and still distinctly new-looking despite the antiquity of the building material.

John was fairly silent as they approached, his father noted. Whether this was on account of Lord and Lady Madderty or of their daughter remained to be seen.

Their arrival put Lord Madderty in rather a difficult position—as, of course, was not wholly unforeseen. The adopting of his customary haughty line with John was contra-indicated in the company of the only duke in two kingdoms, the man closest to the monarch. A good-looking man of middle years and high colour, he greeted Ludovick almost effusively, declaring the honour done to his poor house. John he acknowledged only warily affable.

"May I congratulate you, my lord, on your enhanced style and dignity?" the Duke said. "Also on this fine new mansion. Well deserved, I am sure." If there sounded almost as though there might have been a question-mark at the end of that, the other could scarcely take it up as such.

"I would hope nowise to detract from the name and repute of Drummond, my lord Duke," was the best that he could do.

"To be sure. You have much to live up to."

Lady Madderty appeared, uncertain as to who was the elder visitor. John she ignored.

"My lord Duke of Lennox, come north with His Majesty, my dear," her husband informed.

"The Duke—here? My lord, here is surprise. We did not know that you were in Strathearn."

"I left the King at Falkland. You do know my son, Sir John Stewart, surely, Lady Madderty?"

"*Sir* John?" She stared. She was a gaunt, fine-featured woman, who had once been handsome, Jane Chisholm, daughter of the late Laird of Cromlix, in nearby Strathallan. "Did you say *Sir* John, my lord Duke?"

"I did. His Majesty, no doubt considering him worthy of the honour, knighted John at the same time as he did Edinburgh's Provost, on his arrival in Scotland. Are you so surprised?"

"No. No—to be sure. But he is young. And, and scarcely . . ." She floundered.

Hastily her husband came to her aid. "This is as excellent as it is unexpected," he declared. "Is it not, my dear?"

"Why, yes. Of course. His Majesty no doubt had good reason for what he did." That sounded less than convinced.

"James always has. Sir John had the privilege of rendering the King some signal services. James was grateful. And, of course, he has a blood relationship to His Majesty."

"H'r'mm, yes." Adroitly Madderty switched the subject somewhat. "We were grieved to hear of the death of your Duchess Jean. And of the two infants. A great loss."

"Ah, yes. That was five years ago and more." Ludovick's second and loveless marriage to the Lady Jean Campbell of Loudoun had been imposed on him by the King for reasons of state and succession, when Prince Henry was sickly and Charles backward. A son and daughter had both died as babies.

"So sad," Lady Madderty said. "Do you consider marrying again, my lord Duke?"

He did not answer but turned to look at his son, to whom as yet scarcely a single word had been addressed. He found John less than concerned, or even apparently very interested, his regard very much elsewhere. The Duke, looking in that direction, saw that a young woman was standing just within the doorway of the castle's hall, listening. She was tall and slender, of a dark beauty which was quietly entrancing. Her attitude there seemed modest, patient, almost self-effacing as she watched—which, considering how eye-catching were her looks, was hardly to be expected.

Observing where the Duke and his son looked, Madderty waved a hand. "Our second daughter, Janet. The first is wed to Andrew Wood of Largo, as you may know."

Ludovick bowed to the girl, rather more deeply than he had done to her mother. "I have heard of this young woman," he said.

She curtsied gravely but did not speak.

"Leave us, Janet," her mother said—and managed thereby to make all three men look displeased.

"A pity," Ludovick shrugged. "She added grace to the occasion."

"You will take refreshment, my lord Duke? And Sir John?" Madderty asked.

"A cup of wine, perhaps—no more. We ride on. We have not long."

As Lady Madderty went stiffly to see to this, her husband asked, "Do I take it, then, that you have some matter to discuss with me?"

"Yes. Sir John tells me that you object to his cutting down of timber in Methven Wood?"

"I would not say that I object. It is, after all, your property."

90

"*His*, my lord."

"Very well, his property. I, and others, would but prefer that Methven Wood remained as it always has been."

"For your hunting's sake?"

"Yes. Methven Wood has always been a refuge for the deer. As has Methven Moss for the wildfowl—and now being drained. We are much the losers."

"That I question. Strathearn has much forest and moss. If the deer leave Methven Wood—and it is being replanted— they will refuge elsewhere in the strath. Your own Machany Wood, or Auchlone. Or even this Wood of Innerpeffray," and he waved a hand northwards. "Or is that too close, too convenient for your own hunting, to allow as refuge? Perhaps you prefer the refuge on *others*' land?"

That was shrewd hitting. The other bridled, but he could not retort as he might have wished. There were some advantages in being a duke.

"None is the same as Methven, which is the largest stretch of the old forest left in the strath. Remove it, and the hunting will, I swear, never be the same."

"We must agree to differ on that. But is there not more to be considered than your hunting? What of grain-growing and cattle and winter-feed, my friend? Do these not mean much to you?"

"I am not a farmer, my lord Duke! I leave such matters to my steward."

"Yet your wealth must come from these, in the first place. From your rents, if not from your own husbandry. It certainly does not come from deer and fowl. All men, even Drummonds, would wish to increase their wealth, I would judge?"

"All this cutting and selling of wood will increase *Methven*'s wealth, I accept—but not mine, nor others'!"

"There again I think that you err, my lord. The timber is being sold in order to pay for the draining of Methven Moss. When drained, the Moss will make excellent grain-growing land. And the grain grown there, on well over one thousand acres, will feed vastly greater numbers of cattle over the winter than can now be kept in the strath. Not only Methven cattle but your farmers' and others'. So you will not have to sell them off, half-grown, in October, as now. Does that not make good sense to you?"

"Methven will not sell its new grain cheaply, I think! And why should the Moss grow good grain, because it is drained. It is no more than rank, sour waste, peat-bog and reeds."

"No, my lord—hear me," John urged, his first intervention. "There is little or no peat there. I have tested the Moss in many places. Drilled holes and dug deep. Below the reeds and bog-cotton and mud there is good rich soil. Level and sound and deep, loam and silt brought down over the years by the Cowgask and Pow and Balgowan Waters, flowing to Earn. Drain the water from it, plough deeply, and it will make the best tilth in the strath."

"You hope so, Sir John—but may be wrong. Is it worth destroying Methven Wood and all our sport to find out?"

"It will not destroy your sport, my lord. The deer and fowl are not so easily driven off. I know—for they are eating *my* farmlands bare, and have been doing for years, kill them as we will. I have great deer-drives as you will know . . ."

A servant came with wine. Lady Madderty did not reappear.

Sipping, their host changed the subject to the King, his health and that of Prince Charles.

Fairly quickly Ludovick finished his wine. "Time that we were on our way, John," he announced briskly. "I do not think that we are going to change my lord's mind on this matter. You must just go on with your labours and prove him wrong, hoping that he will thank you one day. My lord—your servant. Our respects to your lady . . ."

Madderty saw them out with evident discomfort.

"I see what you are up against, lad," the Duke said as they rode away. "These people resent you—and that is *my* fault, in the first place. And Madderty has no interest in improving his land or in aiding his people. He will only be convinced by proven facts—and his wife will not be convinced by anything! So you must show them how wrong they are—if it means sufficiently much to you. Ignore their disfavour. They cannot stop you."

"No, but they can turn others against me. The entire clan of Drummond, and their friends the Grahams."

"Surely not? The Drummonds are good enough folk. I have always found them fair neighbours."

"Yes. But they are great on the hunting. And Lord Madderty has great influence. Their chief, the young Earl of Perth, is his nephew—and much interested in his Cousin Janet."

"Ha—is that it? You do find problems for yourself, lad! Well, I was young myself once. I . . ." He paused, and pointed. "Do you see what I see, Johnnie?" They were riding westwards along a grassy bank above the curves of the Earn, and a little way ahead, below them, a slender figure in light clothing was walking slowly along the riverside.

John nodded but said nothing.

"Myself," his father mentioned, "I am going to have a look at the Drummond graves at Innerpeffray Chapel, yonder. Most interesting. You, now, will have seen them many times. Why do you not go down there and pay your respects, and mine, to that young woman who was so shortly dismissed by her mother? I say that she deserves some small civility. See you, there is no haste. The graves will occupy me for some time. Come when you are ready."

"I thank you," his son acknowledged, and reined his horse left-handed.

John rode down into the haugh and on to the winding path which followed the bends of the river. The young woman heard his horse's hooves and turned to wait, smiling. And her smile was a joy.

"Janet!" he said.

"John! Or did I hear aright, back there? Should it now be *Sir* John?"

"Not to you." He dismounted and stood before her, looking doubtful.

"What . . . how did it come about? This knighting? You must tell me." She sounded eager to know.

"It was nothing. Or my part in it was. Little worth the telling. It was all a foolish mistake. At Edinburgh. They had arrested the King, and . . ."

"Arrested? The King! Surely not—that cannot be so? You cozen me . . . !"

"It is true. They did not know that it was the King. A mistake, as I say. I was able to put the matter to rights. Then later I was able to do him some other small service. And when he was knighting Provost Nisbet he called me to him and knighted me also. That is all."

She stared at him. "I cannot believe that it was all so simple as that, John." She had a warm, throaty voice which affected him not a little. "You are not telling me the half of it! What really did you do?"

"Just what I say. I had to knock over the constables who were taking the King away—that is all. He is a strange man, easily affrighted. He was most foolishly grateful."

"You knocked over constables? How many?"

"Only two. It was not difficult."

She wagged her lovely head in exasperation. "So you are a hero—but you will not tell me! This is unfair, unkind! What was the other service you did King James? I must hear."

"That was afterwards. After the knighting. And still less worth telling. Merely bringing the Earl of Buckingham to him, the King. And halting the cannonade at Edinburgh Castle until he came."

"I see that I shall have to discover all this from others! That was your, your father, the Duke, with you, was it not? Did he see all this? Is he still with my parents?"

"No. He is gone to the chapel. To see the graves. We saw you down here, so . . ."

"So?" She considered that, and him. "He went on and left you to come to me here? I think that you must have a more accommodating father than have I, Sir John Stewart!"

He found nothing to say to that, and they walked on together along the riverside in silence, he leading his horse.

"Your mother and father, I fear, do not like me," he said at length. "What I am, nor what I am doing."

"I am sorry," she told him, not attempting to deny the truth of it. She sounded as though she meant it.

"I tried to tell him—your father. As did the Duke. About

94

Methven Wood and Moss. But he would have none of it. He can see no good in what I do."

She nodded. "I also have tried to tell them. The worth of it. But I am only a girl, a lassie who knows nothing of such matters."

"I thank you, at least, for the trying."

"You will continue with your labours?"

"Oh, yes."

"You are a determined young man. I have noted it before!"

"I cannot stop now, having put my hand to it. Would you have me otherwise?"

"Does it matter how I, or any, would have you?"

"It does, yes. It matters . . . much. To me. How *you* would have me."

She looked away. "Is . . . is that wise, John? As matters are?"

"Wise? I do not claim wisdom, Janet. But . . . I cannot help myself in this."

"You mean, of Methven Wood and Moss?"

"No—of you. Of your regard and, and esteem. Your well-wishing."

"You have these, John—my esteem and good wishes. You must know that. Not that they can greatly serve you, I fear . . ."

"Not that. I mean more than just good wishes, lass." He reached out and caught her hand. "I seek more than that."

She looked troubled but did not disengage her hand. "John—what can I say? You have my regard, my very real regard, my friendship indeed. But—you must face the situation, the facts . . ."

"Is it not fact enough that I love you, want you?" He drew her to him, strongly, dropping the horse's reins. "My dear—can you not see? I love and want you, need you . . ." Urgently he pulled her round, to kiss her brow, her eyes, her lips.

For moments she was unresistant in his arms. Then she twisted and drew away, shaking her head. "John—no! Please, no! This will do us no good, no service. You must know it, as I do." Anxiously she stepped further away, to look back. "If anyone should see us—my father! Or mother!"

Only the topmost storey and roofs of the castle were still in sight, so it was unlikely that they could be observed.

He sighed. "No one will see us here. But . . . if I have offended, I am sorry."

The young woman bit her lips. "Not offended . . . but, but misjudged, John. This is folly. Will bring but pain to us both. Surely you can see that?"

"I can see only that I love you. And believe that I can make you love me."

"Even if you do, and could, what good would there be in it? My parents would never permit our, our coming together. They are set against you. And they have . . . other, other plans for me, I fear . . ."

"So? You accept them, then? Their prejudice and dislike for me? I would have believed you made of stronger stuff than that, Janet Drummond!"

She shook her head, silent.

"Is this to be the end, then? You offer me no hope? Nothing to sustain me? No word that even you wish me well?"

"I do wish you well, John—that you may be sure. But to what end? Wishes will not change anything for us. I am in my parents' hands. I am but nineteen years. What *I* wish is of little moment. You are determined on this Methven project. It will bring you into even greater enmity with my father . . ."

Abruptly he turned away and flung himself up on to his horse in one lithe if complicated bound. He reined the beast round.

"You say that I am a determined man," he exclaimed. "I tell *you* that I am determined in more than Methven Wood and Moss! Think on it!" And, waiting for no more, he spurred off to climb the grassy bank and make for Innerpeffray Chapel, riding fast.

She gazed after him unhappily.

As though to prove something, as much to himself as to the whole strath perhaps, John organised a great deer-drive for four days later, and invited all who cared to attend, near and far. Ostensibly it was to celebrate his father's return to Methven; but the Duke could take hunting or leave it, and was far from the moving spirit.

In the event, a large number of hunters turned up from up and down the strath; but it was noticeable that there were no Drummonds amongst them, and precious few Grahams either. They assembled, on a cool grey morning, on the high ground of Drumbuich and Keillor, north of Methven some three miles and about three hundred feet higher, between the straths of Earn and Almond, more than one hundred men, apart from the beaters. Of deer-hounds and other dogs there were as many.

This was no conventional hunt on horseback such as King James delighted in, but a drive after the Highland fashion. There was sport in it, but the object was to kill deer, many deer, rather than to prove the superiority of individual huntsmen or their hounds, a means of keeping down the great numbers of deer which roamed the hills and mountain-sides and descended on the farmers' crops to decimate them. The programme was to have an army of beaters march, in close-ordered but extended lines, across hillside and woodland scrub, with their dogs, with much hallooing and shouting and barking, to drive all the deer out before them. Permanent barriers of turf and peat, known as deer-dykes, were placed at strategic points, high enough to dissuade all but the most agile animals from trying to get over, and at carefully selected spots in these there were gaps left open, usually at right-angled bends and re-entrants, through which the fleeing deer might bolt. Here the hidden huntsmen placed themselves, armed mainly with bows and arrows and some cross-bows, and sought to bring down the running quarry. It still demanded good archery at swiftly-moving targets, and most escaped. But with some half-dozen barriers and as many gaps, the total bag could be quite large, for there was seldom any lack of game.

Today John had selected his dykes and gaps with much care. Normally the ultimate objective was to force the deer ever downhill, through various stages and shooting-points, until eventually they found sanctuary in the extensive glades and aisles of Methven Wood. But on this occasion that was not desired. John's purpose was to force the creatures to select other refuges throughout the strath, to prove his assertion that they were not dependent on Methven and that they would go to ground in other woods and wastelands. The entire operation was designed to demonstrate this and also that there was no lack of deer.

The forenoon's drive was a marked success, with forty-three beasts accounted for out of perhaps a couple of hundred driven past, John himself, no mean shot with a bow, having brought down four, from his chosen position in the rear of the beaters' line, where he could superintend the advance and at the same time deal with any game which might break back.

At this stage Mary Gray and a company of women arrived with pannier-ponies laden with a welcome repast of cold meats, oat-cakes, honey and ale. Less welcome was the news that a royal courier had arrived at Methven Castle with a message from King James at Dundee. He had changed his mind about going to Aberdeen, as taking too long and shortening his hunting at Falkland, and intended now to be at Perth on the last day of May, where he expected the Duke and his son to join him. He was due back in Edinburgh on 3 June.

This distressing news meant that they had only one further clear day here, for this was the 29th of the month. That John was expected to appear also, anticipated by his father as it was, was far from welcome to his mother and received with mixed feelings by the son. In a way he would not be sorry to get away from Strathearn for a little while; on the other hand, there was so much to be done here, so much to be sorted out . . .

That afternoon's sport was as productive as earlier but two at least of the sportsmen now lacked enthusiasm.

At least the day's proceedings confirmed John's claims as to the deer, so far as it could go at this stage. Next day reports came in from all over mid-strath of large numbers of the animals being seen in various localities and coverts. Clearly denial of Methven Wood had not caused them to flee the strath as yet. Whether this would last, of course, remained to be seen; but it was a hopeful start.

The following morning the Stewarts reluctantly set out for Perth, Mary Gray deciding to accompany the two men. Since the King was going to be attending the parliament in Edinburgh, the possibility was that he might remain in that city for some little time—although James being James, he might at any time decide to cut short his visit without notice, and depart. At any rate, Mary felt that the opportunity to have a few more days in which she might see at least something of Ludovick was not to be rejected. So it was to be Lady Tippermuir's lodgings again. John would have liked to get a message to Janet Drummond, but did not see how it could be effected with any dignity in the circumstances.

5

Actually Mary did rather better with Vicky than she had anticipated at Edinburgh; for, after a day at Perth and another at Stirling, with much public laudation and spectacle and banqueting, James was glad to escape to the Douglas Earl of Morton's castle of Dalkeith, some six miles south-east of Edinburgh in the valley of the Esk. From there he could ride into the city in under the hour for sundry appearances and activities, but could get away again when he had had enough, which was a notable attraction. Also there was good hunting to be had in the vast park and up the Esk valley into the skirts of the Pentland Hills. But Morton's castle, although quite large, could by no means house any major proportion of the royal entourage; so the King was able to leave most of the unwieldy company at Holyrood, or in whatever quarters they had been able to find in the city, to his great relief, and surround himself with only his special cronies and drinking companions. Indeed, at this stage quite a number of the great crew were missing anyway, for, not desiring to spoil the hunting at Falkland by large numbers, nor anxious to expend much good money on catering for them at the hunting-palace and vicinity, James had got rid of many, especially of the English courtiers, by sending them on ahead on the long road north to Aberdeen. The fact that he changed his mind about going there himself—if he had ever truly intended to do so—worried him no whit. They would find their way back to Edinburgh in course of time, undoubtedly.

So, with accommodation at Dalkeith at a premium and hunting still the preferred order of the day, the Duke and John found themselves but little in royal demand, and were able to spend much time and most nights with Mary at her lodgings in the High Street.

They had a full week of this before repercussions from Aberdeen developed to interrupt the pleasant pattern. The missing English courtiers arrived back, somewhat disgruntled—but nothing to the disgruntlement of the Aberdonians who came with them, the commissioners for the parliament, the Town Clerk, the deacons of trade guilds, and oddly, the Rector of the Grammar School. These came to protest, in no uncertain terms, that the northern city, seat of learning and torch of episcopal probity, had been insulted. King James had visited Edinburgh and Dundee, Perth and Stirling, even Linlithgow and lesser places still—not visiting Glasgow, a mere bishop's burgh, hardly counted—but had avoided Aberdeen, preferring to chase four legged brutes in Fife. It was to be deplored. Great celebrations had been prepared, no expense spared and a notable presentation arranged. In fact, the senior Englishry arriving had all been made honorary burgesses and freemen of the city, and were loud in their praise of Aberdeen hospitality and generosity—which only made matters worse.

Not that James himself was greatly concerned. He did not think that he had missed much—Aberdeen, although fond of bishops and fish, he had heard, was a cold and draughty place and too full of Gordons for his liking. However, he was a little worried about that notable presentation which had eluded him; and, hearing that the deputation had brought something for him south with them, he was persuaded to put on a special reception and entertainment for them at Holyroodhouse. Sundry other ceremonies and presentations could be effected at the same time and got out of the way, and it would be a full-scale royal occasion. The Duke and his son were commanded to attend.

It got off to a good start when, after a moderate meal— when James was host he did not approve of squandering good siller on filling clamorous bellies—Sir Thomas Hope of Craighall, a notable lawyer, Advocate-Depute to Tam o' the Cowgate and likely to be that magnate's successor when he could be persuaded to relinquish the lucrative office of Lord Advocate, presented a handsome book of his own verses to the monarch, with a flowery oration in mellifluous Latin which even James could find no fault with. There followed a lengthy poem, also in Latin, by Patrick Nisbet of Eastbank, another advocate, which the King had his doubts about, and said so. Then the Earl of Morton asked leave to present the Dalkeith parish minister, Master Andrew Simpson, who had an offering to make. When Majesty graciously acceded to this request, a burly individual was produced, obviously by pre-arrangement, who in a broad Lowland Scots voice declared that he was Andrea Simonedes and would gie them *Dalkethensis Philomela*, of his ain compose.

There followed another lengthy dissertation, in execrable Latin, which soon had much of the company groaning through it and talking to their neighbours, to James's outraged cries of Shush! Shush! and beatings on the table with his tankard—ale was being served at Holyroodhouse, not wine, in the interests of royal economy. Whether the homespun composer actually finished his rendering, or merely gave up in the face of competition, was not clear, but at any rate James thereupon took the opportunity to expand upon the superior virtues of Scottish education whereby even rustic, groundling folk such as this could compose and expound in excellent Latin for their edification.

Even John Stewart, whose Latin was only moderate, swallowed somewhat at this attribution of excellence by one whose critical faculties were to say the least pronounced. The English present no doubt groaned again, if only in spirit.

At a sign from the King the Lyon King of Arms announced that the worthy citizens of Aberdeen now had something to say.

Some shuffling took place down near John's fairly lowly position toward the foot of the palace's central courtyard— for this affair was being held in the open air of a warm June evening—and the group from Aberdeen moved out and up to front the monarch's table. After waiting for quiet, the Town Clerk, a tall and dignified individual, declared in an accent which many of the southern visitors failed to understand and assumed to be probably more Latin or even Hebrew, that he was privileged to represent the ancient and important metropolis of the north, the largest centre of population beyond Forth. Unfortunately the Provost himself was unable to attend on this occasion, he having arranged to go hunting in the Forest of Glentanar. The Bishop of Aberdeen also was at this great hunting. But no doubt the King's Grace would recognise the conflicting demands of the situation, and understand?

There was an appalled silence from at least the Scots present at this extraordinary announcement—a hush which was broken, to the surprise and relief of all, by a cackle of laughter from the monarch.

"Hech, hech!" he cried. "Droll—aye, right droll! Continue, man—continue."

The Town Clerk bowed stiffly. "Aberdeen, however, has sent the Rector of the Grammar School—since the Chancellor and Rector of the University were unfortunately detained—to present Your Majesty with a token of the city's esteem. We had, to be sure, arranged great things at great cost. But . . ."

"Well, man—well?" James was looking wary now, one eyebrow raised doubtfully. Of the row of Aberdonians only one appeared to be carrying anything, a small but substantial man with a small but noticeably insubstantial satchel.

This character stood forth, and announced that he was David Wedderburn, Rector of Aberdeen Grammar School, and drew from his satchel a roll of parchment. This he unrolled and began to read—one more ode in Latin.

James glowered and a shudder and moan ran through the assembly.

The Rector's eloquence went on and on, for this was a very long poem indeed. The Latin was good too. But the subject matter was different from usual, a deal less florid and flattering. Indeed it reserved its encomiums for Aberdeen itself rather than its liege-lord, and, while not specifically criticising the King, went into some detail as to how other monarchs had esteemed and favoured the northern seat of learning, how loyal it had always been, how firm in its adherence to the episcopal authority, all calculated to make James uncomfortable. There was even a reference to the superlative hunting available in the neighbourhood and enjoyed by previous royal visitors.

When at last it was over, all who had understood what

was said were eyeing the King. This was something new, for him and for them all.

James tipped forward his high hat. "Are you finished, man?" he demanded. "Is that all you have brought me frae Aberdeen? Words? Aye, and ower mony words! Is that the best you can do? You have come a gey long way to bring me that!"

"Yes, Sire. We have made the journey that others failed to make, at great expense. We . . ."

"Ooh, aye—great expense! Like this entertainment and gastrosophy, aye. Gid Murray—where's Gid Murray o' Elibank, wi' the siller? Gie them fifty merks, Gideon, for their trouble. To see them back to their precious Aberdeen! Fifty, just." Abruptly he rose. "Noo, I'm for my bed. I've had plenties o' this—aye, plenties. Steenie, you come wi' me . . ."

All rose in some confusion—especially William Douglas, Earl of Morton, who had been expecting the King to return with him, as usual, to Dalkeith for the night.

After this sudden royal departure, as often happened, the evening's proceedings rapidly deteriorated, as men relaxed—James's entertainments tended to be all-male gatherings. There was noise, horseplay, raillery, squabbling. The English, in especial, had frustrations to work off, having had to put up with endless Latinity, uncouth accents and the alleged superiority of Scottish education. Now, restraint removed, they sought to get a little of their own back—and they were, in fact, in the majority there. And the ale was now circulating freely.

So there was argument and invective and contumely. Duke Ludovick, up at the royal table, sought to catch his son's eye to signal a discreet retiral, when a group of young English courtiers of the second rank began to shout for Tony Weldon to favour the company with his panegyric on Scotland and the Scots. Loudly they clamoured and presently a slender young exquisite was hoisted up on to the table-top, down near John's seat, clutching a paper. Sir Anthony Weldon, from Kent, was Clerk of the Green Cloth, and had been knighted only at Berwick-on-Tweed on the way north. He boasted literary leanings.

Beaten tankards gained him approximate quiet, and with pretended reluctance and in fashionably weary tones and clipped voice, the more emphasised in that he was slightly drunk, announced that they had had to listen to a devilish lot of utterly incomprehensible oratory and endless articulation in foreign tongues. It would do them all a power of good, he swore, to hear some simple sentiments in good English, Queen Elizabeth's English if not King James's, on the subject of this curious northern kingdom, by a long-suffering visitor. He did not accord his blank verse a title, anything such was beyond him quite. They could all choose their own titles hereafter. He commenced to read, with frequent pauses and hiccups:

> Scotland—too good for those who possess it,
>   Too bad to be worth conquering.
> Its air might be wholesome,
>   But for the stinking people who inhabit it.
> Their beasts are small, women only excepted,
>   Of which there are none greater in all the world . . .

Noise prevented further delivery for a while, fury from the Scots and cheers and laughter from some, though not all, of the orator's fellow-countrymen.

He managed to continue:

> They set great store of fowl, as foul houses, foul sheets and shirts,
>   Foul linen, foul dishes and pots, foul trenchers and napkins,
> With which sort we have been forced to fare,
>   As the Children of Israel did with their fowl in the wilderness . . .

The pauses became more frequent and prolonged as the reactions mounted. Soon half of the distinguished company were on their feet shouting and fist-shaking and the other half on theirs egging Weldon on. This looked like developing into the most serious international clash since the Union of the Crowns, and in Holyroodhouse of all places.

> As for trees, had Christ been betrayed in this country,
>   As doubtless he would have been had he come here as a stranger,
> Judas had sooner found a tree of repentance,
>   Than a tree to hang himself on . . .

John found his father at his elbow, in the uproar. "Time we were out of here," the Duke said. "Better to know nothing about it, in the morning, when James gets to hear."

As they made their way out, with fisticuffs breaking out all over the courtyard, it was to be noted that not a few of the guests, English as well as Scots, were like-minded. The hotheads were being left to fight it out.

Lady Tippermuir's lodging seemed a good place to be in.

On the morrow, when the Stewarts presented themselves at the palace again, at a respectable hour, it was to find matters already well advanced. The King, up with the sun, had announced that he was going to visit St Mary's College, seat of learning and enlightenment at St Leonards, and to take the wretched Aberdeen schoolmaster with him to perhaps improve his Latin. But first he had had business to attend to at the palace, where his royal bed-going had been shamefully disturbed by satanic noise and wicked bedlam from the central courtyard. Displeasure had been pronounced, and investigation made. Anthony Weldon had been promptly sent packing back to Kent, with one or two of his friends—apparently they were gone already. It was gathered that a new Clerk of the Green Cloth would be appointed, soon.

The Duke, who had anticipated something of the sort and timed their present arrival accordingly, set off with John for the university.

Thirty-four years before, in 1583, Edinburgh had decided that, as now the accepted capital city, it could no longer give place to St Andrews, Aberdeen and even Glasgow in matters academic, and must have a university. This had been started in a modest way, using the old Romish church of St Mary's in the Fields and its grounds, near where James's reputed father had been blown up, and no longer required, between the Cowgate and St Leonards. With a bequest of 8,000 merks from Robert Reid, Bishop of Orkney, they had begun with one professor and five lecturers. James himself had been a supporter of the project. Now it had grown considerably and required larger premises, the King's aid being called for.

They found James, typically, lecturing the lecturers, and on the subject of meteorology allied to astrology, with asides on Egyptology, Assyrian and Babylonian culture and other matters little more obviously related. Most of his hearers were looking dazed, Master Wedderburn from Aberdeen lost.

At sight of the newcomers, the monarch broke off his discourse, censoriously to accuse them of the sin of sloth, of lying like hogs in their beds when more well-doing folk were up and about God's work. They had missed much enlightenment on the sciences, of which he had small doubt they were in considerable need, and would be well advised to bestir themselves betimes in future—especially a young man with his way to make in life. Having delivered himself of this rebuke, James returned to his theme. Ludovick murmured that they had got off lightly and that it was well worth this to have escaped the morning's upheavals at Holyroodhouse.

The dissertation had reached the first manufacture of papyrus in the valley of the Euphrates and the probability that its inventors would speak the Gaelic, this being un-doubtedly the site of the Garden of Eden and Gaelic the language of Heaven when—this appearing to remind the Lord's Anointed—he announced that he had expended enough time on them already, he hoped to good effect, and he must be off to inspect the paper-mills of the Water of Leith. When the Principal of St Mary's pointed out, in some distress, that a special meal awaited the royal visitor and his company, he was informed that the last thing that dedicated academics should be concerned with was the stomach—besides which, some of those present could only recently have finished breaking their fast. With which thrust he headed for the door, only pausing therein for a moment to call back that, in future, the establishment would be called King James's College instead of St Mary's—and let all make fell sure that they did credit to the name, and put yon so-called university at Aberdeen in its place.

No one could say that the monarch's interests and con-cerns were not catholic, all-embracing. Paper-manufacture was now the theme. James had, in 1590, introduced paper-making into Scotland, importing two German experts, and had established mills at Dalry, a village a mile or two to the west of the city, near the Water of Leith. To these he had given the contract—at a price—for the supply of paper for his many books, indeed providing them with a monopoly which was very profitable, and in which he made sure of sharing. He even had his own personal watermark. Finding paper-making almost non-existent in England, when he went south, he had not been slow to perceive the opportunities of the Scots' monopoly, and ordered extension of the Dalry mills. This was to be inspection-day.

He was not, of course, going to have a lot of Englishry, nor Scots either indeed, ferreting out the processes of this valuable trade. So he forthwith dismissed such courtiers as had attended him to the college, with the wretched Aberdonian, back to Holyroodhouse or wherever they liked to go, taking with him only Steenie, Fyvie, the Duke and John—with whom presumably he considered the paper-making secrets safe.

As they rode westwards through the city for the West Port, unrecognised, James held forth on the uses of paper, not only to write and print upon but for an endless variety of purposes, ever increasing. In the Low Counties they were even making boats of a sort out of paper; and the Moors were said to be using it to make cannon, scarcely to be believed as this was, as it did not overheat as did iron. In Florence, he was assured, they painted it and hung it on palace-walls instead of tapestry and arras. He had a notion that paper would be used instead of siller and gold coins in due course, not just as notes-of-hand of the sort Geordie Heriot used to accept, but as a kind of currency, if backed by signatures of true worth and wealth—although the danger of forgery could not be overlooked. It would require much thought but he believed that it could be effective and was a notable thought to think. Other uses he envisaged. He foresaw the day when paper would be as commonplace as woven cloth. And Scotland, this Edinburgh, could be the great supplier, sending paper all over his kingdoms, and other kingdoms forby. Think of it, money to be made in a bit mill . . .

If three of his four companions were not greatly interested, having sufficient money for their needs from more conventional sources, John *was* interested, being himself concerned with the creation of wealth in a small way and local prosperity. James, approving, went into details of manufacture and production, having the young man to ride alongside and banishing the others to the rear.

From the West Port they rode down to the village of Dean, deep in the valley of the Water of Leith. The King had recollected that there were tanneries and flour-mills here, some of them decayed, which he wondered whether might be converted into a new paper-making complex. The quality of the water was of the utmost importance in the process. They must inspect and consider.

So, down at the riverside, amidst the tannery stinks, the monarch and his new knight got down from their horses to paddle and puddle about in the river. James, who asserted that water was harmful to the human skin and to be avoided, waded in in his boots, although John took his off to go barefoot—whilst the others sat their mounts and looked elsewhere, as though to disassociate themselves from the entire undignified proceeding.

The King, splashing about on slippery stones, peered into pools and runnels, sniffed and muttered, exclaimed over a drowned cat, concerned lest he wet even his fingers, kept urging John to taste the water to try its freshness, to smell it for purity, and so on. A number of the villagers drifted down to stare at the unchancy sight of gentry paddling in their river, children to hoot and cheer, dogs to bark.

James ignored all, but sadly came to the conclusion that the water was insufficiently pure, fouled by these filthy folk, and they would need to go further upstream.

They rode on, three-fifths of the company thankfully, and presently turned off up a side-stream southwards, called the Rose Burn, eventually to reach the milling hamlet of Dalry. There were five mills here, only two of them making paper, and James was quick to suggest that these corn-grinders and flour-makers should be switched to more important and profitable work. However, this proposal was soon negatived, when the papermakers themselves informed the royal visitor that the quality of the last consignment of paper sent down to Whitehall Palace, and apparently complained about, was due to the deteriorating state of the water here, which each year became more polluted, as more houses were built further upstream. Indeed they were seriously considering leaving

Dalry and seeking new sites for their mills much further up-river, perhaps at Hailes or Currie.

This much concerned the King and he promptly began to suggest other locations—which, considering that it was fourteen years since he had left Scotland, revealed a remarkable memory for places and scenes. His enthusiasm mounting, he dwelt on the possibilities of the Lothian Esk, on which Dalkeith was situated, the only other major river near Edinburgh, pointing out that, although it rose in the same Pentland Hills, its fall was swifter than that of the Water of Leith and its tributaries, and therefore the water ought to be fresher. He declared that he would explore the Esk for possible mill-sites whilst he was bedding at Dalkeith, immediately enrolling John in this project.

They toured the mills, examining the entire process of manufacture and having it pointed out to them how vastly important water was and how much was used. Certainly there seemed to be a great deal of washing and boiling and draining in the various stages of production, John counting eleven different occasions in which fresh water had to be fed into the tanks and sinks and boilers and sluices, all pumped in through the action of paddle-wheels in the stream. Since all this water was drained back into the river, milky white now, after use, it did not take much deduction to recognise why the Water of Leith, down at the Dean village, was less than pure. This paper-making process, then, if it was to expand, must demand continued upstream development, which in turn would invalidate the mills further down. He said as much, whereupon James, nodding, commended his perspicacity and pointed out the lesson—that John must look for sites in major side-streams of the Esk, just above their junction with the main river. Ideal would be a forking-place where the river gained three tributaries and so three mills could be sited in some proximity, to their mutual advantage, producing different qualities of paper for different uses. John noted that it was he, it seemed, who was to do the looking.

These Dalry mills were making linen paper, the best, naturally, for the royal use, and required a large and continuing supply of linen rags, which was another preoccupation of the manufacturers. This required the mills to be sited near a city or other large source of the material, with collectors touting for rags. Part of the washing process was thus explained, with bleaching and caustic-soda applications to remove dyes and colour. James waxed eloquent and instructive on all this, and went on to proclaim the disadvantages and relative costs of other materials—different kinds of rags, fibrous grasses, straw and even certain barks from trees.

Steenie yawned aloud at one stage and earned a dressing-down—although presently the monarch was patting his padded shoulder, saying that he forgave him and that his young dog could not be expected to understand all its master's concerns.

Soon thereafter James announced that he was hungry. Had his Germanic papermakers no bit of provender to offer their royal benefactor?

Much put about, their hosts foraged around and produced large swatches of distinctly stale bread and cheese, which the monarch attacked with gusto, his companions with varying degrees of appreciation. Some potent and rough home-brewed ale helped to wash it down.

Then they were on their way. They would skirt Edinburgh, to the south, they were informed, and call at yon limmer Napier's house of Merchiston, who had died as recently as April last. Many was the tulzie Majesty had had with that skellum in his day—too clever by half, mind—on the subject of arithmetics and the science of numbers, and his contrive that he called logarithms. He would pay his respects to the chiel now that he was departed to a realm where he would learn that he was not always right, and his royal master no fool. Also seek to see if he had left behind any papers concerning his claim that there was gold buried at yon Fast Castle—before his son Archie Napier got at it. They might be a whilie at Merchiston, to be sure—but that need not delay Johnnie Stewart, who should get back to Dalkeith instanter to start his survey of the Esk.

Duke Ludovick smiled gently.

So commenced an odd period in John's career, wholly unexpected and for which he was nowise equipped but

111

which proved interesting and quite pleasurable—more so than hanging about at court, certainly. He was given but cramped quarters to sleep in, little more than a cupboard in the thickness of the walling of Dalkeith Castle, but spent the June days riding around the quite large area between there and the Pentland Hills, assessing, noting, a tract some eight miles long by four wide rising through some 700 feet. He discovered that there were two Esks, or at least that the main river split into the North and South Esks just below Dalkeith itself. He found the north branch much more hopeful than the other for paper-making purposes, at least as far as his own untutored eye could discern, with more water and water-power, steeper flow, more tributaries and more villages for the necessary labour. Each night, whatever the hour of the King's retiral, he was summoned to the royal presence to report and be questioned. And the more he saw of his peculiar liege-lord, the more he came to respect his shrewdness, sagacity and far-sightedness, to say nothing of his knowledge. The wisest fool in Christendom he might be called, but his folly seemed to John to be superficial and his wisdom deep—whatever his personal habits, which could be off-putting to a degree.

Meanwhile, Ludovick and Mary were enabled to be alone together much more than they had hoped for.

James told John that he wanted a final report, with recommendations, two evenings before the day he opened parliament, for there would be no time thereafter to go into the matter. John therefore produced a list of possible sites, mainly where tributaries joined the main North Esk, from Lasswade and Polton up to Auchendinny and Penicuik. The next day, the 16th of the month, he conducted the King, with a very small party, which included the Earl of Morton who owned most of the ground concerned, on a tour of inspection. James saw, weighed up, commented acutely and expressed himself as pleased, commending John and declaring that he thought that they might set up the first Esk mill possibly at Polton—and only in passing mentioned that this was a good augury for the work he would have for John to do in London.

As the significance of this remark dawned on the young

man, he grew the more perturbed. Did this mean that the King expected him to go back to England with him? And, if James expected it, that was as good as a royal command. The thought took him aback. How could he leave Methven and his mother? So much there depended on him. Besides, he had no wish to go to London—even though it would be good to see more of his father.

Greatly daring, he put it to the monarch. "Sire, you said London? If I heard aright? I, I would not think that I would go there. I have Methven to see to, so much to be done there. I . . ."

"Hech, lad—to be sure you must return with me to London. You have proved useful and proficuous, aye right proficuous. In mair ways than the one. You will be a right convenience at my court—a deal mair so than maist there, I jalouse! I can do fine wi' the likes o' you in yon London."

"But, Your Majesty—Methven! And my mother. She needs me there. And I have great matters afoot. I cannot just leave all . . ."

"Greater matters than your sovereign-lord's service, Johnnie Stewart? Na, na—*sic volo, sic jubeo*! Methven will no' run awa', man. It managed fine before you were born, I mind! As for yon Mary Gray, she can look after hersel' good and well—has done a' her days. Or she wouldna be Patrick Gray's daughter!"

"But, Sire . . ."

"Say nae mair about it, man. I can use you at Whitehall. Now, awa' wi' you—I'm for my bed. You'll attend me to the parliament the morn. We ride early for Holyrood, mind—so no biding in your bed the way your faither does . . . !"

And that was that.

The Riding of Parliament was a traditional prologue to the first sitting of any new parliamentary session, designed to emphasise the importance of the occasion for the people as well as the participants. Normally all representatives of the Three Estates of Parliament, lords, commissioners of the shires and the burghs—these last having at the Reformation replaced the Estate of Holy Church—assembled at

Holyroodhouse and rode in procession up the almost-mile-long Canongate and High Street to the Parliament Hall beside St Giles High Kirk. But on this occasion there were two innovations, by royal command. One was a religious service for the members, some two hundred of them, held in the palace chapel, which had been formed out of an aisle of the burned and ruinous Abbey of the Holy Rood—and this set the cat amongst the pigeons straight away, since the service was conducted by William Cowper, Bishop of Galloway, with the English Bishop of Ely making an admittedly brief address. Moreover the chapel proved to be decked with sculptured figures of the twelve apostles and the four evangelists, specially sent up from London by the King; and, worse still, an organ, or kist o'whistles, as it was called, defiled the worship. Worst of all, the Communion was administered to the recipients kneeling, the King leading the way, anathema to the Presbyterians, who proclaimed the custom as the worship of material idols and a supporting of the abhorred doctrine of transubstantiation. So quite a number of the commissioners, having entered the chapel, promptly marched out again, others stood about looking severe, refusing either to sit or kneel, and some partook of the bread and wine, but standing not kneeling. Altogether it made for awkward worship, however blessedly curtailed. It was, of course, the Scots who displayed protest; the English, being all Episcopalians of one sort or another, anyway, accepted all as normal.

The other innovation followed, and may have had something to do with the first's reception. For although this was the Riding of Parliament, James announced that he alone would ride and everybody else would walk, all horses to be left at Holyrood. This aroused further consternation on all hands—not so much that the distance of less than a mile was too much but that it would look undignified, especially as many there were dressed unsuitably for walking, the lords in their full ermine-trimmed robes, the great officers-of-state more decoratively-garbed still in wigs and brocaded gowns. Even the bishops, James's favourites, were upset, for they were the most elaborately turned-out of all, in full canonical fig, highly impracticable for walking Edinburgh's refuse-strewn streets. But the monarch was adamant, he himself, as always over-dressed but in the same clothing he had worn for all occasions, hunting, feasting or inspecting paper-mills, and now distinctly soiled to say the least. And the same old high hat. No doubt if anyone had dared to suggest that he might be differently clad for this occasion, he would have answered, as he had done more than once before, that fine dressing was for the increase of ordinary men's dignity; whereas he had no need for dignity, being the Lord's Anointed.

So a move was made, amidst much grumbling, already late—but then the parliament could not start without them—Steenie walking at the King's stirrup, clad all in white satin and gold. The English, of course, were not robed, save for Bishop Andrews of Ely and Dean Laud, having no part to play in a Scots parliament—although there were one or two rather unsure of their status, to whom James had given Scots peerages.

After the King came the great officers-of-state, High Constable, Lord Lyon King of Arms, Chancellor Fyvie and the rest. Then the judges, Lords of Session and the Provost and magistrates of the city. The Duke of Lennox then led the lords of parliament, one marquis, earls, viscounts and barons. The Scots bishops joined this group for the occasion, their position delicate. Since the Church was reformed, bishops and priors and the like had lost their seats in parliament; but James had insisted that, since the English bishops were Lords Spiritual and had seats in the House of Lords, their new Scottish episcopal counterparts were entitled to a similar status. This was hotly contested, and undoubtedly a majority of the parliament would refuse such the right to vote. However, James had the ultimate sanction of being able to create lords of parliament, and could, if driven to it, make all the bishops such lords and none could say them nay. So there was a sort of uneasy truce in the matter.

Behind this colourful and lordly company came the ranks of the county lairds and then the chosen representatives of the towns, these certainly the best clad for Edinburgh's cobblestones. There followed a great straggle of English

notables, sauntering and laughing, with sundry mere privileged spectators such as John Stewart. A detachment of the
royal guard went before and after all, mounted on fine
horses, to the resentment of the pacing parliamentarians.

The citizens were out in force to cheer them on, with
frankest commentary. Mary Gray waved from Lady
Tippermuir's window.

At Parliament Hall much time was taken in arranging the
seating, with precedence very much to the fore—and nowhere more particularly insisted upon than amongst the
burgh representatives, with royal burghs, however small,
consigning others ten times as large to lesser placings, and
the dates and seniority of burgh charters being vehemently
emphasised and demanded. The spectators, from their
various perches, were able to consider all, and marvel.

The Scots parliament was unlike the English one in many
ways. First and foremost, its true title was The King in His
Estates, and the monarch sat in and took part in the proceedings. Indeed, if the King or his appointed High Commissioner was not present, any assembly of the members,
however validly called, was not a parliament but only a
convention, and incapable of law-making. Secondly, all
members, lords, lairds and townsmen, sat together in one
assembly, with no Houses of Commons or Lords. There was
no Speaker, the business of the session being conducted by
the Chancellor, with due deference to the Throne, which
could always intervene, advise, or call an adjournment.
Many rules were different. It could be argued that it was
more democratic than the English model in that every man,
from duke to small town representative, had an equal voice
and vote. But the Crown remained very much in command,
so that there could be no continuing battle between King and
Commons as had prevailed for so long in England.

On this occasion James took very personal charge right
away, being able to dispense with all the formalities of the
last fourteen years, of the High Commissioner reading out
his credentials, delivering the royal injunctions, announcing
details of agenda and procedure, and the like. The King
plunged straight in, although he spoke with unusually careful enunciation, at first at any rate:

116

"My lord Chancellor, my lords spiritual, temporal, my good and leal friends and subjects all," he said, patting his hat more firmly on his over-large head. "We do rejoice, aye rejoice, to preside over this our parliament and assembly of our ancient realm once again. Would to God Almighty that we could do the same over our English parliament, to the better government of that realm!" And he glowered from his throne at such English subjects as he could place about the hall. "Aye. But we are right pleased to be here. We admit our natural and salmon-like affection and earnest desire to visit again our native land. Aye, salmon-like. *Amicus humani generis!*"

He peered round, to observe the effect of that on his audience, but perceiving little appreciation, straightened his hat again, which always tended to tip back, and continued.

"Aye,. well—there is business to be done. Plenties of business. We will do what we have to do and leave what we have not. Mind that." With this peculiar warning, he abandoned the royal we and spoke in his more normal and slobbery voice. "In this business I would counsel all to be brief, succinct and laconical—aye, laconical and inflatulent. If we Scots have a fault it is to be ower disputatious and largiloquent. Unlike my guid English subjects who get by wi' but a pickle o' words, and them gey clippit! Mind, they hae much to teach us, I hae found, if no' just in matters educational and scholastical. Some o' them are here to instruct us, and we maun learn frae them. Learn how we may reduce the barbarity o' this Scotland to the sweet civility o' England! Aye, if the Scots nation would be so docible as to learn the goodness o' the English, I might wi' mair facility prevail in my desire for the weal o' this mair ancient realm. Ooh, aye—much to learn, my friends."

There was a shuffling and stirring from the crowded benches at this, frowns and murmurings. John Stewart, who was becoming used to his liege-lord's ways, recognised this as satire but most of the company did not.

James warmed to his theme. "Such Scots as did accompany me to London already hae learned much—how to drink healths and to wear coaches and gay clothes. To tak tobacco and to speak neither Scots nor English! Mony siklike benefits they have to confer. Forby, mind you, I am beholden to the English for their love and conformity wi' my royal desires—in especial, *their* parliament! *Dictum sapienti sat est!*"

At last the Scots perceived the royal humour and that it was the English and not themselves who were being ridiculed, and the laughter rose. It is to be doubted whether the said English, in fact, were any the wiser.

Having prepared his ground, as it were, James suddenly came to business. "This parliament will consider and ratify sundry matters o' Church government; the selection and appointment o' bishops and archbishops; the abolition o' hereditary sheriffdoms, now maist outdated, and the institution o' justices o' the peace, for the better administration o' my justice; approve the renewal o' the sanctions and decrees against yon limmers o' the Clan Gregor, still a thorn in the flesh o' my honest subjects; consider the matter o' further monopolies and permissions for trade and manufacture and the revenues to be gained therefrom. Aye, these and other competent matters which may be brought up and which I may permit—competent, mind! My lord Chancellor—you may proceed."

Lord Fyvie cleared his throat at this abrupt and crisp directive. "To be sure, Sire." He sat at a table below the throne, flanked by clerks. He shuffled his papers. "His Majesty has certain proposals for the better regulating of Christ's Church in this realm," he announced, in his pleasantly cultivated voice, in such notable contrast to that of the monarch. "These are . . ."

"No' proposals—requirements," James interrupted.

There was a gasp from the benches, smiles swiftly wiped off all faces. James's choice of this subject to start with, and now this prompt and downright challenge, let everyone see that this parliament was going to be a battle. It also demonstrated a side of their liege-lord's character which few there knew. Probably all present had heard of the Five Articles of Perth, since they had been denounced from the vast majority of pulpits in the land in the two weeks or so since they were promulgated in that city, after having been proposed by the King in St Andrews, as it were between hunting-bouts.

They were elementary and to the point. Communion to be received in the kneeling posture. Private communion for the sick. Private baptism where called for. Confirmation by bishops restored. And the festivals of Christmas, Good Friday, Easter, Ascension and Whitsunday or Pentecost to be observed.

As the Chancellor, distinctly unhappily, read these out, uproar erupted throughout the hall, with men on their feet everywhere, furious shouts resounding, fists even being shaken. This amounted to demanding that parliament approved of the imposition of episcopacy, and in the most unsubtle and downright fashion. Yet three-quarters of the members present would undoubtedly be Presbyterians and would never vote for such measures.

In vain Fyvie banged his gavel for silence and order. James, for his part, took off his hat, examined its inside and put it on again, otherwise apparently unconcerned.

John Stewart, watching and wondering, asked himself why? He wished that he could have been sitting beside his father. What was the King up to? Quite clearly he could never get these five demands accepted by this gathering and must have known that from the start. It looked like utter folly—but then, he was discovering, so much of James Stewart looked like folly and was not. There must be method in this seeming madness.

When at length the Chancellor succeeded in obtaining quiet and order, asserting that this was a parliament and not a bear-pit, calling for reasoned and responsible discussion, there was no lack of proposers and seconders that a direct negative of the five principles should be carried, and notice-ably fewer who moved otherwise. Although many cried out for a vote right away, the King, mildly enough, called for debate. And, as this proceeded, certain facts became evident to the observer. Despite the obvious preponderance of feeling on the opposite side, much more time and elo-quence was being devoted to the episcopal case. This was because the balance of expertise was most unfairly weighted. All the clergy present were bishops, eleven of them. The Kirk did not have representatives in parliament, having their own and powerful General Assembly. So the opposition point-of-view had to be voiced by laymen. And, whilst these were sufficiently vehement, they inevitably tended to lack mastery of religious doctrine and phraseology. They could, and did, state feelings and convictions, but scarcely reasoned argument and dialectics. So that every assertion by the Presbyterian members was countered, authoritatively and at length, by the bishops, to the growing frustration and despair of the majority, and demands that these episcopal interlopers be silenced or even ejected—which of course would involve head-on conflict with the Throne and probably closure of the sitting.

It was James himself who resolved this difficult situation. After an hour or so of it, during which he had sat unspeaking and unusually non-fidgety for a man who so quickly tired of speech-making other than his own, he intervened. He declared that it was clear to him, as no doubt to all, that this debate was proving unprofitable and getting them nowhere. No reasoned and reasonable case was being put by the opposition—no doubt through lack of theological education. No decisions, they would all agree, should be taken on blind prejudice alone. Therefore he proposed that these matters should be referred by this parliament to a specially-called General Assembly of the Kirk, where there would be a sufficiency indeed of informed divines to make decision, such decision to be accepted as the expressed will of parliament. How said they all?

There was almost as astonished reaction to this as to the initial challenge. Men stared at each other, wondering. After all, a General Assembly of the Kirk could be expected to be even more anti-episcopal and anti-liturgical than was this parliament; so it was as good as the King conceding defeat there and then. It did not take long for loud cries of assent to resound from all over the hall, and these were finally endorsed by a mover and seconder and carried by a large majority. It was notable that the bishops did not protest and of course did not vote.

Nodding amicably now, James added that it seemed to him that the election and appointment of bishops and archbishops would come into the same category, and so should also be referred. They would move on, therefore, to the matter of the proscription of the Clan Gregor, of ill fame. The Chancellor to proceed.

Fyvie, with a sigh of relief, launched forth. This subject undoubtedly would cause no trouble, indeed obviously was going to be highly popular with all. Although it was a parliament of the nation, there were very few Highlanders present, nor ever were, most chieftains and clan-leaders having no least interest in what went on south of the Highland Line, save for the Campbells and one or two allied names, who were non-Catholic anyway. Ninety per cent of the clans were Catholic still and of course Gaelic-speaking, and, whilst this made them uninterested in the Lowlands and the parliament there, it had the reverse effect on the Lowlanders, who hated and despised the Highlanders, looking on them as barbarous and little better than vermin. It so happened that the acquisitive and ever-more-powerful Campbells had progressively dispossessed the clan of MacGregor from their ancient Argyll lands and pushed them ever further south and east towards Lowland territory; and there the small but spirited dispossessed clan, descended from a son of Kenneth MacAlpin, first king of the united Picts and Scots, maintained themselves by foray and theft, their staple support the stealing of Lowland cattle. So they were a convenient object of Lowland hate, and the nearest available Highlanders, and inveterate law-breakers at that, fit to be hunted down like wolves. The year he went south to London, James had proscribed the very name of MacGregor after a massacre of Colquhouns on Loch Lomondside arising out of some clan feud. It became unlawful even to use the name, it carried no weight on a legal document and all of the rascally race had to take other surnames, or hang—this in an attempt to stamp out clan-spirit and cohesion. Drastic as it was, this had been only partially successful, for the MacGregors remained as large as life and remarkably resilient, still a thorn in the flesh of their neighbours even though they now had to sign their names as Greigs, Gregorys, Griersons and the like. All this the Chancellor recapitulated, and declared that it was necessary, not only to renew these measures but to make others still more severe and effective. Proposals were called for.

So the assembly went into happy conclave, thinking up ways of dramatically reducing the numbers of these Highland savages, ingenuity blossoming, everybody at one in this vital and pleasurable endeavour.

John Stewart, who suffered from MacGregors himself, felt that some of the suggestions went rather far.

With everyone in an excellent mood now, the King again intervened. Time was wearing on, he pointed out, and the inner man deserved sustenance. They probably had achieved enough for the first day. But, before they retired for well-deserved refreshment, it might be as well to appoint a small committee to consider details of this last debate, and others to come, so that the main parliament need not be cluttered with lesser matters and minor particulars, and so be able to devote itself to the broad and important issues of the nation. He therefore proposed a committee of, say, thirty-two delegates—eight lords, eight knights of the shires, eight burgh commissioners and eight bishops, under Lord Binning the Secretary of State as chairman. This should be more than sufficient.

This, as it happened, in the MacGregor euphoria, was accepted without debate.

James, thanking all present, rose, tapped the top of his hat, and shambled off to his private door. Parliament stood adjourned.

Later, eating at his mother's lodgings, John questioned the Duke on the King's extraordinary behaviour that day, nonplussed at his changes of stance and mood. His father shrugged.

"There you saw James at his cleverest," he said. "It was a brilliant performance."

"I do not understand," John admitted. "It seemed as though he started out strong and determined and then weakened and conceded defeat."

"Seemed—and meant to seem. James knew that he could not prevail on this parliament to vote for the Five Articles of Perth. And yet they require parliamentary sanction to be enforceable as law. So he misled all into thinking him defeated, as did you, made sure that his bishops would make the debate seem loaded against the majority, and then got parliament to refer all to a General Assembly of the Kirk, and to *accept* such Assembly's findings. In other words, parliament has surrended its power in this matter to the Assembly."

"But . . . a General Assembly will be even more set against those proposals than is this parliament!"

"Will it? Clearly James thinks otherwise. And I swear he knows what he is at! The Crown can bring much pressure to bear on many attending an Assembly, particularly parish-ministers. At our glorious Reformation the patronage of innumerable livings fell to the Crown or the Crown's nominees, instead of the Catholic bishops, abbots and priors. James, if he wished, could unseat great numbers of ministers. Others he could greatly impoverish by sanctioning the witholding of tithes and teinds. Others he might merely bribe. The reformed clergy are much more vulnerable than the old Romish ones, who were backed ultimately by the power of the Vatican. And they are in the main poor men. James will control preferment with his bishops. Needy but ambitious ministers will not lightly offend the monarch in this, I think."

"Your father is right," Mary Gray said. "*My* father always said the same. Not all the parish-ministers are such con-firmed Presbyterians as are the college divines and the like. How could they be? Most were reared as Catholics. Many would change only because it was politic to do so. King James knows what he is doing, in this. I have no doubt."

"And this committee under Tam o' the Cowgate—that was a masterstroke," Ludovick asserted. "It will rank, like the Lords of the Articles, as what they call 'an epitome of parliament', speaking with authority *for* parliament and interpreting the decisions thereof to its own satisfaction. And eight of the eleven bishops to sit upon it! These may have no vote in parliament itself, but on this committee they can have enormous influence. Especially as Tam Hamilton will select his other commissioners with the greatest of care, you may be sure. The MacGregor business was no more than a bait to trap our unsuspecting parliament into assenting mood. The Scots, I think, have forgotten just how shrewd a monarch the house of Stewart has spawned!"

"I would never have thought of all this," John said.

"Then you will have to learn about James, everything you can, lad, if you are coming to London with us," his father warned. "Otherwise you will be at the greatest disadvantage—for he will use you shamelessly. James *has* no shame, and uses everyone he can. So it behoves us all to look after ourselves!"

"I wish that I was not going."

"Do you truly?" his mother asked. "Or do you but say that? It will be a great adventure for you—sorry as I am to be losing you."

"Not losing me, I promise you. I will be back. I will not stay long . . ."

"That depends on the King, Johnnie, not on you," the Duke pointed out. "As part of the court, you are at James's command. We all are. You cannot announce one day that you are for home, and go, without the royal permission."

"Then I wish the more that I was not going. I said as much to the King, but he would not hear me."

"Can *you* not speak with him, Vicky?" Mary asked. "Convince him that Johnnie should remain at Methven. That he will make but a reluctant courtier."

"I can try. But I have little hopes of changing James's mind. Once he decides on a matter, he is hard to budge. He may say that he will consider it, then merely goes the same road by another door. He has taken a great fancy to John—thank God, in no indecent fashion—and considers him useful. And if James does that, then the useful man will not escape. I *know*—who have been useful for a score of years!" He smiled. "But do not look so woeful, lad—most young men would give much to be in your shoes, in this."

His son remained unconvinced.

"There is an aspect of all this which requires consideration," the Duke went on. "In London you will require money and some position—or at court you will find yourself at much disadvantage. The English are hot on position and title, on siller too! You are a knight now, yes—but that carries little weight at court, where all are knights if they are not great lords. And their greater ladies! James may give you some minor dignity, Extra Gentleman Usher, or

Deputy Cup-Bearer or the like—but he is ever short of moneys, the English parliament keeping him so, and you will gain little from him. You will have to dress well and live in a style suitable for a courtier—and my son!"

John's frown grew the darker.

"I have been considering what we can do. Methven cannot spare sufficient with the castle to maintain and your great drainage scheme. It occurs to me that Dumbarton is the answer. I have long been hereditary Governor and Captain of the royal castle of Dumbarton, with its revenues and dues. It is a gift of the Crown, of course. But I should not think that James, in his present mood, would object if it was transferred to you. I have not been near the place for years, and have to pay a deputy-governor—as you would have to do. The remaining revenues, rents and harbour-dues are not great, but sufficient for your needs in London, to be sure. And to be Sir John Stewart, Governor and Captain of Dumbarton Castle, would give you some standing at court. How think you?"

"But . . . but . . . how can I be governor of a royal fortress?" John demanded, astonished. "I know nothing of such matters. It is a great citadel, with soldiers and cannon, is it not? It controls the Clyde firth . . . ?"

"You can be governor, in name, as well as I can—from London! Continue to pay William Middlemas, the present deputy—he is called the Constable—and all will be as before. I will be glad to be quit of the responsibility, to tell truth. And when you escape from court, if so you wish, you can take your governorship more seriously. There might be quite great opportunities for you there. If James agrees—as I would expect him to."

Mary laughed amusedly. "You see what it is to have a duke as father," she said. "However illicit!"

6

John Stewart had had enough of attending parliament as a mere spectator, and, since the King did not seem to require him at this stage and during the sessions, nor even to remember his existence apparently, he decided to slip away back to Methven for a few days before the projected move south. Although he still hoped that somehow he might be able to avoid making that uncalled-for journey—not that it seemed likely now that his father had succeeded in arranging the Dumbarton business with James. Mary Gray remained in Edinburgh, where the Duke of course was still attending the parliament.

So John had to go on the assumption that he would be gone from Methven for some time and to make the necessary arrangements. Especially for the reclamation work on Methven Moss to continue, with the tree-felling to pay for it, as well as sundry other essential matters. Still more urgent, perhaps, was the need to see Janet Drummond.

He put considerable thought into how this last was to be achieved, without upset, since he could hardly just present himself at Innerpeffray Castle again and expect to be well received—even though Lord Madderty was attending the parliament in Edinburgh; unfortunately his lady was not. Eventually he hit on the idea of seeking the good offices of a mutual friend, a young woman with whom he had done some juvenile sweethearting, Alison Moncrieff by name, now safely married to the old Lady Tippermuir's grandson and mother of a bouncing boy. He would request her to call at Innerpeffray and ask Janet to take her to see the chapel, where long generations of Drummonds were buried, and where, since the Reformation, services were no longer held, and it was kept locked; like most other denizens of Strathearn, Alison had some Drummond blood in her veins. John would be waiting for them there.

When he called at Tippermuir House, Alison, incurably

126

romantic, was only too happy to oblige the King's new knight, for old times' sake. She would go the very next day.

So, the following afternoon, John hid his horse in the surrounding woodland and stationed himself amongst the Drummond gravestones to wait. There was a distinct possibility, of course, that his plan might fail. Janet might not agree to come. After their last meeting and his abrupt departure, she might feel disinclined. She might be away from home or otherwise engaged.

However, in due course, the two young women came walking along the riverbank, and John's heart bounded. Their greeting, nevertheless, probably disappointed the romantic Alison, for Janet was restrained and John was stiff, despite feeling as he did. After a distinctly formal exchange of courtesies, a disconcerting silence developed.

Alison plunged in volubly. If Janet would give her the key to the chapel she would go look. No need to accompany her—indeed she would rather be alone. With the past, you know, the dead . . .

They were left most evidently alone.

They both started to speak at the same moment, and both stopped.

Almost roughly John took the young woman's arm to lead her further away from the chapel. She did not hold back, but she gently disengaged.

"It was good of you to come, Janet," he jerked. "After . . . after my leaving you so, last time."

"Alison was very pressing," she answered.

"Yes—I asked her to be. She is kind. I had to see you. I am going away."

"Oh!" she faltered in her step, just a little.

"Yes. The King commands that I go south with him. With my father. To London. I do not want to go, to tell truth, but have no choice. It is a royal command."

"I see. Will you be gone long?"

"That is the difficulty of it. I do not know for how long. It seems that I cannot leave the court without the King's permission. And James can be exacting, contrary. So nothing is certain."

"That must be . . . unsettling for you."

"Yes. It is."

They had halted at the graveyard wall. Abruptly John lost patience with this polite exchange.

"Look you, Janet," he cried, "this is damnable! To be leaving you like this. At such time. Leaving all at odds between us."

"As well, perhaps," she said, low-voiced.

"No! It is not. To be parted, with nothing resolved."

"More resolved than you think, John, I fear! My mother and father . . ."

"Your mother and father do not approve of me, no. I am not good enough for their daughter. A bastard—aye, and son of a bastard mother! But hear you this. The King has appointed me Captain and Hereditary Keeper of Dumbarton Castle, with its duties and revenues. So, so . . . !"

"So you are a great man! All that!" She seemed less than elated.

"But—do you not see? Could this not change all? The knighthood and now this. It gives me standing. A namely position. That is why it was done, to give me a position at court. But it will serve as well nearer home, some position in Scotland. One of the royal officers. And the revenues. I have now the wherewithal to marry. I would not be too humble to wed even Lord Madderty's daughter!"

She shook her head, unhappily. "No—do not think it is that. I am glad for you, John—believe me. But I fear it cannot be . . ."

"Why not? Does this not change all? Your father cannot . . ." He paused. "Or is it *you*? You who will not have it?"

"No, no—not that. Or, leastways . . ."

"See you—it would be good for more than just our, our joy. If I could tell King James that I must come home here to be married, that all was arranged, he would surely never hold me in London. We could decide on a day, and so I could get away. If you do not wish to dwell in my mother's house of Methven, we could live at Dumbarton Castle . . ."

"John—hear me. Listen to me. You do not understand. I am to be married—but not to you! My father has hastened to arrange it. I, I blame myself. After that last day, I told

128

them that I . . . that I was fond of you. I protested at how my father and mother had dealt with you. They were angry, berating me. Hard words were spoken. And thereafter my father went off and arranged a marriage between me and David Drummond, my cousin. Or half-cousin."

John drew a long quivering breath.

She looked at him quickly, and then away. "Davie is the son of my father's cousin, Drummond of Dalpatrick. You know him. His lands adjoin ours. My parents look on it as an excellent match!"

John still could not trust himself to words.

She touched his arm. "I am sorry, John—sorry! This is no wish of mine, I promise you. I like Davie well enough, but . . ."

"Davie Drummond!" he got out, through clenched teeth. "That, that . . ." He swallowed the rest.

Janet was silent, now, unhappy.

For a while there seemed to be nothing to say. Then, level-voiced, John spoke.

"You are prepared to abide by your father's wishes in this? To be, to be exchanged for property, like some dumb beast!"

"That is unfair!" she declared, but not hotly. "I can do no other. You know it. I am not yet of age. My marriage is in my father's hands, his right. He may give me to whom he will. Do you think that I have not pleaded with him, besought him?"

"Yes. I am sorry. When is it to be—the wedding?"

"Soon. He says the sooner the better."

"So there is an end to it? Nothing to be done? We accept all, as of the will of God!"

"Can *you* think of anything that can be done?"

"Aye. We could go off together. Secretly. Run off. Leave all, to be together."

"You, you would do that, John? For me? Abandon Methven? Offend the King? Throw aside your position at court? Lose this of Dumbarton Castle? For Janet Drummond?"

"Yes," he said shortly.

"Then I thank you. With all my heart. But—Janet

Drummond would *not*! I would never do that to you, John—never! You must know in your heart that I would not, could not?"

"I know nothing such . . ."

"Surely you must. No honest woman could."

"Do you refuse for my sake? Or for your own?"

She hesitated. "For both. This is not the way for love, John—true love. To ruin a man's life. Possibly to ruin mine also. For could love survive that? The loss, the hurt, the dashing of hopes . . . ?"

"You say love, Janet? True love. Do you mean that? Do you indeed love me, then?"

She swallowed and bit her lip. "Yes," she got out at length, strangled-voiced.

"Dear God!" He swung on her, to grasp her to him. "Oh, Janet, Janet!" Hungrily he kissed her, her hair, her brow.

She did not struggle nor push him away. But she kept her head down, denying him her lips. He felt her trembling in his arms.

At length, as on that other day, she gently disengaged. "This serves nothing, John—will only make it worse. I think that we should go find Alison. We but hurt ourselves."

"If you truly love me, how can you do this, Janet? Send me away and wed another?" He sought to hold her back.

"I can because I must. One of us has to be strong. Do you not see? It is fated this way. Whatever we feel, we were not meant for each other. I am my father's daughter, in his hands. And you are . . . Sir John Stewart of Methven!" She moved on.

Shaking his head helplessly, he followed on.

Alison was waiting patiently just inside the chapel doorway. She looked from one to the other eagerly, almost anxiously. Her face fell at their expressions. She did not speak.

"I think that we should go home now, Alison," Janet said evenly. "Sir John and I have had our talk. If you are ready?"

John took his leave of them, where he had met them, almost as stiff and formal as had been his greeting. Long he stared after them as the two girls walked off along the river-bank. Alison looked back once, but Janet did not.

He went to mount and ride back to Methven, features set.

PART TWO

7

Despite his father's warnings, John Stewart was disappointed with his first impressions of London. Used to Scottish cities and towns, which tended all to be set in or around dramatic natural features, great defensive rocks, hill-passes, river-crossings and the like, the low and level lands of southern England offered little challenge to the eye. Used by now to the more humdrum appearance of English towns, having been all too long, as it seemed to him, on the way south from Carlisle through the Midlands, nevertheless, without consciously thinking about it, London, he had assumed, would be different, one of the great cities of the world. Yet, as the royal train made its approach, there was little to arrest the attention save far-flung building, admittedly punctuated by church-spires and towers, and smoke, a vast pall of smoke, for it was now autumn and fires were necessary; and, as they drew nearer, smells. Never had John smelled such comprehensive and enduring stink. Edinburgh could smell sufficiently badly, admittedly; but there, like elsewhere in Scotland, the wind always blew, on account of hills and sea, and tended to disperse the odours of humanity in the mass, with its livestock. Here there was little or no wind apparently and the stench was appalling. The river, when they reached it, the renowned Thames, seemed to be if not the main source of smells, then the principal repository and amplifier thereof, receptacle for all the filth, refuse, carcases and scourings of the vast city. Gagging, John rode on, in his fairly humble position in the lengthy cavalcade—even so, much smaller than that which had arrived in Scotland, for many of the English notables had dropped off on their progress down through England.

They wound their slow way through seemingly endless narrow streets, mere lanes most of them, by the West

Bourne from Dudden Hill and past Campden Hill to Bridge Creek and Chelsey, and so along the riverside to Whitehall. These streets were even more congested than Edinburgh's, more crushed and crowded-seeming, largely because the houses were built of wood, not stone, and above the ground floor at street level each storey was projected somewhat on, as it were, brackets, so that by the time they reached the top, these galleries were all but touching those on the other side of the street, cutting out daylight and putting all below into a sort of twilight—also enclosing the stinks.

The royal guard cleared the way for them as best they could through all this—at least, for the King at the head of the column, the narrowness of all lengthening the procession to a mile at least, with John perhaps halfway down. No crowds cheered them on their way—there was no room for that, even if the Londoners were so inclined—although folk hung out of windows, some screeched, and urchins managed to run alongside, often amongst the horses' legs, dogs barked and church-bells rang as welcome.

At length they turned in from the Thames to the palace, through a vast tilting-yard flanking splendid gardens out of which rose no fewer than thirty-four stone columns, each topped by a heraldic beast. Whitehall looked almost like a town of itself, huge, sprawling, with liveried guards and attendants everywhere, musicians playing, courtiers milling around and confusion reigning. Sundry great lords were already greeting the monarch as John rode up, and he heard them acquainting James with what presumably was the latest news—Queen Anne was unwell again at her own palace of Somerset House; Charles, Prince of Wales, was at Theobalds Park, or Tibbalds as the King called it; the Earl of Pembroke had suffered a fall from his horse and damaged his shoulder; the Attorney-General, Sir Francis Bacon, had produced a new addition to his essay on the *Advancement of Learning*, dedicated to His Majesty—but was at the same time condemning the system of monopolies. And so on. James seemed interested in little of this, although he frowned darkly at the monopolies item. As for his wife's health, he declared that it would just be the gout, and hadn't he himself been suffering from the same disorder all the way from

Carlisle, and that compounded by the arthritis, forby? What he *was* concerned with was whether that limmer Walter Ralegh was returned yet with his treasure from yon Orinoco place? That was fell important. The information that there was no word of Ralegh yet sent James stamping into his palace, muttering.

John was fortunate in being able to obtain a room in his father's quarters in Whitehall, for despite its size the palace was apparently full to overflowing, and the King was not the man to demean himself by finding accommodation for hangers-on. Except for the Villiers family, that is. An entire clan of them seemed to have taken up residence, mother, brothers, sisters, uncles, aunts and cousins, to the undisguised disgust of most of the court, especially of the Howard faction, who were also there in strength and sounding so greatly more important, the most illustrious house in England even if somewhat waning in influence.

John quickly learned that the Palace of Whitehall was in fact something of a battleground and that the wise newcomer would be well-advised not to get involved if he could help it. The main factions were the Howards and the new Villiers and their supporters; but there were others also, at differing levels, all seeking to attain power and prestige by influencing the King. At first John was looked upon by almost all with grave suspicion, as yet another personable young man to whom James had presumbly taken a fancy. But the fact that he was the Duke of Lennox's bastard and therefore in some sort of blood relationship to the monarch, helped, especially as Ludovick was assiduous in letting it be known that James was not interested intimately in his new courtier.

In fact James did not appear to be interested in the newcomer in any other way either, as the days passed. If the King was aware of his presence in the palace he did not show it. John asked himself, and his father, why he was here at all, what was the point in bringing him all this way just to ignore him? The Duke said to be patient, James would call for him in due course—whereupon John perversely wondered whether he would not prefer just to be forgotten and rejected so that he could go home to Methven unhindered. He was, of course, in a distinctly disillusioned frame of mind these days. Janet Drummond, although unreachable and so very far away, was seldom long out of his mind.

The fact was that the King, as well as suffering from his gout and arthritis, had returned to two pressing and immediate concerns. One was a quarrel with his Privy Council over money, or at least the means of raising it—for parliament still continued to keep the royal purse-strings tight; and this of Bacon's campaign against monopolies was very relevant. The other was the marriage of Steenie's brother John Villiers, which James had promised to stage, if that was the word, and for which the most ambitious plans were well ahead—and which was going to cost a lot of money, nothing apparently being too good for Steenie and his family. These preoccupations helped to explain James's disappointment that Ralegh had not yet returned from Spanish America with the ships' loads of gold and treasure which he had promised to bring the monarch, in exchange for his freedom from the Tower of London and sentence of death. The wedding had been fixed for 29 September, at Hampton Court Palace—part-reason for some of the haste of the return journey from Scotland—and all the court was commanded to attend. John could not understand why the King should be so concerned about this marriage of a young man whom he himself termed a witless loon, to a daughter of a man whom he had always disliked, Sir Edward Coke, formerly Lord Chief Justice. His father explained. Apart from the fact that James doted on Steenie, the bridegroom's brother, politics and rule entered into this. The King was anxious to limit and indeed reduce the enormous power and influence of the Howard family and their allies, who between them controlled far too many of the high places of state, with no fewer than five earldoms and the suppressed dukedom of Norfolk. The last favourite, Carr, Earl of Somerset, was their nominee, married to one of them, and he was now in the Tower, after scandals amany. James was now seeking to raise up a new dynasty, dependent upon himself—as the Howards were not—to counter their influence and wealth. But shrewdly he did not want this to *replace* the Howards in entrenched power, so he was using the comparatively humble, little-known and not notably clever Villiers tribe, whom he could manipulate and use, and when necessary put down again, without difficulty. He had learned the lessons of divide-and-rule in a hard school, in Scotland. This wedding was a step along that road.

Just how important a step James considered it to be was demonstrated the day before the ceremony, when the monarch sent for Ludovick Stewart and commanded him to repair to Somerset House and escort Queen Anne to Hampton Court. He added that Annie likely would be stickit and awkward, for she did not want to go, being wickedly incommodious towards Steenie. But she was to be fetched, willshe, nillshe—and Vicky was the only one to whom he could entrust the task. She must attend.

So to Somerset House the Duke went, that same day, and John with him. Anne of Denmark had had her own palace and small court for years now, in general distinctly out-of-sympathy with her husband and his ways—as perhaps who will blame her? She went her own way, was not always the soul of discretion and was wildly extravagant; but she was the Queen and, almost more important, the King of Denmark's sister—and had to be humoured to some extent. But every now and again James put his foot down, as on this occasion.

John found the Queen to be of middle years, growing plump, plain of feature and with a long pointed nose, but autocratic of nature—and not very welcoming on this occasion, since she well knew why the Duke of Lennox had come. Normally she got on well enough with Ludovick—who was admittedly easy to get on with.

"You are sent to drag me to this stupid wedding, Vicky Stewart," she declared, at sight of them. She had never lost her foreign accent, but overlaid by a Doric flavour from her years in Scotland, a curious blend resulted, often quite unintelligible to English ears. "I do not wish to go. I am indeed *unable* to go, a sick woman. You may tell James so. Not that he cares for my state."

"I am sorry to hear that, Your Majesty—the more so since you look so well," the Duke said, diplomatically. "No doubt it is your spirits which are low. The wedding will do you much good, I swear. There will be much to entertain, masques and play-acting, dancing and pageantry—all to Your Majesty's taste."

"Perhaps. But I shall not be there!"

"Surely you will come, Anne? If only for my sake! For James will never forgive me if I do not bring you. He said as much."

"Why does James want me to go there? He requires no wife, with those shameless young men! I am not to be insulted so. Who is *this* young man whom you have brought here? Do not say to me that you too, Vicky Stewart, have become so, so . . ."

"This is my son. By Mary Gray, whom you know, Anne. John—Sir John Stewart of Methven, now Keeper of Dumbarton Castle."

"So—your by-blow, is it? And so good to look at! Mary Gray I remember well, a woman of much worth and cleverness—despite her father, the man Gray."

"Yes. Although Patrick had his points, see you."

"You, young man—what brings you to London? Not King James's favours, I hope, no?"

Embarrassed, John looked away. "No, Your Majesty. Or . . . not that, no. The King has been kind . . . or, leastways, gracious. I, I . . ."

His father came to his rescue. "John was privileged to do James a useful service. More than one. At Edinburgh. James insisted that he came south with us."

"Ah. And what does he find for you to do, in this wretched London, young man? No good, I would jalouse." That sounded odd on guttural Danish lips.

"Nothing, Majesty," John told her, simply.

"Nothing? He has nothing for you?"

"No doubt in time James will find occupation for him," Ludovick said.

"But what occupation? I do not trust James's occupations for young men. I have it better, yes. You will come to me, Sir John. Yes, that is it. I could use so goodly a young man in this Somerset House. I have too many women here. And old men whom James he has sent to spy and keek upon me.

Evil old men! That is it, yes—you will come to me, Mary Gray's son, Patrick Gray's grandson. To be one of my gentlemen. How say you?"

Bewildered, John stared first at the Queen and then at his father.

That man looked thoughtful. "This is kind, Anne—but requires thinking on," he said. "James might not like it."

"James! James has eyes only for those odious Villiers! The King has not offered you any position at court, Sir John? Nor employment?"

"No-o-o. Save this of Dumbarton Castle, Highness."

"That is in Scotland, not London. So—all is well. I offer you position first—Gentleman-in-Waiting. You cannot refuse—it is the will of your Queen! You shall wait on me, Sir John Stewart, and we shall do most well."

John looked uncertain.

Ludovick proved himself to be something of an opportunist. "If that is Your Majesty's will and command, I am sure that my son will feel honoured. And will accompany you to the wedding tomorrow. It will be a good opportunity for him to commence his service."

The Queen considered the Duke narrowly and then shrugged. "Very well," she acceded. "Sir John, you will attend me tomorrow, to Hampton Court. I shall, I think, not remain there long. Thereafter you will make your biding here at Somerset House, as one of my household. You understand?"

"Yes, Your Majesty," he said, if doubtfully.

They withdrew.

On the way back westwards to Whitehall, the Duke sought to reassure his son—who suspected that he might have been sacrificed in order to get the Queen's agreement to attend this wedding. But his father said that this appointment to Anne's household might be an excellent development, not only giving John employment and added status but possibly would draw James's attention to his neglect, and produce some advantage in that quarter. He was amused that his son seemed to have this facility of making swift good impressions upon Queen as well as King. What was the secret of it?

The younger man did not know, nor consider it much of an asset.

So the next forenoon father and son embarked on one of the gaily-painted and canopied royal barges, at the Whitehall steps, manned by the King's liveried watermen, and were rowed in state down-river the mile or so to Somerset House again. Ludovick had decided to come along too, partly because that had been James's original command, but also in case Anne turned difficult and John could not cope. As a personal touch he hired four musicians, with lute and flute, to accompany them, and these practised their repertoire on their brief eastwards journey.

They found Anne not resiling on her commitment but far from ready to go. Indeed the Stewarts were ushered, presumably on royal command, directly into the Queen's bed-chamber, where they found her, in a state of undress, being prepared for the occasion by a twittering clutter of females and as yet undecided as to which gown she was going to wear—a situation which obviously held no embarrassment for Anne, who whatever else she was, was no prude, however much it disconcerted her new gentleman. Clearly they were not going to get away for some time, and the Duke grew a little anxious, which was not like him, for the wedding ceremony was due to start at one hour after noon. James, of course, might himself be late, as he so frequently was, having little regard for mere time—but on the other hand he might be early, in which case all would have to begin forthwith.

The Queen, practically naked as to her top half, and no very delectable sight, demanded of all present which she should wear of fully a dozen splendid gowns laid out—which evidently she had been doing of her flock of ladies for some time previously—and the Duke, to save further debate, chose a heavily-jewelled confection in purple taffety, Anne being partial to jewels on a daunting scale. However, this was laughed to scorn as dowdy, ageing and quite inappropriate. Whereupon Anne pointed to John and declared that her new Gentleman-in-Waiting should choose.

Appalled, the young man swallowed and gestured blindly to the nearest of all the dresses to himself, lying over a settle, a thing in pink and sewn pearls; where upon the Queen clapped her beringed hands delightedly, announced that it was quite the best choice, the youngest-looking gown there, and trust a young man to know what a woman should wear. Only, she might have difficulty in containing herself within it—this to fits of almost masculine laughter.

Her ladies shook censorious but helpless heads.

Anne insisting, she was pushed, pulled and constrained into this pink creation, amidst much royal gasping and indeed profanity. It did not take long for John to see what the Queen had meant by non-containment, for her large and sprawling bosom was alarmingly under-controlled and over-exposed, with any incautious movement liable to allow one side, or both, to bulge free.

Anne, however, presently declared herself to be satisfied, and, donning sundry ropes of pearls and a furred robe for the journey, and a high hat rather similar to her husband's, conceded that she was ready for the river.

And now a new problem delayed them. It seemed that fully a score of her ladies expected to accompany the Queen, and the royal barge just would not hold them all. There was a great to-do, and Ludovick eventually sent John to try to hire another boat locally. This proved to be quite difficult, for all who mattered in London appeared to be going to Hampton Court, and much the quickest way was by water. After considerable efforts and at some expense, he managed to engage a very indifferent wherry, smelling of fish, and manned by a ribald crew. Reaching Somerset House steps with this, he found the royal barge gone—it was, he supposed, unthinkable that the Queen should sit and wait for anyone so lowly. Instead he had about ten disgruntled females, those rejected for his father's boat, to escort to Hampton in a smelly rough craft oared by leering characters outspoken with their comments.

It was an uncomfortable journey in every way.

Amidst the ladies' complaints about the wretched boat, the uncouth crew, the stink and the effect on their fine clothes, one Scottish voice sounded. This belonged to a quite handsome young woman, auburn-haired, with a bold eye and a fine figure. She came and sat beside John in the stern and seemed less critical than most of her companions. She introduced herself as a Hamilton, Margaret, daughter of the late Sir Claud Hamilton of Shawfield, brother to the first Earl of Abercorn. Her father, who had died three years previously, had been a Gentleman of the King's Bedchamber; and, left alone, her uncle had procured for her the appointment of Extra Maid-in-Waiting to the Queen. She seemed a lively and quite attractive young woman.

It was a dozen miles by river to Hampton Court and the boatmen were in no hurry, so that the journey seemed interminable and John was glad enough of the Hamilton girl's chatter, which at least passed the time and helped to insulate him from the older women's censure—for they seemed to blame him for current disappointments. Margaret, who appeared to know everybody who was anybody in London, was able to identify most of the well-dressed occupants of the innumerable other boats which passed them—and the fact that they did pass them only added to the general complaint.

At last they came to the great palace, in its magnificent gardens, which Cardinal Wolsey had built for himself and then presented to Henry the Eighth—who had later condemned him to death. Even here there was delay and frustration, with long queues of river-craft awaiting to disembark, the major portion of the landing-area being railed off for the arrival of the King's barge, James not yet having put in an appearance, although fully an hour late.

In consequence much concern and upset prevailed at the palace, with the Queen insulted, Steenie's and the bridegroom's mother, the Lady Compton, a masterful woman, in major offence, the bride's father, Sir Edward Coke, gobbling like a turkey and the groom already the worse for liquor. Ludovick was seeking to pour oil on troubled waters, with only limited success. Of the bride there was no sign.

Fortunately the royal barge, all banners and gold-tasselled awnings, surrounded by a positive flotilla of escorts including two boatloads of musicians and singers, and another with two Muscovy bears for baiting and a fourth full of dogs, arrived soon thereafter, and the nuptials could approximately proceed. Only a very small proportion of the crowd could get inside the palace chapel, of course, and John for one did not try. He went exploring the vast building, the largest that he had ever seen, and was much impressed by this at least. The furnishings, the eastern carpets, the tapestries, the paintings and statuary, were an eye-opener indeed as to what an acquisitive Prince of Holy Church had been able to accumulate.

The wedding ceremony itself must have been very brief, for a great noise drew John back sooner than he expected to the main state apartments, where the King and Queen and bridal party were now congregated in high-spirited din. Conceiving that it might possibly be expected of him, in his new capacity of Gentleman-in-Waiting to the Queen, he made his way through the throng to a position not far from Anne's side, arousing some hostile reaction in the process. He was scarcely where he sought to be when chaos was let loose in that banqueting-hall—or, more accurately, it was the two bears which were let loose by Steenie Villiers and some of his youthful relatives, as some sort of prank, and the chaos resulted. There was a great scramble to get out of the vicinity of the lumbering animals, amidst much jostling and shouting, women screaming and John getting his first sight of the bride, a pale and anaemic-seeming creature of no more than sixteen years, as she was hoisted up on to a table-top amongst the viands and flagons, where other ladies joined her, including even her new mother-in-law, yelling shrilly as any fish-wife, at her sons.

John got himself to the Queen's side in case she required help. But the sea-king's daughter was not to be frightened by any pair of semi-tame Muscovy bears and, although looking disapproving, stood her ground. She acknowledged John's attendance with a nod but was clearly concerned with what was going on nearby.

A slight and thin young man, with rather soulful eyes above a petulant mouth, gorgeously clad in gold satin, was berating the Earl of Buckingham for this escapade, declaring it to be unsuitable and unseemly immediately after holy worship and divine service. He should be ashamed of himself, putting the bride in fear and his own mother likewise. And so on, Steenie scowling but not replying.

The objector did get his answer, however, for King James, who had been standing behind and listening, and watching with sardonic eye, suddenly stepped forward and cuffed the thin young man over the ear, and in no playful fashion.

There was an appalled silence in the immediate circle, broken by the Queen's cry of outrage. In her anger she burst forth in Danish but quickly changed to her own brand of Scots-English.

"How do you dare to do that, James Stewart!" she demanded. "Strike Charles! Strike my son—the Prince of Wales! How do you dare! And for this, this upstart!"

"Och, I dare fine, Annie—fine! I'm the King, mind—as well as the laddie's faither. I'll dae mair'n that, if need be. If this son o' your's—and mine, is he no'?—clacks his tongue in *my* presence, he'll do so to my liking! You hear that, Charlie Stewart?"

The prince inclined his head, lips tight.. But his mother was less easily silenced.

"You insult my son, you insult me, the Queen! It is not to be carried, no. I will leave this place, and all these your creatures . . ."

"Na, na—you'll no', Annie. You'll bide. And that's my royal command, see you. Aye, and you'll cover yoursel' better, woman; you're no' decent, for guidsakes!"

Anne drew a gulping breath—thereby exposing still more of her frontal development—but she did grab a silken shawl from one of her ladies, to wrap tightly around her.

John glanced guiltily over at his father, standing beside the King. He felt some slight responsibility for having chosen that gown.

James nodded, and turned to Buckingham. "Steenie—best you get yon critturs out o' here. You've had a sufficiency o' sport for this present. Vicky—hae these women doon off the tables—it's no' seemly. And hae nae mair skirling and yowling. We'll now eat—if we can win room on the boards for female bodies! Aye." And he tapped his hat more firmly on his head and moved round to his throne-like chair at the top table, all put to rights.

Perhaps it was as well that there had been this encounter

144

between King, Queen and Prince, since it ensured that one of the principal problems as to seating for once did not arise. Always the matter of precedence tended to be a headache, and the Master of the Household had the unenviable task of sorting it out, never to everyone's satisfaction. This being a wedding, the matter was complicated by the claims of the principals and the bridal families. The Queen and the Prince of Wales, of course, were normally entitled to pride-of-place, even though James frequently decided otherwise. But today these two chose ostentatiously to distance themselves as far as possible from husband and father, without leaving the top table. Which was a major easement. James did not like Sir Edward Coke, the bride's father, nor Lady Compton, the bridegroom's mother—indeed he found most women unprofitable table-companions being good neither for drinking nor erudite conversation, in his opinion. He did not think much of the bridegroom either, but for the look of things put him on his right, with Steenie on his left. But there was the Archbishop of Canterbury, to make matters difficult; he would go on the other side of John Villiers, with Coke. The rest could fight it out between themselves and the Master of the Household.

This they did, with considerable argument and protest. Ludovick's services as ducal arbiter and peacemaker were much in demand. James ignored all, and began to sample the wines.

John Stewart had found himself a suitably modest place well down the hall where there was no competition, when the young woman Margaret Hamilton appeared at his side to say that the Queen required his presence up beside her at the top table.

Reluctantly he rose. He could have done without this.

He imagined that all eyes were on him as he followed the young woman up to where Anne sat with Prince Charles at one extreme end of the table. The Queen smiled on him graciously and pointed to the crosswise extremity, where presumably he was to sit. He beckoned one of the servitors to fetch him a chair, and sat, feeling very conspicuous. He had no doubt that this was not being done out of any affection or esteem for himself but merely to let the King see that the Queen had taken him over. Charles could not have looked less interested.

The Archbishop said grace-before-meat, at considerable length, seeking God's blessing on the happy couple in the by-going; James, who had started beforehand, continuing to eat and drink throughout. Thereafter the banquet proceeded, accompanied in the central space of the hall by jugglers, acrobats, dancers and music.

John had ample opportunity to survey the scene and consider his fellow-guests at this the first major function he had attended in England—for, having got him up to this prominent position, the Queen saw no need to converse with him; and, seated at the table-end, no one else was within reasonable speaking-distance save the Prince of Wales, who sulked. The bride and bridegroom he judged, perhaps unkindly, could be dismissed as nonentities, their only significance being that they were Villiers. Lady Compton, formerly Lady Villiers, was a small, waspish, determined-looking woman, notorious for her anxiety to screw the utmost advantage out of the King's infatuation with her second son, trying hard to have herself appointed, retrospectively as it were, Countess of Buckingham, suggesting that Steenie might well become a duke, and angling at least for a peerage for her new husband, the amiable and inoffensive Sir Thomas Compton. Ludovick said that James loathed her but believed that he could make use of her drive and ambition.

Sir Edward Coke, now large and gross, was also ambitious and had achieved much. An able lawyer, he had been one of the late Queen Elizabeth's bright young men and had been Attorney-General when James succeeded. He had risen to be Lord Chief Justice but the King never got on with him and he still awaited the peerage which normally would have come his way before this. No doubt he hoped this marriage-link with the rising star of Villiers would improve his fortunes.

Beyond the Archbishop was a darkly handsome man, all in black and gold, whom John knew to be Diego, Count Gondomar, the Spanish Ambassador, said to have an unsuitable influence on James, with whom he discussed diablery and witchcraft, astrology, mythology and the like. Gondomar was angling for a Spanish alliance—which would hopefully stop the English privateers' continuing attacks on Spanish treasure-ships from the Indies—and of course was much concerned over the outcome of Sir Walter Ralegh's venture. If Ralegh failed, all said that Gondomar would have his head.

At the far opposite end of the table was a splendidly-dressed and confident-seeming group which John assumed to be the Howards—at least he recognised one as Thomas Howard, Earl of Suffolk, Lord Treasurer and acting Earl Marshal. These had with them a most eye-catching figure, a glorious youth, clad all in pale blue satin, quite the most beautiful male John for one had ever set eyes on. He noticed that the King not infrequently looked in that direction—as indeed did Steenie. For that matter, John was equally aware that James occasionally cast his eye thoughtfully in his own direction.

Presently however the monarch seemed to remember that this was a wedding-feast, tapped his hat more firmly on his head and flapped a hand at the Master of the Household, who in turn waved to his trumpeter who sounded a brief fanfare. Silence achieved, the King, still lounging back in his seat, scratched his wispy beard and nodded portentously.

"Aye," he said, thickly but conversationally, "we've had a marriage this day, a right auspicious occasion, representative of a deal mair than this bit laddie and lassie you see before you—and who maybe do not look fell auspicious!" And he glanced from the owlish-looking bridegroom at his side, seeking to find the shrinking bride. "These twa are but symbols, this day, o' a much greater signification in marriage—aye, and maybe shilpit symbols, you'll jalouse? But, och—*non omnia possumus omnes!*"

James always waited hopefully for appreciative reaction to his Latin asides, however seldom he got it.

He sighed and went on, "Aye, well—marriage, holy matrimony, between a man and a woman, represents first and foremaist the union between Christ-God and His Church. And, secondly, the union between an anointed monarch and his people. These are baith sacramental relationships, mind—and let nane forget it! *I* do not!" That last was accompanied by a glower round the great company, as though in warning, lingering it seemed especially on Queen Anne and then on the Howards.

"As Christ's Vice-Regent on this pairt o' God's earth, and sovereign-lord o' this realm, I am consairned that these twa aspects o' holy matrimony shouldna be owerlooked on sik-like an occasion as this, lost sight o' in wedding and bedding and haughmagandie—forby, whether these ensamples o' wedded bliss this day will be fit for much o' that last, I hae my doubts! The Church was committed to my keeping by Almighty God at my coronation, and I'll see to it that she isna set aside, imposed upon or robbed, aye robbed, by any. Let a' tak tent! The guid Archbishop here may rest assured, never fear."

A pause, as the gathering listened enthralled, all knowing of current moves by the Howards, the greatest Catholic family, to win back by legal process some of the lands taken from them at the Reformation and handed over to the new Church of England.

"Aye, and as husband o' my people, it likewise behoves me to look to the common weal and see that there's nae diskindness and exploitation o' my folk, as I hear tell of in certain parts and offices. Even in the realm's Treasury itsel', I'm told!"

All eyes were again on the Howards, with Suffolk Lord Treasurer.

Having thus given the clearest public indication yet of his attitude towards the mightiest family in England, James changed his tone somewhat. "Mind," he went on, "marriage can be a right lottery—we a' ken that, even the Lord's Anointed!" And he chuckled, gesturing amiably towards the Queen. "It's a fell kittle affair at times, and nae mistake! But we maun warstle through, aye recollecting that the husband is head o' the wife, just as Christ is head o' the Church and the King is head o' the people. If we mind that, we'll no' go far wrang! Eh, Annie?"

The Queen, shocked and flustered, half-rose in her chair, gasping for words. But James flapped her back.

"Na, na, bide your time, woman. I'm no' finished yet."

He turned towards the bridegroom. "You, Johnnie Villiers—a bit word on this your wedding-day. You dinna seem to me to be like to make one o' the props and stays o' my kingdom, just! But maybe there's mair to you than strikes the eye, since you're ain brother to my Steenie, Earl o' Buckingham, who has his pairts—ooh, aye, he has his pairts! Sae, maybe yoursel' also. I'm hoping so, leastways, for I can use some stout props and stays in this realm o' England, that will serve me honestly wi' mair consairn than just to fill their ain pouches! Sae I've hopes for you, John Villiers, for your brother's sake. Aye, and in token o' my hopes, I hereby name, appoint and create you Lord Viscount o' Purbeck. An act o' faith, as you might say! My wedding-gift to you and your lassie."

John Villiers was by now too far gone in liquor to do more than goggle at his sovereign-lord. But James appeared not to notice any lack of appreciation from the new viscount, for his glance was wholly on Sir Edward Coke beyond, a leering glance, almost triumphal.

The former Lord Chief Justice's highly-coloured and bejowled face was indeed a study. Here was the peerage, which he himself had sought for so long, and surely earned, conferred as though by a mere whim on this whipper-snapper, who had done nothing to deserve it, nor likely ever would. He, a mere knight, had now to call his son-in-law my lord, his daughter a viscountess.

John, for one, was sorry for Coke. He had no doubt that the King had done this deliberately to humiliate him rather than to honour Villiers. The banqueting-hall buzzed like a beehive disturbed.

Since James appeared to have finished, the Queen arose, not to speak but to sweep off towards the door, leaving her ladies in twittering uncertainty behind her. As she passed John she signed peremptorily for him to follow her. The Prince of Wales sat still.

John unhappily rose, bowed towards the King, and hurried after the Queen.

He had almost reached the door when a hand gripped his arm. He turned, to find the Master of the Household at his elbow.

"Sir John," that dignitary said stiffly. "It is not permitted that any leave the royal presence without the King's express permission."

"But . . . the Queen . . ."

"The Queen may do as she thinks fit, sir. But you are the King's subject, before the Queen's."

Looking after Anne's disappearing person, John shrugged and turned back.

At least he did not have to face the battery of all eyes, as he feared, for attention was now concentrated on what was happening up at the top table. The Howard group, or at least the men thereof, had risen from their places and moved up to stand around the King, and with them the beautiful youth in blue. Suffolk was doing the talking, clearly presenting the young man to the monarch, who was eyeing him up and down critically. Steenie was looking on, his eyes like daggers.

Resuming his seat more or less unnoticed, John was near enough to hear most of what was said in the King's vicinity.

". . . most able and of excellent wits," the Lord Treasurer was saying. "Good on a horse and a notable dancer. Your Majesty will find him well endowed in every way."

"Is that a fact?" James said. "You're no' for selling me a blood horse, nor yet a trained chase-hound, are you, Suffolk?"

"Indeed no, Sire. This is a most noble youth, William Monson by name, who should add lustre and relish to your court. He comes from a good family. His uncle indeed is a servant of Your Majesty's own, Sir Thomas Monson, Master of the Armoury in the Tower . . ."

"Aye, well, my Lord Treasurer," the King interrupted, "wherever he comes frae, you can tak him back there again!"

"But . . . Sire . . . !"

"Nae buts, my lord! You've misjudged in this, you Howards. Aye, and no' for the first time. You misjudge *me*, man, in this as in much else. And that isna wise, mind."

Even the Howard confidence was wilting. Suffolk looked strained and the ageing Earl of Nottingham, Lord High Admiral, stammered something incoherent.

James nodded. "Sae, if you hae any commission wi' this

young man, I'd advise him, right perfumacious as he smells, to forbear his company in my royal presence hereafter. You have it, my lords? Guid—then you hae my permission to retire frae this place, all o' you. And tak the limmer wi' you!"

Scarcely believing their ears, the princely Howards stared. But if they were in any doubt that James was serious, his flapping hand shooing them away as though they had been barnyard poultry, convinced them. In much confusion, bowing, they backed away, to collect their womenfolk and make for the nearest door, whilst the great company looked on in astonishment.

Thereafter the entertainers proceeded with their acts, but James was restless now and presently rose, and of course so must everybody else. The jugglers stopped juggling abruptly, and, as the King made a shambling exit, the Master of the Household hurriedly announced that the bear-baiting would take place outside.

John found his way to his father's side, in some anxiety as to what was now expected of him. Was he due for reprimand from the King, or was he to follow the Queen, as she had commanded? Ludovick sympathised with his son in becoming involved in a tug-of-war between James and Anne, but advised him not to distress himself unduly. The King would probably forget the incident and the Queen would hear that he had been summoned back. His counsel would be to go now to Anne, and keep out of James's sight meantime. He himself would have a word with their lord, in due course.

So John went in search of the Queen—only to discover that she was gone from Hampton Court already. In high dudgeon she had swept down to the riverside, alone apparently, and commanded the royal barge which had brought her and the Duke to take her back to Somerset House there and then, waiting for none.

Whilst John was digesting this information and wondering what to do now, the young woman Margaret Hamilton descended upon him. The Queen's ladies, she asserted, were urgent to be after their royal mistress, and looked to him to transport them. He protested that he could not be held reponsible for what had happened or for getting them all back to Somerset House, but the girl assured him that these were the orders of the Countess of Arundel, principal Lady-in-Waiting, and was he not now in the Queen's service?

The wherry which had brought them there was waiting, amongst all the other boats, to be hired for a return journey; but, since it had scarcely been a success coming, he thought to effect some improvement for the journey back. However, ask as he would amongst the watermen, all were already engaged to carry back those they had brought, or at any rate not prepared to abandon probably richer pickings later. He toyed with the idea of seeking the King's permission to use one of the royal barges, but decided to keep his distance from James meantime. So he had to fall back on the fishy-smelling wherry, anticipating the comments which would be forthcoming from his passengers.

He had not over-estimated the offence. When they all came flocking down in loud-voiced complaint at every-thing, the Howard Countess of Arundel very much in command, deploring the wedding arrangements, the King's behaviour, the insult to the Howards and so on, the sight of their transport drew wails from the previous passengers and haughty protest from the more senior ladies—for now, of course, John had the Duke's boatload to take back as well. So the wherry was grossly over-laden, to add to the rest, with the boatmen demanding extra payment. But, with no alternatives evident, everybody eventually piled in, and the return journey commenced.

By the time that they reached Somerset House, John realised something of what being Gentleman-in-Waiting to the Queen meant. Whether it was better than having nothing to do at Whitehall was a matter for debate.

Finding that Anne had taken to her bed declaring that she was ill, and that no arrangements seemed to have been made for his accommodation at Somerset House, he was glad enough to slip away thereafter and back to his father's quarters at Whitehall Palace. Sufficient unto the day . . .

8

Next morning John was in something of a quandary. The wedding over, King James decided to go to Theobalds Park in Hertfordshire, his favourite resort, where the hunting was excellent, and most of the court would go with him—but not the Queen, who would remain in London. What was John to do, he asked his father?

The Duke advised a quiet departure for Somerset House. If the Queen had no quarters for him there, he could continue to use the Lennox rooms at Whitehall. If, of course, she had changed her mind about the gentleman-in-waiting appointment, he should just come on to Theobalds. Ludovick always made life sound easy and simple.

John was very doubtful as to which eventuality he would prefer—indeed wished that he was back in Scotland. However, the matter was resolved for him almost immediately, for a summons came for him to attend on the monarch forthwith.

He found James in a gallery of the palace superintending in person the extension and deepening of a wall-chamber, with masons and carpenters busy excavating and hammering—or would have been busy had the King not been so assiduous in interrupting them with new instructions, alterations and improvements. To his much relief, John was welcomed almost with enthusiasm, James explaining what was being done, in some detail, how the mural-chamber was a mere garderobe which was to be extended right through to the walling and panelling of the room behind. When John looked mystified over the point of this, the monarch drew him aside and in a stage-whisper revealed that the apartment beyond, with the panelling, was an ante-room to his audience-chamber, where petitioners, suppliants and litigants waited until he was ready to hear their pleas and requests. It would be a right convenience, he pointed out, to know what they were saying privately beforehand, with their advisers and lawyers; so he would have some small little holes bored in the panelling at eye- and ear-level, to enable him to see and hear what went on, if he came round into this bit closet. The workmen were not to know about this, of course.

Much impressed by his sovereign-lord's perspicacity, John made appreciative noises. But if he imagined that such considerations wholly preoccupied the royal mind, he was disillusioned. James turned abruptly and poked him in the middle with a jabbing finger.

"Now, my mannie—what's this you've been at wi' the Queen, eh?" he demanded. "For why hae you attached yoursel' to my Annie? Yesterday you marched oot o' my royal presence without leave nor allow. Yon's no' permitted and you must have kent it."

"But, Sire, the Queen summoned me. I had to go. I could not disobey the Queen's Majesty."

"Could you no', then, Johnnie Stewart? And what o' the *King*'s Majesty? Whose subject are you—Annie o' Denmark's or your sovereign-lord's?"

"Yours, to be sure, Sire. But the Queen has appointed me her Gentleman-in-Waiting and . . ."

"Ooh, aye—Gentleman-in-Waiting. Man, that sounds grand, grand! But she was a wee thing late, was she no'? Were you no' my gentleman first? Who brought you to this London, eh?"

"You did, Highness. But there seemed to be nothing for me here, nothing for me to do. The Queen said that she required me . . ."

"Impatient, eh? Impatience can be a sin, mind. I'm dis- appointed in you, Sir John. It wasna well done."

The young man bowed his head, tight-lipped.

"Aye, well—I'll gie you a chance to redeem yoursel', lad—even if you dinna just deserve it. I'm off to Tibbalds. But you'll bide here. You'll go and discover for me certain matters, fell important matters. About these monopolies, as they ca' them. Like the paper and the salt we considered at Edinburgh. That's what I brought you to London for,

154

mind. See you, the monopolies here in this England are no' sae well contrived as in Scotland. I didna get my due and proper share. So you've to put that to rights, Sir John Stewart. Thae Howards are getting ower much that should be mine. They've got their long fingers in every pie! But it's gey hard to get at the figures, the details. You are to go discover them for me. Mak lists. Goods. Names. Moneys. I want to ken it all. Then I withdraw the monopolies and issue new ones. Wi' right and proper sharcs fo· me. Somehow I maun keep this ship o' state afloat, wi' yor. parliament no' voting me the siller."

John stared. "But how am I to do this, Sire? I know nothing of it all. Where do I start? Surely some of your clerks here, your officers who know the English and their ways, would better serve . . . ?"

"Know, perhaps—but are known themsel's! I choose you because you are *not* known, man. You can learn much. A Scot concerned wi' trade. You will be that. And I can trust you—can I no'? Sae many others are in the pockets o' the Howards and their like. You're no'. Use your wits, laddie."

He wagged his head. "Where do I begin, Sire? Knowing nothing of all this?"

"Begin wi' the man Mansell. Robert Mansell. He's held the glass-making monopoly for years. The woman Elizabeth gave it to him lang syne. Through the Howards. She didna ken how to use siller, that one. She was a' for glory, was Gloriana, wi' nae money-sense. Did you ken that she left me wi' £400,000 o' debts? Guidsakes, think on that! Aye, well—begin wi' Mansell and the glass. And there's William Cockayne and thae Merchant Venturers, as they ca' themsel's. They hae the monopoly o' the export o' woven cloths, for dyeing in the Netherlands. Look you into that. I was to get £300,000 frae them—and I havena' had a tenth o' it. Cockayne's the man. He keeps the Howards in siller, I swear! There's others—ships' ropes and cordage. Aye, and canvas—right lucrative. The import o' whales' oil, skins frae Muscovy and plenties more. Start wi' Mansell and Cockayne. And watch out for the Lord Treasurer's men, the Howards, laddie. You watch!"

John swallowed. "Where? Where do I do all this, Highness?"

"Go you to St Paul's. Geordie Heriot aye said that he could learn half the secrets o' this England at St Paul's!"

"You mean the *church*, Sire? St Paul's Church?"

"Just that. You start there. This very day."

"And, and the Queen?"

"The Queen? Och, that's your affair, laddie. If you're sufficiently unwise—aye, and if you've any time—to serve my Annie, after you've done *my* business, you do it, Sir Johnnie Stewart. Be her Gentleman-in-Waiting, if you must. But mind—you're my servant first and foremaist, even though you dinna tell them that at St Paul's. And I expect results. You have it? Aye, well—off wi' you."

A distinctly bemused young Scot backed out of the royal presence, and the King returned to his hole in the walling.

Making his way to Somerset House, John found the Queen still confined to bed, allegedly in much pain—although whether this was a genuine or a diplomatic ailment was open to doubt. At any rate, he saw it as adequate excuse for him to presume that he was not required there and then in any capacity, and to be able to go about the King's business without having to make awkward explanations. He did, however, seek out Margaret Hamilton to tell her of his call, in case the Queen asked about him. Directed to her chamber, in a wing of the great house, he found her with a man— from whom she somewhat hurriedly distanced herself, rearranging her neckline—a rather fine-looking man in probably his early forties, sensitive of features, slender and elegant.

Margaret quickly got over any embarrassment she might have felt, intimated that the attendance of two gentlemen might even be preferable to that of only one, and introduced her companion as Sir William Alexander of Menstrie, one of the Prince's gentlemen, now appointed the King's Master of Requests.

John was surprised. He had heard of this man. Menstrie, after all, was no more than thirty miles from Methven, near Stirling; and Alexander was moreover a poet of some renown. By his appearance he had assessed him to be one of the many English exquisites with which the court abounded.

"Ah, the King's new paladin, who rescued him from unknown perils at Edinburgh!" the other greeted, smiling. He had a good Scots voice, at least. "I saw you yesterday at that peculiar wedding!"

"No doubt. I was forced to appear somewhat kenspeckle. No wish of mine, I promise you."

"Are you of the King's household, or the Queen's, Sir John?"

"I wish that you could tell me, sir! The King brought me south. The Queen said that I was to be her Gentleman-in-Waiting. And now the King requires me to serve him. It is . . . difficult."

"You are bespoke for the Queen," the young woman declared strongly. "You cannot betray her, now!"

"Our Margaret means, I think, that you are not to disappoint *her*!" Sir William observed, with a flourish of his hand. "She is a young woman jealous for her men!"

"*I* am not one of her men, sir," John said, rather shortly. "I am merely here to inform her that, since the Queen has taken to her bed, I cannot think that she requires my poor services today. So I am off on the King's business, as he commanded. I shall call again tomorrow."

Margaret eyed him thoughtfully. "We do not know, Sir John, that the Queen does not require you this day. She may have errands for you, messages to deliver."

"Then I am sure that Her Majesty has a sufficiency of servants to act messenger. After all, she did not know that I existed two days past!"

"You are not going to Theobalds with the King, then? Since you say that you will come tomorrow," Alexander said.

"No," John agreed, but did not elaborate.

"Nor, as it happens, am I," the other informed. "Like you, I share my services. But between King and Prince. Which can have its difficulties, I agree. That is why I am here, on Prince Charles's behalf, to his mother. *He* does not go to Theobalds. And the King, I cannot think, requires his

Master of Requests whilst chasing deer! Where do you proceed on the King's business, Sir John?"

John was cautious. "Here and there about London," he said.

"Just so. Well, I have my barge at the steps. Or, I should say, the Prince's barge. If I may convey you anywhere, sir, it will be my pleasure."

"But, Will—do you not stay?" the young woman protested. "Need you go so soon . . . ?"

"My dear Meg—I have other errands to run, on the Prince's behalf. Much as I enjoy your excellent company. Most urgently I have to call upon Charles's money-lender, in Carter Lane. Charles is ever needing siller, for the King keeps him very short . . ."

So despite Margaret Hamilton's disapproval, the two men took their leave. Alexander was clearly disposed to be friendly, and John, although careful, perceived that the other could be good company and just possibly useful. So far he had made no friends since coming to London.

Sir William gestured towards the riverside steps and asked which part of London John was making for. He saw no harm in mentioning that it was the St Paul's area, and the other declared that this was entirely convenient, his money-lender's place-of-business being in that vicinity—as indeed were most of the city's trading and financial concerns.

They went down-river, then, in one of the smaller royal barges, painted with the Prince of Wales' feathers, and conversed amicably enough, both of London and of Scotland. Alexander obviously knew a great deal about England and the English, having come south in 1604, and John was tempted to seek his advice in his present quest; but he decided that he must not risk taking even the King's Master of Requests into his confidence. After all, if James had fully trusted this knowledgeable and experienced individual, why had he not given *him* the task of enquiring into the monopolies position?

About a mile down, they landed at Blackfriars and thereafter the older man conducted John through the network of narrow and seemingly mean streets until they could see the spires of St Paul's Church ahead. There the other left him to return to Carter Lane, telling him that they must keep in touch, two fellow-Scots with much in common. He said that he had always admired the Duke of Lennox and wished that the King had more close associates like him.

Unsure just what he was looking for at the great church, John was astonished at what he found. He had assumed that James meant that its environs, churchyard and even steps were the meeting-place of merchants, dealers and the like; but, although men did stand about talking outside, clearly the great numbers going in and out of the church itself were not all worshippers, by their appearance. When he ventured inside, he was almost shocked to discover that the huge building was full of men, in groups and pairs, walking up and down, sitting in the side-chapels, talking, bargaining, declaiming, even buying and selling. The noise was as bad as in any market-place. John thought of the money-changers in the Temple at Jerusalem. He had never heard of a Scots kirk used thus.

With no preconceived notions as to how to set about his task, he wandered around the church for some time just looking and listening. This produced no enlightenment other than that innumerable deals, sales and contracts were being fixed up there and then, these sacred premises used as a centre of exchange. He heard one or two Scots voices, and eventually sought the advice of the owner of one of these.

"Friend," he said, "your pardon. I hear that you come from Scotland. Can you help me? I look for a man named Mansell. Robert Mansell. Do you know him?"

"Know him? Na, na, I dinna *know* him. It's no' for the likes o' Dand Pringle to ken Robert Mansell! But I ken *of* him. We all ken o' Robert Mansell, laddie."

"Is that so? Can you tell me, then, where I can find him? Is he here?"

"He could be—forby I've no' seen him, the day. Hae you tried yon bit chapel, yonder? St Bart's or some such nonsense, they call it. Yon's his favourite howff when he's here."

Thanking him, John made for the indicated side-chapel, one of many. Only two men sat therein, in earnest converse. When he asked if either of them was Robert Mansell, he was stared at as though witless, and then waved away with head-shakes.

He went back to the man Pringle, to ask where else he might look for his quarry.

"Och, the man has warehouses, booths and chambers all ower London," he was told. "And manufactories, forby. I'd hae jaloused that anyone seeking Robert Mansell would have kent as much! What do you want wi' him, lad?"

"I am new to London," John admitted. "And am recommended to him. Is he so notable a man?"

"He is one o' the richest merchants in all England. You must be weel-connected, young man, if you're recommended to Mansell!"

"He has the glass monopoly, I'm told?"

"Glass, aye—and much else. Saltpetre for gunpowder, spices, silks—a wheen mair."

"How did he gain all these? One man?"

"It's easy seen you're new to London, lad. If you're close to my lord Suffolk, your fortune's as good as made!"

"The Lord Treasurer? And this Mansell is?"

"They say he's a by-blow o' one o' the old Howards."

"So! That is how it goes? And this other? Cockayne. William Cockayne—what of him?"

"Guidsakes—Will Cockayne, now! Fegs, young man—but you fly high! Dinna tell me you're recommended to him, forby?"

John coughed. "Well, in a lesser way. Is he another Howard liegeman?"

"He's a sheriff o' this city and like to be Lord Mayor—that's who Will Cockayne is!"

"Ah. But another of the monopolists, I take it?"

"Oh, aye, he's that, right enough. He's head o' the Merchant Venturers Company, just."

"And they are important?"

"Lord save us, lad—for one wi' recommendations to Mansell and Cockayne, you're gey ignorant about this city o' London! The Merchant Venturers hold the biggest monopoly of all—the export o' woven cloths. And the dye franchise."

"What is that?"

"Where do you come frae in Scotland? The farthest Hielants, that you dinna ken about dyeing cloth! The Dutch hold the market for dyestuffs—especially reds. Scarlet, crimson, turkey. They dinna let others ken their secrets. All guid woven cloths have to go to Holland to be dyed—and through the Merchant Venturers, both going and coming. For they hold both the export monopoly and the Dutch dye franchise."

"Lord! For all England? There is nothing like that in Scotland. We dye our own cloths well enough. Consider the tartans. This broadcloth I wear was woven and dyed in Scotland."

"I ken it. But that's small stuff. Simple dyes made frae lichens and mosses and heathers and the like. You'll be a laird's son, by the looks and sound o' you. Maist o' the Scots folk wear homespun. Dyed, if at all, wi' plant-dyes. Here it is different. There's ten times the numbers. And the Dutch do the dyeing."

John shook his head. "I did not know that there were so many barriers and monopolies. It seems wrong, foolish, making trade difficult. And all goods more costly for most, whilst making fortunes for some."

The other looked at him curiously. "If you're commended to Mansell and Cockayne, I'd reckon you'd be unwise to speak that way!" he advised. "See—there's Elias Woolcombe. He's one o' Will Cockayne's chief men. Yonder, wi' the Jew, Levison. He's your man. He'll tell you what you need to ken. The fat one."

John was a little doubtful about approaching one of Cockayne's people directly and delayed somewhat whilst he thought up some story which would not sound too hollow. When the stout individual parted from the handsome Jew, John moved in.

"Sir—you are Master Woolcombe, I am told? Of the Merchant Venturers. May I have a word with you?"

"To be sure, youngling. One word—or even two! But words are dry goods—and I think to moisten my gullet with a sup of ale. You join me?"

"Here, sir? In the church? If that is possible, then let me play host. My pleasure."

"To be sure, friend. Follow Elias Woolcombe and you'll be apt to find good ales!" A belly-laugh seemed to establish the other as a jovial character, but John was aware of a very shrewd eye upon him.

An inconspicuous stairway off a minor aisle led them down to a crypt, already full of drinkers all seemingly on business bent despite the leaden coffins on which they either sat or placed their beer-mugs. Commerce clearly was thirsty work. Master Woolcombe found them a corner, and a coffin, and ordered two great tankards of strong ale, one of which he drained there and then without so much as a pause. John ordered and paid for another, and sipped tentatively at his own. When the fat man had half-finished his second tankard, he set it down on the dented coffin-lid with a hollow bang, wiped his mouth with the back of a great paw, and declared himself as now fit to discuss business.

"It is scarce that. It is more guidance that I seek," John said carefully. "I am from Scotland, as you will have guessed. I was advised to seek out the Merchant Venturers."

"To what end, friend? What is your interest?"

"Paper," he was told, briefly.

"Paper, heh? Paper. Paper comes from the Hansa, the Germanies."

"Also from Scotland."

"Do you tell me so? That I did not know."

"I think that few know of it, here."

"Ah." The large, red moon-face looked thoughtful. "And what sort of paper? What quality?"

"The best. The sort that the King uses."

The other picked up his tankard but put it down again without drinking, an indication, it seemed to John, that his interest was well aroused.

"The King, heh? Quality paper, from Scotland. Are you in this trade, young master?"

"Say that I know something about it. And who is behind it."

"And you ask for the Merchant Venturers?"

"Yes." He took a chance. "Or, perhaps, Robert Mansell."

Woolcombe frowned. "Ah," he said again, but with a

different intonation. "I would not recommend Mansell, sir."

"No? Why?"

The other did not answer that. "What is proposed? As to this paper?"

"I but make enquiries. There could, I think, be a much enlarged market. In England. Who handles paper? Is there a monopoly?"

"No-o-o. Or . . . not yet! Many import it. From the Hansa people. Hamburg, Bremen, Danzig, Lubeck. They have it all in hand, the Germans. Mansell does much trade with them."

"Then perhaps he is the man to speak with? If he already trades in paper?"

"No. Better not Mansell. He has too much to handle already, has Robert."

"You mean, in monopolies? What does he control that paper would be too much for him?"

"Why wines, Rhenish and Portugee. Lace, pillow-lace, from Mechlins in Flanders. Needles, likewise. Whale-oil. Fish-nets and hooks. Soap. Raisins and dates from the Barbary Coast. Cinnamon."

"Save us—all these? One man!"

"More, if you make count of other lesser men he controls. Sol Karter has the licence for importing inks. And Stanton Lewis has the monopoly for certain spices."

"And all these Mansell gained through the Howards?"

The fat man looked somewhat disconcerted by this question, which evidently was not appropriate. He reached for his tankard.

"So you think that Master Mansell is not the best man to approach on this matter of paper?" John went on. "With over-much already on his hands. Who, then?"

"Well, now—the Association might be interested, young sir. In paper."

"The association . . . ?"

"The Association of Merchant Venturers."

"Ah. Of which you are a member? But, Master Woolcombe—are your association's hands not also already full? What monopolies do *you* hold?"

"Why, we hold some, yes—and great ones, see you. But we *are* an association, with many members. And so may, shall we say, do justice to more commodities than such as Robert Mansell. Many members, sir."

"But all under one man also—Will Cockayne?"

Woolcombe finished his liquor before answering that, but John saw his shrewd little eyes considering him over the tankard. He beckoned for more ale.

"Will is Master of the Association, yes," he agreed. "But only first amongst many, Master . . . ? I do not have your name, sir?"

"Methven—John Methven. Come from Edinburgh, where it is planned to extend paper-making in the North Esk valley. Master Cockayne is first amongst many? But am I not right that it is through him that these monopolies are . . . acquired?"

"Perhaps, Master Mervyn."

"Methven, sir. And what monopolies does your Association already control? Would paper fit in well with the rest?"

"We hold the export of woven cloths, Master Methven, and the import of dyed cloths and dyestuffs. Also tobacco-leaf from the Western Indies, a growing market. We share the sugar monopoly with the new East India Company, they east, we west. Also indigo. We hold the lead export franchise. We are developing cotton and seek the monopoly for that. And others, of lesser account."

"Cloth, dyestuffs, tobacco, sugar, indigo, cotton. With all these, sir, you still would have the time and concern to handle paper?"

"To be sure, Master Methven. That is, if we considered it a sufficiently large trade to be worth our while. We should require much information, see you."

"Quite, sir. But if you could sell Scots paper, of all qualities, instead of importing it from Germany and paying their prices, this would interest you?"

"Indeed yes, sir. If the quantity and quality was there, I think that I can say that we would be much interested."

"As to quality, I could bring you some ensamples to consider. On another occasion."

"Good, good. I am here each noontide, sir. Tomorrow, shall we say?"

"I cannot be sure of tomorrow, Master Woolcombe. I have other calls to make, persons to see . . ."

"Master Methven—you have spoken of this to none others? As yet? Nor will? Until we have considered the matter more fully?" The stout man sounded all but agitated. "That could be important. None others, I beg of you, meantime."

"You see it as another monopoly, sir?"

"Why, that would probably be best. For all our interests, friend. Why share the proceeds amongst many, when the Association would handle it to best advantage?"

"You are sure, then, of the security of your monopolies, Master Woolcombe? After all, they come from the Crown, do they not? And if the Crown can grant them, the Crown could take them away again, could it not?"

"I think that we need not fear or trouble our heads on that score! Parliament would have some say in the matter, I swear! And we have sufficient votes in parliament to keep us safe, I think!"

"Ah. In the House of Lords? The Howard influence? But what of the Commons?"

"The Commons, also, friend. We keep the honourable members sweetened—why have a sugar monopoly else!" He laughed heartily and finished his third tankard. "Leave the Commons to us."

"Very well, Master Woolcombe," John said, rising. "We shall speak of this again. I bid you good-day."

"Tomorrow?"

"As I say, I cannot promise tomorrow. But shortly, never fear."

John Stewart made his way out of St Paul's Church thoughtful indeed. He was in a hurry now, in haste to get on paper all that he had learned while still he remembered the details. The King had asked for lists, names, goods. Well, he had made a start. Moneys he had not yet discovered but that might come. This was all bigger than anything he had envisaged—perhaps even than James envisaged. He hoped that the monarch would be appreciative.

It occured to him, as he made his way westwards for Whitehall, to wonder what he had let himself in for over this business of the paper, and whether he could handle it, with these sharp London merchants, without it becoming apparent that he was a fraud? Also what King James would say . . . ?

Next morning, John presented himself at Somerset House again, and to a different reception. Summoned to the Queen's bedchamber, he was berated in front of the gallery of females for having neglected his duties and abandoning Anne in the time of need. This was not to occur again. The Queen would not listen to his pleas about the King's service, declaring that he was now part of *her* household, not James's, and as such must hold himself available for her commands at all times. He would occupy quarters here in Denmark House—Anne called it that, although to all others it was still Somerset House—to which Margaret Hamilton would conduct him forthwith. He was dismissed.

Smirking somewhat, Margaret took him again through the corridors and passages of the huge house, to the same wing overlooking the riverside gardens where he had seen her the day before. There he was ushered into the very next room to her own.

"You will be fine and comfortable here, Sir John," she told him, cheerfully. "Better than Whitehall, I swear! And if you require anything, I am just next door!"

He looked at her doubtfully, and then around him. It was certainly a quite handsome apartment, a deal larger than his cramped room in his father's quarters at Whitehall, indeed larger than the Duke's own chamber, and seemingly well-furnished also. The young woman went about straightening and patting things, demonstrating that all was in order, indeed announcing that she herself had seen to all.

John was perhaps less appreciative than he should have been. Obviously he was being taken over by these women, and he did not like that. He would see about this—but meantime he presumably would have to seem to go along with it.

He pointed out that if he was to be lodging here he would

166

have to go back to Whitehall for his things and his horse. She admitted that this seemed to be indicated, and said that she would go and ask the Queen if it was permitted.

"See here," he jerked, "if I am to be the Queen's Gentleman-in-Waiting, I will wait on her myself, not through yourself or other."

"You, Sir John, or other man, will not enter the Queen's bedchamber without being summoned. I may. You have, I think, much to learn!"

"This is ridiculous!" he exclaimed. "And requiring permission to leave this house. Like some child!"

"You went off yesterday without Anne's leave. She did not like it. You have yourself to blame. Do I go, or not?"

He shrugged. Dipping a mocking half-curtsy, she left him.

He prowled round his fine apartment, something like a caged lion. Here he was, Sir John Stewart of Methven, Keeper and Captain of Dumbarton Castle, treated like some unreliable menial! It was not to be borne. He kicked an embroidered footstool from one end of the room to the other.

The clatter of it had its effect. He forced himself to calm down. This sort of reaction would get him nowhere, he recognised. He must use his head, not his feet. Some men, he supposed, would give much to be in his situation, given position in the Queen's household, provided with excellent accommodation, an attractive young woman readily available. Perhaps he should seek to make the best of it, instead of kicking stools.

So, when Margaret returned, he was rather less unforthcoming. But promptly reverted to stiff arm's-length when, with permission granted to go, she suggested coming with him to Whitehall to help collect his baggage. He could do that very well on his own, he asserted, and marched off.

In fact, having escaped temporarily from Somerset House, he decided on a detour further westwards still. He had scarcely time to go to St Paul's looking for Woolcombe and company; but he thought that a brief call at St James's Palace might possibly be worth making. This was where the Prince of Wales roosted, in what had been Prince Henry's quarters, and where presumably he might find Sir William Alexander. It occurred to John that Alexander might be able to advise him in his predicament.

So he made his way to that small and inconvenient old palace, almost on the edge of the countryside, and was fortunate in catching Alexander just as he was preparing to depart. He greeted John warmly, however, and assured him that there was no haste about his errand. The Prince had decided to go down to his mother's weekend house, which Inigo Jones had built for her at Greenwich, and he was to repair there first and see that all was in order. And what could he do for Sir John?

"I require advice," he admitted. "I seem to be caught, as it were, in a trap. But it occurs to me that others must have been caught in the same way before. You have been at court for long and must have seen it happen. So I seek guidance."

"I would have thought that your father, the Duke, would better guide you?"

"My father is the King's cousin and close friend. And none can command him save King James. His problems are not mine, nor mine his. Besides, he is gone to this Theobalds."

"And your problem is this of the Queen's service? You feel trapped between the Queen and the King?"

"Yes. The King gives me a task to perform. But the Queen says that I must remain at Somerset House, lodge there and not leave without her permission. I am only out now to collect my things from Whitehall. That Margaret Hamilton is like a watchdog set to mount guard on me!"

"Oh, Meg is all right. She is . . . generous! Give her a kiss or two and a fondle now and then, and she will be your friend. And a watchdog that is a friend is none so ill! Kiss her, Sir John!"

"As do you?"

"Why, yes. Amongst all those countesses and female dragons of the Queen's, Meg is as a well in a dry land! You will find it so."

"A well at which all may drink?"

"Oh, I would not say that. Wells have various functions,

have they not? They may be admired, sat by, dabbled in, sipped at or quaffed deeply."

"I see. But that is only a small part of my problem, Sir William. How am I to escape from Somerset House every so often to be about the King's business? Without trouble?"

"Meg Hamilton can probably help you there, too. This business of the King's—what does it entail? Where do you go? Do you have to be away from Somerset House for long at any one time? If not too long, it might be arranged."

"I think that, meantime at least, it need not be for long. To go down to St Paul's, meet people there, discuss certain matters. It need not take so long. Two hours, three."

"I am intrigued—as to what the King requires at St Paul's. It is not to borrow moneys? But surely this could be contrived? It occurs to me that this of the Prince going to Greenwich might be used. The Queen and Charles are close. With Anne ill, the Prince could be expected to be anxious. To wish to hear of her state daily. That is why I was there yesterday. I could come up from Greenwich every second day, and then you come down there every other day. How would that serve? How ill, think you, *is* the Queen?"

"I do not know. At first it was thought that it might be but a sham. But she vomits much, I am told, and her physicians attend her daily."

"Then Charles has reason to be anxious. I think that this could be managed. Greenwich is an hour's sail down-river, a little more coming back. It would give you time enough. For your . . . discussions."

John decided that, since he was going to require Alexander's co-operation, he would have to confide in him to some extent, perhaps to further advantage. Anything else would seem uncivil to a degree.

"The King is concerned about the monopolies position," he revealed. "There is much that is wrong there, he says. So I make enquiries. But secretly."

"Ah, the monopolies! Yes, all know that there is corruption. Fortunes to be made."

"All may know, yes. But the details are not so easy to come by. Not for the King, at any rate. So I have to resort to guile. I make myself as one involved in the paper-trade—one John Methven. In that process the King himself is concerned. In Scotland I visited paper-mills with him. I have managed to arouse some interest, yesterday, at St Paul's, in a representative of the Merchant Venturers—and learned not a little."

"The Merchant Venturers? Are they not the greatest of the monopolists? You have not wasted your time, Sir John! Or Master Methven!"

"There is a deal more to discover. The King wants details—names, amounts, goods, sources. So I must learn much from them, if I can. I must lead them on, over this of the paper." A thought struck him. "Perhaps you might help me? And therefore the King? I must seem young to these merchants to seem to speak with any authority. I fear that they may doubt my tale. If you, Sir William Alexander, were to appear with me on one occasion, then it would seem to give me credence. A man of substance."

"Strange that the King's Governor of Dumbarton Castle should require the warranty of such as myself! But, yes—I will come with you, one day."

"I thank you. And you will let me know if this of visiting Greenwich is acceptable to the Prince?"

"I cannot think that it could be otherwise. I will call at Somerset House tomorrow. Do you go there now? I take the barge to Greenwich, so could set you down in passing."

"No. I must go to Whitehall now for my belongings and my horse. I thank you for all your help . . ."

Back at Somerset House that evening, John had his first experience of being an actual member of the Queen's Household. He sat down to an exceedingly dull repast in magnificent surroundings, one of a company of about a dozen women and two other men, both elderly, Edward Somerset, Earl of Worcester, Master of the Queen's Household, and John Chamberlain, her Comptroller. Clearly neither approved of the new arrival—nor apparently had most of the ladies forgotten or forgiven him for the unfortunate wherry-journey to and from Hampton Court. The meal seemed interminable and John felt that he could not be the first to leave the table. The idea of this sort of situation continuing was scarcely tolerable.

When at last a move was made, he found Margaret Hamilton's company a positive relief—bold, provocative but at least lively and cheerful. She suggested a stroll in the gardens, the Queen being unlikely to have any duties for either of them at this hour. She tucked her arm in his, companionably.

So they wandered through the riverside grounds pleasantly enough, while the young woman chattered. She told him that she was now twenty-one years old, how she had been brought up at Shawfield, in Lanarkshire, with six brothers and two sisters, and how when her mother died four years before her father, Sir Claud Hamilton, had brought her, the youngest, to London where he was Gentleman of the Privy Chamber to the King. Then he had died the following year, and, left alone, her uncle the Earl of Abercorn had gained for her this appointment of Maid-in-Waiting to the Queen. She did not greatly enjoy her life amongst all these elderly dames, but managed to find diversions now and again and here and there. At that, she squeezed his arm against her prominent and shapely bosom, and chuckled.

Despite himself, John was impressed by her uncomplaining acceptance of these family complications and bereavements and her lot generally, and asked himself how his own attitude to a much more fortunate life bore comparison?

He was in a more receptive frame of mind then when, passing a seated leafy bower on the river-bank, guarded by somewhat indecent statuary, Margaret drew him towards it, suggesting that they might sit awhile and watch the to-ings and froings on the Thames. At least there would be no midges to bite them here, as would be the case in Scotland.

He could scarcely say no but would have preferred a seat where the white marble embellishments were less prominent and explicit, especially when his companion herself was sufficiently explicit. She snuggled up close to him, one arm around him, a warm thigh pressed against his own, one shoulder on his chest so that he gazed down the cleft of her breasts which seemed to heave with a life of their own.

John was no prude and had had his youthful amatory adventures in Strathearn; but he was still very much in love with Janet Drummond, however hopeless his case. No doubt Margaret found him somewhat unresponsive.

She asked him about his life and background, but seemed to know already more than he would have expected. He wondered where she had got her information. Guarded in his replies, she did not glean a great deal more. However, on the physical side she did rather better, for in that position, and holding his hand, somehow without too much encouragement the hand came up gradually to rest upon her chest, and once there tended not so much to rest as to stir and stroke and stray, as of its own volition, an entirely natural reaction. Which, in turn, had its side effects, of course. So that, when after some nibbling at his ear-lobe and tickling his jawline with the tip of a pink tongue, her pouting lips were upturned close under his own, it seemed the most obvious thing in the world to kiss them—as Alexander had advised. And, with the response encouraging, not to say eager, matters proceeded on their predictable course.

How far they would have gone there amongst the foliage and statuary is a matter for speculation, considering that it was a long time since that young man had done any woman-ising, thanks to Janet Drummond, and he was entirely normal in his appetites. However, it was Margaret herself who called a halt presently, not in any prohibitory fashion but by announcing that she was beginning to feel cold and that they should go in—which seemed strange in that she did not feel cold to the touch nor in demeanour. Uncertain whether he felt relieved or cheated, John expressed suitable concern and bestirred himself. He offered her his doublet to wrap around her, but learned that this was not necessary.

On their way back to the palace, still hanging on his arm, she revealed that she would have to go to the Queen's apartments to discover whether there were any duties required of her before retiring for the night. Declaring that he could not believe that anything such was expected of *him*, he gave her a chaste goodnight salute and left her for his own chamber, vaguely dissatisfied.

He was in his bed and feeling less than somnolent when

he heard her come back to the next room—any duties she had had presumably brief. He wondered about her, wondered what a young woman like that felt about love and marriage as distinct from this purely physical traffic, wondered what would be expected of him hereafter and whether he had let himself in for a progressive relationship, or merely intermittent, and what Sir William would advise now.

His wondering ceased there, for the door of his room opened quietly and as quietly closed again. He sat up in bed. It was not quite dark, and he could see a shadowy figure standing there. No question who it was, however shadowy. In fact the shadow very quickly materialised, and changed shades also, from dark to pale, glimmering white, as some sort of bed-robe was dropped and Margaret, unclothed entirely ran across to launch herself bodily upon the bed and himself, laughing deeply in her throat.

After that, to be sure, wondering was uncalled for, with everything proceeding in straightforward and predestined fashion. She certainly made both a challenging and a satisfying armful, rounded and smooth but active, demanding, enterprising.

It was a full and educative night, and dawn before she left him for her own room.

Sir William Alexander duly arrived next noonday, with solicitous enquiries from Prince Charles as to his mother's state. He was admitted to the Queen's bedchamber, and when he came out was able to assure John that the suggested arrangement had been agreed. Anne was pleased at the concern shown by her son, and well content that her Gentleman-in-Waiting should share in the task of keeping the Prince informed. The timing was left open—apparently the Queen had no other urgent duties in mind for John— which confirmed that young man in his belief that his appointment had been made, not out of any real need but purely as a gesture to annoy King James.

Alexander had even taken the opportunity to improve on the situation by asking, and gaining, permission to take John with him that day, to show him how to get to Greenwich and where the Queen's house was situated. So they would be off, right away. Margaret thought that this would be a pleasant outing for herself—her duties at Somerset House seemed to be conveniently vague and elastic—and it took both the men's efforts to persuade her that it was inadvisable on this occasion.

John went to his apartment to collect the paper he had fetched from his father's and the King's own quarters at Whitehall. But, although Alexander looked about the room with interest, the younger man forbore to inform him of what had gone on there the previous night—although he did not put it past Margaret herself telling. Then they made for the barge at the steps.

"Can we go straight to St Paul's?" John asked.

"Surely. That was the design. Will your merchants be there?"

"I am hoping so. When I did not come yesterday, it is my hope that they will be the keener. Woolcombe said that he was there most days."

John's hopes as to keenness were not misplaced. They had scarcely mounted the steps to the church-door when Elias Woolcombe came bustling forward to greet them, obviously relieved. He looked a little doubtfully at Alexander but, when John introduced him as Sir William Alexander of Menstrie, Master of Requests to His Majesty, he was suitably impressed.

He led them, this time, through the crowd, not downstairs to the crypt but over to the same side-chapel where John had searched two days before. Again two men sat therein—but not the same two. One rose at their appearance, the other did not.

"Here is Will Cockayne, High Sheriff of this city and Master of our Association," Woolcombe said. "And Luke Cardell, Deputy-Master. This is Master Methven, from Scotland. And another, Sir William . . . ? I did not get the rest, but Master of the King's Requests."

The seated man, obviously Cockayne, nodded but said nothing. The other bowed, especially towards Alexander.

"I am glad to see you, gentlemen," John said. "Sir William Alexander of Menstrie is also from Scotland. And knows of the matter of which we spoke."

174

"Paper," the man Cockayne said briefly. He was a thick-set, florid individual with a bull-neck and a mane of greying hair. "Elias Woolcombe says that you have a proposition to make?"

"Scarcely a proposition, sir. I was sent but to make enquiries. To sound out possibilities."

"He represents paper-making interests in Scotland," Woolcombe put in, much more eager-sounding than Cockayne. "Of which we did not know."

"You mean to say that you did not know that we made paper in Scotland? Excellent paper?" Alexander remarked, politely incredulous.

"No, sir. Not on any scale."

"That is the point—how large is the scale? And what is the quality?" Cockayne demanded. "Sit down." He appeared to be a man of few words but incisive manner.

"As to quantity, sufficient is made to supply our needs. We could make more. And more. And new mills are planned."

"In the valley of the Esk," Alexander added, knowledge-ably, having been primed on the way. "In Lothian."

"And the quality?"

John reached into the bag he carried and brought out a selection of sheets, which he tossed down in front of Cockayne casually enough. He said nothing.

"Sufficient quality for the King's Grace," Alexander murmured.

Clearly the others were impressed as they handled the papers, passing them one to another. They should have been, for it was the best in the royal archives-room.

"These are excellent papers, all of them," the man Cardell said. "But perhaps too fine for most trade."

"We make lesser qualities, to be sure."

"How much?" Cockayne asked. "How do you sell this? This quality?"

That was the crunch, of course. John had no idea. "I have nothing to do with the price," he declared, as authoritatively as he could. "That is for others to settle. To negotiate. My mission is to discover whether there is any demand for the papers. And, if so, what quantities would be required."

"Before we can tell you that, sir, we have to know the

175

price. Surely you must know what is your normal selling-price? In Scotland?"

"Ah, but in Scotland we have the monopoly. That is something else I have to know. Would there be a monopoly here? It would much affect the price, you will agree."

The three Englishmen·looked at one another.

"I take your point," Cockayne said, after a moment or two. "We certainly would not wish the paper to be sold on an open market. Let us say that I believe that a monopoly could be arranged."

"*Could* be, sir? I will require to take back more than that!"

"Will be, then, Scotchman—will be, if you prefer it!"

"I do, yes. You seem very sure?"

"I have reason to be."

"You know to whom to go? To gain the royal authority?"

"Shall we say, the Lord Treasurer's authority. Kings do not concern themselves with such matters. Eh, Sir William?"

"Perhaps you are right, sir," Alexander nodded. "But I have heard that my Lord Suffolk is somewhat out-of-favour, and has retired to the West Country."

"So I understand. He remains Treasurer, however. And John Bingley remains at the Treasury—which is what signifies."

"Ah, yes—the Deputy-Treasurer. Lady Suffolk's friend!"

"Precisely, sir. I think that your young friend here may rely on monopoly prices."

"Good," John said. "Then I would think that our Scots prices will work out a deal less than what you are paying the Germans, sir. What is their present price? For quality paper?"

Cockayne looked at Cardell.

"About 120 shillings the packet of five reams, at today's price. It varies."

"One hundred and twenty shillings sterling the packet? And it is sold on the open market at whatever it will fetch? If you gain a monopoly, what price would you think to charge?"

"We would still have to compete with the German paper. And to outsell you they might lower their price somewhat. Unless, with a monopoly, we could have their imports prohibited. With a monopoly I would say that we would double that price of 120 shillings."

The others nodded agreement.

"Two hundred and forty shillings for five reams? Quality paper. Is doubling a usual oncharge in your English monopolies?"

"It varies. Do you do better in Scotland?"

"Likewise it varies with the commodity. We would expect some share in this oncharge."

"That, like the price, would be for negotiation, Master Methven."

"To be sure. Then it seems that this is as far as we can go, at this time. I must now consult with the others."

"Master Methven," Cockayne put in carefully. "We must hope that, by consulting others, you mean your paper-making friends in Scotland—not any other interests here in England? If we are to do business on the best terms, then all this must be kept a close secret. If it leaked out, all could be put at risk. I am not prepared to chaffer and haggle with others. The Association can offer you the best terms, since we are the largest, with most members, all over the country."

"I understand."

"Will you leave these ensamples of paper with us? For us to consider, test and cost?"

"Certainly. Perhaps you will set down the order of their value to you and probable demand, for our guidance? And I will collect it, say, two days hence?"

"Very well. Two days . . ."

There seemed to be no more to say, so they rose and took their leave, Woolcombe escorting them to the church-door.

"That took less time than I had feared," John said, out in the churchyard. "Having Cockayne there in person probably helped."

"A hard man to handle, that! Are you satisfied? Was it successful?"

"Oh, yes—learned more than I had expected. I think that your presence was an advantage. They accepted me the more readily."

"For a man who knows nothing about the paper-trade, I thought that you sounded most expert and confident! King James chose well, I swear!"

"That was but mummery, play-acting, asking suitable questions. What was that of *Lady* Suffolk?"

"Oh, the Countess has this lap-dog, the man Bingley. He does her bidding without question. Suffolk has made him Sub-Treasurer, and so Catherine Howard manages all at the Treasury. She has a better head for affairs than has her husband, all say."

"This is interesting. Is it the Countess rather than the Earl, then, who contrives to cheat King James out of much of his revenues?"

"It could be. Since it seems that this Bingley does the arranging. He is very much her creature. Thomas Howard tolerates him, no doubt finding him useful for filling his pockets . . ."

Back at the barge, they proceeded down-river. John had never been thus far and was interested in all that he saw— the great Tower of London, of ominous repute, which disappointed, looking nothing like the mighty rock fortresses of Edinburgh and Stirling, as he had visualised; the marshy reaches beyond, of Wapping and Rotherhithe— which Alexander called Redriff—flat and waterlogged; and then the great U-bend, made up of Greenwich and Blackwall Reaches, still in desperately flat country, with the river ever widening.

When they landed, on the south shore now, John was further surprised when they passed the sprawling ancient palace which Henry the Eighth had renamed Placentia and came to a comparatively tiny house, some distance apart, handsomely built but a mere miniature, in fact with only three bedchambers although with rather fine reception-rooms. Anne had had this built for her a few years before by Inigo Jones, where she could get away from the ongoings in James's huge establishment. The Prince of Wales, who was of a fastidious and rather solitary nature, much at odds with his father's, also found this little retreat to his taste.

His reception of John held no pretence at warmth or even interest. He was obviously regarded merely as a messenger being shown route and destination. Not that this concerned John in any way, who did not find Charles much to his taste either, actually preferring his odd sire. He was dismissed quite quickly, Alexander conducting him back to the barge and assuring him that the Prince was none so ill-natured once one got to know him. He was shy and self-conscious—in fact, he had never really got over early impediments in health and abilities; he had hardly spoken for the first six years of his life indeed.

The barge would carry John back to Somerset House and would call for him again two forenoons hence.

So he returned, to write up his findings for King James in detail, now much fuller and more circumstantial than he could have hoped for a few days earlier, covering several sheets of the good Scots paper. In this task Margaret Hamilton was less than helpful, coming to interrupt him frequently—and, he had to admit, not entirely un-welcomely. And she came to his room, of a night, without fail.

The Queen seemed to have no other duties for him mean-time than messenger to Greenwich. She was now evidently a very sick woman—no sham invalid. Even Margaret began to look concerned about her.

Two days later John was back at St Paul's, where he found Woolcombe and Cardell awaiting him with evalu-ations of his paper samples and some other informa-tion which he could add to his dossier. So that, when presently he reached Greenwich again, it was to seek Sir William's advice on the next problem—how he could get to Theobalds Park to present his findings to the King? Alexander said that he would think about it.

The day following, when that resourceful individual appeared at Somerset House, in turn, it was with a sugges-tion. It was clear that the Queen's deteriorating state should be brought to the King's notice, Charles reluctantly agree-ing. He, Alexander, himself had contrived it so that he could not be away the at least two days necessary to reach Theobalds—so what more natural to put to Anne than that her own Gentleman should go? Would he ask the Queen?

Anne, in low spirits, acceded—but asserted that James would not be interested even if she lay at death's door. John would start off next morning, with the physicians' report.

9

Theobalds Park, which King James had acquired from his late and long-suffering minister, Robert Cecil, first Earl of Salisbury, in exchange for Hatfield, had been coveted by the monarch not because of any architectural or other excellence but because it bordered on and indeed included part of, Enfield Chase, with a ten-mile wall around it to ensure that its deer remained exclusive. This was the finest hunting area within reasonable reach of London. Here James could indulge to his heart's content in his favourite occupation, and even with advancing years and deteriorating health he could still spend long days in the saddle, from the crack of dawn until dusk, before hard-drinking sessions and then bed. To this programme all at court had to adjust as best they could, the King insisting that he could rule two kingdoms from the back of a horse.

John, arriving in mid-afternoon of a golden October day, discovered this. But his father, who was rather less keen on the chase, had excused himself that day, as so often he did, and to him John was able to unburden himself and to ask whether he could not, somehow, help him to get out of the Queen's service. He went to some lengths to describe the problems and restrictions of life at Somerset House—although he did not feel it incumbent upon him to go into the amenities supplied by Margaret Hamilton. He indicated that he would not object to visiting Somerset House from time to time, but found immurement there trying indeed.

The Duke said that he would see what he could do.

However, when his son gave him some summary of his investigations into the monopolies situation, Ludovick, much impressed, thought that the King would not require great persuasion to enroll John permanently in his own employ, as much more useful than most of his Household.

John was not too happy about that either, especially the use of the word permanent. After all, his aim was to get back to Scotland and Methven.

He had to wait until late for his interview with James. He could not, of course, approach the monarch personally; and, at the meal after the hunt got back, he noticed that James had his eye on him more than once in his lowly seat, but did not summon him. It was far into the evening, and his thoughts turning towards bedding down in his father's room, before the command came. Sir John Stewart was to attend in the royal bedchamber.

He found James looking even more incongruous than usual, sitting up in bed, in a vast, shadowy room, in night-gown and bed-robe, but still wearing his high hat, beaker of wine in hand. Steenie was hanging about, looking sulky. But at John's appearance he was dismissed and bluntly told not to come back until sent for.

"So, Johnnie Stewart, you're here," the King observed. "You weary o' my Annie's service, eh? Is that it?"

"Not entirely, Sire," John answered carefully. "The Queen is very sick. That is why I could come to tell Your Majesty. She is grievously unwell."

"Annie's aye unwell—or says she is! All her days that has been the way o' it."

"This is true sickness, Sire. Constant vomiting. Much pain. Her Majesty's physicians are greatly troubled. They have sent a report . . ."

"Aye, aye—that's no' new, either. Dinna tell me that's all you've come to tell me, man?"

"No, Sire. But this was the reason for me getting away."

"Excuse, you mean! Come on, laddie—out wi' it. You've been active, I hope? As I bade you. No' wasting your time on sickly women! What's in yon satchel you've got?"

"Papers, Sire. Certain papers I have put together. As you commanded me." He laid his bag on the royal bed and drew out a sheaf of close-written sheets. He held them out to the monarch.

One glance was enough for James. "You tell me, lad. My eyes are no' just what they were. And it's gey dark in here, mind."

"There is much here, Highness. Too much just to re-count . . ."

"*I'll* say what's too much—no' you, boy! Gie me the meat o' it. What have you uncovered, eh?"

John cleared his throat. "Majesty, the monopolies, I find, are rich and powerful and have all well in hand. Nor fear interference. They have parliament, both Lords and Commons, well sweetened, as they say—to vote in their favour. The great ones, Cockayne and his Merchant Venturers, and Mansell, have all the most profitable trade neatly parcelled out between them, with the East India Company coming third. Only the less profitable trades are left to the smaller men. But—they mislike and fear each other. That could be their weakness."

"Go on, man. Maist o' this I ken already."

"Yes, Sire. I learned that Lady Suffolk is perhaps more powerful in this matter than the Earl. You know of this man Bingley . . . ?"

"Ooh, aye—we a' ken Jack Bingley. Kate Howard's play-marrow!"

"More than plaything, Highness. As Treasurer-Depute he it is whom the monopolists work through. When I suggested a new monopoly, they assured that all could be arranged through this Bingley."

"So-o-o! Bingley, eh? And Kate Howard. Mair fly than Tom! Tom Suffolk will no' soil his lily-white hands—but he'll tak the siller! Ooh, aye—he'll tak the siller. That should be mine!"

"Yes, Sire. In these papers are lists of the monopolies. And, so far as I can find out, who holds them. The goods and trade. There must be a great many that I have not discovered, but these are the main ones."

"And the monies, man? The siller? How much? What did you discover there?"

"Figures, Highness, are not bandied about. But I learned that, with such new monopoly as I suggested, they would double the price at which they bought. Double! I gathered that this was normal."

"Double, eh? One hundred per centum. As much as that? That is a fair return, aye, fair."

"I would name it robbery, Sire!"

"Aye, maybe. But what *you'd* name it, Johnnie Stewart, isna just the vital issue! And what's this o' a *new* monopoly you speak of? What's this?"

John trod more carefully than ever. "I had to have excuse for my enquiries, Sire. So that they would talk. At St Paul's, as Your Majesty suggested. I have little knowledge of trade and manufacture but *you* had taught me something about paper. So I used this knowledge."

"Paper, eh? That was apt, man. Shrewd."

Relieved, John went on. "It was Your Highness's own teaching—all I could speak of. I learned that here in England almost all paper is bought from the Hansa merchants in Germany and the Baltic coasts. At a price—for *they* have the monopoly. These London men knew nothing of Scots paper-making. So I made so bold as to suggest that they might buy cheaper from Scotland. Hinted at a new monopoly for them, in paper from Scotland. They jumped like salmon to fly! These Merchant Venturers—they wanted to know qualities, quantities, prices. I could not tell them, to be sure, not knowing—but I took them some of Your Majesty's own papers, and my father's from Whitehall, as ensamples. They were much impressed. So they told me much that I could not have learned otherwise. Did I do rightly, Sire?"

"Aye, ooh, aye. Leastwise, maybe." It was James's turn to be careful. "A paper monopoly, eh? How much did they want?"

"I know nothing of quantities nor price. You did not inform me as to that. I had to . . . dissemble. But I understood them to be eager for as much as the Scots mills could supply. If the price was right. They would then double the price for their own market. I declared that the Scots paper-makers would expect to be given some share in the doubling of price."

"Assuredly! Maist right and proper. We'll hae to find out how much they want, lad. And how much the mills can gie them. Difficult."

"Is that necessary, Sire? In bringing this monopoly corruption to an end? I only used the paper suggestion to win information out of them."

"Tut, man—first things first! There could be siller in this, much siller. Paper, as I told you, is a right useful commodity. Its uses are aye growing. If we could stop the import o' this German paper and supply these English frae Scotland instead—man, wi' a properly contrived monopoly, we could coin siller, just. Aye, coin it!"

John stared. "You mean . . . ? I thought that Your Majesty wished to end the misuse of these monopolies? And to stop the Howards' control of them. Not to, to operate one yourself!"

"Fegs, Johnnie Stewart—be no' sae mealy-mou'ed! You sound like any Kirk pulpiteer! To be sure I'll end a' this corruption. Aye, and put thae Howards in their place, forby—and that place is the Tower o' this London, I'm thinking! But that's nae reason for rejecting a bit honest trade—which will help Scotland, mind. Trade's right necessar. And if I put you in charge o' it—*if*, mind you—you'll no' do too badly out o' it your ainsel', lad!"

John was silenced.

"Aye, well—we'll hae to see about that. These folk at St Paul's—when do you see them again?"

"I left it open, Sire. Told them that I would have to make enquiries, as to quantities and price, before we could go further. I would guess that they think that I am going back to Scotland to do this . . ."

"And they're right, Johnnie man—they're right in this. For that's what you are going to do. You're going back to Scotland to discover just that—quantities and prices. Back to yon Water o' Leith millers frae the Germanies. If thae Merchant Venturers need mair information, the mair so do we! You're to get it."

Head spinning, John swallowed. "My, my service with the Queen, Sire?"

"Och, leave you that to me, man. You've mair important affairs to be at. How soon can you leave? The morn? Aye, the morn—the sooner the better. This mustna run stale on us, mind."

"But . . ."

"Nae buts! There's just ae thing. We'd be best no' to be right out o' touch wi' these merchants at St Paul's meantime, see you. Keep them interested. How could we contrive that? If Geordie Heriot had been alive . . ."

"I do not think that they will lose interest, Sire. But if you would wish someone to keep in touch with Cockayne and Woolcombe, there is Sir William Alexander of Menstrie. He accompanied me to St Paul's, on one occasion. I felt, at my age, that I needed credence, a man of some substance with me. They know him now."

"Alexander? Him? Is he to be trusted?"

"He is your Master of Requests, Sire."

"That's no' to say he's honest! He was one o' Johnnie Mar's recommends, coming frae Stirling. He writes poetry, forby! Is that in his favour, for the likes o' this?"

"So do you, Sire!" John said, greatly daring.

"Aye. I' ph'mm. Well, I'll hae a word wi' him. Now, off wi' you. And nae dawdling in Scotland, nor on the way. I want you back wi' this information at the soonest. How much o' the different grades o' paper they can supply, and at what price? How much mair they could supply without new mills? How long to get new mills built and working on the Esk? A' that. You have it? Right—and if you spy yon Steenie Villiers lurking around outby, send him in. A guid night to you, Johnnie Stewart!"

"Thank you, Sire. And . . . you will tell Her Majesty?"

John hurried back to his father's room, for the most part delighted. He was going back to Scotland, even if only for a brief spell; and the problem of Somerset House was solved, meantime at least. Whether this paper monopoly involvement was good or bad remained to be seen, but it had gained him an unlooked-for advantage here and now.

What Margaret Hamilton would say when he went to Somerset House the next day, for his gear and horse, was open to question.

John arrived back in Edinburgh less than three months after leaving it, having made a reasonably speedy ride up through England, blessed by crisply golden autumn weather. He had never appreciated his own land and the northern capital so greatly, with its breezes and vistas, its hills and valleys, the city's soaring tenements and dominant castle.

185

As his father had suggested, he went to ask if he might lodge with his aunt, the Countess of Mar, in her fine town-house in the Cowgate, and was well received. Ludovick's sister Mary seldom accompanied her second husband to London, finding him trial enough when he was at home, as she explained frankly. But as the King's own cousin, sister of the realm's only duke and wife of the King's foster-brother, she was the uncrowned queen of Edinburgh society.

Despite all this, the Countess was agog to know of all that went on at London. And John, for his part, heard of much that had transpired in Scotland, that his mother was well, and also learned quite a lot about Sir William Alexander, whom his Aunt Mary knew well and obviously much admired.

Lady Mar however knew nothing about the paper-trade, nor any other, and said so with some vehemence.

The next day he rode out westwards to the Dalry mills where, after some little difficulty in getting the two Germans to take him seriously, despite assuring them that he came direct from King James, whom they had seen him with previously, at length got them down to details. And, when they recognised that he was visualising a great and protected trade with England and a vast expansion of their industry, they became prepared to sit down and answer questions.

He had come well armed with these, of course, and by dint of putting his points in careful sequence and being ready with supplementaries, he was able to amass practically all the information required in a remarkably short space of time, ridiculously so considering the distance he had come to glean it. He learned that although paper was sold by the ream and quire to ordinary buyers, to large traders it went by pounds and tons. The standard unit of such sales was 1,000 sheets, sheets being the pieces which emerged from the manufacturing process, after drying, and usually measuring about six feet by four, although different types and qualities tended to have their own sizes. The number of sheets per pound or ton varied with quality and weight, naturally, as did the price.

As to the export situation, he was told that these two

Water of Leith mills produced at present very little low-quality paper, concentrating mainly on three high grades, selling at 39, 36 and 33 merks per 1,000 sheets, that is £26, £24 and £22 Scots respectively. Output depended upon demand, and at present ran at about 300, 1,200 and 2,000 packets of the three grades, annually. In addition they made the special extra-fine linen weave for His Majesty, with his own water-mark, this not being available for others. As to production, they could, if the demand justified it, more than double, perhaps even treble their output in these two mills without too great difficulty.

John, taking hurried note of all this, enquired about less expensive paper and was told that, yes, they could produce it if there was sufficient market, as was not the case at present. In the Germanic states much low-quality paper was produced, printing-paper in especial, but there there was infinitely greater demand. Indeed they would be quite happy to extend their premises and installations for this purpose, since it would allow them to use up much of the rags and material brought in by their collectors, unfit for the highest quality papers; and also could make use of water which was insufficiently pure for the best grades.

On the subject of new mills in the North Esk valley, they could not be so specific, of course. How long it might take to establish such would depend on many factors. If existing meal-mills could be taken over and converted, much time would be saved, needless to say; but there was the matter of trained and skilled labour. Paper-makers were not to be produced over-night, and, since these two Water of Leith mills were the only source of skilled men in Scotland at present, no manning of new mills could be arranged without affecting the production here. Any expansion to the Esk would have to be a very gradual process.

With this John had to be satisfied. Indeed he was more than satisfied, grateful that he had got all that he needed so swiftly. He had ascertained that the export of paper to England was quite possible and would be welcomed. It might not be very large, in English monopoly terms, but could be increased and adjusted in time. He did not tell the Germans anything about sharing any special English

187

surcharges—that was no part of his present fact-finding mission—and the others did not raise the point, the assumption being that they would charge the same prices as they were doing to Scots buyers.

In no more than a couple of hours, then, John had learned as much as he required to know, at present, and took his departure. This speedy result meant that he could proceed on to Methven with a clear conscience. He had determined to do this anyway—but now he could go in less haste. The King had not commanded him to be back in London by any given date, but he knew his monarch well enough by now to be sure that any undue delay would be frowned upon.

His mother was as delighted as she was surprised to see him, having assumed that she would be deprived of the company of her son until the winter was over, at least. Mary Gray was a self-sufficient creature, but those whom she loved she loved dearly. Mother and son were very close.

It grieved her, therefore, to tell John that Janet Drummond was already married—although sooner or later made little difference, did it? Her parents had hastened matters, undoubtedly, occasioning the usual talk. She was now living with her husband, David Drummond, at Dalpatrick. No, nobody suggested that she was particularly happy.

John tried not to show his feelings.

His mother had other news which affected him. There was trouble connected with Dumbarton Castle. The Deputy-Keeper, William Middlemas, was apparently behaving badly, and there were complaints being made, even to the Privy Council, of oppression. As the new Governor, some responsibility inevitably lay with John. This Middlemas had never been really satisfactory, but Ludovick, at hundreds of miles distance, had been insufficiently firm with him. Now, it seemed, matters had come to a head.

John agreed to pay a visit to Dumbarton.

For the rest, all went on at Methven more or less as before. The work of draining the Moss proceeded, the good summer aiding. The wood-felling had been halted meantime but would resume soon. The farming activities had also benefited from the good weather and both the hay and the corn harvests had been good. And so on. It seemed to John almost as though Methven could get on quite well without him.

Nevertheless, he spent three days, dressed in old clothing, playing the country laird again, inspecting, directing, planning and using his muscles—and finding it all a deal more to his taste than the life of a courtier. But he was haunted by the thought that Janet was only a few miles away and yet to visit her was quite out of the question.

Three days, then, and he bade farewell to his mother and set off south-westwards. He made an early start, for it was all of sixty miles to Dumbarton. He rode by Gask to the Earn, across it and down Strathallan to Dunblane, then through Menteith and up the Forth valley to Aberfoyle, MacGregor country where it behoved a man to gang warily, even though the Children of the Mist were now proscribed in law and deprived even of their name. However he suffered no interference, and continued, skirting the head of the great Flanders Moss, and so to the Drymen area—from which the Drummonds had taken their name. After that it was a fairly straightforward ride down through Lennox and the Vale of Leven to Dumbarton town. He had made good time.

John had been here only once before, as a child with his father, but he well remembered the mighty conical rocky hill which soared above the Clyde, dominating all and guarding the upper estuary. The obvious site for a fortress, it had supported such since Pictish times, and now was festooned with the oddly scattered and individual buildings of the royal castle. It had a different aspect from the other great citadels, less of a piece, inevitably, because of the conical shape of the rock, which disallowed clustered towers and keeps within a lofty curtain-wall, forcing the buildings to cling wherever they could, at various levels, and the enclosing wall to encircle the hill, part-way down and erratic, the defences strongest at the most vulnerable points.

Avoiding the town, John rode over the causeway and up to the first of the fortified gatehouses in this perimeter wall. The drawbridge was down, and the great gates stood open. He rode in, unchallenged.

Some way up the zigzagging climbing track which linked

189

the buildings and levels of the rock, was a second gatehouse, likewise open and unguarded. Beyond this, John came across a man lying sprawled at the pathside. Presuming that he was sick or in some trouble, he dismounted, only to discover the individual to be in fact blind-drunk. Leaving him, he came to a third gateway, again open and unmanned; and here he had to leave his horse hitched at a row of stabling, for the further ascent was only by steps cut in the naked rock. At a sort of terrace here there was at least a sign of life, a building, some sort of guardroom on the left, from which shouts and skirling emanated. Going to enquire therein, he found five men and two women, in various stages of undress and intoxication, sprawled around a table laden with flagons and beakers and dripping spilled ale. Banging on the open door, he called to ask where might be found William Middlemas, Deputy-Keeper, but was answered only by hiccups, grunts and leers. For a royal fortress, Dumbarton appeared to be in doubtful hands.

Still higher, the steps now only wide enough to take one person at a time, John reached the chasm between the two peaks of the hill, twins which at certain angles appeared to be only one but which from here could be seen to be of rather differing heights. In the gut of this steep-sided saddle was, strangely, a tiny lochan, the castle's water-supply. And on a shelf above this stood a house, part-fortified, of some pretensions considering its difficult approach, if not the Governor's residence at least the most substantial building the visitor had come across so far. However strange its site, the prospects were magnificent, up and down the Firth of Clyde and north and westwards to the Highland mountains, lovely in the late afternoon sunshine.

The door of this, like the rest, stood open, but there was no answer to John's knocking. He moved inside—after all, he *was* Governor here.

The interior was untidy, neglected-seeming, although the room-proportions and furnishings were good. There was no sign of life. He moved upstairs, by a turnpike in a turret—and on the landing heard the murmur of voices. He went over to a closed door from behind which the sounds emanated. He knocked.

This time he got an answer. A volley of oaths assailed his ears and he was instructed to be off unless he wanted a horse-whipping.

John Stewart was no busybody nor yet an intruder on others' privacy but he had been greatly shocked by what he had seen at this royal castle, and recognised that he had a responsibility in the matter. Also, he did not like being sworn at.

"Come here," he called, as authoritatively as he could at the closed door. "Come out. I require speech with you."

That produced an even more virulent outburst.

John opened the door and entered.

A man was sitting up in bed, a woman beside him, both seemingly unclothed. The man was corpulent, red-faced and prominent as to jaw.

At sight of John this character leapt from the bed and came at a run towards the door, stark naked. John took an involuntary step backwards at the sheer ferocity of the man. He fumbled for the dirk which always hung at his side when travelling, seldom as it had ever had to be drawn.

"Out! Out!" the apparition shouted. "Before I break every bone in your body, by God!"

"You are Middlemas?" There was no answer to that, and, with the other almost upon him, John got his dirk out. "Halt you—in the King's name!" he exclaimed.

More likely it was the naked steel than the royal authority which gave the man pause, in his notably unprotected state. But at least he halted, fists clenching and unclenching, features working—clearly an individual of strong emotions.

"*Are* you William Middlemas?" John demanded. "I am Sir John Stewart."

"I'm no' caring whether you're the Angel Gabriel! Out o' this house, fool!"

"*My* house! Since I am the King's Governor here."

The fat man goggled.

"If you are Middlemas, you must have heard of Sir John Stewart of Methven, son to the Duke of Lennox, now Governor and Keeper of this Dumbarton Castle. I am here on the King's business." And when still there was no reply,

191

"Now, sir—go and clothe yourself. I do not discuss affairs with folk in your state! I will await you downstairs—but not for long! Or I shall be up again." And, without waiting for reply now, he turned and made for the stairs.

He had less time to wait than he might have anticipated, in the untidy main chamber. Middlemas came down scowling but at least part-clad. What he had done with his doxy—men did not usually entertain their wives in bed in late-afternoon—John did not enquire, or at least not directly.

"I walked in here through three gates, quite unchallenged," he said, levelly. "And up to your chamber. Is this a royal fortress or a whorehouse, Middlemas?"

The man shrugged heavily. "I am no' expecting an armed invasion!"

"I have seen but six men—and all drunk. You are paid to have a garrison of eighteen men. Where are the rest? All abed?"

"They have duties. No' in the castle. Collecting taxes, dues, casualties. In the port and town."

"Ah—so that is what they are doing? But lacking your supervision, sir! It is *you* who have the commission to so collect, is it not?"

"They'll no' cheat me, young man, never fear!"

"It is not you I am concerned as being cheated, but the King's subjects. Or even His Majesty's self."

"Then you needna be!"

"You collect these revenues in the name of the Keeper and Captain of this royal fortress. And I am that Keeper and Captain. I expect better service than this."

The other said nothing.

"Besides that, I am here on another matter. There are complaints against you by sundry folk of Dumbarton. That you oppress and extort in *my* name. That you put the people of this town in fear and distress."

"Lies!" Middlemas said shortly.

"Yet the complaints are many. And detailed. And from some substantial citizens."

"If you heed such, more fool you! They refuse to pay their rents and dues. Rogues, sorners, knaves!"

192

"That is not as I heard it. And what I have seen here today scarce reassures me, sir!"

"I have been Deputy-Keeper here for long. Before you were weaned, belike! Are you teaching me my business?"

"If you do not know your business, or abuse it, then I must. And you were my father's deputy, never mine."

"I hae a paper saying that I am Deputy-Keeper, signed and sealed. That is enough for me."

"Not if I appoint a new Deputy."

"You canna do that."

"I can and probably shall—since you inspire me with no confidence."

"I'll no' accept it. I'll protest to the Duke. Aye, even to the King himsel'!"

"Which will serve you nothing. I *come* from the King, I tell you. And my father. And return to them shortly."

"I hae my friends."

"They would have to be powerful ones, to save you!"

"We'll see about that."

"We shall, yes. You will hear from me, in due course, Middlemas. Meantime, I do not think that I have anything more to say to you. Since we scarcely seem to speak the same language! But I warn you—your days as Deputy here are numbered. So watch how you step, for such time as is left to you!" And, turning on his heel, John strode out.

Unwilling to put up anywhere in that castle, he found a tavern down near the harbour from which, after a scratch meal, he sallied out to make a few enquiries in the town about the regime at the fortress, not revealing his own identity. There was no question as to the unpopularity of the man Middlemas, with his minions, who, on the strength of his position as Deputy to an absentee Governor, had been behaving like a tyrant, not only as regards the castle, with its dominant influence over the town, and as tax and rent gatherer for the crown, but in affairs of the community in general. There were many instances quoted of misbehaviour, harshness, even savagery and rape, as well as extortion and sheerest fraud. Nobody seemed to be in a position to effectively counter the man. Incidentally, John discovered that the Duke of Lennox, by association, was almost equally

193

unpopular, no one in Dumbarton apparently having heard that he was no longer Governor.

Clearly drastic action was required here.

Next morning he rode off eastwards, over the waist of the land, to Edinburgh, and the day following was on his way back to London.

10

Having enquired in the area on his way, and learned that the King was still at Theobalds Park, John presented himself there on a chilly, wet November afternoon. Like the weather, he found the atmosphere at court changed for the worse. James was ill, confined to his bed, and proving difficult. He had stopped all hunting, and, there being little else to do at Theobalds, his courtiers found time hanging heavily and wished that they were back at Whitehall—indeed many had already gone, for James did not relish feeding what he called idle mouths. Moreover, Prince Charles had been summoned from Greenwich, and come unwillingly, and the father-and-son relationship not being of the happiest, the atmosphere was not improved.

Ludovick at least was glad to see his son, although perturbed to hear about the Dumbarton situation.

As he awaited a call to the royal bedchamber, his father told John about developments. The King's crony, Count Gondomar the Spanish ambassador, had concocted a scheme with James whereby the proposed Spanish alliance could be consolidated by a marriage between the Prince of Wales and the King of Spain's daughter, the Infanta Maria. James had become very keen on this, however unenthusiastic was Charles, mainly because this daughter of the richest prince in Christendom was to bring with her, as well as a fabulous jewellery collection, £600,000 as dowry, which would be paid to her prospective father-in-law not her husband. Presumably Gondomar had arranged this with Philip beforehand. Charles, of course, had really no choice in the matter; but Steenie Villiers, oddly, had been selected for the task of persuading him to accept his fate with a good grace, and ordered, in the process, to attend upon the prince at all times. So these two young men, formerly enemies, were now seen constantly in each others' company, neither most evidently enjoying the situation—which again did not make for joy at court.

John was also surprised to learn that the Queen had been moved from Somerset House to Oatlands, a royal seat in Surrey, her physicians advising that a change to country air might do her good.

The call to the royal presence did not come that night, nor yet by noon next day, and John was ruefully wishing that he had taken at least another day at Methven. Then, in late afternoon, the summons arrived.

He found James in the same bed in which he had last seen him, surrounded by books and papers and still wearing his hat. He looked neither worse nor better than when last seen, but welcomed his young visitor with a powerful fit of coughing, hawking and spitting into a most unsavoury bowl, catarrh apparently being one of the current maladies. Tears in his great lachrymose and soulful eyes, he confided to John that he was a done man, overtaken before his time by the pains and paiks of managing two unruly and ungrateful kingdoms. Did he, Johnnie Stewart, realise that he, James Stewart, was so weak of the legs that he had had to have them tied beneath his horse's belly when hunting or he would have fallen from the saddle? *Quantum mutatus ab illo!* Having got this off his chest, along with the phlegm, Majesty blew his nose between finger and thumb into the useful bowl and sat up more brightly.

"Well, man—well?" he demanded.

"Very well, Sire—as regards the paper. All in order. I have written down the details for Your Majesty, as to qualities and quantities, weights, prices and production." He brought out a paper from his doublet, which James consigned to the litter already decorating his bed. "As to new mills, the principal problem will be the training of people to man them. This will take time, without injuring the production of the two mills already working."

"Houts, laddie—any fool could jalouse that! What o' monopoly surcharges and the like?"

"I did not mention that to them, Sire, considering it no concern of mine. And they did not raise the matter. They think to sell the paper to the English at the same rates as they do to the Scots."

"Aye, i'ph'mm. Maist right and proper. For *them*! We'll likely can double that, eh? So that's that. We can now proceed wi' thae Merchant Venture rogues. The mannie Alexander's been to see them and they're keen, keen. Aye—but, before you go treat wi' them, I've another ploy for you, Johnnie. It has come to my lugs that there's a bit paper-mill here in England, after a'. At Dartford, in Kent. A right scunner! Yon Elizabeth Tudor, it seems, when she had her wits aboot her mair than latterly, brought a mannie ower frae Gelderland, in the paper-trade, and set him up at Dartford. Name o' John Spielmann. Gave him a monopoly forby. But och, it came to naething much. She lost interest in it. I told you, the woman had nae head for affairs—it was a' glory, glory! Hech—you'll no' butter much bread wi' glory, without siller! So this Dartford mill never came to much. Indeed the man Spielmann became a jeweller, they tell me, court jeweller to Elizabeth, and did better than wi' his paper. But, och, the mill's still there."

John looked thoughtful. "This could alter things, could it not?"

"It could, aye—it could. But it mustna, Johnnie Stewart—it mustna! So you're to awa' doon to Dartford and see what's what. We don't want this Spielmann making trouble. Cockayne and the others canna ken about him or they'd hae been on to him lang syne. They mustna learn now."

"I see that, yes. But what have I to tell the man, Sire?"

"Tell him naething. Your task is to find out, no' to tell. *I'll* decide what's to be done wi' this Hollander. Now—there's another matter. On your way back frae Dartford you're to repair to Oatlands Park. Hae you heard tell that my Annie's gone there? Mair fool her! It's in Surrey, beyond Hampton Court a wee. Near to Chertsey, on the Thames. Her witless physicians hae sent her there for to get a change o' air! And that's no' the worst o' it. Can you credit it—they've set her, a near-dying woman, to sawing wood, I'm told! Aye sawing wood! As guid exercise for her. Guidsakes, they'll finish her off in nae time at a', wi' yon! But afore she

197

ends up, there's some information I'm needing, see you. And you're to seek it out for me. You're still one o' her household, mind."

John swallowed. "I thought . . . I had hoped, Sire, that you would have arranged it otherwise . . ."

"Och, she kens you were awa' on a mission for me. Time enough for the other. Fegs—belike there'll no' *be* a Queen's household for much longer, wi' this traipsing the country and sawing o' wood, for a sick woman! So—I want to ken whether my Annie's made a will and testament, or no. And, if she has, what's intilt."

"But . . . !" John stared. "But . . . !"

"Wheesht—you're aye butting, Johnnie Stewart! You've got sound enough wits, or I wouldna be employing you. So use them and spare us the buts. See now—Annie has been buying jewellery a' her days—aye, and costing me a bonny penny! She scatters diamond-rings as though they were poultry-meal! Forby, she owns much property in her ain name. This Oatlands itsel'. And the housie at Greenwich. Aye, plenty other lands. And her movables amount to over £400,000, they tell me. Now, it would be maist unfortunate, aye and improper, if she in her half-wit state was to leave it a' to other than her lawful husband and lord. You canna but perceive that, Johnnie man? It wouldna do. But she's head-strong and has taken a mislike to me, for some reason. Och, you ken women! So I need to ken whether she's made a will, or hasna. And if she has, who gets what."

John bit back his buts. "I do not see how I can discover such a matter, Sire," he declared, helplessly. "I may be in her service still but I am not close to Her Majesty . . ."

"No—but you're close to yon lassie Hamilton, are you no'? I heard you'd been bedding her! Maist improper!"

That effectively silenced John Stewart.

"Aye, well—are you thinking o' wedding the quean?"

"No . . . no, Sire." he got out.

"No? You could dae worse, man. She's nae siller, mind. But she's the niece to the Earl o' Abercorn. And the Hamiltons are a right canny lot. And clannish. They mak guid friends and bad enemies!"

When that produced no comment, the King went on,

"The lassie could be useful in this pass, see you. She has quick wits, I'm told—as well as other parts! And a right loving nature, heh? Forby, she's in and oot o' the Queen's chamber a' the time. Close to a' Annie's ladies. If there's a will, it will hae been witnessed. Some o' thae auld bitches will hae witnessed it. Maybe the lassie hersel'. So you find out, Johnnie man—next time you're bedding her!"

John bit his lip.

"Aye, well. But a word in your lug, lad. Watch out for yon Anna, the other one. The Danish maid, who's been wi' the Queen ever since I brought her frae Denmark. She's a right dragon, that one. She helps hersel' to my Annie's jewels, I ken fine. The Queen fair dotes on her. I wouldna put it past her, mind, to leave the crittur a right whack o' her gear and siller! Shamefu' as that would be! Her and the Frenchie she ca's Pierrot. Maist o' the jewellcry could go that way. Aye, and I'd no' be surprised if she thought to leave her lands and properties to Charles. She's aye been soft on Charlie. So—you're to find out, for me. But discreetly, mind. She's no' to find out what you're at, or she'll likely do worse, just to spite me! You have it?"

Dumbly John nodded.

"Aye—then begone, boy. You tire me—for I'm a sick man, mind. Wi' ower much on my mind. Off wi' you . . ."

John backed out from the presence of a remarkably spry-looking invalid, thoughts in a whirl—an effect James Stewart was apt to have on folk.

Ludovick Stewart, long past being surprised at anything, was much amused.

Dartford lay some seventeen miles down-river from London, and to reach there most expeditiously from Theobalds, without traversing the city and obtaining a barge, it was necessary to make for the nearest crossing of Thames, at Chiswick Bridge, and then to proceed eastwards by Mortlake and Lewisham and Bexley. John's own beast being tired and a little lame after its long journey from Scotland, he borrowed one of his father's horses.

The weather was still grey, chill and misty, so that the thirty-mile and five-hour ride was scarcely enjoyable, although John was interested in all he saw, particularly the Kent farming scene with its oast-houses, apple-orchards, brewhouses and cider-presses, so different from anything in Scotland—although the cattle, he noted, were no better than his own at Methven.

Dartford proved to be much different from his anticipation, after the flat country he had passed through. Although scarcely hilly by Scottish standards, the land hereabouts became folded into a sort of downland, through which the River Darent, swift-flowing compared with the other sluggish streams he had seen, ran in a narrow and shallow valley. And some couple of miles from the river's confluence with the now estuarine Thames, the thriving little market-town clustered around an ancient church and former monastic buildings, the Chantry of St Edmonds.

John had no difficulty in finding the paper-mill, some way upstream, where the water was comparatively uncontaminated. There were other mills, the Darent's flow making this the best water-power for a large area, but the paper-mill was larger than those for meal and flour. But obviously it was not working, the premises shut up although clearly not abandoned. He made enquiries at cottages nearby, and learned that the mill worked only intermittently. But, if he wanted to speak with the miller, he would find Master Vandervyk's house in the High Street—or more likely at this time of day he would be in the Bull's Head tavern. When John mentioned that he thought that the name was Spielmann, he was eyed somewhat askance and informed that Sir John Spielmann had died years before—although Lady Spielmann still lived in Park House up the valley. Master Vandervyk had run the mill for long, even before Spielmann died.

So John went back to the town centre and found the Bull's Head inn prominent in the market-place. Within, the innkeeper directed him to a heavily-built, middle-aged man drinking ale in company with two or three other substantial-seeming citizens in a corner of the premises. Ale and trade, in England, appeared to be inseparable.

He introduced himself as John Methven, from Scotland, interested in paper. The big Dutchman made room for him at his side, ordering more ale, his companions decently moving off to another table.

John explained his quest thus: he had links with the paper-trade in Scotland, but had come to London where he had kin. He was interested to know whether there was any opening for further paper-making here in the south, and had been told that Spielmann's was the only paper-mill in all England. Could Master Vandervyk give him any useful advice and guidance?

The other appeared only too ready to do so. Forget it, John was told, in a thick foreign accent but eloquently enough. Paper and England just did not go together. There was not enough trade to keep *his* mill going six months in the year, without any other starting up. Anyway, it would not be permitted. All the paper used in this country came from the Germanic states, with the Hansa merchants holding a tight grip on all the trade. His own sales were confined to certain private buyers who required a special quality linen paper, mainly in the West Country, such as the Germans did not make in any quantity. Indeed, he had thought of transferring his mill to Devon, but doubted whether it was worth it, the trade being so small and even declining. Probably he would be wiser just to close down altogether, or change over to milling grain. Certainly there was no opening for another mill, here or elsewhere.

John sought to sound suitably disappointed. Why should this be, he demanded? Surely much paper was used here in England? Why not produce it here?

The other shrugged great shoulders. It was all a matter of monopolies, he said, making something of a mouthful of the word. The Hansa papermakers had a close monopoly, and appointed their own distributors in each country. No one else could break in. Even the Dutch and Flemish millers —who had trained him—had to export their paper through the Hansa merchants. The only reason why his mill was able to survive was that old Spielmann had himself been granted a monopoly by the late Queen Elizabeth, to collect linen and make linen-paper, and this charter he still held, even though Spielmann himself had given up paper-making for more profitable jewelling and money-lending in London—being a wiser man than he, who had taken over the management of the mill! So this mill could not be closed down by the Hansa traders nor their distributors in London. But it was scarcely worth running.

And did Master Vandervyk know who were the London distributors—who presumably themselves knew about this mill?

The Dutchman made no bones about that. Mansell held the distribution of paper in his fist—Robert Mansell. And a tight fist it was.

So, John saw it all. Why Cockayne and his associates were so eager. This was all to be part of their war with Mansell. Presumably *they* did not know of this Dartford mill; but even if they did, they probably would not consider it of any significance. It was an alternative *import* monopoly they were concerned with, which would avoid the Hanseatic strangle-grip and Mansell's share in it. The issue was clear enough now.

Feigning grave disappointment, John bought the Dutchman some more ale, and took his departure.

The King ought to find all this to his taste and relief.

It was much too far to consider making for Oatlands that day. John rode back to Bexley and put up for the night at an inn there.

Margaret Hamilton welcomed him at Oatlands Park next afternoon, clearly delighted to have some young male company again. This Oatlands, a vast sprawling mansion in extensive parkland, was not her idea of paradise, cut off from all the excitements of London life and with no other associates than the Queen's ageing attendants. Country life, she asserted, was not for her. And she had missed John, she averred, all but purring, and rubbing against him like a cat.

The Queen's condition was not good, she reported, this place by no means helping her, despite her physicians. Could he believe it, they had had her up and outside and sawing wood, logs for the fire! That had all but killed her, and for days after each attempt she was prostrate—so that at least had been discontinued. But she was still being wheeled out, in a day-bed, to partake of the country air, chill November as it was, and she was often blue and rigid with cold.

John was suitably shocked and declared his lack of faith in all physicians, leeches and blood-letters. But what about his own position, he wondered, somewhat warily? What was the Queen's attitude towards him now?

Laughing pityingly, the young woman told him not to think so highly of himself as to imagine that, in her present state, Anne was in any way concerned with him. Her mind was wholly on her own state. Margaret had not heard John's name so much as mentioned since they came to Oatlands. Why? Was he anxious to come back to the Queen's service?

Not so, he asserted, probably too hurriedly. The King was altogether too demanding of his time. He did not go into details of his activities and the young woman did not enquire.

Margaret, in fact, was concerned about her own future. The Queen's illness might well prove fatal, she admitted—and then what was to happen to her? This household would be broken up and she would be without employment. She would have to consider what she was to do. She might even consider marriage!

John still more hurriedly changed the subject, or at least its direction. Something would turn up, he asserted. Was not her uncle the Earl of Abercorn, a great man in Ireland, practically ruling in the north there?

She dismissed her uncle. He had no concern for her, with innumerable sons and daughters of his own to settle; moreover he was said to be failing in health. Besides she had no desire to go to Ireland, nor even to leave London, where life was to be lived. Oatlands was quite sufficiently countrified for her, thank you! No, it might have to be marriage. Had he any suggestions?

John definitely had not. He asked urgently whether there was not some other great lady's household where the Queen's Maid-in-Waiting would be welcome? What about the Marchioness of Winchester? She was rich and powerful enough.

Margaret snorted indelicately over the Marchioness, a puling, fashionless creature! To be in *her* household would be as bad as being buried alive! No, it was marriage for her—unless some opening could be arranged in the King's court? Since John was so far ben with the King, could he not contrive something for her?

That young man's mind worked quickly, assessing, balancing. He had to get her off this talk of marriage, somehow. So far as he knew, there was no position at James's establishment for women, save as mere servants. There were women about the court, of course, but these were only there as the wives of courtiers and visitors. On the other hand, this might be the opportunity he required to introduce the subject of the Queen's will. He had been wondering how to bring it up without making the point too obvious. This might serve—and possibly James might be persuaded to show some gratitude towards the girl thereafter?

"I do not know," he answered carefully. "But there is one matter which occurs to me, in which you might be of use to King James. And which might cause him to favour you in some way. He is concerned about the Queen's health, naturally, even if he does not show it openly! But he is also concerned about her affairs. He does not know what she aims to do with her properties, her lands and moneys. Apparently she has not told him. He does not know even whether she has made a will. Nor what her debts may be. You will understand that it is important for him to know. If he is responsible for her debts . . ."

"Oh, I can tell you that," Margaret interrupted, without more ado. "Anne will not make a will. She has said that, often. Declared that it would be as good as signing her own death-warrant! Some of her countesses have urged her to it, saying that otherwise the King will take all. But she refuses to set anything down on paper."

"You are sure of this?"

"Oh, yes. They rally her on it—the ladies. But all know that she intends that Prince Charles shall have all her properties. Including this Oatlands, I suppose. Her jewels will be shared out amongst us, I think—if Danish Anna does not get to them first!"

"So-o-o!" In these two brief sentences, surprisingly, John had practically all that he had come for. He nodded. "Then, if you learn more of a will being made, or any word of bequests, let me know. I think that the King will be grateful."

"You will speak to him, of me, John?"

"Yes. But, of course . . . this may be all a, a beating of the air! The Queen may recover and live for years yet. She is none so old—still not fifty years, James says. Then you would need no new position. And this talk of wills unnecessary."

"Perhaps, yes. We shall see. But still I might be wise to find a husband . . . !"

They left it at that, meantime.

John, of course, had no room allotted to him at Oatlands, but it was late to ride the near thirty miles to Theobalds that night, and Margaret appeared to take it for granted that he would share her bed. The great house was sufficiently large for privacy, and she had elected to occupy a wing well removed from the rest of the now reduced household, no doubt advisedly, being the young woman she was. Without ever making his presence known to the Queen herself nor to her elderly attendants, and eating in the kitchen premises, John more or less inevitably spent the night with Margaret—and would have been hypocritical to assert that he had not anticipated it or that he did not enjoy the proceedings. Free with her favours she might be, and not altogether to his taste in some other ways—but she was very good in bed and whole-hearted in her physical enjoyment.

Not too early in the forenoon following he set off on his return to Theobalds.

James, still abed, was delighted with both items of information brought by John, although as ever he hedged about his satisfaction with reservations. He declared that he could well believe that his Annie would be feart to make a will—women were right irrational creatures at best. But John was still to keep his lug to the ground—or at least to the person of the lassie Hamilton, which he gathered would not be too unpleasant—in case the Queen changed her mind, if that was the right word.

When John tentatively suggested that perhaps His Majesty

205

might wish to remember Margaret Hamilton, if it came to the Queen's household being broken up, James eyed him shrewdly and declared that, if he was so concerned for the lassie's future well-being, would the best thing be not to just marry her? Marriage was a lottery, mind—but most men had a try at it, if only to produce lawful heirs. And at least this quean was bedworthy, by all accounts, and well-connected, if penniless. Johnnie could do fell worse.

This subject seeming to dog him, John made non-committal noises and reverted to the matter of Master Vandervyk at Dartford. Did His Majesty not think that this royal charter, which the man held from Queen Elizabeth, might present a problem?

The King agreed that steps would have to be taken to deal with it. He would consider the matter and decide what was to be done. Meanwhile, perhaps Johnnie Stewart should likewise do some considering on the subject of marriage and his future. After all, as Governor of Dumbarton, and who kenned what else might follow in time, he would look better as a married man, less of a laddie. Forby, the Hamiltons were a well-doing lot and could prove useful to have links with. Such matters deserved serious thought. Aye, and while he was at it, he should tell his ducal father that he too should be thinking about marrying again. He had no right heir to the royal dukedom, save for a brother in France whom nobody knew, and said to be an arrant Catholic at that! Which would not do. A lawful son was what was required. So Ludovick Stewart should marry again, some suitable woman to be a royal duchess. Yon Mary Gray was all very well for a concubine, but in bastardy she could not be a duchess.

Tight-lipped, John withdrew.

Later, indignantly, he passed on to his father the King's comments—without mentioning the marital advice to himself.

"Ah—so James was at that again, was he? He keeps reminding me," the Duke said, casually enough.

"You *would* not marry again, would you? Or . . . anyone but my mother?"

His father shrugged. "I have no desire to, John—none at

206

all. But, you know the position. Mary will not consider marrying me—never would. I suppose that she is right in that. It would not serve. For a royal duke. James would never accept it—have it annulled if we were to do it. The marriages of members of the royal family are subject to the King's authority, to be lawful. Yet James wants me to produce an heir to the dukedom. I am, after all, third in line of succession. Charles is not married yet—and his sire, who scarcely dotes on him, doubts whether he *could* produce a son! And Elizabeth, his only daughter, is wed to the German Elector Palatine, and James is by no means sure that his kingdoms would accept a German as heir to the throne. So it would much strengthen his dynastic position if I, a Stewart, had a son born in wedlock."

"That may be so. But he cannot *make* you wed again!"

"Perhaps not. But he could make life very comfortless for me! He could strip me of revenues and position. He could banish me the realm, both realms. He has put folk in the Tower for less. He could even forfeit Methven, if so he thought fit. James may usually seem something of a simpleton and a figure-of-fun, but never forget that he has enormous power if he chooses to wield it. And, in a matter such as this, where his dynasty is concerned, I think that he would not hesitate."

"But you are his friend, as well as cousin . . ."

"True. He *might* spare me. But he would probably say that friendship should cut both ways—that I, as his friend, owe him this, owe the Stewart line this. That it would be no great sacrifice—he has already said so, more than once. It would be a marriage in name only, make no real difference to Mary and myself . . ."

"I say that it would."

"But then you, John, are prejudiced. And, shall we say, not greatly experienced. I would be making a new duchess, that is all. And, hopefully, an heir to the dukedom. I have had duchesses before, two of them, and they did not come between Mary and me."

"You are set on it, then?"

"No, I am not. But it looks as though James is. I would prefer not. And have nobody in mind. I can satisfy my bodily needs, whilst I am separated from Mary, readily enough without marriage. As, it seems, can you!"

A change of subject appeared to be advisable.

John reverted to the matter of Dumbarton. What was he to do with the man Middlemas?

The Duke shrugged again. "You must get rid of him, evidently."

"He declares that I will find that difficult. Claims that he holds a commission from you which secures his position."

"A commission granted can be revoked. Although you may have to pay him some compensation, since it is an office of profit—the tax-gathering. As he seems to be ensuring!"

"M'mm. How much? How much compensation?"

"Lord knows! That kind of man will ask much, I have no doubt. And you must needs beat him down."

"Why did you appoint such a man?"

"He was recommended by Johnnie Mar. And seemed none so ill, then. Myself being far away all these years, he has thought himself safe, no doubt. Perhaps I have been remiss. But I have over-many offices to grace! I am Lord High Admiral of Scotland—did you know that? Also Great Chamberlain. And Master of the Horse. Not to mention Keeper of the King's Falcons! Give me time and I will recollect others!"

"All of which bring you profit!"

"A little, lad—a little. Or, most of them."

Not for the first time John felt at odds with his father's attitude to life. "Do you find all this to your taste, admirable?" he demanded.

"Admirable? Perhaps not. But necessary, in the circumstances, John. The moneys and therefore the offices. I require all, for James's service is expensive—as you will find out! Parliament keeps him so short of money that he is in no state to pay his helpers and servants. So we must make what we can. A bad system—but the blame must lie with this English parliament."

John was not entirely convinced, but he returned to the problem of Dumbarton. "How do I set about getting rid of Middlemas?" he asked.

"Find a replacement. Someone whom you can trust with the task. Then send him to my Deputy-Sheriff of the Lennox, since Dumbarton is in the Lennox. That is Robert Napier of Kilmahew. *I* am Sheriff of the Lennox as well as Duke, and will write you an authority for Napier. He will then go to the castle and expel Middlemas and install your man."

"You make it sound simple," his son said, grimly. "I fear that it will be otherwise."

"Napier will have the authority. As Deputy-Sheriff he can call upon whatever force is necessary, if Middlemas proves difficult. Have you anyone in mind for the task? Your Deputy-Keeper?"

"I have not thought on it. But—would Sandy Graham, at Methven, serve? The minister's son. He has always been my friend. He is honest and no fool."

"Like yourself, on the young side. But, why not? If you think that he is sufficiently strong. For it is a task which calls for a strong hand."

"I hope that *I* shall be there, or thereabouts, much of the time. To be my own Keeper."

The Duke eyed him thoughtfully. "You do not think to remain at court, John?"

"No. This is no life for me. I wish to be back in Scotland. I am hopeful that the King will let me go, before long. I long for Methven and the Highland hills. I am no courtier."

"Perhaps you are right. I have often wished the same for myself. But I am saddled with a royal dukedom, and you are not."

"Will you help me with the King, then? Convince him to let me go?"

"If you wish it, I will try. But James is . . . James. It may not be easy, whilst he finds you useful here. It will be a question of choosing our time . . ."

Clearly that time would not be in the immediate future. John did not doubt that he would be required for further errands on the subject of the paper-trade—and he had not long to wait. Two days later he was sent for by the King, still in bed. James was fond of his bed, and when not able to hunt was apt to spend much time therein—so that there were occasions when his alleged sicknesses might be no more than excuses to lie in. Indeed he transacted much of the nation's business thus.

Buckingham was not present on this occasion; his orders were to be much with the Prince of Wales—which must in some ways have been a blessed relief for that young man, however much at odds he had been formerly with Charles. Now they were reputed to get on well together—by royal command.

"Aye then, Johnnie—I have our ploy worked out for your mannie at Dartford—what was his name?" James greeted.

"Vandervyk, Sire—a Hollander."

"I'ph'mm. Well, you're to go back down there and you're to tak him up to Scotland."

John stared. "Scotland . . . ?"

"That is what I said. I have decided that is best. You're to take yon Will Alexander wi' you, to Dartford. No' to Scotland . . . or, we'll see. As coming frae mysel'. The Hollander thinks *you're* in the paper-trade, mind. So you'll need someone who looks mair substantial, frae me."

"But you'll dae the talking. You're to tell the mannie that I've heard well o' him, and that he's to go to Scotland to help wi' the paper-making there—help train new men. And then likely manage one o' the new mills on the Esk. Is that no' a right notable conceive? It gets him awa' frae his Dartford mill, so that nae mair paper will be made there—and at the same time aids in our paper-production in Scotland."

"But . . ." Hastily John amended that. "He may not *wish* to go to Scotland, Sire."

"Then you'll hae to see that he does, laddie. For that's where he's to go. Och, he'll like it fine, once he's there. You'll offer him compensation for his mill. And you'll get the woman Elizabeth's bit charter back frae him. You have it?"

"And if he *refuses* to go?"

"You'll tell him it's a royal command, whatever—or Alexander will. He's to go to Scotland—and there'll be nae mair paper-making in England. And that's that!"

"Yes, Majesty." John was learning to keep his emotions under control, where his sovereign lord was concerned at least. Although, of course, concerned about how he was to achieve this latest task, he was lost in admiration for the cleverness of the scheme, and the wits which had devised it, bringing down two birds with one arrow. And delighted, to be sure, at the thought of returning to Scotland again so soon—although winter travel might be unpleasant.

Sir William Alexander came to John next day, saying that he had orders to accompany him to Dartford. When would they go?

John was for setting off right away, but the other pointed out that it looked like rain and it would be sensible to wait till the morrow in the hopes of better travelling conditions—no point in making a misery of it. This was not John's reaction to royal commands, but the older man seemed calmly assured, and the Duke did not indicate otherwise.

So the following morning they set off in slightly more favourable weather. They did not hurry, as John would have done by himself. Alexander, it seemed, seldom hurried. Nevertheless, November weather was not for lingering, and they reached Dartford in mid-afternoon. They went straight to the Bull's Head tavern, where they would stay the night. And there was Vandervyk sitting at the same table, tankard in hand, as though he had not moved since the other day. Obviously he was a man who took life very much as it came.

If the Dutchman was surprised to see John again, and so soon, he did not show it, acknowledging their arrival by promptly ordering more ale.

John, being the young man he was, plunged in right away. He introduced Sir William as Master of Requests to King James, who had a message for him from His Majesty. Vandervyk guffawed at that, but pushed the ale across to Alexander.

"It is so," John insisted. "The King is interested in the paper-trade, and has sent Sir William to speak to you. He has an offer to make to you."

"Indeed, yes," Alexander said, taking his cue. "Mr Methven has told His Majesty about you and your mill, and how you have insufficient trade, because of the monopoly, to keep it running as it should. Now in Scotland where we—and the King—come from, they make paper, and do not recognise this German monopoly. The King wishes you to go to Scotland and aid them there."

"Me? Go to Scotland?" The Dutchman snorted.

"To be sure. Your knowledge would be valuable there. It is wasted here."

"Valuable, heh? Valuable to who? Not to me!"

"Yes, valuable to you," John said. "The King intends much to increase paper-making in Scotland. To set up new mills. You could much assist in this. And you would be well paid. Earn much more. There are two German millers, only, to teach the Scots the trade. You would make a third. You would be important there, busy instead of all but idle here."

"Do I want to be so busy, Master Methven?"

"Why not? You are a paper-maker, are you not? You did not come here, from your Netherlands, to idle your days away, I think?"

"I do sufficiently well, young man. I have my good house, my friends and my ale. Your Scotland is far away."

"Do not tell me that you would not wish to be doing what you were bred to do, what you can do so well, what you came to England to do? That I will not believe!"

"You—or your King—must want me very much in this Scotland, I reckon."

"We do, yes. But—it is good to be wanted, is it not?"

"I am no longer a young man, to dig up my roots and move to another land. They say that Scotland is a hard land, cold . . ."

"No colder nor wetter than Holland, I think. And the folk are more like the Dutch than are the English, they tell me. And we have good ale there, stronger than here."

"Man, man, do you never take no? When I am well enough content here?"

"It is the King's wish—and these are royal commands, Menheer Vandervyk," Alexander mentioned warningly.

"His Majesty will compensate you handsomely for your mill and property here," John put in quickly. "You will gain much, in all ways. How much would you desire, in money, for your mill and house? How much, think you?"

The other rubbed his chin thoughtfully, eyelids narrowed. Clearly this was different, a new note struck—pounds, shillings and pence. "Now, that," Vandervyk said, "that would take me a little time to reckon. Yes, indeed—a little time."

"Then take you your time, friend," John said, finishing his ale. "We bide here tonight. Sleep on it, if you will."

"Do that," Sir William added. "But recollect that this is the King's wish. And His Majesty likes to have his wishes carried out."

They left it at that, and Vandervyk to his consideration.

Alexander made John excellent company and they spent quite a pleasant evening setting the world to rights in the Bull's Head.

In the morning, they had to wait quite some time before the Hollander appeared at the tavern. When he did, he was amiable enough but non-committal, avoiding any real discussion of the situation, so that presently Alexander began to register impatience. But when Vandervyk suggested that they paid a visit to his mill, John felt encouraged. Why should they go to the mill unless some positive reaction was envisaged?

So they walked up the riverside and were shown over the mill and warehouse, with the paper-making process explained to them in some detail. John was concerned to make knowledgeable comments and to ask questions, suitable to his role as one already in the trade—although once or twice he caught the Dutchman looking a little strangely at him.

At the end of this, however, Vandervyk, scratching his chin, observed that the mill was a valuable property, representing much labour, knowledge and experience, as well as the mere buildings, equipment and stock; very valuable, not to be disposed of lightly or for a mere pittance.

John, catching Alexander's eye, knew that they had won their case.

"Oh, I agree, friend," he said. "We never thought otherwise. How much do you value it at, then?"

The other's keen glance darted. "Difficult, sir—yes, difficult." That was the first time that he had called the younger man sir. "Much to consider. But . . ." He took a deep breath, and plunged. "Two hundreds of pounds!"

John pretended to debate, scratching the ground with his boot. He looked at Alexander.

"I know nothing of paper-making," that man said. "But £200 seems a lot of money."

"It *is* a lot of money," John agreed.

"But this is the only paper-mill in England," Vandervyk pointed out.

"That is so. But no more paper will be made here. This is compensation, not a trade sale."

"I . . . I could accept £190. No less."

"M'mm. I think that might just be possible. If . . ." It was John's turn to be slightly hesitant. "If the charter, the Queen's charter, of fifty years ago, is handed over, with the mill. Just in case . . ."

"That old paper? Yes, yes—I will find it somewhere. In some box . . ."

The younger man swallowed. Was it possible that this, the kernel of the entire matter, was going to be so easy?

"That is well," he said. "If you can get me that, I think that I can promise you £190 of compensation. When would you be ready to leave?"

"Leave . . . ?"

"For Scotland. I will be taking you there."

"By God, man—you go fast! Is there so much haste?"

"Perhaps not. But the King likes his affairs to be dealt with expeditiously. And this is His Majesty's business."

"Who knows, he might show some special favour towards you, Menheer," Alexander added, significantly.

"A sennight, then? Will that serve?"

"To be sure. I will come for you seven days from this, with horses for your belongings. But first, will you find me that charter . . . ?"

As the two Scots rode back for Hertfordshire that afternoon, the Elizabeth monopoly in John's pocket, they congratulated themselves on a successful mission. Alexander declared that he could do with a visit home to Menstrie, where he had not been for three years; he would see whether it could be contrived that he accompanied the other two. Now that Prince Charles was so much involved with Steenie Villiers there was the less need for his own services. And, as the King's Master of Requests, he was scarcely kept busy.

11

It was not the time of year that anyone would have chosen for a long journey but, since the King would hear of no delay, John accepted that it was an unlooked-for opportunity to be home at Methven for Yuletide. It would be cutting it fine, for the heavy Vandervyk was no horseman, and they had a groom and three pack-horses bearing his gear. Also travelling conditions were scarcely favourable for long days in the saddle; in fact the days were the shortest of the year, so that twenty miles each day was a good average—and they had over four hundred miles to go to Edinburgh from Dartford. Fortunately they had no snow and not a great deal of rain, mainly still frosty days, with long evenings in country inns and parish rest-houses. The Dutchman proved to be quite good company, however averse to haste; and Sir William's groom, a Hillfoots Scot, had a rich tenor voice and a talent for singing old songs of the countryside, which helped to pass many a long mile, and evenings by an innkeeper's fire. They seemed to drink an inordinate quantity of ale.

In the event it was 20 December, the Eve of St Thomas, before they reached Edinburgh and, anxious to be home before Christmas Day, John decided to postpone introducing Vandervyk to his new paper-making colleagues and establishment and to take him up to Methven with them for his first Yuletide in this strange land. This, however, meant informing him that he was really Sir John Stewart thereof and no Master Methven, and this took a little explaining away, although he was able, and truthfully, to lay the blame on their sovereign-lord. Vandervyk made little comment. John invited Will Alexander also, since that man had nobody particularly close at Menstrie Castle and he seemed glad to accept. John knew his mother well enough to reckon that she would not object.

They spent a night at Menstrie, near Stirling, on their way north, where an aunt kept house for Alexander in a grey, L-shaped fortalice in the plain of Forth directly under the steeply-rising Ochil Hills. A smaller place than Methven, it seemed to crouch beneath the great escarpment, whereas Methven stood high and proud above its loch.

They made it to Strathearn the next day, where Mary Gray welcomed them joyfully, obviously not at all put out by the unexpected guests. She declared that the King's service seemed to entail a lot of travelling—which suited her, so long as the traveller came north to Scotland thus frequently. From the first she got on famously with Will Alexander, and charmed the more stolid Vandervyk. Clearly the Yuletide was going to be a pleasant one.

Asking for Janet Drummond, John learned that his mother had seen her recently and had found her quiet, subdued but wearing a sort of applied serenity. No, Mary would not say that she was positively unhappy; but nor was she the joyful young wife. David Drummond, Younger of Dalpatrick, was a decent and moderate man, and she might have done so very much worse. Moreover, Janet was a strong-minded young woman. But . . .

John was sorely tempted to go to see her, but decided that this would help neither of them. However, the matter was taken out of his hands. The cold, dry and frosty weather continued and intensified, and three days after Christmas all the ponds and shallow lochans were frozen hard. It so happened that the largest of these lay on Methven Moss, really only a winter-time overflow of the Cowgask Burn, a favourite venue for the sport of curling when weather conditions were propitious. If this coincided with Yuletide, when folk were in holiday mood, then a bonspiel, as a major curling gathering was called, was always held, expected by all. So John was more or less bound to organise such an event, the more so as he had always been keen on the roaring-game.

So, on Hogmanay, the last day of 1617, all Strathearn and district flocked to Methven Moss, some to curl, some to sledge, some to skate, others merely to watch, to meet folk, to gossip and feast—for it was traditional that great fires should be lit around the rims of the ponds, and beef, venison and mutton roasted on spits for all to partake, with hot stew for those who preferred it, and barrels of ale to wash it down.

This took a deal of arranging and served to keep John's mind from too much preoccupation with his lost love. Will Alexander entered into it all with much goodwill and even Vandervyk played his part.

Great crowds turned up, on a still, cold day of pale blue skies, gleaming white mountains and glittering ice, the ordinary folk mixing easily with the lairdly ones and gentry, children sliding and shouting, dogs barking, even fiddlers playing for dancing on the ice. There were skating contests, sledge-races, the sleds being pulled by teams of husky young men, skirling females aboard, tugs-of-war with more on their bottoms than on their feet, and other games adapted for the ice.

The curling, of course, was to be taken more seriously. Teams of four-a-side, under a captain or skip, competed from up and down the strath and all its side-glens, almost every estate and lairdship producing its quota. A dozen matches went on at once, each of two teams, the winners of each bout meeting other winners until the championship was decided. Each pair of teams competed on a rink forty yards long, playing from opposite ends, using heavy curling stones of polished granite, shaped like Gouda cheeses, each weighing up to fifty pounds, with iron handles. These were propelled over the ice, demanding much skill and no little force, with a fascinating ringing sound, rather in the manner of a game of bowls but with very different aspects and scoring. The skips were very much in command, ordering each shot and pointing out where a cannon-shot from one of his team could knock an opponent's stone off course. All contestants were armed with brooms or besoms, with which to run in front of their stones to sweep away snow, ice-crumbs or anything else which might impede, with shouts of "Soop! Soop!", cries of encouragement or groans of disappointment. The object was to get one or more of a team's stones as near centrally, as was possible, into a circle drawn on the ice at the head of the other's rink, forty yards away. It was all a noisy, inspiriting affair, demanding skill, energy and much liquid refreshment.

John was skip of his own Methven team. They had won their first two matches when, glancing up after sending down a devastating riding-stone to scatter two of his opponents' stones, he saw Janet Drummond standing watching him from only a few yards off. Their eyes locked.

For a few tense moments curling and all else was forgotten, the acclaim for his cannon-shot fallen on deaf ears, the demands of his team for what to do next ignored. The young woman, cheeks flushed with the cold, eyes gleaming, bare-headed but her person wrapped in furs, had never looked more lovely.

He forced himself back to present realities. Scores of eyes were upon him, possibly on her also. Any failure in his curling enthusiasm would be noted and discussed. He must behave normally, keep his mind on the game . . .

It is to be feared that John was rather less successful in that than he would have wished, however hard he tried, for after a good start, his team lost the match by a mere couple of points; and, moreover, lost the next one also, which put them out of the running for the final. Whether anyone, his team-mates in especial, recognised that the trouble started from those few moments was not to be known, although nobody actually reproached him.

Curling over, he looked for Janet but she was no longer where she had been standing. Against his own probably wiser judgment, he could not restrain himself from going in search of her amongst the crowd.

He saw her husband presently, talking with a group of Strathallan gentry, but he and David Drummond had never been friendly and he could avoid him without comment. He found the young woman at one of the fires, nibbling at a venison rib in company with his mother and Will Alexander, and was grateful that he could thus approach her without it being in any way noteworthy — which no doubt was Mary Gray's intention.

"Janet!" was all that he could find to say — and he kept his clenched fists close to his sides.

"John — you look well. It is good to see you," she greeted

219

him, voice steady, carefully controlled. "London life must serve you kindly."

"No," he said. "It does not."

"Oh, I am sorry to hear that. But . . . at least you can get back not infrequently. You came before, did you not?"

"Yes. Two months ago."

"I heard that you had been."

"I could not . . ." He left the rest of that unsaid.

"No. I understand."

"You are well?"

"Thank you, yes. But I have always been a healthy creature."

"Yes."

"For how long are you to be back at Methven?"

"Two or three days more. That is all."

"So soon to go? A pity."

"It is, yes. We have to return. To the King."

"A long journey. At this time of year."

"Yes."

Mary Gray came to their rescue. "John—have one of these roe ribs. Cooked to a turn. I am going to introduce Sir William to a bowl of our Strathearn stew, yonder. They may not make it in the Carse of Forth. We will be back." And she took Alexander's arm and moved away.

Janet and John searched each others' faces, eyes.

"You . . . you are more beautiful than ever!" he got out—which was hardly helpful, nor indeed what he had intended to say.

"Oh, John . . . !" she exclaimed, swallowing, her voice quivering now.

"I should not have said that. I am sorry. But—I could not help myself."

"I know . . . how it is. But we must not . . ."

"No. That is why I have not come. To see you. This time, nor the last. Hard as it has been. But that cannot stop me from thinking of you—nothing can do that. Even if I wished it."

"I should not say it—but I am glad."

"You are? Thank God!" He shook his head at himself, glancing around to ensure that no one was near enough to

220

have heard. He lowered his voice. "How do you fare, my dear? As, as you now are?"

She bit her lip. "Say that I fare . . . none so ill. Davie is a good man, and none so hard on me. But—do not call me dear, John—for I cannot bear it!"

"Very well. But nothing will make you otherwise, to me. I saw David back there. I could not speak to him."

"No? But it is not his fault, John. We must just thole it."

"More easy said than done . . ."

His mother and Alexander returned, timing judged, bearing bowls of the rich hot stew for four, with horn spoons.

"How are your parents, Janet?" Mary asked. "I heard that your mother was less than well . . . ?"

When they had finished their stew, the younger woman said that she must go find her husband; and, when John did not propose to escort her, Alexander gallantly offered his arm.

"Goodbye, John," Janet said. "It has been good to see you . . . I think!"

"Yes." He gripped her arm briefly, then all but pushed her away. "So much . . . unsaid."

She nodded. "I wish you very well. In England. A good journey. And, and . . ." She shook her head, and turned away.

Will Alexander led her off.

"Too much of this would not be good for either of you," Mary Gray observed, but kindly. "Come and talk to Master Graham, Sandy's father. About your Dumbarton . . ."

After that, John was for getting away from Strathearn as quickly as possible, and two days later they were on their way. Now they had another companion, Alexander Graham, Sandy, the parish-minister's son and John's friend from boyhood, whom he had persuaded, albeit doubtfully, to take on the position of Deputy-Keeper and Constable of Dumbarton Castle. This, despite the opposition of Sandy's father, who considered it far too responsible a position for a young man of Sandy's age who had no experience of life outside Strathearn. John had pointed out to both that, if *he* was old enough to be the King's Governor and Keeper, then Sandy, six months older, could surely be Deputy. Moreover, although admittedly this new role would call for rather different qualities than the work Sandy had been doing for the last years, that is combining farming with supervising the drainage of Methven Moss and the marketing of the estate's timber, nevertheless these duties had involved the management of many men and a good deal of judgment and responsibility. The principal requirement at Dumbarton was surely that whoever held the position should be responsible, trustworthy and able, and Sandy was all three.

So they rode south by west again, for the Clyde estuary, to eject Middlemas and install his replacement, before turning east for Edinburgh, there to install Vandervyk. John had a feeling that Will Alexander's presence might well be a help in the former, at least.

Just how much help he required, John had not quite anticipated. After spending the night at Aberfoyle, they called at Kilmahew, west of Cardross, to collect Robert Napier, the Sheriff-Depute, to provide due legality to the proceedings. Thus reinforced, even though Napier was scarcely a vehement character, they made the final five miles to Dumbarton and its fortress.

There, at the foot of the great rock, John experienced a very different reception from the previous occasion. The massive doors at the outer gatehouse of the perimeter wall were shut and barred. At first, he assumed that Middlemas had accepted his dismissal and departed without further ado, shutting up the castle behind him—until Sandy Graham pointed out the smoke which was rising from an inner gatehouse chimney, and also, it could be seen, from the hallhouse high on the hill. So the fortress was not in fact deserted.

Nobody came in answer to their shouts and bangings on the iron-bound door.

At a loss as to what to do, they presently went back down to the nearest houses, a pair of fishermen's cottages on the shore between castle and town, demanding of the occupants to know what was going on. The cottagers were reluctant to talk, obviously frightened of Middlemas and his crew;

but, when Sheriff Napier threatened them with the sanctions of the law, they capitulated and informed that four days earlier the Constable, Middlemas, had suddenly closed and barred the castle-doors, which had always stood open hitherto. There were about a dozen men within, with some women. The fisherfolk heard them emerge at night sometimes, no doubt to collect food and change the women; but otherwise the castle remained closed and silent.

"So-o-o." John commented. "They lock themselves in. A state of siege, almost! Four days ago, you say? I wonder why then? Middlemas must have heard, I think, that I was back at Methven. And guessed that I would be coming for him."

"This is crazy-mad!" Alexander declared. "The King's royal fortress held against the King's Governor and his Sheriff! And by a mere deputy-keeper. This is beyond belief!"

"He is a hard and violent man. I do not know why my father appointed him. But I did not judge him capable of this. I am at a loss what to do, if he will not come to speak with me."

"He may not hear our shouting. It seems a long way up to that large house."

"If we had a trumpet, to blow as summons?" Napier suggested.

"I fear that none of us carry trumpets around with us!" John said. "I suppose that it might be possible to find one in the town."

"A ladder," Sandy Graham proposed. "If we could get a ladder to scale this outer wall."

"It would scarcely look dignified for the Governor of Dumbarton to enter his fortress by climbing a ladder, man!"

"*You* need not do it. I will climb up. And Pate, here." Pate was Alexander's groom.

"I too," Vandervyk declared, laughing heartily, clearly finding the situation highly amusing.

"Well . . ."

They went back into the town, John at least feeling distinctly feeble. There they divided forces, Sandy and Pate to search for a long ladder, Napier to try to find a

223

trumpet, and the other three to enter an ale-house, to wait, in an effort at dignity. This affair was going to resound round Dumbarton inevitably.

They had quite a while to wait. A sufficiently long ladder to scale a twenty-foot-high wall was not readily to be found, and eventually Sandy and Pate came back with a pair of grinning stone-masons and two twelve-foot ladders which, bound together with rope, ought to serve. The Sheriff-Depute could not lay hands on a trumpet, either, but had uncovered an old Highland hunting-horn, which at least would make a loud noise, he averred.

Thus equipped, they headed back to the castle-rock—unfortunately now an enlarged company, a small crowd having assembled, to follow them, agog.

At the gatehouse, whilst the ladders were being tied together, sundry members of the party took turns at blowing on the horn, some more successfully than others. A variety of noises resulted, squawks, moans, gurgles and wails, few really impressive, although some were probably loud enough to reach the upper hallhouse. The delighted cheers of the onlookers, however, more than made up for the less-than-effective horn-blowing, and no doubt carried further.

No response was evident from the castle, to either.

The ladder ready, it was set up a few yards from the gatehouse, its topmost rung reaching to within a few inches of the wallhead. Sandy volunteered to climb first, and amidst renewed cheers started up. But he had not risen more than a few steps when two men appeared on the parapet-walk which topped the wall on the inner side and, leaning over, pushed the ladder sideways. It toppled and fell with a clatter, throwing Sandy Graham in a sprawling heap.

Great was the uproar.

The position was now clear, at least. There could be no pretence at not knowing nor hearing on the part of Middlemas and his minions. He was openly defying John's and the Sheriff's authority, prepared even to use violence apparently.

Whilst the ladder was being re-erected, John went close up to the gatehouse and cupped hands to mouth.

"William Middlemas," he shouted. "I, Sir John Stewart,

the King's duly-appointed Governor of this hold, charge you to open these gates to me, in the King's name. Or else suffer the dire consequences. Open, I say, in King James's royal name!"

There was no least reaction.

Pate the groom was now eager to try the ladder. He pointed out that, if others climbed close behind him, the extra weight could make it difficult for the men at the wallhead to push it over. Vandervyk—asserting loudly that he at least had plenty of weight—Sandy and even some of the townsfolk agreed to back him up. Pate started his climb.

But the people above recognised their danger and, before the groom was halfway up, with only Vandervyk able to be off the ground, they bent to their task, a third man coming to assist them now, and again managed to tip the ladder sidelong and over with apparent ease. Great was the fall, with Pate crashing down on top of the Dutchman, amidst yells. Two rungs where the ladders were joined, were sprung loose.

Vandervyk was winded, his laughter quenched for the moment, and Pate had hurt his leg. John called a halt on any more ladder-work, and returned to vocal efforts.

"I warn you, Middlemas, that you put yourself, and these fools who support you, in the greatest peril," he cried. "You cannot hope to continue to hold a royal fortress in defiance of the King's authority. You will be ejected in due course, and suffer the fullest penalty—all of you. Open now—or meet your doom hereafter!" He felt something of a fool shouting that.

Alexander joined in. "I am Sir William Alexander of Menstrie, Master of Requests to the King," he called up. "Do not think that you can expect any mercy if you do not yield up this castle at once. Do you wish to hang, for your insolent folly?"

He received no more response than had John.

Napier was not to be left out. "I am the Sheriff," he declared—and then, coughing slightly, amended that, in present company. "The Sheriff-Depute. This holding of the King's citadel against the King's Captain and Governor could be adjudged high treason. And you know the penalty for treason is death! Open, I command you."

They all might have been talking only to the ancient masonry for all the effect they appeared to have.

John spread his hands. "This is useless. They are not going to heed us. We are not going to get in, that is clear. What to do now, God knows!"

"What says the Sheriff? Can he bring armed force to bear? With the law being flouted?"

"I have no armed men, Sir William. I could enrol a few constables—but what would that serve? It would take a siege to reduce this place. I cannot mount that. It would have to be the Privy Council. And you, Sir John, will have more authority with the Privy Council?"

"Is that what I must do, then? Appeal to the Privy Council?"

"Yes. Or, I believe so. I have never known the like of this before. But I can see no other course, in law. The Council is bound to act, since it is the King's business."

"Very well. We are going to Edinburgh. I will demand that the Privy Council takes action against this madman. There is nothing more that we can do here . . ."

Authority, looking and feeling distinctly sheepish, made its way back to the town, the crowd vociferous behind.

The urge to be out of Dumbarton was now pronounced. Surely never had a Keeper of the proud fortress been so humiliated. But, before they left, John had Sandy sworn-in as Constable and Deputy-Keeper, before Sheriff Napier, so that at least in law he replaced Middlemas and had authority to act when he had any power to do so.

They then set off eastwards, taking Sandy with them meantime.

Installing Vandervyk at the Water of Leith mills, in comparison presented no problem. The two Germans appeared not in the least to resent the Dutchman's arrival, especially when they learned that he was to be concerned mainly with a training programme and the setting up of new mills.

Thereafter they spent a couple of days, in wintry weather, inspecting the Esk valley, from Dalkeith right up to the Pentland Hills, with the Dutchman and Germans, and settled on two or three suitable sites for mills, at Lasswade, Polton,

Roslin and Penicuik. Final decisions would be left to the papermakers.

This aspect of the King's business duly performed, John set about seeing to another, that of the royal fortress of Dumbarton. It was all very well to declare that he would involve the Scots Privy Council in the affair, but that august body consisted of prominent individuals who met only infrequently and were scattered over the face of the land. John was advised that the procedure was to see the Secretary of the Council, in the first place, to have the matter put on the agenda of the next meeting. Nobody suggested that there would be any very swift and decisive action.

The Secretary proved to be James Primrose, a lawyer and small Fife laird, renowned for his enormous family of nine-teen and the fact that his eldest daughter had been wed to the late George Heriot, the King's banker and crony. Primrose, however, appeared presently to be at his West Fife property of Burnbrae, in the Stewartry of Culross; so John had to make another journey, Alexander, having nothing better to do, accompanying him.

They found the Secretary to be a fussy, tetchy little man with a notably downtrodden wife, living in a tumbledown house on a small estate which appeared to consist of little more than a steep wooded valley down which a stream tumbled in almost a prolonged waterfall, hence the name of Burnbrae, flanked by only one or two meagre fields. He was not really helpful, and as good as stated that it was the Keeper's and Captain's business to maintain due discipline at Dumbarton and keep his Deputy in order, not to come bothering the Privy Council. When John demanded how he was to take order with Middlemas, barricaded and defiant inside the fortress, the other shrugged and said that this ought never to have been allowed to develop so far. If Sir John was incapable of keeping the castle for the King in good order, or found it impossible to do so from far away London, then he ought to resign the office to someone better placed.

In a sneaking sort of way John agreed with this, but could not say so. The fact remained, he insisted, that this royal strength was being held unlawfully against due authority, to the hurt of King James; and the Sheriff-Depute concerned asserted that it was a matter for the Privy Council. Would Master Primrose, as Secretary, take the necessary steps to bring the matter before the Council? Or must His Majesty, in London, be informed of this non-co-operation and take the necessary steps from there?

Will Alexander backed up this strong line in suitably authoritative fashion, and he could have a notably lofty way with him; and the little lawyer testily acceded. But he would have to take down a proper deposition of the case, with the complainer's assertions and relevant substantiatory deponings by witnesses. Also the Sheriff-Depute's observations. All this could certainly not be done here and now, and must await his, Primrose's, return to Edinburgh the following week. The due processes of law had to be observed.

It is to be feared that John made less than courteous reply to this. But Primrose was not to be moved. The two friends parted from their host in no great mutual esteem.

So they had to kick their heels in Edinburgh for quite some time. However they lodged very comfortably with Lady Mar and found sufficient to occupy their time pleasantly enough. As Alexander pointed out, they were almost certainly much better entertained here than if they were back at James's court in London. They took the opportunity—although Primrose undoubtedly would not have approved—to inform two prominent members of the Privy Council who happened to be in Edinburgh, one of them the Chancellor himself, the former Lord Fyvie and now Earl of Dunfermline, of the Dumbarton situation, and were more sympathetically heard than by the Secretary. Sheriff Napier was duly summoned from Kilmahew.

Eventually they got their depositions, deponings and witnesses' statements duly set down, signed, sealed and certified. How long it would be before relevant action would be taken was not indicated.

There appeared to be nothing more that they could do, meantime. Snow held up their departure for a few more days. Then they started on their long return-journey to London in uninviting weather conditions, duties performed.

12

So it was March before the travellers got back to Whitehall—only to find that the King and court were at Theobalds Park again in Hertfordshire. They had to turn around and retrace some of their steps.

Although scarcely the time of year for serious hunting, the breeding-season, James was not to be denied his sport, and considered that falconry could be pursued satisfactorily at any time. But the day of their arrival at Theobalds, in blustering rain and wind, even James stayed indoors. Nevertheless, sport was still his preoccupation it seemed, only the theory rather than the practice—and, as it affected the laws of the land, oddly enough. Something being called the Declaration of Sports was being debated, as a mixture of judgment and exercise in government, and sundry authorities had been summoned to discuss and comment. The said authorities had been at Theobalds for a week but had had to kick their heels most of the time, the King being more concerned with the practice than the theory, in this instance, and the weather having permitted the former in preference to the latter. But this cold, wet day was apt enough for the business. They had had one session in the morning, it appeared, before the travellers arrived—and Ludovick of Lennox had looked in on it and been mildly intrigued. He suggested to his son and Alexander that they could do worse than attend the afternoon session and learn how their liege-lord decided on matters of state policy. They could possibly make their due report to James thereafter. He explained that the question was to do with religion, strangely enough; churchmen's attitudes varied on the subject of engaging in sports on Sundays, and the Puritan element was lobbying parliament, where they were fairly strongly represented, to forbid all Sunday sports and games.

James personally had other views, indeed hunted and hawked regularly on the Sabbath, after due attendance at divine service, with no inhibitions.

When the Duke ushered the two younger men into a crowded dining-hall of the palatial mansion, it was not into any very evident atmosphere or judicial enquiry nor yet learned debate. Great log-fires blazed and crackled in the two huge fireplaces, and tables were laden with bottles, flagons and beakers. Clearly the discussion was going to be thirsty work, at least for the non-Puritans. The company assembled was a very mixed one, dignitaries of the Established Church of England in soberly rich garb, Romish clerics in cassocks and birettas, Presbyterian divines in stern black-and-white, Puritans in aggressively mouse-like anonymity, and courtiers in padded and slashed extravagance and every colour under the sun. The noise was remarkable.

Knowing that James would be in no hurry to appear, after a mid-day nap, Ludovick brought them in a good half-hour after the session was due to start. But even so it was almost another half-hour before the King tottered in, leaning on Steenie's shoulder—whom he had recently promoted to be Marquis of Buckingham and Lord High Admiral, much to the latter's disappointment and more so to his mother's, who had wanted him to be a duke. As the noise died away, James could be heard telling his favourite not to sulk and that this debate might well be good for his young soul—if the good God had seen fit to lend him one . . .

It took some further time for the monarch to settle himself at the dais-table, test the various wines and spirits on offer, fill his beaker, tip forward his high hat to scratch vigorously at the back of his head, and eye all from under his brim, critically.

"Aye, then," he said, at last. "Let's hear you. And you'll oblige me by talking mair sense and less whummle than you did this morning. I never heard so much daft-like blethers! A' we learned was that there is mair folly talked in the name o' religion than even Almighty God could have jaloused! Archbishop—you perhaps will talk sense?"

John knew George Abbot, Archbishop of Canterbury,

slightly, for he was a friend of Queen Anne's and visited her frequently—which may not have been a recommendation in the monarch's eyes. He was a large, heavy, slow-spoken man.

"Sire," he said, "this morning we heard the differing views of what the Lord's Day should represent. Few agreed on all aspects—save that it was essentially a day for the worship of God. Some saw it as *only* that with nothing else to be engaged on by any—this, if necessary, to be enforced by the laws of this realm. Others saw it as a day of rest, celebrating the Biblical account of the Creation, when the Creator is said to have rested on the seventh day. Others again saw it as a continuation of the Jewish Sabbath and would apply to it all the exercises and also the bans and prohibitions of that ancient and non-Christian people's worship of Jehovah . . ."

"Aye, man—aye," James interrupted. "Just so. But we had a' that this morning. Guidsakes, we dinna need to hear tell o' it again!"

"No, Majesty. But bear with me, I pray you, for just a little longer. Some of us, I think, need to marshal our thoughts from this morning's much talking, to remind ourselves what are the options before us when we make our decisions . . ."

"*My* decisions, my lord—mine! As the Lord Christ's Regent and Vicar in this realm, and head o' its Church, *I* mak the decisions, I'd remind you and all. You are here only to advise."

The Archbishop inclined his head slightly, but made no comment.

"Well, man—well! Proceed."

"Yes, Sire. Still others this morning appeared to see Sunday as a day for recreation and enjoyment, with worship only a very modest part of it, if at all. So there are widely opposing views, and men will continue to hold these opposing views, no doubt, whatever we here decide . . . or advise. As I see it, that is not our real concern here. What we are concerned with is to draw up a Declaration as to what should be the *realm's* attitude to behaviour on the Lord's Day, whereby basic guidance shall be given to all, but none shall be able to enforce their own particular views on others, save by honest persuasion. Thus men's consciences left free in this matter. We are not here to decide Holy Church's views on the matter—although the Church's attitude must, I say, be taken into account—but only the state's, since the matter will come before parliament. This morning, many seemed to have forgotten this."

There were murmurs amongst the company.

"I said a' that myself when I opened this perquisition and postulation this morning," James observed severely. "Lord help us—we're no' to go havering ower the same ground again, are we? See you—these attitudes we a' heard a sufficiency about can be shown to be mainly untenable and fallacious—aye, fallacious. Item—" he ticked off his points on long and slender but distinctly grubby fingers—"a day for the worship o' God. That it is, and maun be. But nae man, even your maist perfervid Puritan, some o' the by-ordinar holy Reformers in Scotland, or even the Pope in Rome, can worship God a' day without cease, for twelve hours or mair. It's no' possible. So what do they dae for the rest o' the hours? Stare at the wall? Plague their wives? Fill their bellies? Or what? Item: The day o' rest and recreation. Some would celebrate that in their beds, alone or wi' another—aye, recreation, indeed! Then there is recreation o' the mind, as well as o' the body. And, if the good God created this world in six days, they must ha' been gey long days, each a wheen thousand years. So the seventh day would be as long—you'll no' deny that? You'll no' hae us resting for the remainder o' our lives? Forby, the Creator didna start again on the Monday and create it a' once mair, each week! So we'll no' be slaves to siklike theoretics. Item: The Jews' Sabbath. I'm thinking that maist o' the Sabbatarians who never get past the Auld Testament, hate the said Jews and fair persecute them! The first to cast yon stane the Lord Christ spoke about. They canna have it both ways. So there's the matter. *Graviora quaedam sunt remedia periculis!*"

There was a suitable silence after this profound exposition, whilst James deservedly slaked his thirst.

Sir Francis Bacon, recently created Viscount Verulam and Lord High Chancellor, spoke up. "Now that we are all

232

refreshed at the very Fountain of Knowledge, as at the Source of Wit and Learning, it but remains for us to ask what need has His Majesty for any guidance or advice from such as ourselves in this, or any other, matter? I feel sure that parliament will now be entirely informed on the essence of the business and able to take the required steps. It seems to me that there is little more to be said."

The King narrowed those great liquid eyes of his and tapped a tattoo on the table-top. He had on more than one occasion expressed his doubts about Francis Bacon, declaring him to be too clever by half, reminding him of that other clever rogue, the Master of Gray, now happily gone where a sarcastic tongue would serve him little good.

"My Lord High Chancellor goes ower fast," he said. "We have yet to consider which sports and recreations are to be permissible on Sundays. Or better, which are not. Which would tend to be an offence in the eyes o' maist reasonable men. I do not say in the eyes o' God, mind—for, if a sport or recreation isna an offence to God during the week, I dinna see why it should be so on a Sunday, provided that the sporter or recreationist has attended his public worship and service to the Almighty beforehand. But men are apt to be less reasonable than their Creator—even such as the Lord Chancellor and Archbishop perhaps—and sadly we must legislate for men, no' God! Especially in this England! You agree, my lord Archbishop?"

Cautiously Abbot made a non-committal gesture.

"Aye, well—it seems to me that the dividing-line, as it were, must be between the individual and the crowd or concourse. What causes an assembly and heightens passions can provoke an uproar and public upset, unsuitable at any time but especially so on the Lord's Day. So no horse-racing for wager, no prize-fighting for purses. And siklike ploys. Again, no public wrestling, quarter-staffery or football—the which can arouse fell to-do. Aye, and cock-fighting. But a decent bit game o' golf, now, is guid for the soul, in that it breeds patience and a proper recognition o' a man's ain shortcomings—it does that! Likewise archery, flying a bit hawk or falcon, bowling, putting the weight—although you dinna do much o' that in England nor yet tossing the caber or even curling. Och, you're right backward at the sports, I've discovered. Aye, and there is tennis and quoiting and . . ."

"Shame! Shame on you, I say!" a quivering cry interrupted from the back of the room. "Tennis! Quoits! Bowling! On the Sabbath! Here is very damnation! To provoke the All Highest. The very promptings of Satan himself . . . !"

There was uproar at such outburst against the monarch's observations. But not from James Stewart himself. That man appeared to find something like satisfaction in this eruption. He even grinned.

When he could make himself heard, he spread those eloquent hands. "You a' perceive now how these Puritans are without reason—for I swear yon was a Puritan. Was that Christian charity, I ask you? Some might say it was contumacious and even subversive, aye. Subversive, if no' actually treasonable towards mysel', the Lord's Anointed. *I'm* no' asserting so, mind. But in case some here judge the speaker to be but a puir witless loon and no' representative o' other Puritans, hear this. I call upon one Maister Edmund Troutbeck, of Bramham in Yorkshire, to give evidence."

A fine-looking elderly man, dressed in good country fashion, moved forward through the press, and bowed to the King.

"Your Majesty, my lords and gentlemen," he said, in very Yorkshire voice. "Although no trouble-maker, I deem it my simple and loyal duty to give this evidence of shameful and disgraceful conduct relative to what we have been here discussing. I squire a few acres at Bramham Manor and attend regularly at divine service at the parish church there, where the Vicar, the Reverend William Clough, is one of these Puritans. And on many occasions I have had to listen to the most distressing statements from the pulpit, to my extreme displeasure and that of other parishioners. On one occasion in especial, on the first day of August last, I was so incensed at what I heard that I went home after service and wrote down what the Vicar had said, and later had it witnessed to by a neighbour, William Oglethorpe, also present at church. Have I Your Majesty's permission to read out some part of what was said at service?"

"Aye, man Troutbeck—read you."

"I warn all, it makes ill reading, Sire. Here is some part of the Sunday's discourse from the pulpit. Thus: 'For the Father, the Son and the Holy Ghost, I care not for them all three a rye or brown bread toast!' Later, he went on . . ."

Squire Troutbeck thus speedily had to pause, so great was the noise provoked, some of it laughter admittedly but most shock and outrage. The King had to bang on his table for quiet.

"Later in the same discourse, Majesty, the Vicar went on: 'I am a priest after the order of Melchisideck; and you . . .' meaning, Sire, his congregation, ' . . . you are devils after the order of Beelzebub.' Hear me out, my lords and gentles —there is more. He was preaching on the text, Thou Shalt Keep my Sabbath, and said: 'Now indeed the King of Heaven doth bid you keep His Sabbath and reverence His Sunday. Now the King of England is a mortal man and he bids you break it. Choose you whether of them you will follow. Now I will tell you the reason why the King of England makes laws against God's laws in that behalf. The reason is the safety of his own body in his progresses.' Yes, Sire, so he said, and more railing than that, which I did not write down. As Will Oglethorpe here present will vouch for."

In the renewed uproar, James called upon Squire Oglethorpe to homologate.

A squat man, almost as broad as high, shouted out in what was almost a farmyard bellow that what Squire Troutbeck had said was God's own truth. He added that Vicar Clough had further said that it was more than the King could do to make such laws. And that in ancient times kings were subject to the laws of priests and not priests to the laws of kings.

More noise, after which James asked Troutbeck if he was finished.

"Only a little more, Your Majesty. When one member of the congregation, an aged lame man of good repute, rose to make protest there and then—as myself did think to do—Vicar Clough shouted him down, saying: 'Thou bald-pated buzzard, thou wilt go to the Devil like a bald buzzard! Thou goest limping upon the earth but thou wilt go leaping to the Devil!' I could say more, Sire, but believe this is sufficient."

"Sufficient indeed, Maister Troutbeck. I thank you. How say you, my lords? Do we tak cognisance o' the views o' siklike gentry in our Declaration on Sports and Recreation?"

The anticipated answer was loud and prolonged, although one or two voices could be heard asserting that such sentiments were scarcely typical of Puritan clergymen. James asked the Archbishop whether he had any comments to add.

Abbot could do no other than declare that what they had just heard was disgraceful and as offensive to Almighty God as it was to the King's Majesty and all decent men. He deplored the Puritan element in the Church and believed that such should indeed be expelled from the Church of England. But he could not believe that there were many parish incumbents so shamefully unsuitable as this. He would write to his brother of York—unfortunately sick and so unable to be present this day—and urge him to hail the man Clough before the Ecclesiastical Commission for the archdiocese of York, where no doubt he would be duly and drastically dealt with.

"Aye, you do that, Archbishop," James nodded. "And now, my lords and friends, I jalouse that I have savoured a sufficiency o' views and advisings on this matter o' Sunday observance, to enable me to put a Declaration before yon parliament o' mine. My clerks will draw up such document, and nae doubt the good Archbishop and the Lord Chancellor and others concerned will add their supporting signatures. So—that's plenties, aye plenties, for the day. Now—refreshment awaits you. And fell needed, I swear, after a' that ill and seditious report. Set to, my lords and gentlemen, set to . . ."

Ludovick of Lennox turned to his son. "I promised you that you would see how our liege-lord manages the affairs of state. I swear that the late Will Shakespeare himself could not have stage-managed this affair better! No doubt he brought these Yorkshiremen all the way down here precisely for this meeting. James gets his way, as ever. Save perhaps with parliament. We have yet to see how this English parliament will take the issue. He is constantly at war with it. Now—do you wish to make your report to him? Come, we will try him . . ."

But the King was surrounded now by lofty folk and, though the Duke was able to push his way close, and indeed got Steenie Villiers to tug James's sleeve for attention, the monarch was clearly in no mood for listening to any account of his Scottish affairs. He did, however, nod briefly to John and Will Alexander, said that he had noted their presence there, and told John to wait on him next day at the hawking, if the weather permitted, when he would hear what he had to say. Then he flapped them away.

The following morning, grey but still and not raining, the royal hawking-party set off at first light—quite a small company, for falconry is no sport for large numbers and most of the court were glad to lie late in their beds. This apparently included Will Alexander, John noted.

James, in the saddle, was a different man, impatient, decisive, less wordy. He ignored John, paying more attention to his head-falconer and the men in charge of the birds than to such of his courtiers as had turned out. Indeed he set off before most others were ready and mounted—which was awkward, since nobody knew just where he was heading.

John, who was hawkless, positioned himself close behind the monarch, with two under-falconers and half-a-dozen hooded birds and a few dogs. He soon found himself out-of-sight of any others in the woodland. It looked as though this was not to be the usual competitive and wagering hawking.

They were heading south-by-west, presumably for a specific destination. There were no lochs in this part of the world and there was no point in flying hawks in woodland, where they would just disappear. So they must be making for some open space.

After three miles or so they came to an uninviting area of swamp and sedge, with only a few scrub hawthorns, the vistas sufficiently wide for falconry—part of Hadley Wood, according to the Earl of Montgomery, who along with two or three others had now caught up with them.

James apparently was out to test and compare his own hawks today, not to challenge others, and required no gallery of spectators and critics to assist, quite brusquely dismissing such of the company as had managed to follow him, flapping them away with the declaration that surely Enfield Chase was extentatious enough for them all to have their sport without ruining his?

As the courtiers departed, in some doubts, John was equally doubtful as to whether he was to stay or go. But the King told him to wait that, since his faithless dog Steenie had not seen fit to accompany him this day, too great now that he was a marquis, he would just have to make do with his mere knight Johnnie Stewart as dog, for the nonce.

It was not long before John discovered that being the King's dog—an endearment he often used for George Villiers—could have a fairly literal translation. He, in fact, with one of the under-falconers, was to act dog-handler, to take the animals and use them to beat out the scrub woodland to leeward of the swamp area to put up the game. But it had to be done carefully, he was left in no doubt, only one strip of wood roused at a time, so that all the birds did not fly up at once, and the sport was decently spaced out. So the dogs had to be kept under strict control and not allowed to go splurging off, spoiling all. It was John's turn to be flapped away.

Fortunately he was used to hunting-dogs, at Methven, and knew how to keep them approximately in order. But he was not clad for ploutering about in scrub and undergrowth, especially when it transpired that this woodland was itself not much better than swamp and he had to splash and wade much of the time—which did not do his fine new thigh-length doe-skin riding-boots any good at all. He had to quarter that covert methodically, putting up duck and other waterfowl and herons—deer too, and lesser creatures, but these could be ignored—but had to pause whenever the head-falconer blew his horn, for the hawks could not cope with constant flighting, and renew his efforts when signalled again.

It was scarcely suitable employment for a knight, and Governor of Dumbarton Castle at that; but since the King had made him both and this was the King's command, John could not very well complain.

It made a slow and slaistery business, for there was a lot of this marshy scrub; but at long last the horn blew a succession of short blasts for the recall, and thankfully the weary beaters made their way back to the monarch at the horses, heavy-footed, mud-covered and wet.

James, still in the saddle, eyed his young kinsman critically. "You sent them out ower many at a time, man," he complained. "Confusing the hawks, just. I didna want *flocks* o' ducks and the like, but ones and twos. You should have kent that. And you're right clarty, fair covered in glaur! What have you been at?"

John controlled his voice with difficulty. "Those trees are growing out of water and mud, Sire. It is all flooded. And the birds are *in* flocks, not conveniently in ones and twos! Nor do I think that the dogs can count!"

"Hey, hey—hoity-toity, eh? You'll no' speak that way wi' *me*, your liege-lord, Johnnie Stewart! Watch your words."

"Yes, Sire." That was scarcely humble, however.

James eyed him thoughtfully, then without another word, wheeled his horse round and spurred off. Hastily John had to mount and follow.

The King now seemed to be heading approximately back on their tracks, towards Theobalds; but at a sort of cross-roads of woodland-rides, in the depths of Enfield Chase, he drew rein. There he sent off the falconers and the dogs, left-handed, for the palace, whilst he turned to the right, beckoning John up to ride at his side.

"There's a bit place I ken, no' far frae here, where we can get a sup o' quite fair ale," he disclosed, in confidential fashion now. "You'll can do wi' a sup, Johnnie? And we dinna want crowds, thirsty crowds. I aim to hear what you've been at, up in Scotland. And nae long ears to listen to us, mind."

"There was nothing very secret, Sire . . ."

"That's a' *you* ken, laddie! Yon Frankie Bacon, who's too

239

clever by half, is making a great stramash o' this o' the monopolies, a right campaign. He's gathered a great faction in the Commons against the monopolies, envious, aye envious o' their wealth. I made him a peer to get him oot o' the Commons, but he's still at it. Mind, I've no love for the monopolists my ain self, especially as so muckle o' the siller goes to the Howards. But I wouldna like our bit paper monopoly to go doon wi' the rest. That's why I wanted it a' shifted to Scotland. Bacon's no' going to be content until the parliament here maks monopolies illegal, just. But they canna legislate for Scotland, Johnnie—no' for Scotland. So we'll keep the paper-making there, see you—and mak a bit honest siller for oorsels oot o' it, as well as paper!"

"But, Sire, if the monopolies are to be put down here, then *anybody* can make and sell paper in England. Who will want the Scots paper?"

"Och, it will be a gey long whilie before that, man. There's naebody in England who kens how to mak paper, for a start. Why I wanted yon Vandervyk man awa' north. They'd have to bring in men frae the Low Countries and the Germanies—and that's something I can maybe discourage, eh? Forby, setting up mills is no sae easy, as you ken—aye, and wi' pure water less plentiful here than in Scotland— och, the rivers in this flat land are little better than stanks, just. Na, na, there'll be nae English paper-making in my lifetime. And after that, God help them, wi' our Charlie king! Noo—this o' Scotland . . . ?"

So John gave his account of activities and progress on the Water of Leith and the River North Esk, the which appeared to find approximate royal favour. He was moving on to the more serious matter of Dumbarton Castle, over which James appeared to be supremely uninterestd, when they rode out of the woodland into an open area where were three houses, one most evidently an inn. The King led the way to this, dismounted, and tottered inside, leaving John to see to the horses.

When he followed indoors it was to find the King already drinking from a tankard and eyeing the only other customer, a small, bright-eyed and bewhiskered character, roughly dressed, with a sack and leather tool-bag at his feet, also drinking deep and considering James with equal interest. John was ignored, so ordered ale from the serving-wench for himself.

Presently the King, noting how the other man smacked his lips after each mouthful with such obvious relish, spoke.

"See you, honest fellow—you mak a great splutter and splash! What's in yon jug o' yours that's so much better than in mine, eh? This I've got is gey thin stuff. Thinner than last time, I vow."

The other grinned. "By the Mass, Master, 'tis the house's best brown nappy. Have they given you the less?"

"I declare they have, a plague on it! You, wench—where is she? John—find her . . ."

Their fellow customer beat him to it, however. He emptied his tankard in a great gulp and then banged it on the table to such effect that it brought the buxom serving-girl from the back premises, all but running, her ample breasts bouncing.

"Three pints more of the special brown nappy, lass—and make them as full as your paps!" the fellow cried. "These friends will drink with me. See to it. The best brown."

"Na, na, man," James began. "This shall be *my* pleasure . . ."

"Quiet, you!" he was interrupted. "'Tis mine. Your doublets, friends, may look finer than mine—if not so much cleaner! But I swear my two pence is as good as yours, or any man's!"

"On my soul, there's truth in that!" The King whinnied a laugh, and went to sit down at the other's table. After a brief hesitation, John did likewise.

The girl brought them three brimming tankards slopping on a tray, and was rewarded with six pennies and a pinched bottom—for which she delivered a playful slap as change.

"My, oh my," James said, rolling his great eyes. "You're nane sae blate, man. You ken what's what, I can see that."

"A tinker learns what's what wi' his mother's milk, or don't survive! Here's to you, friend—Scotchman by your voice or none!"

James shot a warning glance at John. "And to you, honest man," and raised his tankard in turn. "A tinkler, eh? Yon'll be a rough trade?"

"None so rough, I'll thank you to allow. There's many rougher, by the Mass. It's honester than some! And yours, my masters?"

"Ah." Another glance at John. "Ah, paper. Paper, aye. This young friend o' mine is consairned wi' the making and selling o' paper. Isna that so, Johnnie?"

John nodded, unspeaking.

"Paper, is it? You will not sell much paper in Enfield town, friend, I think. You'd do better mending pots!"

"Aye, maybe." The King raised his tankard again. "Here's to the tinkler's trade."

"And to the paper-trade—though I'd say God help it!"

They drank to that. Then James looked at John. "Your turn," he said.

John eyed his ale for a moment, then raised it. "To King James!" he said solemnly.

The monarch pursed slack lips. But their companion nodded.

"I'll drink to that. They do say that he's none so far away—a-hunting the deer in Enfield-town Chase this day. He's an odd gudgeon, they tell me, this King. Fonder o' the deer than some o' his lords, they do say. Not that I'd blame him for that. You can have all the lords in this kingdom, for me!"

"The deer are out o' season," James reproved. Then, in a different voice. "So you prefer your King—gudgeon was it?—though he may be, to your English lords?"

"That I do. I'm told he's a middlin' honest man, wi' some care for the poor folk. Have you heard that?"

"Precisely! Exactly!" the King exclaimed approvingly. "Or, that is, so it is purported."

"I wish that I could set eyes on him, the while he's in this Enfield Chase. Think you there is any chance? I've travelled the land, and other lands too, but I've never seen a king in all my born days."

James cackled. "'Deed, aye! 'Deed, aye! Can you bestride a horse, my fine tinkler? Then you'll mount behind my

Johnnie here, and I'll bring you into the presence o' your sovereign–lord Jamie! I ken where he is. How say you?"

The other stared. "How can *you* know? The Chase is big. They could be anywhere . . ."

"Och, I hae a right good notion where they will be. There's no' that many bits o' this wood that's clear enough for hawking—and that's what the King will be at. They'll be down yon Bush Hill way, tak my word for it. Come—drink up, and we'll be on our way."

Doubtfully as to two–thirds of the party, they moved outside, and John was peremptorily ordered to help the tinker with his clanking sack and leather tool–bag—which the other protested he could manage perfectly well on his own. At the horses, John was further told to mount and take up the sack of pots before him on the saddle, as there would be no room for it when the tinker was up behind.

If John could not actually protest, however sour he looked, their new friend was under no such compulsion. He declared that he had not really meant that he was all that keen to see the King, that he had no wish to put their young friend out, that he was not used to sitting on horses' rumps, and that it was time that he was on his road to Barnet anyway.

But James, once launched on a project, was no easy man to counter, king or none. "Up, you!" he commanded, more regally than suited a paper–merchant.

"But, Master—he'll be surrounded by all his lords. We'll not get near him. Besides, how shall we tell him from them? They'll all be fine as peacocks."

"You'll see, man," he was told. "The King will have his head covered, the lords will all bare theirs." And, tapping his hat on more firmly, James trotted off.

John had no option but to help up the tinker, tools on his back, and balancing the pots and pans before him as best he might, rode after his monarch.

James, as before, seemed to know where he was going, south–by–west through the greenwood, by rides and bridle–paths. It was his own property, of course and he had hunted here for years. Beyond an initial grumble or two, the tinker, jolting about behind, held his peace.

After some twenty minutes, the land, although still tree-covered, began to rise slightly but steadily, and soon the trees were thinning out to a fairly bare, downlike ridge. It was not much of an eminence by John's standards but apparently this was Bush Hill. Beyond, the land sank again to a level area dotted with small ponds. And down there, sure enough, horsemen could be seen, and dogs.

They trotted down, and were soon spotted. The King's unmistakable posture in the saddle identified him while they were still some distance off, and hunting-horns started to sound. So there was quite a group of courtiers assembled when the odd little party came up, and promptly all hats were doffed. John had to pull off his own flat velvet cap dutifully.

The tinker behind him scanned the richly-clad throng looking for a man still wearing a hat, and could see none.

"He is not here," he said. "The King."

"Oh, but he is that," James assured.

"Then where is he? They are all dressed so fine."

"That's only their bodies, man. 'Tis their heads that signify. I told you, did I no'—he who's covered."

"But they are all uncovered."

"On my soul—so they are! Then . . . then it must be you or me, eh? You, or me. We are the only two wearing our hats."

The tinker stared, appalled, as it dawned. "Is . . . is it true?" he whispered, at John's ear.

"True, yes. This is the King. I would have told you, but he signed me not to."

The man groaned and slipped to the ground, tool-bag and all, and made a grab at his sack. Clearly he was going to bolt.

"Na, na, my mannie—wait you!" James said. "Come here, tinkler."

In a panic now, the other hesitated, and then ran forward to fall down on his knees beside the King's horse. "Mercy, lord . . . !" he gasped.

"Tush, fellow—what's to do?" the monarch asked, innocently. "Up wi' you. Or . . . na, na, bide there. You'll do fine there, on your knees. Aye. Johnnie—here to me. Gie's

244

yon bit dirk. It's no' a sword, but it'll hae to serve. Forby, he's only a tink, the mannie."

The kneeling man let out a wail.

John handed over his dagger, all that any of them might carry in the royal presence, save Ludovick with his sword. Seeing it, the tinker cowered back, hands up beseechingly.

"Still, man—still!" James exclaimed. "Or you could get hurt. Bide where you are. What do they ca' you? Your name, man?"

"John, lord," the other got out. "John o' the Dale, lord. Spare me. I'm an honest man, I swear, lord. But a mender of pots and kettles. Never harmed any . . ."

"Wheesht, you—wheesht! Come closer, John o' the Dale—I canna reach doon to you, there, can you no' see?" With a sudden swoop down with the dagger, bending low from the saddle, the King made a pass at the kneeling man's shoulder, barely managing to touch it as the other shrank away.

"Och, you're a right fearty sumph!" Majesty declared. 'But it'll hae to serve. Like the dirk. Guid enough for the likes o' you! *Exitus acta probat*, eh? Arise, Sir John o' the Dale—and be as guid a knight as you ken how! As guid as any o' these, I'll be bound!" And he scanned the astonished company of courtiers critically. "Guidsakes, yes! On your feet, man—did you no' hear? Tak up your pack. Aye, we a' hae to tak up oor packs and paiks in this life, mysel' as well as you, mind, even though it's a different pack! Go you to my house o' Tibbalds, and tell them that you're Sir John o' the Dale, new-knighted. And they'll gie you royal pots to mend for the rest o' your days! You're the first man ever bought me a pint o' brown nappy!"

The bewildered new knight rose but stood as though rooted to the spot.

James thrust the dirk back at John, blade first, and wheeled his horse round. "Enough o' this," he jerked. "Come you, Johnnie Stewart—I'm hungry."

As they rode back towards the palace, the King beckoned John closer and at the same time waved more illustrious folk back.

"You'll be wondering why I knighted yon tink, I've nae

245

doubt? If you're like your faither, maist like you'll be judging that it wasna weel done, debasing the honour o' knighthood for a stupid bit whim. Eh?"

Since that was exactly what John had thought, he could scarcely deny it. "I . . . ah . . . no doubt Your Majesty had your own reasons," was the best that he could do.

"I had that. Just as I had when I knighted *you*, Johnnie Stewart! Mind that. See you, there are two-three fine fowl in this company behind us who reckon that they are entitled to honours frae me. No' for anything byordinar they've done, but because o' *who* they are. Yon Jermyn wants a knighthood for his son—and forby reckons he himsel' should be upped frae baron to viscount. He's aye at Steenie to persuade me—pays Steenie guid siller for it! And Harry Cooper, him that's Deputy-Wardrober, is another—he would bribe any close to me to get him made *Sir* Harry. Och, I ken fine what they're at. So I teach them that I honour who *I* wish, no' them. And that nane can rely on advancement because o' who or what they may be. You tell Vicky that, or he'll be at me again ower this, for certain sure. He's a' right auld wifie, some ways, is Vicky Stewart!"

"He . . . he greatly regards Your Majesty."

"Aye, weel—maybe. Anyway—keep you an eye on our tinkler-knight, if he bides about Tibbalds. I may hae uses for the likes o' him . . ."

13

Strangely, it was not at court but on one of his trips to
St Paul's, to keep in touch with the Merchant Venturers
over the Scots paper-supply situation, that John got his first
news about Sir Walter Ralegh. He found the great church
buzzing with talk and speculation, most of which was incomprehensible to him. He knew of the great, veteran wit
and explorer, of course, one of the few surviving ornaments
of the Elizabethan galaxy; knew that he was out of the
country; but had not heard him referred to of late. He
sought enlightenment from Elias Woolcombe.

That cheerful character told him, almost with relish, that
it looked like disaster for Ralegh this time. That his ship,
from the Americas, had limped into a West Country port,
and with a tale of woe. The Orinoco adventure was a
failure, it seemed—and heads would fall, Ralegh's own
amongst the first, for sure. Not wishing to betray his
ignorance, John did not question further. He had heard
nothing of this from his father—but presumably these
Merchant Venturers had sources of information denied to
others.

Back at Whitehall, he told the Duke—and was surprised
at that man's reaction, he who was usually so imperturbable.
Ludovick was much upset. If this was true, he said, there
would be trouble, serious trouble.

When his son expressed incomprehension, the other explained. Ralegh was a great man, yes, but not always wise.
In 1604 he had got himself involved in the so-called Main
Plot, a conspiracy to depose James and put Arabella Stewart,
his cousin, daughter of Darnley's brother, on the throne. It
was a stupid business, and came to nothing—save for the
deaths of the major plotters. Ralegh himself was condemned
to death but the sentence was never carried out—mainly

because James feared popular anger, for Ralegh was then beloved by the people, a notable figure. So he had been merely confined in the Tower, a long imprisonment, but in not too grievous conditions. John must have heard of that?

It was James's chronic shortage of money which got Ralegh out of the Tower. He came up with a scheme for an expedition to the Orinoco River, in South America. He had been there in 1595 and had heard about an Indian city, up-river, where the streets were literally paved with gold—Manoa, it was called. All the natives knew of this place, apparently. If he could sail out there and take his ships up the great river, he could fill them with gold, silver and jewels sufficient to solve all the King's money problems.

James had been doubtful. George Heriot, his banker, had advised against it as an impractical dream. Also James's friend, the Count Gondomar, the Spanish Ambassador, who saw it as an infringement on the King of Spain's territories. But, as the financial situation got worse, and the Scottish visit was planned—and going to cost a great deal—parliament in its running battle with the monarchy refusing all provision, and Heriot dying, James agreed to allow Ralegh his attempt. At least, he said, he would not have the expense of keeping the man in luxury in the Tower. Ralegh could fit out an expedition—at his own expense. But he was not pardoned. If this proved to be a wild-goose-chase, he would pay for it in more than expenses!

John still did not see why his father should be so concerned, even if the expedition *had* turned out a failure and Ralegh had to go back to his Tower. It was scarcely an earth-shattering development?

Was he overlooking the Spanish situation, the Duke asked? That had developed much in the meantime. James was now eager for Charles, Prince of Wales, to wed the Infanta of Spain, with her dowry of £600,000—which was to come to *him*, not to Charles! The Spaniards did not like Ralegh, who had plundered their shipping in the past, and disapproved of this entire expedition. They looked on South America as theirs, even though they had done little about it. So long as Ralegh was successful, James was prepared to risk Spanish displeasure—but he did promise Philip that, if Ralegh so much as harmed one single Spaniard on the venture, he would send him in chains to Madrid for Philip to hang! So, failure could mean dire trouble—and not only for Ralegh.

They debated as to whether John should go to tell the King about what he had heard, since fairly obviously no word of it had yet reached court. But, on the principle that bearers of ill-tidings were seldom popular, they decided to let James find out from his own sources—which no doubt would occur soon enough.

Meantime, John was despatched on a mission to Hampton Court, where Queen Anne had been taken—Oatlands having proved too 'exposed'. Anne's condition was giving continued cause for anxiety—especially on the financial aspect, as far as her husband was concerned—and he wanted something positive done about the jewellery. James calculated that she had spent over £300,000 on jewellery with George Heriot alone, and, although she had undoubtedly given much away, much must remain. Somehow this had to be saved before, as the King put it, the rats got at it. John was to go and see Margaret Hamilton again, apparently the only possible weak link in the Queen's household.

This time he travelled up-river in better style, in one of the King's barges. But he found Hampton Court very different from heretofore. The great house seemed almost dead, with the Queen and her reduced staff roosting in only one corner of it. The air of gloom was tangible.

Margaret was delighted to see him and made no secret of it. She was distracted with boredom, she announced, tired to death of sickness, crabbed, aged, haughty females, hushed voices and general misery. This vast empty palace was worse than Oatlands. There was no company for her, no young people anywhere, nothing for her to do. Where had he been all this time? Why had he not come before? He had promised that he would speak for her to the King. She had looked for him, for weeks.

John sympathised with her—and his sympathy was genuine. For he could imagine few fates less tolerable for a lively young woman than to be entombed in this huge echoing house with a dying Queen and her sour and anxious ladies.

Margaret wanted more than sympathy, however, and almost dragged him off forthwith to a far wing of the palace where, in a chamber with a large bed, already somewhat rumpled he noted, she only paused in flinging off her clothing to help him discard his, entirely single-minded about the business.

After an active, indeed almost breathless but admittedly pleasurable half-hour, during a lull, he revealed his present mission.

"I would think that the King would have more to worry about than a few jewels! The state of his own wife's health, for one thing."

"Yes, it is strange. But—he is a strange man. And desperately in need of moneys, it seems, always. It is one long battle with parliament, over funds. Things are done differently here than in Scotland. Anyway, he needs money. And reckons that the Queen's jewels should be worth as much as £200,000."

"All that? But they *are* the Queen's jewels, not his."

"He says that the Queen, in her present state, can have no need for jewellery, nor interest in it."

"*I* say that he is a cold-hearted monster!"

John stirred uncomfortably beside her. "I do not like it, my own self. But he is no monster, however strange. He sees things differently from others. Perhaps all kings do. But—well, that is no business of ours. He is the King and we must do as he tells us."

"You must, perhaps—not I."

"You are his subject also, are you not?"

"What does he want of me, then?"

"He says that you must know where the Queen *keeps* her jewels. And are in and around her rooms every day. It should not be difficult for you to, to move them. Or some of them. A little at a time. Without it being noticed. To, to somewhere else . . ."

"Into the King's hands, you mean? Steal the Queen's jewels? I, her own Maid-in-Waiting!"

"Not steal. Abstract was the word he used! He is a great one for words, is James. It is to save them, so that the *wrong* folk do not steal them."

250

"I mislike this. If I do, what reward will I receive?"

"The King says that some position at court will be found for you."

"He does? What position?"

"He did not say what. But something. He will show his gratitude. *Do* you know where the jewels are kept?"

"Oh, yes. Or some of them. It is no secret. They are in a dressing-room off the Queen's bedchamber. Along with her gowns. But to get them will mean to get past Danish Anna."

"She it is James distrusts most of all. She cannot always be on watch."

"She sleeps, after midday, for a while. They all do. This place is like a kirkyard, then! It would have to be done very gradual. A little at a time . . ."

"Yes—the King understands that."

"The great and favourite pieces would have to remain. On top. So that the loss of the others might not be noticed."

"The Queen will not inspect her jewellery now? When she is so ill?"

"No-o-o. But I do not know how often Anna may do so. As personal maid. She may deem it her duty. Indeed I have seen her wearing some of it, at times—the odd piece. Perhaps with the Queen's permission. They are close, both Danish."

"Aye—that is partly what troubles the King. What of the others? Her ladies, the countesses . . . ?"

"I think that none would touch anything—meantime. But when the Queen is gone . . . !"

"Exactly! You will admit that James has reason for his fears. So you will help?"

"I will try. On condition that you, or the King, find me a place at Whitehall. And a good place. But, see you—it occurs to me, John, that *all* the jewellery will not be here. It was not all taken to Oatlands. A deal must still be at Somerset House. The Queen was ill when she left there and has been ever since. Abed, not wearing jewels. So much is probably left."

"Ha! That, now, will interest James."

"Yes. Well, remember to tell him that it was *I* who told

251

you! Now—enough of that." Her hand became busy under the bed-covers, and John had to put aside statecraft and high finance for the time-being.

That his representations had not been wasted, however, was proved before he had to leave for his down-river journey. Presently Margaret left him on the bed, saying to wait there and she would endeavour to find some food and wine before he went. Nothing loth, he lay—for it had been quite an exhausting interlude, what with one thing and another—and indeed he dozed over before the young woman returned. She bore a flagon of wine and some wheaten cakes and cheese, very acceptable. But, even more so, she presented him with a pearl necklace, a couple of diamond brooches and four gold rings, to take back to the King. Having been to the kitchens, she had gone upstairs to the Queen's suite, found all there having their afternoon sleep, including Anna Thorsten, and had taken the opportunity to slip into the dressing-room and 'abstracted' these items from one of the many drawers full of jewellery.

John was much impressed by this practical initiative and effectiveness, and said so. She told him pointedly that she looked for more than thanks and honeyed words. Her future was at stake. If the King wanted more where these came from, he must assure that future.

John returned to Whitehall with mixed feelings, his errand more successful than he could have anticipated; but he did not like this mission of filching a dying woman's belongings. And he was becoming uncomfortably aware of a steely ingredient in Margaret Hamilton's character, which might have to be reckoned with.

James, in another bedchamber interview, was delighted with his young kinsman's report, with the samples brought, and especially with the suggestion that there was probably much jewellery left at Somerset House, declaring that he himself would pay a visit to that establishment and see what was to be found. Meantime, Johnnie would make journeys up and down to Hampton Court every day or two, and ferry back all that the Hamilton lassie could extract.

John had some difficulty in penetrating the royal euphoria to the extent of getting it appreciated that the said Hamilton lassie was no meek and mild maiden, to do just what she was told, but a tough bargainer, almost he judged to be compared with Alderman Cockayne and the Merchant Venturers.

The King huffed and puffed at that, going on at some length about the insolence of underlings, his God-given authority to command all his subjects, and what could happen to those who did not obey. Then he changed to a more typical, jollying stance, suggesting that any man who was bedding a quean—as he wagered John was—and who could not get her to do more than open her legs for him, was unworthy to be called a man, especially a Stewart! It was John's turn to huff, although he could not demonstrate it in present company quite so openly as he would have wished; but he could show enough to indicate displeasure both at the implications and the crudity. James perceived it, of course, pulled at his lower lip, and surprisingly came out with a promise that he would make an arrangement whereby the young woman would have a place in his household. John could tell her that—his royal word. When, would depend upon the Queen's state, naturally.

With that John had to be content.

Next day the news of Ralegh burst upon the court, and for the time-being all else almost went into abeyance. The ship had finally docked at its home-port of Plymouth, and the news therefrom was all bad. Not only was there no gold, but two of the vessels had been lost. Almost worse, the expedition had, for some reason, attacked the Spanish town of St Thome, near the mouth of the Orinoco, and caused much damage and casualties. That Ralegh's own son had been killed in the process, gained him little sympathy— although this happening was alleged to have taken the heart out of the veteran explorer and almost certainly contributed to the lack of success thereafter.

James seldom actually showed anger, however frequently he demonstrated disapproval. But he was angry now; Ludovick said that he had never seen him so wrathful. The disappointment over the complete collapse of high hopes was bad enough; but it was the assault on the Spanish settlement which infuriated the King, after his assurances to Philip and warning to the expedition's leaders. Ralegh's immediate arrest was ordered. He would return to the Tower—for onward delivery to the King of Spain, as promised.

So Whitehall was in a high state of tension, for Ralegh's fate could affect many and much. He was no ordinary man but a former national hero, beloved of the populace, who saw him as a link with Gloriana in her time of splendour. Parliament, always looking for sticks with which to beat the King, would undoubtedly rise to the defence of Ralegh, especially as most members disapproved of the proposed Spanish match for Charles, with its Catholic associations. The idea of sending him to meet his death in Spain would undoubtedly create uproar.

John, like everyone else, was affected by the atmosphere at court, and in the days that followed came to look forward to his visits to Hampton Court and Margaret's un-complicated love-making—although that was hardly the phrase, for love did not come into the sheerly physical pleasure. The jewellery-extraction went on. She was taking items from various drawers and caskets, never the principal or favourite pieces. But on each occasion the young woman grew more apprehensive over discovery. It was only a question of time. And then, what? She wanted John to take her back to Whitehall with him one of these days, and soon.

This request he passed on to the King, along with the jewellery, but James ignored it. In his present frame of mind, this was perhaps hardly to be wondered at—although he still grabbed the proceeds eagerly enough.

John asked his father for advice. Ludovick agreed that matters could not go on like this. It was foolish to wait for James to act over the young woman. She should be brought away from Hampton Court at once, before the losses were discovered. Then she—and John—might never be linked with the wretched jewels. But her removal would have to be effected discreetly. It would be unwise for John to bring her away—he would then be saddled with her, every finger pointing at an affair of the heart.

Wholeheartedly his son agreed. Who, then? How could it be contrived? And where would she be lodged? This palace was over-crowded already.

What about his friend, Will Alexander, the Duke suggested? He was friendly with Margaret Hamilton also, was he not? As one of Charles's gentlemen, he had quarters in St James's Palace, a great rambling place. Plenty of room there.

John was doubtful. Could he ask that of Alexander? Would not the fingers then point at *him*?

His father smiled. Will Alexander's back was broad enough for that! He was a noted lady-killer, living apart from his wife. None would raise an eyebrow at him.

So John went round to St James's, distinctly diffident. But his father was right. Sir William chuckled when he heard his young friend's predicament and what he had been up to, and made no bones about going to Hampton Court and fetching Meg; it would be a pleasure, and might well be rewarded. As to accommodation, he did not foresee any difficulty in finding her a corner in this ramshackle palace, temporarily at least. Charles used only a very small part of it, with no large number of attendants—and no interest in women—and besides was seldom there, preferring Greenwich or even Steenie Villiers' quarters at Whitehall, these two being now great friends.

Thus, next day when John proceeded to Hampton Court, he was able to tell Margaret that Will Alexander would be coming for her in a day or two and thereafter she would be lodging at St James's until the King's plans for her future were made clear. She was delighted, and showed him even more than usual favours, in consequence. She was relieved too, for she suspected that the loss of the jewellery had been discovered. On the last two occasions when she had taken items, she had been fairly sure that someone else had been investigating the contents of the drawers in the dressing-room. One ruby-and-pearl pendant on a chain, which she had thought of taking once or twice, was no longer there. One or two other pieces, with which she had become familiar, she could not now find.

Much perturbed, John asked whether she thought, then, that the game was up? To which the young woman answered that there had been no outcry as yet nor private accusation. It could be not so much that the game was up as that there was another player! Danish Anna might have guessed what was going on and decided that she might as well profit in a similar way.

Uneasy as John was on his way back to Whitehall, it did occur to him that this development could at least serve as an excuse, such as he needed with the King. So that night, when he proceeded as usual to the royal bedchamber with the latest takings, somewhat meagre, he was armed with a version of the situation which enabled him to gain James's approximate approval instead of the reverse that he had feared.

"Sire," he said, handing over a few rings and gems, "I fear that this will be almost the last of it. The loss of the jewellery appears to have been discovered. So far no accus-ation has been made against Margaret Hamilton. But she expects that all will now be watched, by Anna Thorsten or the ladies, and she dare not take more."

James frowned. "Unfortunate. A right pity, that. When it was going along nicely. But we've saved a fair whack o' it. And I got a deal mair frae Somerset House. Man, you'd scarce believe the amount o' costly gew-gaws and toys my Annie had amassed, aye amassed. Guid kens what she thought to dae wi' them a'. She couldna wear them a' if she spent the rest o' her days trying! She's aye been a right expense to me, has Annie. *Varium et mutabile semper femina!*"

"Yes, Sire. Women appear greatly to covet jewels, for some reason. But—this situation could be dangerous, High-ness. For your royal . . . credit. It would not do if Margaret Hamilton was caught and admitted that she had been taking the jewels to pass on to you. It would . . ."

"Guidsakes, it would not!" the monarch exclaimed in-dignantly. "Maist inappropriate. I told you, man—my name mustna come into this matter, at a'. D'you hear? I warned you—this is a fell private matter."

"Yes, Highness, I understand. So I have taken certain steps to, er, keep it that way. In consultation with Sir William Alexander. Clearly Margaret Hamilton must be removed from Hampton Court before this gets any further, before there are any developments or accusations. Sir William is going for her tomorrow or the next day. We thought it better that *he* should bring her away, not myself, in case my links with Your Majesty should be remarked upon, and having been seen with her frequently. Suspicion falling on me would not be to your advantage, Sire."

"U'mm. No. That is wiselike, aye."

"Sir William will take her to St James's Palace, meantime. Until Your Majesty decides what to do with her. It is the best that we could think on, Sire."

"Aye, well. We'll see. The lassie will be fine at yon St James's. She'll no' get much out o' Charlie! She'll hae to fend for hersel' meantime, see you—but I jalouse that yon one will be guid at that! For she winna hae you nor yon Alexander-man to dance attendance on her for a whilie, mind. You'll be otherwhere."

"Otherwhere, Sire?"

"Aye—in Scotland. The pair o' you. It's this o' Dumbarton Castle—a right hash and munsie you and Vicky ha' made o' that! There's a summons come frae my Scots Privy Council, requiring you to compear before it in a month's time, wi' Alexander o' Menstrie as witness, in the case o' yon skellum—whatever his name is? Aye, Middlemas, the fell rogue! It seems that you and the Sheriff-man arraigned him before the Council—and quite right too. But now he's counterclaiming to the Council against *you*, for non-payment o' certain moneys. I canna mind it a'—the paper's about here some place. But that's the meat o' it—siller! It's aye siller that's behind maist o' the ills o' this world!"

"But—how can Middlemas claim moneys? From me? He has been robbing your tax-collection for years, they tell me. Extorting moneys from others. He needn't think that he can do the same with me!"

"Ooh, aye—I hope you're right. You'll need to ask Vicky. He should hang, that Middlemas. If you and your Sheriff had taken and hanged him, there and then, instead o' hailing him before the Council, it would have saved a deal o' trouble! Now, he's claiming wrongous dismissal, or something such."

"But . . . ! He shut himself into the castle. Held the gates against us."

"Nae doubt. It's a' been mishandled, as I say. You'll hae to do better in future, man. But, meantime, you'll need to fight it oot wi' the Privy Council, laddie. So it's back to Scotland wi' you. And yon Margaret Hamilton will be short o' bed-fellows for a whilie! Unless you want to tak her wi' you?"

"No, no—certainly not! That would be unsuitable, Sire. When, when do we have to go?"

"In a day or two, just. And see you, while you're there, I want to ken when the paper is to start coming south, frae the mills. How much is ready to come. The second quality they're producing, for yon Cockayne. The prices it's to work oot at. And how the new mills are coming on. I was thinking of sending you up, anyway—so this nonsense of Dumbarton will serve *some* purpose. They have had time enough, those Germans, to mak plenties o' paper. I want to see results, man—results."

"Yes, Sire . . ."

Again, as so often on leaving Majesty's presence, John was aware of mixed feelings—concern over this Privy Council summons and money claims, alongside delight that he was bound for Scotland again and relief that he would be well out of any complications over Margaret Hamilton and the Queen's jewellery. Margaret might well see it differently.

When he and Will Alexander left, three days later, on the long ride northwards, Ludovick, wishing him God-speed, confessed that he wished that he was going with them. Not only that he too longed for Scotland—or at least Methven and Mary Gray—but because London would be a good place to be out of, in the coming weeks. For although he and others had managed to persuade James not to send Ralegh to Philip of Spain, he was determined that the man should be executed. There was no need for a trial and all the upheaval that would cause. His previous sentence of death for the Main Plot had never been annulled, only postponed. He would die, and that was that; but, until it was all over, Scotland would be an excellent place to be.

14

They were in plenty of time for the Privy Council hearing at
Edinburgh, but imagined that there would be preliminary
interviews and proceedings to go through. However,
although this might be so, they discovered that little could
be done about it all beforehand. The Clerk, James Primrose,
was, as before, at his Fife lairdship, and was not expected
back much before the meeting on 8 August—and neither of
the travellers had any desire to repeat their previous experience of Primrose hospitality. So, while John spent a
couple of days with the paper-makers, Alexander actually
went off for a brief visit to his estranged wife, who lived
with her parents, also in Fife. He never spoke of his marriage,
and John did not question him.

John found all well at the Water of Leith mills, with
Vandervyk settled in comfortably, on good terms with the
Germans and apparently spending most of his time in the
Esk valley, converting two corn-mills. The work was well
ahead, and he hoped that these would be producing paper
before the year's end. The existing mills had manufactured
the new second-grade paper such as the English appeared to
want, and now had quite large stocks of it awaiting export.
John worked out with the Germans a satisfactory price for
this, remembering but not stating that the King would
probably double this price for Cockayne. He then went off
to Leith to arrange shipment from that port to London,
when the price was accepted. This was all perfectly straightforward and should meet with royal approval. Will
Alexander, when he came back from Fife, told John that, as
the working partner in all this evidently profitable enterprise,
he ought to be earning some fair proportion of the proceeds—but did not succeed in convincing the younger man
that he should do anything about it, unless the King himself

suggested it. He looked on all this as merely part of the royal service.

Still with some days on their hands, they decided that it might be advisable to visit Dumbarton and ascertain the situation there, before the hearing. Also to have a word with Sheriff Napier, who presumably would be involved also. So, in the last days of July, they headed westwards, by Forth, Carron and Kelvin, for the Clyde estuary.

They had a very different reception at the great fortress from heretofore; indeed, when they rode up to the first gatehouse, and were admitted by somewhat uncertain guards, Sandy Graham came hurrying down from the Keeper's House, actually to plead with John to go back to the town, to give him an hour or two, and then to return to a proper Governor's welcome. John saw this as quite un-necessary, but, recognising that his old friend was really concerned about the matter, saying that it would be good for the new garrison, give them a sense of the flourish of the royal service, which so far had been totally missing, he agreed. He said that he and Sir William would go on to Kilmahew and see the Sheriff-Deputy, then return in, say, three hours.

They found Napier a worried man, disturbed at the thought of the Privy Council enquiry, to which he had indeed been summoned, and apprehensive that some re-sponsibility might fall on him for the long mismanagement of the castle affairs, particularly the misappropriation of tax revenue and royal dues by Middlemas. Without actually stating it in so many words, he made it clear that he feared that the Duke of Lennox, as Governor and High Sheriff, being much too lofty a figure to be saddled with any blame, the onus might fall on himself. John sought to reassure him.

Napier informed that Middlemas had in fact slipped out of the castle one night, with his minions, soon after the last visit, and had not been heard of since, in Dumbarton at least. Where he was meantime was unknown but he had had the insolence to counter-claim to the Council that he had been wrongfully dismissed from his constableship. It was absurd that the Council should even consider such claim against the King's Governor, but apparently it was proposed to do so. He felt that there must be a reason for this, which was not evident.

They took the Sheriff back with them to Dumbarton, in the interests of legal show, and were surprised at the change of scene on their return to the castle. Quite a crowd had gathered outside the gatehouse in the perimeter wall, and trumpets sounded a fanfare as they came up to a ragged cheer. The gates, found to be shut as the three horsemen rode up, were thrown open dramatically, and the portcullis, which was down for the first time in John's experience, was clankingly raised to more trumpeting. Then, within the vaulted gateway-arch, Sandy Graham appeared, dressed in fine style, with polished half-armour on his chest and sword at his side, a file of a dozen armoured men at his back, one of them carrying a cushion on which were some great keys on a chain. Bowing low, Sandy proffered these to John.

Feeling somewhat foolish and inadequate, the latter dismounted, took the keys and, not knowing quite what to do with them, handed them back to the man with the cushion, nodding. Then he shook hands with Sandy, to more and better cheers from the crowd. Will and the Sheriff dismounted also, and came to shake hands likewise.

"This is all very, er, fine, Sandy," John said. "Most impressive. I . . ."

Graham signed for him to wait. Three more men appeared from the gatehouse, two with fiddles and one with a side-drum, and these proceeded to tune up, before turning round to lead the way into the outer bailey of the fortress and on up the hill. Leaving somebody else to bring on the horses, John and his two companions fell in behind Sandy and followed on, in approximate step, distinctly embarrassed, most of the crowd coming along too.

Once up at the Keeper's House, and thankful to be inside, Sandy explained. For years Dumbarton Castle and its garrison had been hated and feared in the area. The Duke had seldom looked near it and Middlemas had had everything his own overbearing, corrupt way. Now he, Graham, was doing all in his power to change that attitude. He was deliberately seeking to popularise himself and his men in the town and district—not easy, when there were taxes and dues to be collected—encouraging the townsfolk to come about the fortress. This unexpected visit of the Governor was an opportunity to emphasise the royal connection and authority and to bring some colour to the scene. He hoped that John, *Sir* John he amended hastily, did not mind and indeed approved?

John reassured him again, indeed congratulated him on his concern and initiative, admitting that he should have thought of all this for himself. Any help that he could give Sandy, he would.

There were, needless to say, quite a number of questions, problems and decisions which the new Deputy-Keeper and Constable had accumulated for John to pronounce upon; and these they sought to work out thereafter between them with the Sheriff's and Alexander's advice—after the throng had been regaled on the castle's stock of ale and dismissed. But there was something else which had accumulated and which required attention and decision as to disposal—and this was the money, the King's siller, the royal revenues, duties, harbour-dues and the rest, collected by Sandy, and which he did not know what to do with. Oddly enough, neither did John. This was something no-one had thought to inform him on, had scarcely been mentioned save as to Middlemas's misappropriations in a vague way. Sandy revealed that he now had the large sum of £800 locked up in a chest here, with more always being added. What was to be done with it? Who did it go to? Presumably Middlemas had remitted sums to somebody in authority, however insufficient. But he had left no note of it, no records of any sort. Sandy had had actually to ask the tax-payers themselves how much they owed! Nobody official had approached the new Constable for moneys. There was the linked problem of paying the garrison—Sandy had enrolled eighteen new men—and the costs of maintaining the castle. Since Middlemas had left nothing behind him, Sandy had just had to use some proportion of the collected dues for this purpose—which he assumed had always been done. But he would be glad to have directions.

John turned to the Sheriff. Did *he* have any information or guidance on this? Napier shook his anxious head. This did not come within his legal authority at all. He would assume that the moneys should eventually reach the Lord High Treasurer, but through whom he did not know. It was strange that no demands had come in, either to the Constable or to Sir John. But perhaps settlement was only on a yearly basis? However, the Privy Council undoubtedly would inform them when they met it.

John felt instinctively that he would have to go very warily on this matter. He had an uneasy feeling that perhaps his father knew more about it all than he had revealed. After all, this governorship was not merely an honorary distinction but an office of profit under the crown, so that the Duke must have been getting some profit out of it, however inadequate. From whom did he get it? Had it come direct from Middlemas? Or was it paid by the crown, perhaps by the Lord High Treasurer? Ludovick Stewart was no money-grubber but he lived in some style and must have his revenues in some order. He obtained some income from Methven, of course, about half of the annual surplus there; but that would not go far in keeping up the ducal state. John felt that he ought to have been informed on the finances of Dumbarton, at least. His mother might have some knowledge of the matter. Mary Gray had a shrewder head on her slender shoulders than any of them.

He told Sandy to hold on to the money meantime, and to continue meeting expenses from it until a decision on the proper disposal was reached.

They remained two days at Dumbarton, roosting in the Keeper's House, and making a sort of official visit into the town and port to meet the provost, magistrates, guild-deacons and harbour-master; and John gained his first experience of being bowed to and honoured as the King's representative—which made him feel a considerable fraud. But, for Sandy's sake if no other, he was concerned to make a good impression and all went well. Clearly the new Constable was much approved of in the town.

There were still five days until the date set for the Privy Council hearing so, arranging to meet Napier in Edinburgh the day previous, John and Will set off for Methven.

Mary Gray was, as ever, delighted to see them—she and

Will Alexander got on well together—and John slipped back into the routine of property-management as though he had never been away. For perhaps the hundredth time he told himself that this was the life for him, not courts and palaces and cities, or, for that matter, paper or other monopolies. If only . . .

News of Janet was that, although she was well enough and making an acceptable mistress at Dalpatrick, her husband was in trouble. David Drummond had been hunting deer in woodland near Machany when a boar had burst out of a thicket almost beneath his horse's feet, alarming the animal and causing it to bolt. Before he could control it, his mount galloped under a tree with an overhanging bough which David could not avoid and which swept him out of the saddle. He had fallen heavily on outcropping rock and broken his hip-bone and one wrist. In a way, he had been fortunate that the boar did not turn on him as he lay. The wrist had mended, in due course, but the hip had not. It seemed that he was permanently crippled and required sticks to aid him move about, a dire condition for a young man.

John sympathised—but his main feelings were for Janet, married to a crippled man whom she did not love.

Later, he asked his mother whether she knew anything about the money situation at Dumbarton and what proportion his father had received? But she did not know. Tax-farmers usually got about half, she understood—her father, the Master of Gray, had done better, but he was rather a special case; of course they had to pay the expenses of collection and, in Dumbarton's case, the maintenance of the fortress and garrison. That was as much as she knew. She would imagine that the money would go to someone in the Lord Treasurer's office. But she was surprised that Vicky had not told John all about it.

John felt the same way. Did she think that perhaps his father had felt unhappy about it for some reason? Had something to hide, even?

His mother looked at him thoughtfully, and said that that was not impossible. Vicky was a dear and one of the kindest people alive; but he had some odd notions about certain aspects of living, probably because of the way he had been reared, semi-royal, with wealth meaning very little because always readily available. He could close his mind to money matters, she had found out, and to other men's ideas as to honesty. Perhaps all royal dukes were like that, and kings too. She believed that James certainly was.

John nodded. So possibly the answer to his problem lay with the Lord High Treasurer of Scotland or one of his people. The Treasurer was Johnnie Mar, his aunt's husband, John, Earl of Mar, the King's foster-brother and Keeper of Stirling Castle, which made John thoughtful indeed.

The Deputy-Treasurer was Sir Gideon Murray of Elibank, he who had had to find quarters for all the flood of English courtiers at Holyrood. He and Johnnie Mar were both members of the Privy Council—so John could have opportunity to speak with them. But—Mary advised him to be cautious about it. Where money was concerned, and men's credit, it always paid to be careful, especially amongst the highly-placed, she suggested.

After three days at Methven, they returned to Edinburgh, and found James Primrose back in his office in Parliament House and giving John curt instructions to appear in the Chancellor's Room there at noon two days later, with his witnesses. No other guidance was given. John got the impression that the Clerk to the Privy Council just did not like him.

He and Will put up again with his aunt, the Countess of Mar—and from her learned that her husband, for one, would not be at the Council meeting, for he was in London. John learned more than that from the Countess, when he told her of his problems at Dumbarton. She said that she was not surprised that he was having difficulties, for Dumbarton was something of a sore spot in certain quarters—quarters quite near home, too! Her second husband, in fact, had always resented Vicky being given the governorship, for he had wanted it for himself, and latterly for his son by his first marriage, the Lord Erskine. When John had been made Governor, in place of his father, the Earl and his son, her husband and stepson, had been furious, the position having always been looked upon as almost an

Erskine fief. It was scarcely to be wondered at if John's incumbency was not proving entirely easy.

This put a new aspect on the situation, and set that young man's mind working busily. The Earl of Mar, who happened to be Lord High Treasurer, had a grudge against his father and himself, then? Did he, as Treasurer, receive the moneys from Middlemas when Constable?

His aunt could not tell him that, but thought it likely. Not personally, of course, but through his deputy, Murray of Elibank. Or possibly through the said son, Lord Erskine, who more and more was taking over his father's duties and responsibilities as the Earl approached old age. The Countess admitted frankly that she found her second husband tiresome and saw little of him; and that she heartily disliked her step-son. He was half a Drummond, of course, and the Stewarts and the Drummonds had never got on.

Half a Drummond? John pricked up his ears at that.

Why, of course. His mother, the Earl's first wife, had been Anna Drummond, sister of Madderty. Did he not know it?

That information left her nephew all but punch-drunk. Lord Madderty's sister, Janet's aunt. Her son, Janet's cousin, the man who thought Dumbarton should be his—son also of the Lord Treasurer! Small wonder that he, in his innocence, had been finding his role a difficult one. Yet his ducal father, and of course the King, must have known all this and yet never warned him. Wheels within wheels! It all sent John Stewart to bed distinctly bemused and apprehensive too. Likewise angry.

Reporting at Parliament House two days later, at noon, for the hearing, with Will Alexander and Sheriff Napier, they were kept waiting for the best part of an hour in an ante-room off the Chancellor's chamber—which added to the feeling that they were there almost as criminals rather than complainants. When at length they were ushered into the large and handsome apartment, that impression was accentuated by the fact that a galaxy of authoritative-looking individuals sat facing them over a long table, with clerks at other smaller tables, whilst they themselves apparently had to stand, as before a court of law. There was no sign of William Middlemas.

However, at least their reception was civil enough, for the urbane and handsome Earl of Dunfermline, formerly Fyvie, the Chancellor, presided and greeted them courteously.

"Ah, Sir John! And Sir William. And you, Master Sheriff-Depute. A good day to you all. We trust that your journey up from London was not too trying? A long way to come. And that you left my lord Duke in good health?"

"Thank you, my lord. We have been in Scotland for some time. And my father is well," John answered—and, just to even matters a little, added, "as is His Majesty, on whose business I came north."

That produced its effect, and there were some stiff faces and cleared throats along the table.

"Ah, so. We are all glad to hear it," the Chancellor said. "His Majesty's well-being and causes are very close to all our hearts, needless to say. It is as lords of his honourable and secret Council of Scotland that we are here, duly assembled. At some inconvenience, perhaps, to some of us!" And he glanced right and left along the table, smiling slightly. "We understand that you have a petition to make?"

"A petition? Scarcely that, my lord. A request for action, rather. Against one who has grievously injured the said King's cause—which your lordships have at heart." John and Will had decided that in the circumstances they must endeavour to take a strong line from the start; otherwise they were probably going to be browbeaten.

Dunfermline drew a hand over his small pointed beard. "Indeed. A request then, not a petition. You will note that, Master Primrose. For action. By this Council?"

"Yes. Action which, I submit, should have been taken in the matter long ere this."

"Ah. It is a *complaint*, then, that you are making, Sir John, rather than merely a request?"

"Call it that, my lord, if you will. This man Middlemas unlawfully held Dumbarton Castle against the King's officers and Sheriff, refused them admission to the royal fortress and . . ."

267

"A moment, a moment, Sir John," the Chancellor intervened, holding up a beringed hand. "Let us do all in due order. The Council will hear the Clerk read the dittay, as sent to each and all, to refresh our memories. Master Primrose?"

Will Alexander spoke up. "My lord Chancellor—before the Clerk begins, I would respectfully point out that Sir John Stewart of Methven is His Majesty's Governor of the royal castle of Dumbarton and an Extra Gentleman of the King's Bedchamber. And I am the King's Master of Requests, while Master Napier is Sheriff-Depute of the County of Dunbarton. It is surely unsuitable that we should have to *stand* here, before all, while you and even these clerks sit. We are not here as some sort of felons, nor yet as humble supplicants, my lords."

There was some disapproving muttering at the table, but Dunfermline inclined his head. "Master Primrose, have chairs brought for these gentlemen," he directed.

In the stir, while clerks hurriedly brought forward three chairs, John decided to maintain the momentum.

"My lord Chancellor, also before we commence, are we not entitled to know to whom we speak? Your lordship I know. And Sir Gideon Murray there. Also my Lord Binning, I see—now created Earl of Melrose, I am told. But I do not know the others."

Dunfermline, normally so civilly assured, looked a little put out. "If you wish, sir—if you wish. Although I do not know that it is necessary. On my right, here, is my lord Archbishop of Glasgow. Then my lord Earl of Winton. Then my lord Earl of Melrose, Secretary of State. Then my lord Burntisland. And, at the far end, the Master of Elphinstone. On my left, my lord Bishop of Dunkeld. Then Sir Andrew Hamilton of Redhouse, Lord Advocate. Next is my lord Erskine, Deputy-Governor of Stirling Castle. Then Lord Foresterseat of Session. All of His Majesty's Scots Privy Council. Are you satisfied, sir?"

"A most illustrious company, my lord," John said, sitting down—but did not add, as he would have liked to do, distinctly incestuous and no doubt hand-picked. For the Earl of Winton was Dunfermline's own elder brother; Sir

Andrew Hamilton was Melrose's—that is, Tam o' the Cowgate's—brother; Foresterseat was another Hamilton; the Master of Elphinstone's mother was Elizabeth Drummond, sister of Lord Madderty and therefore aunt of Janet; and the Bishop of Dunkeld was Peter Rollo, married to another sister of Madderty. As of course was Lord Erskine's mother likewise. Without having actually to be present himself, Janet's father seemed to be well represented.

"Then we shall proceed, if all agree? Master Primrose—we await your dittay."

"Yes, my lord." The Clerk selected from his papers one which he eyed as though it afforded him no pleasure and in a flat voice proceeded to read. "Complaint of Sir John Stewart of Methven, knight, Keeper and High Constable of His Majesty's Castle of Dumbarton, against William Middlemas, formerly Constable and Deputy-Keeper thus: The custody of the said castle was committed to Ludovick, Duke of Lennox, the complainant's father, by the King's Majesty in time past, but the said Sir John has been in possession thereof for several months, by His Majesty's agreement. Nevertheless the said William Middlemas, who had been removed from office by the complainant, had, while Sir John was absent, made choice to use the time to corrupt certain persons, all servants in the castle, to join him, and, on a day in February last, assisted by the said persons, made himself master and commander of the said castle, seized the ports and gates, munitions, ordnance and weapons and did violently thrust forth the complainant's servants and kept the castle against the King. This on the statement of Sir John Stewart, Keeper, and witnessed by Sir William Alexander of Menstrie, knight, and also of Sheriff-Depute Napier of Kilmahew and others."

There was pause while various of the councillors considered that and murmured to each other. The Chancellor looked left and right, and then nodded.

"Well, Sir John—do you accept that as a true statement of your complaint, as agreed by your witnesses?"

"I do, my lord. Although it could be much added to. In that the man Middlemas also has long improperly defrauded the King and Treasury in his collection of taxation, and oppressed the lieges in Dumbarton town and port. I so informed the Clerk, here, some time ago—but he has omitted to record it. Unless there is more to come?"

Another voice spoke, that of the Lord Erskine, a thin-featured but good-looking man with a notably tight mouth. "I object, my lord Chancellor. That, if considered, would constitute a totally different and separate charge. And not competent to be brought by the present complainant. I move that it be not heard."

"Ah. Thank you, my lord Erskine. Is this your view, Master Primrose?"

"Yes, my lords. If such a claim were made against the defendant, it would require to be put forward and substantiated by the injured party, namely His Majesty's Treasury. Not by Sir John Stewart."

"And this has not been done?"

"No, my lord."

"In the absence of the Lord High Treasurer, who is furth of this realm at present, I ask the Deputy-Treasurer, Sir Gideon Murray of Elibank. How say you, Sir Gideon?"

"I have received no such instructions," that grizzled individual said briefly.

"Very well. That seems to be quite clear. You hear, Sir John? Any such charge should be brought, not by you but by the Lord Treasurer. So far, no such charge has been brought. Therefore this Council cannot consider it. We revert to your original complaint, as read. Is there any defence, Master Primrose?"

"Yes, my lord Chancellor. The aforesaid William Middlemas depones that he has no charge to answer. And that, on the contrary, he has suffered wrongous dismissal at the hands of the complainant, for which he requires due compensation."

"Ha! Wrongous dismissal and a counter-claim. Is the said William Middlemas here to substantiate such claims?"

"No, my lord. I did not consider that was necessary at this stage, believing that the Council would wish to consider the matter further before summoning him and his witnesses to appear."

"Why that, Master Primrose?"

"Because, my lord, the defendant's and counter-claimant's claim is specific and involves other than the first claimant, Sir John Stewart. And such other party, being a member of this His Majesty's Scots Privy Council, but not present this day, it would no doubt be the wish of your lordships to take cognisance of the matter before proceeding further."

"Indeed? And who is this Privy Councillor, not present, whose interests we are to consider?"

"It is my lord Duke of Lennox, Lord High Admiral of Scotland and former Viceroy of this realm, my lords. Father, although not lawfully, of the first complainant."

There was a suitable stir at that—although John was perfectly sure that all were well aware of the situation beforehand.

"In the circumstances, I commend your wise decision, Master Primrose," Dunfermline said. "If my lord Duke is concerned, clearly we cannot make any decision in the matter until his observations and representations have been received. We can scarcely summon *him* from London to appear before us!"

There was much solemn nodding of heads. Then Bishop Rollo of Dunkeld spoke.

"I suggest, my lord Chancellor, that we are entitled, at this stage, to learn what probable substance there is in this counter-claim in which the Duke of Lennox is allegedly involved? Is there any warrant for this, that we should consider it?"

"I have a deposition here, from the said William Middlemas, my lords," Primrose said. "To which he was prepared to come and substantiate before you, with witnesses, if required." He read again. "I, William Middlemas, Deputy-Keeper and Constable of Dumbarton Castle, do declare on oath that I hold the commission of my lord Duke of Lennox, Governor and Keeper of the said Castle, dated 13th October 1615, confirming myself, William Middlemas as Deputy-Keeper, and agreeing that he, the said Duke, shall nowise remove myself from keeping the said castle and uplifting dues and casualties belonging thereto until such time as the Duke, his heirs, executors and assignees pay me, the said William Middlemas, my heirs, executors and assignees in the sum of 3,000 merks due. This sum remains unpaid."

There was silence in the room for a space.

"Thank you, Master Primrose," Dunfermline said, at length. "This, my lords, puts a different light on the entire matter, I think you will all agree. Have you any observations to make on it, Sir John?"

John strove to hide his discomfort. "I know of no such arrangement, my lords," he said, a little thickly. "I can only say that, if such an arrangement was made, it was a private matter between my father and his deputy. *I* am now Governor of Dumbarton and can dismiss or engage whom I will. Is it not so?"

The murmuring at the table was considerable. The Archbishop spoke.

"Such arrangement, if made, was surely a most improper one, between His Majesty's Keeper and Deputy-Keeper. This Council cannot approve of it. However, if so made, and duly witnessed in the name of the Keeper, it is presumably binding on his successor. Is that not so, Master Primrose?"

"I would say undoubtedly so, my lord Archbishop."

"Perhaps another man of law would proffer an opinion?" the Chancellor suggested. "You, Sheriff Napier?"

"I, I should require to see the signed and witnessed undertaking, my lord," that man said unhappily. "But, if such is in order, yes, I fear that it would apply to a new Keeper."

"Thank you, Sheriff-Depute. In the circumstances, my lords, I think that we can do no other than adjourn this hearing until we have the information we require to make a decision. Clearly the testimony and interests of my lord Duke of Lennox must be ascertained. And that will take some time, since he is in London. When received, this Council will meet again to consider and decide whether to hear the man Middlemas in person and to question Sir John Stewart further. Is it agreed? Then, my lords, we shall reconvene at a date to be appointed. You, Sir John, will no doubt hold yourself in readiness to appear, when summoned."

"But . . . !" John was staring. "*When* is this to be? I cannot just wait here, indefinitely."

"*Where* you wait is immaterial, Sir John. But if your complaint is to proceed, you must make yourself available to this Council. You must perceive that?"

"But it will be weeks before you can hear from my father in London."

"Undoubtedly. I would say six weeks at the earliest. Then we shall have to consider the Duke's representations and decide whether to go further, and if so arrange another hearing. This must be apparent to all."

Helplessly John wagged his head. "But, my lord—I am in the King's service. I cannot linger here in Scotland, waiting, for up to two months. I have duties in London."

"I would suggest to this young man, my lord Chancellor, that he has apparently duties in Scotland also!" That was the Lord Erskine, pointedly. "He is, after all, Governor of the King's castle of Dumbarton. If Sir John cannot attend to both his London duties and his governorship, then surely he ought to resign one or the other!"

There was a general chorus of agreement.

"That would seem a reasonable observation," Dunfermline said judicially. "As—was it Extra Gentleman of the Bedchamber, Sir John? As Extra Gentleman, no doubt His Majesty will be able to do without your valuable services for a few weeks while you attend to the affairs of his royal fortress on the Clyde! Unless you wish to journey down to London and then, after a few days, turn round and come back again? The choice, I suppose, is yours."

There were smiles along the table.

Tight-lipped, John glanced at Alexander, but did not speak.

"Then, gentlemen, that is all that we can do this day. You have our permission to retire. No doubt, Sir John, Master Primrose will be able to communicate with you, at any time . . . at Dumbarton Castle?"

Bowing curtly, John led the way out.

He contained himself only long enough to be out of the Council rooms before bursting forth in indignation. It was a scandal—that is what it was! The entire proceedings a contrivance, a mummery and play-acting, all decided on beforehand. Carefully plotted to ensure his humiliation. No doubt by Erskine and his father, with the aid of the Drummonds. It was intolerable!

Will agreed, although Napier was silent. Clearly they would have John out of Dumbarton Castle if they could.

Why? Why? John demanded. It was not so great a plum! Or was it? Was there something about Dumbarton which he did not know? Which made it so desirable to the Erskines?

It could be no more than pride, family pride, Will suggested. If the Erskines had always considered Dumbarton theirs. After all, Erskine House was just across the river. Perhaps they considered that *all* the great royal fortresses should be in their hands—Stirling was theirs hereditarily and the Earl of Mar was Keeper of Edinburgh Castle. That, allied with the offence against John by Madderty and Erskine's other Drummond kinsmen? Or could it be money? Siller? Was it a more valuable appointment than John had realised? If they could find out how *much* revenue it produced they might get nearer an answer to the question! Obviously, the Duke his father was but a babe in all this. Probably he had never known the full possibilities of the appointment. But the Lord Treasurer would know! If the taxes came to him, Johnnie Mar, the King's foster-brother! What if Middlemas was no more than a catspaw? It would account for a lot.

John shook his head at that. He could not believe that it was thus—not corruption. By the Treasury, or the Erskines. They would not descend to that. But they might have been slack, remiss in their dealings with Middlemas, and be anxious not to have it uncovered. The Treasurership was no doubt profitable, but Dumbarton would be a very small part of it. What did Napier think?

Whatever the Sheriff-Depute thought, he did not give tongue to it. Evidently he had perceived the weight of authority ranged against the new Governor of Dumbarton and had no desire to seem to challenge it.

Back at Lady Mar's lodging, they discussed the immediate future. Alexander obviously could not remain in Scotland, hanging about for a couple of months; he had been away long enough as it was, even for the Prince's service. He would have to travel south very shortly. As for John, for him to journey with him and then almost immediately to turn around and ride all the way back again, would be not only absurd but probably playing into his enemies' hands—for they evidently expected him to be at Dumbarton in the interim, and, if he was not, it might be one more stick with which to beat him, a heedless and absent Governor. So he had better stay. Although what the King would say . . . ?

They decided that Will should go quickly, the very next day, so as to get to Whitehall before whoever the Council sent to interview the Duke. He should give Vicky a full account of the situation, warning him of what was involved and seeking his help and information, especially on this matter of the 3,000 merks committment. He must know more than he had told John. As to the King, John would write a letter for Will to deliver, giving him all the paper-milling details and the news that shipping could start just as soon as prices were agreed with Cockayne. Perhaps if he told James that John's remaining in Scotland meantime, and supervising the first shipments, would help, it might soothe possible royal displeasure.

So next day the friends parted. John returned to Methven for another conference with his mother before making for Dumbarton.

It was inside a week when he arrived at the fortress on the Clyde, but even so he found that the Privy Council, or someone influential thereon, had acted swiftly indeed. Sandy Graham informed him that they had visitors, prisoners actually, who had arrived two days previously under guard—two clergymen of all things, parish ministers who had refused to accept the dictates of King James's new bishops and were now arrested and to be confined until they recognised the error of their ways. Sandy had had no idea what to do with them, but had installed them meantime in the Keeper's House, as his guests, waiting John's instructions.

Needless to say, John was astonished at this development. This could be no coincidence, surely. So what was behind it? He went to see the prisoners.

He found two very different reverend gentlemen. One, Master Andrew Duncan, grey, elderly and spare, silent and thoughtful; and Master Alexander Simson, much younger, plump and bustling. Neither gave the impression of being dangerous characters nor fanatic, in need of incarceration, and both seemed to be on excellent terms with Sandy Graham—who, of course, was himself a minister's son.

When John sought to discover the reason for their present fate at the hands of the Privy Council, the younger divine informed him cheerfully that they were in the hands of God, rather, and rejoicing to be used in His service. They were indeed of the elect, having been singled out by the obnoxious bishops to be set up as examples to warn other parish ministers who might refuse to accept the spiritual authority of the King's prelates. They were grieved to be taken away from their flocks, of course, but glad to be banner-bearers of the Lord. And conditions here at Dumbarton were good, much better than at Stirling Castle where they had come from.

The fact that they had been brought here from Stirling, where Erskine was Keeper, confirmed John's belief that this was in some way a move against himself. He offered the prisoners his sympathy, assured them that as far as possible they would be treated as guests rather than prisoners whilst in his care, and wondered whether they had been given any clue as to why they were sent to Dumbarton? They could not help in this, however, but blessed him and his deputy for their goodwill.

What, then, was the point in this transfer—for if Lord Erskine was behind it, some point there was, and scarcely to John's advantage. The more he considered it, the more convinced he became that there were very clever wits at work here. Why ministers, sent to him? There must be a sufficiency of other sorts available, if he was to be given prisoners to tend—felons, rebels, debtors. Surely, because the Presbyterian ministers were directly opposing the King's personal policy. This imposition of bishops on the Scots Church was James's own decision, his assertion that he was Christ's Vice-Regent, ruling by divine right, and therefore entitled to appoint leaders in the Church as well as in the realm. So—the objecting ministers, unlike other offenders, could be claimed to be acting directly against the monarch. This would be why they had been sent to Dumbarton, to be a bugbear and danger. If he treated them well, he was in danger of offending the King. If harshly, he would offend the Kirk and most God-fearing folk in Scotland. It looked like a very cunning device to drive a wedge between John and King James.

If this was so, it seemed as though there was a definite campaign to bring him low. John wondered whether it was worth being Governor of Dumbarton? Which was, no doubt, exactly what sundry highly-placed individuals wanted him to wonder!

At any rate, he did not allow his recognition of all this to prejudice his treatment of his two captives. They remained in the Keeper's House, with such comfort as it provided, took their meals with him and Sandy and had the freedom of all within the fortress walls. Indeed John became quite friendly with them, and spent many an evening discussing the problems created by the King's fondness for episcopacy, which hitherto he had little considered. He discovered that, though the office of bishop itself was frowned upon, their authority in the Kirk disputed and their right to sit in parliament deplored, it was liturgical worship which most grievously disturbed these two, especially what seemed to him the comparatively minor matters of kneeling at communion and private baptism. The King's success at the General Assembly of the Kirk over what had become known as the Five Articles of Perth, foreshadowed at the parliament John had attended, was to them a dire disaster, and treachery on the part of the majority of voting clerics. John found himself being manoeuvred into the awkward situation of using his alleged influence with the King to try to abate this episcopal madness. The two prisoners explained that they, and those who thought like them, were in fact loyal subjects of His Majesty, with no animus against him; but that the Church of Scotland would never accept bishops and prayer-book worship and the King should realise and acknowledge this for the sake of all concerned and the harmony of his ancient realm. John, insisting that his influence with James was of the slightest, especially in such matters as this, nevertheless could not refuse to mention the subject to the monarch in due course. He wondered whether the Erskines and Drummonds had anticipated something of the sort.

In the weeks that followed, John spent considerable time in the town and port with Sandy, investigating the revenue situation, trying to assess the approximate total sums collectable each year from the various sources. He found that the harbour customs represented much the greatest item, much greater than he had visualised, with Dumbarton the main seaport on the west side of Scotland. Since James had united the crowns, its trade had much increased, partly through the King's policy for the Scots development and colonisation of Ulster, and partly through some enhancement of trade with the Americas, especially in tobacco and rum. This latter, of course, was first channelled through English west-coast ports, for the English monopolists were jealous of their colonial rights; but there was considerable transshipment northwards thereafter, most of which came into Dumbarton—and the crown gained a second lot of import duties on the same goods. Moreover, much of the port itself was crown property, wharfs, warehouses and other offices, all built on royal land and paying substantial rents. Even the salmon fisheries at the mouth of the River Leven and along the Clyde shore were leased by the crown and brought in surprising sums. With rentals in the town on more crown property, and casualties of superiority due on a variety of privileges, even pilotage, all in all, apart from direct taxation, the annual total amounted, so far as they could gauge, to at least eighteen thousand merks, or over £12,000 Scots. Whatever proportion of this stuck to the fingers of the collectors, the Dumbarton governorship was obviously a far more valuable appointment than John had realised. The questions were: how much of all this did his father know? How much had Middlemas been retaining? And how much was going to the Treasury—or at least to the Lord Treasurer?

Another interesting aspect of it all was that still no demands nor instructions had come from the said Treasury for payment, and Sandy's hoard continued to grow. This was strange, to say the least, and either indicated extreme in-efficiency on the part of the authorities—or something more sinister perhaps? Could it be that the moneys were being left deliberately to lie, in the hopes that John or his underlings might be tempted to misappropriate these apparently unwanted funds in some degree, and so serve as an added indictment against him? Or was he becoming altogether too suspicious, almost foolishly so?

John paid a couple of visits to Methven from Dumbarton, partly for relief from the pent-up atmosphere of life in the fortress, with its stresses, but mainly to confer with his mother. Also, it had to be admitted, just to feel that he was nearer to Janet, even though he made no attempt to see her. He recounted all the Dumbarton and Privy Council business to Mary Gray, his fears and suspicions, and confessed that he was seriously considering resigning the governorship, or at least handing it back to his father. He would much rather just be back managing Methven—if the King would release him.

Mary sympathised, but urged him to think deeper. Resig-nation on his part would be taken as an admission of either guilt or failure, or both. Probably the Middlemas case would not be proceeded with. Worst of all, it might rebound on his father. From all John had told her, it looked as though Vicky had behaved unwisely, to say the least, over Dumbarton. Probably he had been cheated and misled also; but there must be more to it than that. Vicky must have been aware that all was not aright there. Perhaps he had been receiving more moneys than he should have done? Why had Middlemas been allowed to go on behaving as he did for so long? Now John had come along and upset the arrangement, and many people were concerned. She was not blaming him; what he had done was correct, honest. But clearly there were more repercussions than he had anticipated, and his father would not thank him if he was to be involved in any witch-hunt.

Was she saying that his father might have been a party to some misuse of crown funds, he demanded?

She did not know. But, with her recognition of Vicky's attitude towards money and the King's service, she thought

279

it perfectly possible. He had served James all his life—and got little thanks or payment for most of it, indeed had frequently had to spend his own money on royal affairs, as most who served the King did. If he, on occasion, recouped himself from the Dumbarton revenues, was he to be altogether condemned?

John was doubtful—but asserted that at least *he* ought to have been told, not left to stir up this wasps' bike and deal with all the consequences in ignorant honesty!

She agreed—but observed that the longer he remained in James Stewart's service, the more he would realise that honesty was relative! The King's own interpretation of honesty would be interesting to ascertain! She imagined that it would very much vary with circumstances. She urged John not to be too hard on his father, who had to survive in a much more complicated world than that of Methven! *She* had learned that lesson growing up as the bastard daughter of the Master of Gray!

He went back to Dumbarton perhaps wiser, but little happier.

The summons from James Primrose came on the Eve of St Luke, 17 October, nine weeks after the original hearing. Sir John Stewart was to appear before the Council again in four days' time, 21 October.

Without Will Alexander for support, and having lost confidence in Sheriff Napier, John took Sandy Graham with him to Edinburgh, as witness. Oddly, the same day as this summons arrived, an armed party turned up at the Castle, also from the Privy Council, requiring the handing over to them of the two clerical prisoners for reasons and destination unspecified. John parted with them quite regretfully. He had found their company stimulating.

This second hearing was at the same time and in the same place and company as heretofore, save that Sir Gideon Murray, the Deputy-Treasurer, was not present. This time there were chairs for John and Sandy.

From the start, the Chancellor was more brusque, spoke more quickly and gave the impression that all was to be got over as soon as possible, almost as though he might be uncomfortable about something. Primrose was ordered to read out a minute of the previous hearing, to refresh their lordships' minds—which that man did in a voice devoid of all expression. Then Dunfermline announced that a testimony of sorts had been received from the Duke of Lennox in London, and that this also would be read to them. John sat forward.

Primrose, without changing his tone, quoted from another paper, saying that the lord Duke of Lennox, High Admiral of Scotland, etcetera, testified that, as far as his memory served him for happenings five years previously, he had agreed with William Middlemas, Deputy-Keeper, that he should continue in that capacity for so long as he gave satisfaction to himself as Governor. In the event of him being relieved of the deputy-keepership other than at his own request, some suitable compensation would be paid to him, the sum misremembered at this present by the Duke. That, Primrose added flatly, concluded the ducal statement.

There was a pause thereafter, as all considered this somewhat inadequate evidence. Dunfermline asked if John wished to comment and was answered with a shake of the head. He then asked Primrose whether the man Middlemas was available for questioning and, answered in the affirmative, ordered him to be brought in.

So John came face-to-face with William Middlemas once more, as the man was ushered in, with two companions, identified to the Council as Robert Middlemas, brother, and Robert Cairncross, both servants at the castle of Dumbarton formerly. They stared at each other blankly.

The Chancellor was untypically curt. "You are William Middlemas, lately Deputy-Keeper of the King's castle of Dumbarton, dismissed by Sir John Stewart, Keeper thereof?"

"I am," the other agreed.

"You will add 'my lord' when you answer me, or any other here," he was told. "You now assert wrongous dismissal and claim certain moneys as due to you by Sir John, in accordance with an alleged arrangement made with you by the former Keeper, my lord Duke of Lennox?"

"I do, my lords. In the sum o' 3,000 merks."

"This in the event of wrongous dismissal?"

"Yes, my lord."

"Have you any evidence, other than your own assertion, for this claim and the sum stated?"

"I have, my lord. A signed paper, which I hold. Burnbrae, here, has it."

Primrose came forward with a document, which was passed along the Council table. None more than glanced at it, indication to John that they had all already seen it. Finally it was handed to himself. It briefly stated the terms Middlemas had alleged, with the straggling signature—Lennox at the end, dated 13 October, 1615.

"This document appears to be sufficiently clear and in order as far as it goes, however improper an arrangement," Dunfermline said. "Have you any comments, Sir John?"

"I have, my lord. I accept that this appears to be my father's signature, and, in view of his testimony just read, I cannot dispute that the arrangement took place. But its validity is another matter. The counter-claim by this man depends on wrongful dismissal. If the dismissal was not wrongful, then I submit that the claim cannot stand. I . . ."

"It doesna say that in the paper!" Middlemas interrupted heavily.

"Silence!" the Chancellor rapped. "You will address yourself only to me, and speak only when asked to. Proceed, Sir John."

"If it does not so state in this paper, my lords, neither does it say otherwise. The matter is not mentioned. But in any contract it is surely understood without saying that unlawful acts cannot seek the protection of the law."

"That, I think, cannot be denied."

"Then I assert that William Middlemas has no claim, in that his dismissal was not wrongful. It was entirely necessary and indeed overdue, in that he unlawfully shut up and held the King's castle against the King's lawful Governor and the Sheriff-Depute of the county of Dumbarton. And, further, that he had for long unlawfully mishandled the taxation, customs and revenues of Dumbarton, the which it was his duty to collect and remit to His Majesty's Scottish Treasury."

There was a profound silence, broken at length by the Lord Erskine.

"What proof has Stewart for that statement? I submit that he can have none. For proof could only be produced by the Treasury. And to my knowledge no such proof exists."

The Chancellor tapped finger-nails on the table. "That would seem to be so," he said. "Sir John, can you substantiate your extraordinary allegation?"

"Do I have to, my lord? Here and now? I can bring many witnesses, if need be, from Dumbarton town and port, to testify to extortion and wrongful demands by Middlemas. How much of what he collected he remitted to the Treasury can surely be revealed by the Treasury's records."

"The Treasury's records are a matter for the Lord Treasurer and his Deputy, not for Sir John Stewart," Erskine declared thinly. "So far as I am aware, the Treasury has made no charges against this man Middlemas in his submission of moneys. And only the Treasury has the authority so to charge, not the Keeper of Dumbarton Castle."

"So I would agree," Dunfermline nodded. "I must rule, Sir John, that such charge cannot be considered by this Council. You must withdraw it."

"If I must, I withdraw it as a charge. But I urge your lordships to remember it! However, the charge of extortion and threatening of the lieges remains."

"Perhaps. But cannot be considered by this Council meantime for lack of supporting evidence and witnesses. Our present concern is with your claim properly to have dismissed the Deputy-Keeper, and his counter-claim for compensation. Have you anything to add, William Middlemas?"

"Only, my lord, that I want my 3,000 merks!"

"M'mm. Yes. And you, Sir John?"

"Only to repeat, my lord, that, if the alleged contract was unlawful in the first place, I cannot by law be held to its terms."

"We shall see. Then I think that we may proceed, my lords. Meantime, both complainant and counter-claimant shall retire, while the Council considers its decision. They will be recalled, presently, to hear that decision . . ."

"One moment, my lord Chancellor," Erskine put in. "There is the matter of the prisoners. The Council's consideration on the treatment of these prisoners is relevant to the matter under decision, in that it is perhaps the only guide the Council has as to the fitness or otherwise of Sir John Stewart to occupy the office of Keeper of Dumbarton, and therefore of his fitness to bring charges of *unfitness* against the man Middlemas. This was agreed."

"Ah, yes—the prisoners. They had slipped my mind. Then, William Middlemas, you will retire as stated. But you, Sir John, will remain meantime. Master Primrose—you will see to it."

So Middlemas and his witnesses were led out and from another door the Reverends Duncan and Simson were brought in, looking somewhat bewildered. They greeted John and Sandy warmly but eyed the assembled lords askance, especially the bishops.

Dunfermline looked almost as doubtful as the divines. "You, er, prisoners, Masters Duncan and Simson, have been brought before this Council to testify as to treatment received while in the custody of Sir John Stewart, Governor of the castle of Dumbarton," he announced, scarcely looking at either ministers or John. "What have you to say?"

Alexander Simson, the younger man, did look from his colleague to John. "But . . . we have no complaints, my lord," he exclaimed. "Nane at all. Sir John was kind, maist kind."

"Ha! Kind?"

"Yes. He could scarce have been kinder. Treated us well. As did this other, Alexander Graham."

"You agree with that, Master . . . er, Duncan?"

"I do, sir. Would that we were as well treated elsewhere!" And the older man looked at Erskine.

"This, despite your presence in His Majesty's castle as His Majesty's prisoners, there for disobeying His Majesty's commands?"

"There for ministering to our flocks as laid down by a higher authority in matters of faith and religion, Christ's Kirk in Scotland!" Duncan asserted strongly, even if his old voice quivered a little.

As the bishops present huffed and chuntered, the Chancellor rapped on the table.

"Silence, sirrah! You are here to answer questions put to you, not to make seditious statements."

"We are here to speak, if speak we must, only the Lord God's truth!"

"Away with him—away, I say!" the Archbishop declared, outraged.

"A moment, my lord—not before *we* have established the truth as regards Sir John Stewart," Erskine intervened again. "These two prisoners both testify that while in Sir John's keeping at Dumbarton they were treated, as they say, kindly. Indeed they say that Stewart could not have been kinder! This is their agreed testimony?"

"Indeed, yes," Simson nodded. And, glancing at Erskine, "We were not even required to pay for our board, although we ate at Sir John's table, as we have to pay for poor food in our cells at *Stirling* Castle."

Dunfermline coughed. "Enough! Enough, do you hear? Master Primrose—I think that we have no further need for these prisoners. Remove them."

Although he was indeed very doubtful whether he should thank his late captives, John smiled and nodded to them as they were led out and wished them well.

"Sir John Stewart," the Chancellor resumed. "You have heard the testimony of these prisoners, who were put in your charge, for offences against the King's Majesty, that you not only treated them very kindly but actually fed them at your own table. Do you consider that conduct suitable in a governor of one of His Majesty's fortresses and prisons?"

"I do, my lord. These ministers are not common felons. They may see their duty to God differently from your lordships, or even myself, but they are surely not to be treated like robbers or breakers of the peace."

"That is not for *you* to decide, but His Majesty's judges and magistrates. Your duty was to treat them as offenders against His Majesty's commands. This, most evidently, you have not done."

"As evidently, my lord, as that these two ministers were

sent to Dumbarton for no other reason than to try to trap me! No doubt, if I had treated them *harshly*, that likewise would be considered an offence? Even though they appear to receive harsh treatment at Stirling!"

"Sir John—such talk will do you no service!"

"Do I require your service, my lords? I am here as the King's appointed Keeper of Dumbarton Castle, who has had occasion to dismiss his deputy and appoint another. That is all. The *service*, it seems, is required by William Middlemas!"

"That is a matter for judgment, sir—*our* judgment. I think that I may say that we have heard enough. You will now leave us to consider our decision. It should not take very long."

Bowing curtly, John marched out to the ante-room, followed by Sandy. There was no sign of either Middlemas or the ministers.

They had time only to exchange agreement that it was all a contrivance, arranged beforehand, a plot to discredit John, presumably for some good reason which involved these selected members of the Privy Council, when they were summoned back into the chamber. Obviously no large discussion had taken place.

"Sir John Stewart," the Chancellor said, as though in a hurry now to have it all done with. "We find the contract between the Duke of Lennox and the man Middlemas to be valid and binding, however unsuitable as an arrangement and bargain concerning a house and castle of the King. Also that since it was between the Keeper of Dumbarton and the Deputy-Keeper, it must apply to the Duke's successor as Keeper—yourself. Therefore this Council finds that you owe William Middlemas in the sum of 3,000 merks, and that these moneys must be paid by you to him. Since it is a large sum, we will allow until Whitsunday next for you to find the moneys to pay the said Middlemas. You understand?"

"I understand, my lords, that you choose to support a malefactor and notorious character who held the King's castle unlawfully against the King's Governor, rather than support the said King's Governor. No doubt for your own reasons. His Majesty will be interested to hear of this, surely."

"Your attitude confirms our belief that you are an unsuitable person to be Governor of Dumbarton," Dunfermline went on heavily. "We accept that Middlemas behaved wrongfully in holding the castle against you, and that such action justified his dismissal. But that does not invalidate the money arrangement. As to your treatment of the prisoners just interviewed, we find it lacking in due judgment and a further indication of your unsuitability for the position you presently hold. We will communicate such findings to His Majesty. That is all, Sir John. You may retire."

Without a word, John swung on his heel and left them.

Within a couple of hours he had said goodbye to Sandy and was on his way southwards at last. He felt that it was quite important that he reached Whitehall before the Privy Council's courier. Also, he could do with working off his feelings and frustrations in hard riding.

Exactly a week later, in the vicinity of Huntingdon, John learned that Sir Walter Ralegh had been beheaded three days earlier and that mobs were rampaging in London streets miscalling the King and all his works.

15

Knowing his sovereign-lord and guessing that if there was trouble in London, James would not linger at Whitehall, John made a slight diversion by Enfield and, sure enough, found the court at Theobalds again, and in no carefree state. The King was not only uneasy in his mind of the effects on the nation of the execution of Ralegh, but in trouble with the English bishops, of all people—this over his plans to marry Charles to the Infanta of Spain, and the Church's fears that this would inevitably lead to an increase of Catholic influence in England, the more alarming to them in that the Queen, who still lingered on although ever weakening, was now trafficking with Catholic priests and confessors and had even refused to see the Archbishop of Canterbury; so that Charles, who ever took his cue from his mother rather than his father, might well be affected with the poison of Catholicism already, before any Spanish match. Moreover, the King was suffering from gout—and when James suffered, all suffered.

John had all this unloaded upon him by his father whenever he arrived—and rather got the impression that the ducal eloquence might be partly spurred on by a reluctance to get to grips with the subject of Dumbarton and Middlemas. However, his son was learning in a hard school and was not to be sidetracked.

"Why did you not warn me about Middlemas and your agreement to pay him all that money?" he cut in, presently, on his sire's catalogue of woes.

"Ah, yes—Middlemas. That man was ever a trial," Ludovick conceded. "I had rather forgotten him—and been glad to, you understand, John. It was all a long time ago . . ."

"You mean that you were glad to put off the responsibility

of dealing with him on to me! That is why you gave me the Dumbarton governorship?"

"No, no, lad. You required a position at court, to give you some standing. Also, I had not been able to deal with Dumbarton properly, for long. That was why so much was left to Middlemas. I thought that your fresh hand on the tiller . . ."

"But you did not tell me of this hold Middlemas had on you. Of 3,000 merks. That is £2,000, a deal of money, more money than I have ever possessed! Why, Father—why?"

Ludovick looked uncomfortable and took refuge in vagueness. "It was an old story. Foolish, no doubt. I was not . . . proud of it. And it might well never have come to anything. There was no point in bringing it up unless Middlemas did. And he had not mentioned it . . ."

"Only four or five years. You ought to have told me."

"Perhaps. But I did not know that you would go at it like a bull at a gate, Johnnie—dismissing the man almost as soon as you saw him!"

"He was misbehaving shamefully. I told you. I could not leave him there. And clearly he had been misbehaving for long. You must have known it."

The Duke spread his hands. "Underlings often do misbehave, John. You will learn that. Many of the King's servants misbehave, in one way or another, I know well. And so does James. One cannot watch them all the time. I, for one, have so many offices to fill."

"Why did you sign that paper, Father, committing yourself to pay so much money? There must have been a reason."

"I . . . ah . . . did it without due thought, I fear. A mistake, I see now. Middlemas was very pressing. He was doing all the work, relieving me of much trouble and concern. It seemed but fair that he should have some security."

"My mother thinks that Middlemas probably had some hold over you. That you perhaps had been doing something, well, mistaken. It may be—taking more of the moneys collected than was your due share? And Middlemas knew of it and forced this on you, lest he tell the Treasury? And this, of course, gave the man himself a clear run to misbehave on his own! Was that it?"

Ludovick wagged his head. "Mary thinks that, does she? I am . . . sorry."

"You do not deny it, then?"

"Nor do I admit it, lad. I do not need to deny or admit anything, to you or other. I have had many responsibilities thrust upon me since I came to England with James—and must make the wherewithal to carry them out as best I can. For James certainly will not see to it. You must have discovered that, by now, in your own dealings with him. In this of the paper monopoly, for instance, with Cockayne and the Dutchman and the rest—are *your* hands entirely clean? Aye, and in the matter of the Queen's jewels! James demands service—but leaves the servants to pay for it how they may. It is time that you learned that."

"I cannot pay £2,000. Without defrauding the tax-collection. And that I will not do."

"Do not be *over* righteous, lad."

"It is scarce a matter of righteousness. The Mars want me out of Dumbarton, Lord Erskine in especial. You did not tell me, either, how close linked he was to Madderty and the Drummonds. He thinks that Dumbarton should be his. They will be watching me now, like hawks. So even if I did seek to take overmuch from the taxation and customs, the Treasury would have me."

"Unless the Treasury was . . . accommodated!"

John nodded. "So that is it! I wondered whether it would come to that. You did that—and now it is not being continued? And I am in trouble."

"Scarcely trouble, Johnnie—a mere matter of adjustment! Trouble is something a great deal greater, I can assure you. One learns to give and take, trim one's sails to the winds that blow—or the ship capsizes! I am Lord High Admiral of Scotland, so I ought to know! I have had to do that all my life. I do not expect that *you*, lad, are the one exception to the rule."

It was John's turn to shake his head. Looking at his illustrious father, he perceived, as never quite before, that the only duke in two kingdoms, the Lord High Admiral, the Master of the Horse and all the rest, was in fact, however pleasant a man and good company, weak, weaker than

himself, his illegitimate son. Perhaps he was indeed more
Mary Gray's son than Ludovick Stewart's? In that moment
he was almost sorry for this father of his, knew a sympathy—
and asked himself whether *he* perhaps might suffer in some
degree from self-righteousness, as hinted? He sighed and
shrugged.

"I think that I would give up this governorship of
Dumbarton here and now—were it not that that would
seem like handing all over to the Erskines and Drummonds,"
he said.

"That is the right spirit, boy! You will make do, well
enough, believe me. I will help. See you, as to this money,
I will be in a position to pay it off soon. In a year, say.
Meantime, you keep Middlemas quiet by paying him a
good interest on it. Say one merk in ten—three hundred
merks. He will not refuse that, I swear! I can help you find
that—if you will not pay it out of the taxation."

"M'mm. Where is this access of riches to come from,
Father? In a year?"

"It is a secret, as yet, lad. So let it go no further. But James
has decided that I *must* remarry. Although he is dead set on
this Spanish marriage, that is for the dowry moneys. He is
convinced that Charles is unlikely to ever have a son, and
there is no nearer heir for the succession than myself. He has
chosen a rich widow for me! The second-richest in the
kingdom, they do say—not the richest, who is for Steenie!
So I am to wed the Countess of Hertford, Frances Howard.
This will also help to drive a wedge between the Howards,
our master thinks! The lady has already borne two sons,
so she is sufficiently fertile! And she is renownedly . . .
generous!"

John stared. "And, and you agree to this? To marry
again? And to little more than a stranger. When my mother
looks on you as *her* husband!"

"John—we have been over all this before. You know that
Mary will not marry me—never would. And, if she did,
James would not permit it. This third marriage will make no
difference between your mother and me—the others have
not. Whether I will produce an heir on this female, God alone
knows! But my money problems should be at an end, at

291

least. And that is not unimportant. We cannot all marry for heartfelt love—as I think you will discover soon enough!"

John was silent.

"Now—tell me about your Privy Councillors. Alexander Seton, the Chancellor, is my friend. He would not be happy in this business, I think?"

"No, he did not seem so. But Erskine made the running. His father, the Earl of Mar, was not there, either time. But I felt that he was behind it all, the Lord Treasurer." He paused. "Tell me—how much does a farmer of taxes and customs keep to himself, and how much send to the Treasury?"

"I told you before, it can vary. But four in every ten is usual. This can be bettered, on occasion! Especially with such as Dumbarton Castle to maintain."

"As much as that! Then . . . ?"

"Yes—you see what Dumbarton could be worth to you, properly handled? Have you not been taking the money? You are making the collections?"

"Yes. But have held back, meantime. No word has come from the Treasury. Middlemas left nothing, no guidance . . ."

"Then tell young Graham to send six in ten of all that he has taken to Murray—Sir Gideon Murray, mind you—not Mar. I'd name him middling honest. But to bargain for costs at the castle. You will learn how this game must be played . . . !"

John had his interview with the King the following day, summoned not to the bedchamber on this occasion but to one of the stables, where a favourite mare was in process of foaling, and James was concerned to watch the event. Present, as well as the grooms and stableboys, were two of the King's physicians and an olive-skinned, hook-nosed elegant whom John had seen before but never spoken to, the Count Gondomar, ambassador of His Most Catholic Majesty of Spain, nowadays James's constant companion— so much so that it was said that Steenie was becoming distinctly jealous.

"Aye, Johnnie Stewart—it's yoursel', then? Come and see my Esmeralda giving birth—an exercitation which should consairn you mair than some, heh?" Apart from some slight emphasis on that *you*, the greeting was as though John had not been away for more than hours. The King and Gondomar were sitting on bundles of straw on the stable-floor only a yard or two from the puffing and heaving mare.

"Your Majesty—I hope that you are improved in health? I heard that you were poorly."

"Ooh, aye—I'm in sair pain. But no' deid yet, in despite o' what some folk would wish! You ken Don Diego? He's frae Spain, and right knowledgeable about some matters—but no' all, mind, no' all! *Nec scire fas est omnia*! He's never delivered a foal, see you—is that no' extraordinary? Now, you will ken all about it, eh?"

"I have delivered many, Sire."

"Aye—but dinna sound sae gleg-sure! There's a fell lot you *dinna* ken, as I've been hearing!" He turned. "This, Diego, is a sort o' a misbegotten, far-oot kinsman o' mine, Sir John Stewart o' Methven. Aye, misbegotten—for he's Vicky Stewart's bastard." And, without a change of tone, Majesty went on, "You've been awa' frae our royal presence, lacking oor royal permission, for a gey long time, Johnnie Stewart! We are right displeased wi' you. Months, aye months. You hae forfeited oor royal regard!"

"But, Sire . . . !" John protested, and recollected that the King did not appreciate buts. "It was no fault of mine, Sire. The Privy Council—Your Majesty's Scots Privy Council, commanded me to stay. Ordered me to attend two hearings, over six weeks apart. I could not come back to London in time and then return there. Did Sir William Alexander, or my father, not tell you?"

"I am no' here to be told but to be obeyed, man—mind that. You seem to hae preferred to obey yon Alicky Seton!"

"Sire—I had to assume that the Privy Council spoke in your royal name, in Scotland. I could not disobey my lord Dunfermline, the Chancellor. I did not want to stay."

James turned a padded shoulder on John. "How long now?" he demanded of the physicians.

They shook uncertain but distinctly disapproving heads. "We are not conversant with horses' labours, Highness," one declared.

"Then you ought to be. A mare is one o' God's creatures, is she no'? As much as any woman. Aye, and this Esmeralda's been mair use to me than a wheen women I ken!" James went forward on his knees, despite his gout, pushed aside the stableman who crouched there near the mare's rump, and, pulling up his padded sleeve, lifted the long tail and thrust his hand and arm up inside the animal's rear, feeling around and nodding with every sign of satisfaction. Withdrawing, he wiped off the blood and other smearing on his slashed but already stained trunks. "Coming along fine," he announced. "I could grip the hooves. It winna be long now. You, Don Diego—put your hand up and feel."

Appalled, the Spaniard drew back, shaking his head. "No, no, Majesty—I pray you, no! Not I."

"Come, man—it'll no' bite you! Be no' so nice."

"I beg of you, my lord King . . ."

"Och, weel—I'd gie her ten minutes or so, yet." Pulling down his sleeve, James turned back to John. "The paper? All is weel wi' the paper?"

"Yes, Sire. No difficulties there. Has the first shipment not arrived?"

"Aye—Will Alexander is seeing to that. You'll hae to go see yon Cockayne man, and fix a price wi' him—a guid price, mind. For I jalouse he'll be fair desperate to lay hands on that paper. For parliament's just passed Frankie Bacon's measure banning a' monopolies in England, and Cockayne and his like are like to hae their feet ca'd frae under them. Mind, thae skellums will find a way round it, in time, I've nae doubt. But meantime they'll be in a fair tizzie. They'll be glad to pay whatever price we ask, for oor Scots paper. It's as weel my *Scots* parliament doesna consairn itsel' wi' siklike matters, eh? Save for matters o' religion, mind. In that, they're the spawn o' Satan!"

"Yes, Sire." John wondered if this would be a good opportunity to get back to Dumbarton and the Privy Council. "On the subject of religion, Your Majesty, while I was awaiting the second hearing of the Council they sent me two parish ministers to hold at Dumbarton—at least, I take it that it was the Lord Erskine who sent them, for they

294

came from Stirling Castle. A strange business. They stand accused of disobeying their bishop, I understand . . ."

"Stiff-necked miscreants!" James declared. "Contumacious—maist contumacious."

"No doubt, Sire—but still ministers of religion. I had also no doubt that Your Majesty would not wish them to be maltreated nor used like common felons. I held them secure, but used them honestly, not harshly, even discussing and reasoning with them, as befitted ordained clergy and men of education. Did I do wrong? Now I am accused by the Council of treating them *too* kindly!"

"You tell me that?" The King tapped Gondomar's arm. "This mare is fourteen years, mind. An auld friend."

"No doubt if I had treated the ministers harshly there would also have been complaint, Sire. For complaint was determined on—that I am sure. There was no need to send the prisoners to Dumbarton for that short time. They had been at Stirling and went back there."

"Is that a fact? Would you say that with age and practice, aye practice, a mare foals easier, or the reverse, man? Is age an impediment and coarctation, or no'? I'm told some women slip a tenth bairn as easy as you'd pod a pea!"

"I do not know, Sire. Fourteen years is not too old. I have foaled mares older than that. But—this of Dumbarton. I am convinced that certain people want me out of that castle. And will do much to get me out. For reasons of which I am not certain. Possibly to do with the tax collection . . ."

"Aye, weel—maybe so. But, see you Johnnie Stewart, that is *your* consairn. I didna mak you Keeper there to hae to fret about it my ain sel'. I've plenties on my ain mind, without the likes o' that."

"But, Sire—if there are your royal revenues at risk . . . ?"

"Laddie—*I* see no' a penny o' the revenues o' Dumbarton. Nor yet any other o' my Scots castles and properties. It a' goes—God kens where it goes! But no' to me. The upkeep o' Holyroodhouse and Falkland and the like. Maintaining the royal service in Scotland, as I am told—there's a wheen fine folk to maintain! Ooh, aye—plenties. Including my Lord High Admiral, eh? And the Chancellor. And the Chamberlain. And Lyon and his bubblyjock heralds!

Aye, and a' the pack o' lords o' Session and Justice. Aye, plenties."

"And the Lord High Treasurer himself, perhaps?"

James looked at him directly from those soulful eyes. "Johnnie Mar's an auld friend o' mine, young man. My foster-brother he was. We were skelpit together by yon auld deil Geordie Buchanan. Mind it."

John drew a deep breath. "Yes, Majesty."

"Aye, weel—you didna think, wi' al' that lot to keep in fine fettle, that there'd be any siller left to come to their sovereign-lord, did you? Why I must needs seek it elsewhere. Your faither could ha' told you that, I'll be bound. So—see you to Dumbarton, as best you can. Or we'll hae to find another Keeper."

Digesting that, John said, "You will be getting a report from the Chancellor, Sire—from the Privy Council. It will, I think, be critical . . ."

"Nae doubt, lad—nae doubt. I'm aye getting reports, from this, that and the other, maist o' them critical o' something or somebody! I dinna let them a' come between me and my sleep, mind!" He pointed. "Ha—noo she's coming! Aye, she's on the way. Watch this, Diego man— hooves first I'll be bound . . ."

For the next fifteen or twenty minutes the talk was clinical rather than financial or administrative, as Esmeralda, with a minimum of fuss on her part in contrast to that of her royal master, produced a fine bay colt, hooves first as James had prophesied. He himself did much of the midwifery required, and what he did not actually do he directed and expounded upon, as much apparently to the two physicians as to the Spanish ambassador. He was even more odoriferous and soiled than usual by the time that all was tidied up and dam and offspring re-united—but that was not a matter to concern the Lord's Anointed.

On their hobbling way back to the great house, with James clutching a Spanish and a Scots arm, from excogitating on the interesting relationship in conception, parturition, death and the hereafter, the improbability of reincarnation and the form of the spiritual body, he suddenly dug an elbow into John's ribs, and chuckled.

"You, Johnnie Stewart, should be showing mair interest in this matter, for we've a' go to pass on, some o' us sooner than others—and *you* are like to be consairned in the parturition bit o' it, a' too soon! Ooh, aye."

"I do not take Your Majesty's meaning . . . ?"

"You do not, eh? And you sae gleg! Why, it's marriage for you, man. And without delay. Marriage, aye."

John blinked. "Your Highness jests . . ."

"Not so. You've got yon Hamilton lassie wi' child, and you'll wed her. The jesting's by wi'."

"But . . . but . . ."

"Aye, you were aye a great one for buts, my mannie—but it's *my* turn! I was for you wedding the quean before, you'll mind—but noo it's fell necessar. I'm no' having young females wi' faitherless bairns aboot my court—I am not! I promised her a place, mind—you were strong enough on that, a few months back. Weel—noo she'll be wife to Sir John Stewart o' Methven, Keeper o' Dumbarton Castle! That'll dae her fine. So, you see—conception and parturition are right applicable, you'll no' can deny?"

"Sire! I . . . I . . . this is not right, just. It is unfair. Not marriage. I . . ."

"Dinna tell me you would refuse to mak an honest woman—or sort o' honest—o' the lassie, man? You've lain wi' her, many's the time. This is what can happen when you bed females—is it no', Don Diego? Safer, sometimes, wi' . . . others!"

"But, Sire, she . . . she . . ."

"Na, na—dinna say it, lad! Dinna say anything you might regret. She's going to be your wife—for that is my royal command. So her guid name has its importance, eh? If it's no' too late! You'll wed—that's a' that's to it. And it had better be right soon—before she begins to show. Och, you might dae a deal worse. She's got wits, that one, and plenties o' spirit. And she's weel enough connected. Sir Claud, her faither, wasna very bright but he was a decent-enough man. And his brother, Abercorn's nae fool. The Hamiltons hae some royal blood, mind."

"Are my feelings of no matter, Sire?"

"Your feelings were weel to the fore when you got

yoursel' up under the lassie's skirts, were they no'? Forby, there's mair feelings than yours to consider. So—enough talk. You'll be wed so soon as it can be contrived. You can be off the morn to see Cockayne and his Merchant Venturers, and you can forgather wi' your bit bride-to-be at the same time, at St James's, and decide on a day for it. As to the price you get frae Cockayne, mind to be not ower soft wi' him. *He'll* ca' it a' back frae the folk who need the paper, and plenties mair, you can be sure. Let us see you making a keener paper-merchant than you are a bridegroom! Or a Keeper o' Dumbarton . . . !"

Next afternoon, then, John presented himself at St James's Palace in no very happy frame of mind. He found not only Margaret Hamilton but Will Alexander with her, and two others of the Prince's gentlemen, playing cards and drinking wine, a scene of pleasant relaxation into which it is to be feared he intruded a somewhat souring note, however warm the young woman's greeting. He sought not to eye her lower person too directly—but to him she seemed no different from normal.

Will got rid of the other card-players presently, and then gave John some account of his activities since returning from Scotland. He had given the King and the Duke a report of the situation there. He had seen the Merchant Venturers at St Paul's, not Cockayne himself but Elias Woolcombe, and they were eager for the paper deliveries to commence. The ship from Leith had brought the first cargo into the Thames and the paper was now stored in a warehouse, Bertram's, at the Blackfriars Wharf. Woolcombe had been very urgent to get a price for it, from him; but he had said that was not for him to state. Had John heard about parliament's act ending the monopolies . . . ?

John told him that he intended to visit St Paul's immediately hereafter. Meantime, he desired a word with Margaret.

Alexander took the hint and withdrew.

The young woman, laughing, came to throw her arms around him again and to rub herself against his person. "You are good at getting rid of folk, John!" she said. "So long since we were together. I have missed you."

He stirred uncomfortably in her embrace. "You are . . . well? Or . . . well enough? In the circumstances . . ."

"Oh, yes—never been better. And the more so, now that you are back."

"But . . ." He glanced downwards, where her belly was continuing with a sort of rotation motion against his groin, distinctly disturbing. "Should you be doing this?"

"Why not? Oh—I see. You mean—that? No difficulties there—yet!"

"I am sorry."

"Sorry? Sorry for what, John?"

"This . . . trouble. The child."

"It is scarce a trouble. That is no way to speak."

"Perhaps not. When is it to be?"

"Oh, that? I, I cannot be sure. In the spring-time, it will be."

"You must have some notion, less vague than that?"

"Such matters are not so simple. We were . . . together, many times. Over a period."

"Yes—but you must know when, when . . ."

"John—I cannot tell you the exact time. Is it so important to you? One month, or the next?"

He shook his head. "I suppose not." He paused, and then blurted out, "You know that we are to marry? The King commands it."

"Marry, yes. But not only because the King commands, surely? We talked of marriage before . . ."

"*You* did!"

"You are less than gallant, John, I think! What is wrong with us marrying? You . . . enjoy me, sufficiently, do you not? And I you. We have much in common. The royal service, our Scots blood . . ."

"There is the matter of love."

"Love? What is love, John? We *make* love very well, do we not? We suit each other. We can be sufficiently close in other ways also . . ."

"There is more to love than that."

"How do *you* know? Are you in love with somebody else, John Stewart?"

He looked at her for moments on end. "I am, yes," he said at length.

"So–o–o! Why have you not married *her*, then?"

"I cannot," he said, shrugging.

"Because she will not? Or because she is already wed?"

He did not answer.

"Married, then. Who is this woman? Do I know her?"

"No. Nor shall you! That is my business, only."

"I see. So you are having an affair with a married woman—but it must be kept secret! In Scotland? Is that why you have been away so long?"

"No. Nothing to do with that. And there is no affair—none. I loved her before she married. A marriage forced on her by her father. She is entirely virtuous."

"Virtuous! Yet keeps you dangling! I know the sort . . ."

"You know nothing of it! And knowing nothing, will kindly say no more. It is no concern of yours."

"If I am to be your wife—as the King commands—and you are in thrall with another woman, it does seem to be of concern to me."

"Do you wish, then, to abandon the notion of wedding me?"

"Oh, no, John—oh, no! It is me that you have got with child, not this virtuous wife of another! I need a husband and father for my bairn, and she does not. I also need a place at court. So we shall be wed, as His Majesty decrees. But . . . so long as you remember this other, so shall I!"

He eyed her with the negation of love.

"When shall we have the wedding, then?" she asked, brightly again. "It had, probably, better be soon."

Curtly he nodded.

"Have *you* any preferred day? We are near to November. Yuletide would be best avoided. Do you agree? Then, say, in a month? St Margaret's Day sounds well. Whom I am named for. November the sixteenth. Have you anything against St Margaret? No? Good. But try to sound something more eager as a bridegroom. Sir John Stewart and his lady must keep up appearances, no? Where shall we be wed?"

"I care not. Since it is you and the King who are so keen, you can settle that between you."

"Very well. There will be much to see to before then—and no doubt *I* shall have to see to it!"

"As you say. I have to go now, to St Paul's. On the King's business."

"So soon? After so long a parting? You do not desire some little . . . enjoyment? Of, shall we say, a bridegroom's privileges? It might be contrived . . ."

"I thank you, no," he said stiffly. "I must go, if I am to catch these merchants, at St Paul's."

She nodded. "It is that way, is it? As you will." Then, she reached out a hand to his arm. "John—it will not be so ill—being married. You will see. With an understanding of each other, we will fare well enough. We need not be . . . difficult with one another."

"I hope so—indeed I do . . ."

In consequence of all this, John was not in his most accommodating frame of mind when he reached St Paul's. He could not find any of the Merchant Venturers whom he knew in the throng and was directed to a tavern in Seething Lane, a poor place for such influential traders, but full to overflowing. Woolcombe was there and the man Cardell. When they perceived John they did not delay in detaching themselves from others, and approached him as though he was a long-lost relative. Where had he been? Why the long delay? They had looked for him. His paper was waiting at the Blackfriars.

John told them briefly that he had been detained in Scotland. Had they examined the paper?

Yes, they had. The quality was about right for their requirements. How much?

"How much do you require?"

"We can take all that you can send us. If the price is right. How much money is what I meant."

John shrugged. "Three hundred shillings for the 1,000 sheets," he answered flatly.

The two merchants glanced at each other.

"Three hundred. That is £15 sterling. For 1,000 sheets." Woolcombe gazed into his tankard. "That is, delivered here, to London River? Fifteen pounds the 1,000. Ummm."

"Fifteen pounds . . ." Cardell repeated, examining the ceiling.

"Yes."

"Is there any reduction for quantity? A continuing purchase?" Woolcombe wondered. "We could make it a steady order. For regular deliveries. Some small reduction, sir?"

John could scarcely believe his ears. The price suggested in Scotland had been not much more than a third of that sum—120 shillings per 1,000. He had named 300 merely as an opening bargaining figure, prepared to chaffer. But they seemed to be taking it seriously. This monopolies ban must be hitting these people hard, that they were so eager. He would have thought that prices would be coming down, not going up. He took a chance.

"No, sir—no reduction. That is our price. Take it or leave it. We would have no difficulty in selling the paper elsewhere."

"This price will stand for further shipments?"

"In the meantime, yes."

"How many? How much in each cargo? And how often?"

"There are 30,000 sheets in this first consignment. We could send more, at a time. How often would you wish deliveries? Monthly?"

"We could take more."

"Fifty thousand sheets monthly, then? At 300 shillings per 1,000. Present quality."

"So be it. If that is the best that you can do for us. But, see you, Master Methven—there is one matter more. We would not wish you to sell to others also."

"I understood that monopolies were now to be unlawful?"

"No doubt, sir—but this is scarce a monopoly. But a private arrangement between buyer and seller. As all trade must be."

"Very well. Let us say that we shall consider no other sale in England without first informing you."

"It is agreed, then?" Woolcombe held out his great paw. "We'll shake on that, Master Methven. It's a bargain. We will seal it with the best ale. When can we have delivery?"

"When you have payment to hand."

"The morrow, then? At Bertram's, in Blackfriars. At twelve noon? Thirty thousand sheets. At £15 the thousand

That is £450 sterling. You will have the Merchant Venturers' note-of-hand for the sum, then. Made out to whom? Yourself, Master Methven?"

"No, sir. Made out to Sir John Stewart, Knight."

"*Sir* John? A knight . . . ?"

"Yes, In Scotland we do such things differently. You have the name? Stewart."

"Stewart it is, yes. Four hundred and fifty pounds. Tomorrow noon. Yes, Master Methven. Now—ale!"

Sir John Stewart, Knight, returned westwards with mixed feelings again. King James would be happy, at least. Even at 120 shillings there would have been a fair profit. But at 300, if he calculated aright, there would be no less than £270 profit. In sterling. For this load. And at 50,000 sheets a load, £450 profit. Each month. Surely the King would not grasp it all, thirled to money as he was? Some ought to come to himself—to help pay off Middlemas. And him soon with a wife to keep . . . !

16

They were married on St Margaret's Day in the private chapel of St James's Palace, a small and rather shabby sanctuary, now but little-used, and cold on a chilly mid-November day. Nor was there any large crowd to fill and warm the place, only a handful of guests, however distinguished some of them. One of the King's favourite chaplains, Valentine Cary, Dean of St Paul's, officiated, and made fairly short work of it. Will Alexander was groomsman and one of Margaret's cousins, another Margaret Hamilton, coltish, plump and plain, was bridesmaid. Another cousin gave her away, in the absence of his brother, the new Earl of Abercorn—the old one had died, in Ireland. He seemed almost glad to be rid of her. Ludovick was there and one or two of his friends at court. Otherwise most of the congregation appeared to be grinning young men, who were presumably friends of Margaret's, since John did not know any of them.

Margaret herself was certainly looking at her best, high-coloured, bold-eyed, smiling, scarcely a demure bride but clearly pleased with life—and no sign of pregnancy was evident. John, having taken himself in hand, put the best face on it all of which he was capable, and sought to look reasonably cheerful even if less than ebullient.

The King did not grace the occasion; perhaps that could hardly have been expected, however much of it all was of his engineering. His contribution was the wedding-feast at Whitehall, to which the court had returned for the winter, the Ralegh furore having died down. This proved to be a fairly modest affair of no great munificence, over which Ludovick presided and which fairly quickly became noisy, with the liquor flowing and only the two females present, neither of whom were shrinking violets. Presently, possibly attracted by the noise, James himself turned up, with Steenie Villiers, and, after proposing a toast to Sir John and Lady Stewart, settled down to some steady drinking.

John, in fact, could have done without this expression of royal goodwill, for it meant that he and Margaret were now stuck at this table until such time as the monarch might choose to remove himself, since none could leave before the King. And, once James started serious drinking, he could keep it up for hours.

However, Ludovick, recognising his son's lack of enthusiasm, not being a drinking man, presently had a word with James and then announced to all that he conceived that it was just possible that the bride and groom might be growing slightly impatient to proceed further with this auspicious day's, or night's purposes, and he suggested that, with His Majesty's permission, they should be allowed to get on with it. Whereupon, amidst the shouted rudery, James beat on the table with his goblet and declared that the vital, aye vital, matter of the bedding should not be longer delayed; and that it would be their pleasure and privilege to assist the happy couple to due fulfilment thereanent. Although, mind, he jaloused that this fine pair would require but little instruction and advice, being possibly already as expert at the business as any present! To loud cheering, all rose, eager to co-operate.

John had been afraid of something of the sort being envisaged, and had been ready to reject it in no uncertain fashion. But this of the King changed all; he could not flatly refuse a royal proposal. He had heard about these nuptial beddings, and wanted no part in one. But how could he avoid it, especially with Margaret showing no signs of alarm or reluctance?

"I thank you, Sire," he said, raising a hand. "But, since no guidance in the matter is required, as Your Majesty says, the lady and myself would prefer to take our departure in more private fashion. And not to disturb the feasting of you all. If you please . . ."

"Nonsense!" the new Marquis of Buckingham declared loudly. "You misjudge your lady, so soon! Meg Hamilton is none so ill-humoured, I swear!"

"I misjudge nothing, my lord. Would you deny me my first exercise of a husband's authority?"

"Na, na, Johnnie," James intervened. "*You'll* no' deny us *oor* right in this fell important matter? You've been wed before these witnesses. Now you'll bed before the said witnesses, in the guid auld-fashioned way. So, nae mair havering. Let us dae oor duty by these twa, friends a'."

So, like it or not, bride and groom were grasped and propelled from that dining-hall in triumph, and all but carried along corridors and down stairs of the palace to the very modest bedchamber prepared for the happy couple, John set-faced but Margaret laughing amiably. With the King nowise backward in the proceedings, John came to the perhaps jaundiced conclusion that this was indeed why James had come to grace the occasion.

Beside the large bed, the party divided—on this occasion very unevenly. Practically all the men took Margaret and began to undress her; there being only the one other woman, however, Cousin Margaret, John would have had sole attention had not the King and Steenie come to assist her, whilst Ludovick stook back, looking sympathetic. Great was the hilarity on the other side of the bed, the bride being notably more co-operative than her groom. John, normally no prude, found it all distasteful to a degree. Strangely or otherwise, he resented Steenie's fumblings much more than the young woman's.

Margaret was stark-naked first and being vociferously acclaimed—as indeed she deserved to be, with a well-proportioned, full-breasted and satisfying figure, adequately endowed in all respects, which she made no feeble attempts at covering, confidence in her own physical attractions entirely obvious. John, of course, was less confident, the male partners in these trying occasions more often than not tending to worry about their masculinity demonstrating itself, as it were to order, desire in the circumstances apt to be at a lowish ebb, however vigorous it might have been had they been alone. This was the situation now, and loud and detailed were the comments and instructions of the onlookers.

At this stage there was usually some spirited argument, on the part of the bedders rather than the bedded, as to which should be placed where, and when. Now Steenie, undoubtedly intent on getting his own back for that memorable occasion in Edinburgh's Candlemaker's Row, took charge, declaring that there was no question but that the bridegroom must be deposited first, and on his back, if there was going to be any sport at all, since assuredly he was in dire need of assistance. As it happened, this announcement proved to be something of a kindness to the victim, however unintentionally, for, in a sudden burst of real anger, John twisted round, fists clenched, and would have struck the Marquis had not the King hastily put himself between them, flapping beringed hands and babbling admonitions; and the spasm of wrath had the effect of deflecting John's preoccupation with physical problems for the moment and contributing some useful spirit to the situation.

James beckoned to some of the bride's supporters for aid, and a little reluctantly two or three of these young men relinquished their grip on their delectable quarry and came round to assist the bridesmaid to hoist John on to the bed, and there to hold him down, on his back, Steenie now keeping warily out-of-range, whilst their colleagues on the other side picked up Margaret, squealing with laughter, and deposited her on top of her new spouse. And thus the pair were held in place by eager hands, while advice and urgings were showered upon them and even wagers shouted, complimentary and otherwise.

If this was John's first nuptial bedding, Margaret had undoubtedly attended numerous others and knew what was expected of her. She squirmed about on top of her partner, rotating her stomach in practised fashion, and hoisting herself sufficiently forward to brush her prominent breasts and nipples across John's face and lips, worked into a rhythm which gradually increased in tempo. And, despite himself, the man felt his manhood rising to the occasion—and the development was noted and exclaimed upon by all. Margaret, legs wide, slid backwards somewhat, to regularise the situation, to applause and hand-clapping.

The young woman continued her effective ministrations in less urgent motion.

Ludovick, who had stood back throughout, now asserted

himself, raising his voice. "Enough!" he exclaimed. "We are all satisfied that this match is being properly consummated and looks apt to be fruitful. Our duty here is done. As father to the groom and good-father to this young woman, I declare this bedding adequately performed by all concerned. We shall now leave them to their own devices—with our blessing! Sire . . . ?"

"Devices, aye!" James said, leering. "As to fruitfulness—och, yon's no' hard to prognosticate! Mind, I couldna see much sign o' it, as yet—I could not!"

"Time enough, James. Now—let us return to the table . . ."

The King allowed himself to be led off, with backward glances—and none could refuse to follow the royal example, even though one or two parting kisses were deposited on Margaret's plump and busy white buttocks. At last the door closed behind the last of them.

"Lord, John," the young woman gurgled, "that was touch and go! I feared that you were not going to be able to do it! We would never have heard the end of that!"

Without a word, John suddenly and forcibly half-rose, rolled her over, to bestride her and assail her almost violently.

"That . . . is . . . better!" she gasped.

Somewhat to his surprise, John Stewart found his life remarkably little changed for being a married man. Whitehall Palace was not large and had long been crammed to overflowing by the court; the King had been able to provide no extra accommodation for the young couple, or at least had failed to do so. The bedroom they had occupied that first night thereafter was returned to its normal occupants. The ducal quarters were very restricted, like all else, consisting of only three rooms, Ludovick's own bedchamber, a small living apartment and a tiny closet in which John had slept, too small for two; besides, the Duke naturally did not want Margaret roosting in his rooms. So they returned to rambling St James's, where there was at least plenty of room of a sort. But, since the King seemed to require John's services ever more frequently thereafter, as a kind of confidential messenger, not only in connection with the paper-trade but on other errands, and expected him to be almost instantly available, he spent nearly as many nights in his old closet at Whitehall as at St James's. Margaret did not seem to mind.

The fact was that James was initiating a new policy of government, as part of his determination to bring down the power of the Howards and their aristocratic like, who had dominated public office for so long. His aim was now to insinuate almost complete nobodies into significant positions of influence, who would do what they were told, being entirely dependent upon the crown's support; but, whilst having no personal base of great wealth or inherited power, they must be able. And, so that they could be more easily got rid of, should any of them prove ineffective or a nuisance, they must all appear to be recruited by the Marquis of Buckingham rather than by himself; and so any blame for their conduct could be laid at Steenie's door. This was a carefully thought-out and far-reaching strategy, involving numerous departments of government, such as Chancery, the law courts, Customs and Excise, the Admiralty, the Mint, and, above all of course, the Treasury. In this key position, a comparatively new man, Lionel Cranfield, another city merchant, was installed, in place of the Howard Earl of Suffolk, and to him John was a constant courier with the King's secret orders and requirements. Others to whom John beat trails were George Calvert, the new joint Secretary of State, and Henry Yelverton the new Attorney-General. Also he went much to the Tower of London, to Sir Allen Apsley the Lieutenant-Governor, with instructions relative to the treatment and interrogation of the many Howards now in his charge. It was the jest of London that the said Howard faction should set up its own Privy Council in the Tower, since they had there a former Lord Treasurer, a former Lord Chamberlain, a former Secretary of State, a former Lord Admiral of England and a former Captain of Pensioners.

All this, as well as keeping John busy, meant that his initiation into married life was fairly gradual. There was one problem, however, which did come to cause some friction between them, and to concern him somewhat, and this was the matter of suitable employment for his wife. She declared, and he accepted it, that she could not sit all day at St James's twiddling her thumbs, however busy *he* might be; and, for his part, he recognised that, being Margaret, left idle she might well get herself involved in activities unsuitable for the Lady Stewart of Methven. So he besought the King to fulfil his promise, given at the time of the jewellery-extraction, that he would find Margaret some place at court to compensate for her loss in the Queen's service. James brushed this off at first, but, when John enlisted his father's aid, the King eventually came up with the rather extraordinary proposal that, once the Yuletide festivities were over, she should be attached to the establishment of the young Lady Katherine Manners, only child of the Earl of Rutland, and Baroness de Ros in her own right, the premier barony of England, who was to marry Steenie Villiers in the spring, when she reached her fifteenth birthday. Apparently this young person was somewhat odd—as allegedly was her father—had no experience of court or even city life, but was of all things already much interested in witchcraft, necromancy and the black arts. Clearly she must be taken in hand before she, and her great wealth, became the property of the Marquis of Buckingham. So she was to be brought to London and set up at Wallingford House, Westminster, in the care of Steenie's mother. But it was felt that a younger woman was required to be her companion and tutoress in the ways of court and society, and it seemed to the King that Meg Hamilton would suit, Steenie apparently agreeing.

John was doubtful about this. He did not like Buckingham and desired no closer association with him; and the heiress sounded a curiosity. On the other hand, it would solve a problem; and, if he refused agreement, James was unlikely to come up with any other appointment. Moreover, Margaret's down-to-earth outlook on life was unlikely to be affected by this girl's fantasies—as James, who was especially interested in witchcraft and allied subjects, pointed out. So he agreed to put it to his wife—and Margaret accepted the offer with alacrity.

So it was arranged. Margaret would move to Wallingford House, where a couple of rooms would be made available, to prepare all for the young Baroness's and the Countess of Buckingham's arrivals, John still less than easy about it, in his mind.

The Queen died at last, in March, and great was the stir occasioned, not least at Whitehall, where, the King learning that the end was approaching, took sundry steps. He ordered John and Margaret to go to Hampton Court, the moment his Anna breathed her last, to take charge of all valuables there in his name, until they saw what her will said. He ordained a spectacular funeral. And he departed for Theobalds to hunt, pointing out that he misliked funerals, deputing Prince Charles, Ludovick and Steenie to see to all.

So John had the unpleasant task of descending like some vulture on the Queen's possessions almost while her body was still warm, with authority now, but still with distaste. They found little in the way of jewellery, however; most had already gone. James would be displeased. John also was involved in making the funeral arrangements, this entailing much toing and froing to great houses all over London, and the soothing of ruffled feelings over precedence and the like, for in the end most of the arrangements were left to Ludovick, Charles being useless and Steenie bored.

It all turned out to be infinitely more difficult and frustrating than might have been anticipated, this mainly James's fault. For, although he so disliked funerals that he could not attend that of his wife, he nevertheless took all too great an interest in the proceedings from a distance, sending detailed instructions almost daily on how everything was to be done and who was to do what. And his requirements got more and more elaborate, and confusing, as time went on. And time did go on for, although, on his instructions, the Queen's body was brought from Hampton Court to Somerset or Denmark House a week after death, and there embalmed to lie in state, the funeral itself kept getting put off, as ever more ambitious ceremonial was devised; this partly on account of the planning having to be continually changed, but mainly because there was no money to pay for all this flourish. For instance, there was the command that 280 poor women were to form part of the funeral procession, each given a suitable black shawl—where James got the figure

311

of 280, no one could guess—and all the noble ladies in the cortège were to wear twelve yards of black broadcloth over their other clothing, and countesses sixteen. So money was of the essence and parliament would pay for nothing. Although the Queen's personal estate was now being valued at £400,000, with debts of only £40,000 it would be long enough before the bereaved spouse could lay hands on much of that and Prince Charles already claiming his share.

Things got even worse when the King, tiring of Theobalds outwith the hunting season, moved seventy miles further away to Newmarket for the horse-racing. John, for one, came to know that road, by Waltham and Bishops Stortford and Saffron Walden into Suffolk, all too well as the weeks passed.

In the end it was two and a half months after her death before the Queen was finally laid to rest, and in scarcely restful fashion, on 13 May, despite the inauspicious date. The funeral procession formed up outside Somerset House en route for Westminster Abbey, all in theory exactly as the latest commands had come from Newmarket. First of all was to ride the Captain of the Royal Guard, with a mounted troop of his men. Then a detachment of the Yeomen of the Guard from the Tower. Then the Archbishop of Canterbury and the Bishop of London—but not the other bishops, who were to march with the lords. The point was stressed that only the soldiers were to ride, all the rest to walk. Then came Garter King of Arms with his heralds, leading a choir of seventy singing boys chanting doleful music. There was then to be a suitable gap, whereafter would come the Prince of Wales, walking alone. Behind him would be the hearse, drawn by six matching black horses and bearing on top of the coffin an effigy of the Queen, in wax, made at great expense and splendidly dressed. It was hoped that the May sunlight would not melt the wax.

After the hearse would come the Queen's favourite riding-horse, led by her Master of the Horse—who had not had any horses to master for long, and this old beast now decrepit. Then was to follow the principal female mourner, supported by the two most high-ranking nobles in

312

England—both Scots, as it happened, the Duke of Lennox and the Marquis of Hamilton. There had been great trouble over this matter, for in the absence of Elizabeth of Bohemia, the only princess, who had not returned to England, the Countesses of Arundel and Nottingham had fought a virulent war over their respective claims, oddly enough both of them wives of Howards in disgrace. Lady Arundel's husband would have been Duke of Norfolk, Earl Marshal and head of the house of Howard, had his father not been executed by Queen Elizabeth for allegedly conspiring to free the then captive Mary Queen of Scots and put her on Elizabeth's throne. His kinsman, the Earl of Nottingham, had then been appointed acting Earl Marshal and premier earl of England. So both ladies claimed seniority, but James, after much lobbying at long range, had come down in favour of Arundel, since at least her father-in-law had been a supporter of his own royal mother. Lady Nottingham, however, swathed in heavy broadcloth like the rest, stalked immediately behind, sniffing, and ignoring and being ignored by Steenie, Marquis of Buckingham at her side, dressed at his finest in pale blue satin.

There followed all the other court ladies under their weighty loads of material, most difficult to walk in; and then the ranked nobility and aristocracy of England—such as were not required at Newmarket—with an admixture of Scots amongst them, all in order of precedence, most difficult and time-consuming to arrange, with constant contests and claims to be sorted out, and people like John and Will Alexander charged with the task, all but at their wits end. The bishops were particularly awkward, with much dispute over dates as to the establishment of bishoprics. This section of the procession extended to almost a mile long in itself.

In nice juxtaposition came the 280 poor women, many already fortified for the long walk with ales and spirits and making a lot of noise. Then followed the Lord Mayor, sheriffs and aldermen of the City of London, prominent amongst whom was Alderman Cockayne, whom John was most careful to avoid. Then the representatives of the guilds and liveried companies. James had nominated next what he called 'a host of mean fellows', which was adapted to

313

comprise the royal servants, minions of the lords and assorted churchmen below the rank of bishop.

Finally there came more of the Royal Guard and Yeomen, marking the official end of the procession—although a great assortment of the general public followed on thereafter, almost endlessly and in high spirits, for the Queen had ever been more popular than her husband, and considerably more generous.

This enormous concourse, over three miles of it, escorted James's Annie on her final earthly journey; and, since the distance from Somerset House to Westminster, by the King's defined route, was at least two miles, getting all there was a prolonged and confusing business to say the least, with John and the other marshals continuously hurrying up and down like sheep-dogs with a hopelessly unruly and outstretched flock, seeking to keep it moving at approximately the same pace throughout, preventing hold-ups and pile-ups, straggling, bunching and endless argument. The ladies in their trailing broadcloth particularly found the walk wearing, and few wore suitable footwear for the filthy streets, not being used to this mode of travel, so that much finery was sadly soiled before the Abbey was reached. The two horsed companies at front and rear proved to be a nuisance rather than any enhancement, being unable to proceed at the same pace as the pedestrians; so that those ahead soon disappeared while those behind over-ran the walkers, causing maximum disorder and all but a riot. The head of the procession was in fact almost two hours late in getting started, so that the tail would be much more so; and it was well past five o' clock in the afternoon before the leaders reached Westminster, in a state of exhaustion—although there had developed some hilarity and high jinks en route, by that time, thanks to the enterprise of sundry itinerant liquor-sellers who, having visualised conditions, paraded alongside the mourners shouting their wares.

As a consequence of all this, nobody was in a state for any lengthy obsequies—except perhaps the Dean of Westminster, who had not processed with the rest but met the cortège at the great west door of the Abbey, prepared to do well by the occasion. However George Abbot, Archbishop of Canterbury, who certainly had made the walk in his archiepiscopal splendour, now less splendid, was not slow to inform the Dean that brevity was now the order of service. The coffin, from under its effigy, was carried indoors theoretically on the shoulders of the Marquises of Hamilton and Buckingham and the Earls of Pembroke and Oxford, but the real weight was borne by underlings. At this stage, of course, most of the column was still over a mile away from the church and moving but slowly.

It was quickly agreed by the most authoritative, who of course were all at the front, that it would be highly inappropriate to wait endlessly for the riffraff to come up; and the Dean was given the order to commence forthwith. With new arrivals crowding in all the time, it did not greatly matter perhaps that he had to cut short his service drastically, since few could hear what he was saying anyway; and, when it came to the stage when Archbishop Abbot was to preach his sermon, with further processionists tramping in and objecting that they had not been waited for, he contented himself with a very few words of approximate eulogy—made easier for him by the fact that the ailing Queen had latterly been inclining ever more towards Catholicism, to Abbot's distinct disapproval. Indeed, after certain remonstrances from him, although they had hitherto been on good terms, she had refused him admission to her bedside.

So, with footsore mourners still arriving and the Abbey bells chiming six o'clock, all was expeditiously wound up, with an inaudible benediction, and the tide of mourning humanity put into prompt reverse—to considerable further chaos inevitably. Anne of Denmark and her effigy were left before the high altar, for the Dean, prebends and Knight Marshal to come and bury in Henry the Seventh's chapel at some convenient time later.

It was a pity that King James himself was not present to see and take part; undoubtedly he would have contrived to add much to the occasion.

Weary and bemused, John went back with his father to Whitehall rather than with Margaret to Wallingford House and the Buckinghams.

17

It was not really the paper-trade which got John back to Scotland that spring, but Will Alexander—or, rather, the King's insatiable need for siller, moneys, on this occasion channelled through Alexander. The especial need, this time, was to pay for Steenie's wedding, in which James was taking not only a profound interest but had agreed to pay for all—and George Villiers had ambitious ideas. The famous funeral was not fully paid for, as yet, so financial improvement was urgent; and all at court were besought, indeed commanded, to make suggestions on the raising of substantial funds. Various schemes were put forward, but most were either impracticable, risky or capable of producing only small sums. John's own proposal that a new supply of third-quality paper should be milled in Scotland for sale here in London—which really had been Woolcombe's earlier suggestion—came rather into that last category; it would take a considerable time to materialise, and, although it might perhaps double the moneys being received each month from the Merchant Venturers, this would certainly not be in time for the wedding, and even so would be only a few hundred pounds extra per cargo. Vastly greater sums were required.

Then Will Alexander came up with his scheme. The King had done quite well, many years before, out of his Plantation of Ulster, when he had sold off large areas of land in that part of Ireland, confiscated from the Catholic 'rebels', to colonists of Protestant origin, mainly from Scotland, who were further encouraged to make the risky purchase by being given hereditary knighthoods, or baronetcies, and so could call themselves sir and could also pass on the title to their heirs. This had been a great financial success—if not altogether so politically—but Ulster was not a very large province and they had run out of land there. So no new Ulster baronetcies had been created for years. Now, Will asked, was there any reason why a similar scheme should not be established elsewhere—somewhere plenty of land was available?

James, intrigued, but doubtful, demanded where? All land, unfortunately, was owned by someone. He could not think of any reason for large-scale forfeitures at the moment.

Will had pointed out that this might not be necessary— if the land was overseas, where it would be owned only by heathen Indians, blackamoors and suchlike. The New World—that was where to look, where there was lots of land.

Still the King objected. The New World was already grasped as colonies, save for the most dire wildernesses, by Spain, France, the Dutch and the Portuguese. The English colony of Virginia was of little use—it was already parcelled out to settlers, who were not making all that much of it, unfortunately. Nobody was going to pay good money for land there.

Alexander had agreed, but said that he had been making enquiries. There was one territory, first discovered by the Cabots in 1497—so it should be English, for John Cabot went there under letters-patent from Henry the Seventh. But it had not been colonised. Later the French had laid claim to it—but they had done little more than name it Acadia and visit it occasionally, with no real settlement. This Acadia was composed of two great islands off the coast of French Canada, not mountainous and reputedly containing much good land suitable for cattle and crops, with excellent fishing-grounds around, and all lying empty. Now, if this was to be taken over by the crown, under Henry's letters-patent, and parcelled out to new proprietors at so much a time, with a baronetcy thrown in, much money could be made; for there was a hundred times and more the amount of land there than had been available in Ulster. Will had been talking to a shipmaster who had put in there more than once for water and fresh meats, and he was loud in his praise for the place.

James had been sufficiently impressed to order his Master

of Requests to gain more information; and the more Will had unearthed, the better the prospects sounded. Acadia, all knowledgeable about the New World agreed, was a fair land, the natives friendly and not numerous, and the French doing nothing with it. So the King had agreed to a preliminary survey—not of Acadia itself but of the possibilities of the project being taken up, since it was the money he was interested in rather than any colonisation. But he was still cautious. He was not admittedly, presently on good terms with the French—which was part of his concern with the Spanish match, when the King of Spain's daughter would be old enough to wed Charles, the French and Spaniards being at loggerheads as usual; but he would not wish to provoke any outright hostilities with France on such a matter. So—he would make this, if it came to anything, a Scottish affair, which would allow him to disclaim responsibility, both to the French and, more important, to the English parliament, if trouble arose. A monarch had to consider such matters. Alexander, then, should go up to Scotland and sound out reaction. For this purpose they could call the place, not Acadia but New Scotland—or, since Latin was the more excellent tongue, Nova Scotia—and offer plots of land there at, say, 5,000 merks each for as many acres. No, make it 6,000 merks—which would sound better and even allow a little for Alexander himself on each sale made. And a title to go with it, to be sure. See how many would be prepared to invest. Some of these rich merchants and their sons? They need not actually go to Acadia, of course, so long as they paid. If there was a fair enough response they would set up the scheme forthwith— for the siller was needed promptly. When Will asked what authority he could quote for making such enquiries, he was told that he could, if he wished, call himself Lieutenant of New Scotland, or Nova Scotia, if that would help. And he could take Johnnie Stewart with him, to aid in this matter, and to see to the new paper project at the same time.

So it was Scotland again. In view of the fact that Margaret must be nearing her time, little as she showed it, John only asked formally if she would wish to accompany them on this occasion—to be assured that she would not. She had

318

quite enough on her hands with Katherine Manners and the Villiers woman, thank you! Besides, she was less enamoured of Scotland than John seemed to be.

On the road up, the two friends discussed procedure. John, actually, was not greatly in favour of the entire scheme, taking his father's line that, like the selling of knighthoods, it was a cheapening of the notion of honours and titles, doing nothing for the fount-of-honour himself, the King— save to fill his pockets. Will argued otherwise. In the past men distinguished themselves by slaughtering others on the battlefield or in single combat, and were knighted in consequence. Or were accorded some honour because they were the sons of their fathers or frequently the bastards of the lofty. Was that so much better? Arguably, these people who would pay good money for lumps of land in far places, presumably with the intention of developing it, were more likely to be admirable subjects than those merely born to privilege and position, prepared to exert themselves, to take a risk. And the blood of the nobility and ruling families required constant renewal from more lowly sources or they would become degenerate—as the Howards, for instance, had done. Was this not as good a method as any?

As a bastard of the lofty, John could scarcely contest that.

They drew up something of a list of possibles to approach. James had suggested rich merchants and their sons, and these were presumably to be found most likely in Edinburgh and Leith, in the Fife coastal towns, in Dundee, Aberdeen and the like. Will would tackle this major task, up the east coast; John, since he wished to visit Dumbarton anyway, would, as well as Perth, survey that area, Glasgow, which was growing in commercial importance, Renfrew, Paisley, Ayr and the south-west—although this was probably less hopeful territory. It was decided that they would meet again at Berwick-on-Tweed in a month's time.

John made his way first to the Water of Leith mills, and found all in order there, with much of the premises now converted to manufacture the required second-quality paper, and most of the extensions completed and coming into production, the labour force much increased. The notion of making a still coarser quality product for a new market was accepted by the Germans in principle, for it would enable them to use an ever-widened selection of rags gathered by their collectors. But there was just no room for such expansion at these mills, without affecting the present output. It would have to be done at the new Esk mills, where Vandervyk was now operating, with two mills out of the three working. So next day John rode south to the Esk valley, where he found the Dutchman well established, quite happy in his new life, with a comfortable house at Roslin. He was quite prepared to co-operate and expand. He said that his third mill, at Auchindinny, further south than these at Roslin and Polton, was nearing completion, and could easily be adapted to make the third-grade paper required; and of course the raw material for it and quality of the water was more readily available. He could use coarse rags and the downstream water—which meant that the two old meal-mills he had had his eye on but could not take up because of the less-than-pure water, could be brought into service. Well satisfied, John told him to go ahead.

From Edinburgh John made his way to Dumbarton, where he found all reasonably well, with Sandy Graham now established and quite enjoying his role as Deputy-Keeper. There had been no further word of Middlemas and no major difficulties in the collection of taxes and revenues. Sandy, as instructed from London soon after the Privy Council business, had taken most of the moneys he had accumulated to Edinburgh, where he had handed it over to old Sir Gideon Murray, the Deputy-Treasurer, who had given him a receipt and made no searching enquiries as to deductions, costs and the like, indeed seeming almost gratified to receive anything. The impression given was that the crown finances were in no very thriving state, nor very efficiently handled. There had been no more prisoners sent to Dumbarton.

John discussed with Sandy the New Scotland baronetcies project and gained from him the names of two or three individuals of means in Dumbarton town and vicinity whom he thought might conceivably be interested, his deputy having now become friendly with many in the neighbourhood where, to be sure, he was now an important figure. Next day, John paid a few calls locally, in consequence.

He was not notably successful in his sounding out of reaction—perhaps because of his own lack of enthusiasm. He spoke with four men, two local lairds of broad acres, one of them a cousin of Sheriff Napier; also a rich tobacco-importer and a ship-owner, first swearing all to secrecy as instructed. Neither of the lairds showed any real interest, and the merchant, although he sounded intrigued at first, did not commit himself. But the ship-owner went into the prospects in some detail, asking many questions, and indicated that he probably would be prepared to invest 6,000 merks. Would his wife become Lady Buchanan? He had no son, but his daughter was married and had a son. Could the title descend to him? John said that he was not sure but that he would find out.

He stayed three more days at Dumbarton, on one of them going round tax-collecting with Sandy, interested to see how this went. He found it all a less painful business than he had anticipated. Sandy had instituted a system of payment by instalments, which seemed to meet with approval—if anything could, in tax-paying. Indeed his methods and manner were such an improvement on Middlemas's that he seemed to be almost welcomed.

Sandy had another £900 of collections locked up in the castle. If the ducal four-in-ten proportion for the collection was adhered to, this would mean about £360 for himself—or at least for Dumbarton Castle—which seemed eminently satisfactory. It would pay for the £300 interest which his father had suggested that he pay to Middlemas, on the £3,000. And of course leave £540 for the crown. It had been John's intention to take this money in person to Stirling Castle, there to give it to Lord Erskine or whoever represented him or his father, Mar, the Treasurer, together with the £300 interest—on the assumption that they would know well enough where Middlemas was to be found, which he did not. But now it occurred to him, after hearing of the Deputy-Treasurer's reaction to the first payment, and being so well aware of James's desperate need for money, that perhaps he should just take the £540 south with him and hand it over to the King personally? After all, the revenues, customs and rentals for crown lands were all gathered in the King's name. Yet James had said that he never saw any of this money. It seemed ridiculous that the impoverished monarch of two realms should be reduced to scratching for funds in the most doubtful and undignified fashion when royal revenues such as Dumbarton's were going elsewhere. Just where they did go, John would have liked to know. But at least he could perhaps divert some small proportion into the royal pocket. He would send the £300 direct to the Privy Council, since it was on their order that he was paying it, leave say £60 with Sandy and take the rest to London.

He would pick it up on his way south, for he was going to Strathearn for a few days first.

At Methven his mother was glad to see him, of course, but he sensed that she was less carefree about his arrival than usual. He guessed that it might be because of his marriage, of which she possibly did not approve—he had sent a letter to her at the time. Or it might even be word of his father's impending remarriage which was upsetting her. Always very close to Mary Gray, at table that evening he had to try to get rid of whatever lay between them.

"My marriage," he said, abruptly. "It was . . . perhaps unfortunate."

"Was it, John? I rather feared so."

"Yes. I had been . . . foolish. And the King insisted. I had no choice."

"Save in getting this young woman with child in the first place?"

"Well—yes."

"And you do not love your wife?"

"No. How could I? When . . . !"

"What had the King to do with it?"

"She was the Queen's Maid-in-Waiting. James used her to take some of the Queen's jewellery, when she was sick and like to die. Before others could lay hands on it. And he used me to bring it from her to him. He promised Margaret some place at court, *his* court, if she did this. It went on for some time. We saw much of each other, necessarily—and secretly. I . . ."

"I see. But there was no love? Real love. Does *she* love you, John?"

"No. I am sure not."

"I do not think that I greatly like my new good–daughter!"

"Oh, she has her points. She is cheerful, good company enough, well–connected, strong in some ways."

"When is the child due?"

"That is unsure. I think in June or July."

Mary Gray shook her lovely head. "I am sorry, John— sorry about it all. More than I can say. So much other than what I have wished for you. In especial, now. Now that . . ." Her voice trailed away—which was not like that woman.

"Now that what? There is no use in mourning over what might have been. I have made my bed, as it is said—now I must lie in it."

"What might have been, indeed," she repeated. "John— David Drummond of Dalpatrick is dead. He died a month past."

"Wha-a-at!" Her son rose to his feet, so abruptly as to knock over his chair. He stared at her. "Dead . . . ?"

"Yes. He had been failing. He had never been right since he fell from his horse . . ."

"God! God in Heaven! Janet, Janet is . . . free! And I—I, damned and wretched fool, accursed, lost, *I* am bound! To Margaret Hamilton!" Turning, he kicked the fallen chair out of his way and strode from the table, over to the wall where he laid his brow against the panelling and beat on the wood with both clenched fists. "Christ God!" he groaned.

His mother watched him, with infinite pity. Presently she got up and went to him. "Johnnie, Johnnie! Forgive me for bringing you such tidings. It is hard, hard. My heart bleeds for you. So sore a price to pay, for . . ."

He pushed past her for the door, and out, out into the April dusk, to walk and walk. It was the small hours of the morning before Mary Gray, listening in her bedchamber, heard him come in and go to his room. She longed to go to him, to cradle him in her arms as once she had done—but made herself lie there. She could pray, at least.

Next day John was quiet, withdrawn, seemingly calm, out and about the property. He did not revert to the subject of his marriage, nor David Drummond's death, save, just before his early retiral to his room, he asked his mother whether Janet was still at Dalpatrick or had she returned to her parents' house? She was still at Dalpatrick, Mary said—and almost said more, but did not.

The following morning he rode westwards up the strath.

The house of Dalpatrick was a modest L-shaped fortalice of the previous century, tall and slender with two turrets and a stair-tower and many shot-holes, standing within a courtyard amidst orchards at a sharp bend of the Earn a mile or two upstream of Inchaffray Chapel. Dismounting in the yard, John made for the only door, in the foot of the stair-tower, under its heraldic panel with the Drummond arms. Here a maid-servant came to greet him. Her mistress, she said pointing, was over in the stables where a mare was foaling.

He crossed the cobbled yard to the range of stabling and peered in at an open doorway. He had a mental picture of that other foaling he had attended only months before, at Theobalds Park. This time only two people crouched there, a man and a woman. John's bulk in the doorway blocked out some of the light, and both attendant figures looked up. At first there was no further reaction, then, as the newcomer stepped inside and the daylight illumined his features for them, he heard a gasp, and Janet rose to her feet and came, almost running. Then she halted, staring, biting her lip.

"Janet!" he exclaimed, thickly. He too halted. So they stood, wordless.

Recovering herself, she said a word to the stableman and then came to him, restrainedly now. "A good day to you, Sir John," she said. "It is good to see you."

As he bowed, she took his arm lightly and moved out into the yard.

"Janet!" he said again, in that strangled voice.

"Not here, not now," she murmured, and led him, not to the house but across the cobbles to a side-door in the court-yard walling which gave access to the orchard. Side by side, tense, they walked under the apple trees to still another

324

door, and through into the outer orchard. Here, away from all possible observation, she removed her hand and turned to face him.

He held out his arms to her, features working, but she shook her head, tight-lipped.

"I did not know. That you were here," she said. "When?"

"Two days. I could not . . . wait longer!"

"Your wife? Is she with you?"

He swallowed. "No. God help me—no! I . . . oh, Janet! Janet!"

He saw her lip trembling now, but she controlled herself. "Should . . . you have come?"

"I had to. I had to see you, I tell you. Oh, lass—I *had* to! I only learned . . . two nights ago . . . of, of *your* state. His death."

She looked away.

"Too late. Too late, by only weeks! A month or two. I mean . . ." He held out an open hand to her. "If only . . ."

"If only, yes. If only you . . . had not married."

"I had to, Janet. The King . . . Although, I swear, had I but known, I would have fled the King's service, come here for you, whatever he said. And whatever *she* said!"

"She, yes. What of her, John? This other?"

"Can you ever forgive me, lass? Although I will never forgive myself. I, I lay with her. Margaret Hamilton, one of the Queen's ladies. She was . . . friendly. We had to work together, in the Queen's affairs. Then the King's also. I suppose that I needed a woman. I had no thought of marriage. She . . . offered herself. Very freely. I went to her. Then she became with child. The King owed her a place at court, *his* court. He could not employ a woman with a fatherless bairn. He declared that we must marry. I did not want to, but . . . what could I do? You, the only one I ever wanted to wed, were married. You see . . . ?"

"I see it, yes. A child! And this, your wife? To bear your child? What are your feelings for her?"

"At this moment, I hate her! Though that is unfair, I know. But I have never loved her, never loved anyone but you, Janet. You must believe that."

"I did believe it. And then . . . and then . . ." She pointed to a lichen-grown bench under the trees. "Let us sit, John. And try to think, and talk, more, more wisely. Although I never felt less wise!"

"Nor I. But . . . can you forgive me?"

"For what? Lying with another woman? I had no right to you, in that. I, after all, had lain with another man, my husband. Marrying her? If she was with child by you, I would I suppose, have expected it of you. So what is there to forgive? You could not know that I was to be a . . . widow."

"No. But I do not forgive myself, nevertheless. To have thrown away bliss, all joy, for a loveless marriage! To have squandered all our happiness, so . . ."

"Not all, John—not all. For you have restored to me *some* happiness this day, which I thought that I had lost for ever. This, that you still love me, and me only. It is wrong of me, I know. But always the worst hurt was that you had loved another. Enough to wed her. I did not know about the child. Now, I know that this was not true. That you have not stopped loving me. This may be wicked, to be sure. A man should love his wife, and another woman, myself, should not love him. But . . ."

She got no further. His arms went round her and pulled her to him, on that bench, his lips seeking hers, eagerly, hungrily. And for a moment or two she responded, almost as eager. Then she moved her head away, drew back in his embrace and put a finger up to cover those lips of his.

"No, John—no!" she panted. "This, this will not do. Any more than it did before. Whatever our feelings, my dear, we are still . . . not for each other. You are a married man, soon I suppose to be a father. We cannot shut our eyes to it, whatever we would wish. You have married a woman—as I married David. Without love, but still wed in the sight of God and man. I must not cheat this Margaret, nor must you. Is it not so?"

That, sounding almost like a plea, was hard indeed to agree with, a cry for help rather than any strong assertion. He, who needed all the help that he could get, groaned aloud. "What in God's name, then, are we to do?"

"I do not know. Save—not this! We must be strong,

John—honest. We each deserve it, of the other, do we not? And, after all, we are no worse off than before, are we? Then, I was wed to another and you could not have me. Now, *you* are wed to another and I cannot have you! If we could bear it before, we can bear it now."

Unconvinced, he shook his head, an arm still around her. That she allowed, at least.

"Must I still keep away from you?" he demanded. "As I have had to do, all this time?"

"It would be wise, I suppose."

"Wise! Wisdom I know little of, clearly! I *must* see you, lass, when I can. I will run mad otherwise, I think . . ."

"It will not make it easier for you, John—for either of us. But, I too . . ."

"Where are you to be? Can you remain here, at Dalpatrick? Or must you go back to your parents at Innerpeffray?"

"I cannot tell. As to Dalpatrick. As you know, there is the custom that a childless widow is not put forth from her husband's property for at least nine months after his death, lest she is with child, and a son may be born to heir it. No child will be born to me. But I should be able to remain here until autumn, at least. David had no true heir nearer than his uncle, Drummond of Machany, who has his own greater property. He may turn me out—but I shall have my widow's portion, my jointure. I shall fare well enough."

"If you went back to your father's house, I would never be able to see you."

"That I shall not do, John—whether we see each other or no. I am my own woman now, in that, at least."

"Praise be for that!" He paused, and belatedly asked after her past troubles. "Your Davie . . . ? Was it very grievous? Latterly?"

"It was bad, yes. To see him waste away. To be able to do little for him. Once he knew that he was crippled for always, I think that he did not want to live. He was a man who required to be up and doing always, work and movement. He could not abide being still. He needed the company of others. He was a good man in most things, John. And I was a sore disappointment to him, I fear. I tried not to be. But . . ."

He nodded. "We all were losers in that folly. Why had it to be this way? Why could it not have been as it should? For his sake, as well as ours?"

"I have asked myself that, a thousand times. Profitlessly. No use in such thoughts, John. Tell me of *your* doings. In London. And at Dumbarton . . ."

He remained with her most of that day, although they recognised that this was almost certainly unwise, and that the doings of such a kenspeckle character as Sir John Stewart of Methven, Governor of Dumbarton and Gentleman to the King, would not go undiscussed in every detail in Strathearn, however private their association seemed to be. But each was all too well aware, also, that it might well be long before they saw one another again, especially alone; and they just put off the parting. When finally he left her, it was as though they were being bodily severed however restrained their physical contacts.

At Methven that night, when John appeared for his meal, his mother spoke of this and that, receiving scant response until, presently, she asked outright.

"Well, John—did you see her? And are you more content? Or less?"

"I shall never be content," he said flatly. "But—I am glad that I went to her."

"She received you kindly?"

"Yes. Or . . . sufficiently kindly. I do not wish to talk of it."

"No. But others may!"

"We were discreet."

"As well. For you do not lack for enemies, John, who would use aught against you. In especial use Janet Drummond, if they could."

"Do you think that we do not know that?"

"I speak only for your own good, and hers. What do you intend?"

"What *can* we intend? What can we *do*? We shall see each other, on occasion. At arm's length, Lord help us! But . . . we know that we love each other, despite all. I suppose that that must serve."

"I doubt if it will." But she eyed him understandingly.

"Discretion is apt to wear thin, where love is concerned. *I* should know! Your father and I scarcely maintained *our* discretion! So who am I to speak? But—are you prepared to hurt, and be hurt, further? You will, John, if you continue to see each other."

"You did."

"Janet Drummond is not Mary Gray. Nor you the Duke of Lennox!"

"At least I would not marry again, for the third time. Knowing that you were free!"

She shook her head, but not in anger. "As I say, you are not the Duke. With a duke's responsibilities. I blame Ludovick nothing for this new marriage. He needs an heir—which I cannot give him now, even if he wed *me*. And the King requires it. What I have with your father no other woman can ever share. But—is Janet Drummond prepared to be in that position? Or you to put her there?"

He looked at her but did not answer.

"Think well then, Johnnie. I shall say no more. But think well . . ."

Two days later he was on his way south again.

At Dumbarton he picked up the money and took two of the garrison to act as armed escorts for the pannier-garrons bearing the coinage, until he should meet up with Will Alexander and his groom at Berwick. No one was to know how valuable was the load they carried.

He went by Glasgow and there interviewed a number of possible candidates for the New Scotland project. He obtained a rather more positive reaction than he had anticipated, accounted for no doubt by the fact that a fair proportion of the investors in James's previous and similar Ulster plantation scheme had emanated from this area, and the idea was familiar. Also Glasgow had become very much a trading city since the Reformation, with its eyes on far places. New Scotland might seem not quite so far away, here on the Clyde, as it did elsewhere. And titles could appeal to the intense rivalry of merchants.

He left with fully a dozen probables and as many again showing some interest.

He went on westwards to Renfrew, Paisley and Greenock,

where he did less well. But he felt that he had gained sufficient evidence for the King, and Will, to indicate that the project was probably viable; and he did not think that duty or friendship demanded much more of him. He still was less than enthusiastic. So he did not try very hard at Ayr and the Kennedy country of Carrick further south.

Thereafter, crossing the roof of Lowland Scotland by the Nithsdale and Lowther Hills to the headwaters of Tweed, wild country this, he followed that noble river down its twisting and very lovely hundred miles to its mouth at Berwick. He was two days early for the rendezvous.

Will arrived next day, and John could send his two escorts back to Dumbarton. Will was not exactly depressed, for that was not his nature, but was less enamoured of his project than he had been. He had found precious little eagerness to become involved, in Edinburgh or up the east coast areas. In fact, John's comparative success at Glasgow represented the highlight of the trip, it seemed, ironically. Between them they had raised only about a score of probable investors, and not much more than that of possibles. Whether James would consider that sufficiently encouraging to go ahead with the scheme remained to be seen. However, on his journeyings, Will had composed most of a new poem—which was perhaps more important? It was on the subject of David and Jonathan, which, considering their manly love for one another, he reckoned might appeal to their odd monarch. What did John think?

John, who was no poetaster, murmured something suitable. For his part, Will thought that John's idea, of handing the Dumbarton collections directly to the King, was an excellent one. What Mar, Erskine and the Scots Privy Council would think, however, was another matter.

In due course they arrived at Theobalds Park, to discover that James had left for Whitehall only the day previously. So they rode on to London. At Whitehall they learned that the King was being entertained to a banquet in the city by the new Lord Mayor of London—who turned out to be none other than William Cockayne of the Merchant Venturers, formerly alderman and now newly knighted for the occasion. John did not imagine that paper, its manufacture and pricing, would be discussed at the mayoral table, but with James one never knew.

It was late, in consequence, before the monarch returned to Whitehall, but in excellent spirits. Ludovick, less joyful, came temporarily to his own quarters for money, and found John and Will waiting there. Glad to see them and asking news of Mary Gray, the Duke informed that James, tonight, was in an elevated mood, and was for once shunning his bed and determined to make a night of it, drinking. He was welcome to that but unfortunately he was also in a gaming mood. For the Duke himself playing cards and drinking was a fatal conjunction and he was commanded to take part. Those who played with the King needed a clear head. James liked to win; but he must not be allowed to win too handsomely or his victims could be ruined—and too much liquor could affect Ludovick's judgment in this matter, as he had learned from long experience. In the circumstances, he rather hailed the arrival of his son and Alexander. They should come with him to the royal chamber. They might possibly divert James's mind from the cards and wine, to some extent.

Somewhat doubtfully they went with the Duke.

They found the King settled before a roaring log-fire, although it was a warm May night, in the ante-room of his bedchamber, with two others, Francis Bacon, now Lord Verulam, and James Hay, Earl of Carlisle, one of the King's original Scots cronies. There was no sign of Steenie. Bottles and flagons were ranged conveniently on a table beside that on which cards and coins were stacked.

At sight of the two younger men, James, in the midst of a vehement exposition on something or other, stopped and looked distinctly displeased. Spluttering wetly, he pointed at the new arrivals and flapped a dismissive hand. Lennox, however, was probably the only man in two kingdoms who might ignore such royal gesture.

"These two have arrived from Scotland, James," he said cheerfully. "With good tidings which I think you will wish to hear."

"Maybe so. But the morn will dae fine, Vicky Stewart. I'll see them the morn."

"As you will, Sire. But siller and poetry make an unusual combination. I guessed that you would wish to hear of it forthwith."

"Eh? Eh? Siller and *poetry*, did you say? What's this, what's this? It was yon Acadia I sent them to speir aboot. Whatlike havers is this?"

Ludovick waved an encouraging hand at his two companions.

John and Will exchanged uncertain glances. It was the latter who found words first.

"We attended to the New Scotland project, Sire. And found *some* support. But, on my long travels, I composed a new poem, a heroic work, which I have entitled 'David and Jonathan', or perhaps just 'Jonathan'. And, and dedicated it, in humble service, to Your Majesty." That was the first John had heard of dedication.

"Hech, hech—is that a fact? Maist meritorious—if it has the quality, mind. Yon other bit you did, about 'Monarchick Tragedies' was it, had flaws, mind, flaws."

"Yes, Sire. But I took to heart Your Majesty's wise criticisms and advice and have sought to better my muse accordingly."

"Uh-huh. Creditable. Weel—let's hear it, man."

"Sire—it is a lengthy piece. Covering many pages. I have not brought it on my person. It is with my gear, in my lord Duke's lodging . . ."

James's face fell, even though those of his companions did not. He raised a minatory finger. "You shouldna raise false hopes, man. We are displeased." He turned on Ludovick. "You said poetry and *siller*, Vicky? Is this likewise no' to be forthcoming?"

"My son John will tell you, James."

John cleared his throat. He wondered at the wisdom of saying what he had to say in front of Verulam and Carlisle. But he could hardly voice his doubts.

"We spoke before of the revenues and taxes payable to the castle of Dumbarton, Sire, of which I have the honour to be Your Majesty's Keeper," he said. "I learned that none of the moneys so collected came to Your Majesty's person. This seemed to me . . . unsuitable, when all is collected in your royal name. So, on this occasion, instead of sending it to the Treasury in Scotland, as hitherto, I thought to bring some of it south with me, to hand over to Your Highness."

James stared, slack lips forming a wet circle. "You did that, Johnnie Stewart! How much?"

"Five hundred pounds, Sire. On this occasion."

"Guidsakes—£500!" Majesty looked around him, almost at a loss—which was unusual, to say the least. He took off his high hat, which he was wearing with his bed-robe over partial undress, looked inside it, and put it on again. "Man, Johnnie—a' that?"

"Yes, Sire. Did I do wrongly?"

"Och, well—no, no. Leastways . . ." He scratched at his straggly beard. "Five hundred pounds sterling in siller! No notes o' hand? I could use £500, right enough. But—Johnnie Mar's no' going to like this!"

"Johnnie Mar, I think, has been doing very well for long, James," Ludovick observed.

"Ooh, aye. But he's the Treasurer, mind. Wi' much to see to. And an auld friend."

"I will take it back, Sire, if I erred in my judgment," John said. "And pay it in to the Treasury. As the last half-year's collection was paid."

"Eh? Bide a wee, bide a wee. How much was that, man?"

"Nearly £900 I think, Sire."

"God-a-mercy! Nine hundred pounds—o' *my* revenues! Just frae Dumbarton? That's a fell lot o' siller going some place!"

"So thought I, Highness. Did I misjudge?"

"I'm no' sure, man—I'm no' right sure. Vicky—when you were keeping Dumbarton, *you* never thought on this?"

"I must confess I did not, James. The collection was always dealt with by that rogue Middlemas and sent, after due deductions no doubt, straight to the Treasury. I had little to do with it."

"I'ph'mm. Maybe. But what's the rights o' it? I should get some o' the siller frae my royal lands and customs, should I no'?"

"I would certainly say so, yes."

333

"Frankie Bacon—you're a lawyer and clever, ower clever maybe! What say you?"

"Sire, I would not presume to submit an opinion," Verulam answered genially. "On a matter concerning Scotland. Your law there is different from ours."

"Och, be no' sae nice, man! This is no' a court o' law! Gie's your opine."

"Well, Majesty, it would seem to me that there are two aspects here," he said. "There are royal lands and there are customs and taxation. Without being competent to judge exactly, I would think that they should be separated. Customs and taxation are scarcely a matter for the privy purse, I fear. They are to be used for the needs of the state—through the Treasury, yes. That is as it would be here, in England. But royal lands and the rentals therefore are different. These, it seems to me, might well come to your privy purse, since they are not the state's lands but the crown's. Certain other items, also. I may be wrong, but . . ."

"And you, Jamie Hay?"

"Take it, Sire. Take the lot, I say! And let Johnnie Mar whistle for it!" Carlisle advised, grinning.

James eyed them all. "Aye, well—we'll see," he said. "You, Johnnie Stewart—bring me this £500 the morn and we'll see what's what. I'm no' saying that you've done just right, mind. But there could be right in it. Now—you can be off, the pair o' you. We hae business to transact here. Awa' to your beds, laddies . . ."

Enviously Ludovick watched the younger men bow themselves out.

Late as it was, John left Whitehall for Wallingford House, while Will made for St James's.

At the palatial residence which the Marquis of Buckingham had bought to complement his new state, the servants were used to untimely comings and goings, and a porter on duty admitted John without difficulty. The rooms Margaret had been allotted were in a wing of the great house to the rear, near the servants' quarters. Making his way there by darkened corridors, John entered their outer room, where the remains of a fire still flickered on the hearth. There was just light enough to see that the room was empty but untidy, with platters, flagons and beakers on the table. Lighting a couple of candles from the fire, he cast about for some food, for he had not eaten for long. There were some scraps of cold fowl left on the platters and some broken sweetmeats. He was stepping over to the cupboard to see what might be available there when the sound of movement reached him from beyond the inner door, the bedroom. He went to it, calling, "It is myself, Margaret—John. Just back."

He raised the latch but found that the door was locked. Distinctly he heard whispering beyond.

Frowning, he rattled the door. "Margaret!" he called.

There were further faint sounds from within. Grimly he stepped back, waiting. When the door did not open, he went to pick up one of the candles. There was another door to that bedchamber—most of these apartments were inter-communicating, not having been built as suites—and he could reach that from another room further along the corridor. Moving to their outer door, his candle illumined a chair nearby. Over this was flung a cloak, black, decorated with golden filigree-work. Picking it up, he stared. He knew that cloak.

His hand was on the outer latch when he heard the inner door open behind him, and he turned. Margaret stood there, a wrap loosely thrown around her. Under it, clearly, she was naked, her hair tousled. They gazed at each other.

"I disturb you!" he jerked, gratingly.

"You do, yes," she answered, a little breathlessly. "You, you come at a strange hour!"

"Who else do I disturb?" he demanded.

"No one in particular, John," she said, with an attempt at lightness. "It matters nothing. One of the Countess's ladies. You will not know her. It grows lonely, sleeping alone."

"You lie, Margaret," he declared. "That cloak—it is a man's cloak. George Villiers'. The King gave it to him. He should be more careful with so kenspeckle a cloak!"

She said nothing.

Striding forward, he pushed past her roughly, into the bedroom, still with his candle. The great bed was rumpled but empty. The other door, at the far side of the chamber, was ajar. He hurried over to it, and through. The apartment beyond was empty likewise, but its further door was open. He went to peer through that also but saw nobody.

Back in their own room, he found Margaret sitting on the edge of the bed.

"She has gone. She must have borrowed Steenie's cloak," she suggested, brazenly. "After all, she is one of his mother's people and this *is* his house."

"Spare yourself your inventions!" he told her grimly. "I have a good nose. That was a man sharing your bed—do not try to deny it."

"No—then I will not deny it, John Stewart," she exclaimed. "Why should I? You are a husband only in name! You leave me for weeks, months, at a time. You care nothing for me . . ."

"You are my wife."

"In name only, I say. You are no true husband to me, nor ever have been. I am a whole woman, no shrinking nun! I need a man . . ."

"Damn you—my wife's body is not for other men, Steenie Villiers or any, to use. I . . ."

"You were sufficiently happy to use my body before, when it suited you! I do not recollect you complaining of other men then!"

"Whore!" he cried, clenching fists. He only restrained himself from striking at her with an effort. At the threat in him she rose, as though to dart away, and the wrap she wore fell off.

Tensely they looked at each other, she at his fists and his working features, he at her full and very splendid body, large breasts with dark circular aureolas, and rounded belly above rich auburn bush. And, angry as he was, it was that gently rounded belly which, as it were, brought him up short. He actually pointed at it.

"You . . . you are not . . . with child!" he got out. "Look—you are no different than ever you were. Not pregnant! It would be next month, or the next . . ."

"No," she admitted. "It was, shall we say, a mistake. Such can happen."

"Merciful soul of God—a mistake! A lie, rather—a damnable lie! You never *were* with child. It was but a trap. To trap me into marrying you! Curse you, Margaret Hamilton—curse you, for a liar, a cheat and a whore!"

"And you for a sour, stiff prig! And a fool, likewise!"

"You are right in that, at least!" And, in a different voice, opening those clenched fists to an open-palmed, helpless gesture, he said, "Woman—you have cheated me out of the best thing in my life!" And, turning on his heel, without another word, he left her there beside the bed, to stride off through the outer room and out, slamming the door behind him.

Hunger and weariness forgotten, he walked the streets for the rest of that night, a man all but bereft of his wits.

18

John Stewart was not the man to let matters lie. Out of his wanderings that night and all the turmoil of his mind, two matters were clear to him. His marriage was to all intents at an end; and he had a score to settle with George Villiers. So, in no very composed state of mind, next day he went in search of Steenie. He traced him to Whitehall, indeed to the King's bedchamber. He could not follow him therein, save by royal command; but he could, and did, wait for him in the audience-chamber adjoining, through which the Marquis would have to pass when he emerged. He was not alone in his vigil, for there were always suppliants and litigants tarrying there in the hope of an audience with the monarch or his advisers.

He had quite a long wait, as did the others, for although there was considerable passing in and out of officers and secretaries, the King made no appearance. But John was now possessed of a cold, steely patience. He sat on, as others came and went.

At length Villiers came out, with the Surveyor-General of the royal buildings, one Inigo Jones, whom James was having design him a new banqueting-hall for this palace— although how it was to be paid for went unexplained. Steenie looked as though he was not listening to Jones, who was talking volubly, the company of mere architects being scarcely his choice. John at least relieved him of that burden.

"My lord," he said, rising and stepping directly in front of the elaborately-dressed favourite, "a word with you."

At sight of John, and at the curtness of that address, the Marquis hesitated. Then he waved a hand with a perfumed handkerchief—he was on record as saying that one required strong perfume in the close company of the Lord's Anointed—and waved the interrupter away.

"Another time perhaps, Stewart," he said loftily.

"No—now!" That was harshly enunciated and with no lowering of voice.

Steenie glanced swiftly round the chamber, noting the many watchful eyes upon them. A frown darkened his almost beautiful features. "I said another time. Out of my way, sirrah!"

"You escaped me over quickly last night, Villiers. By a back door! Not today!" John did not move aside, but he did incline his head to the architect. "Your pardon, Master Jones," he said.

That small, dark man, glancing from one to the other, prudently bowed to both and hurried off.

"Have you lost your wits, man? How dare you!"

"I dare much more, I assure you—and trust that you will also! And not in a bedchamber this time!"

"God's Death! I . . ." Villiers, again glancing round, restrained himself, shrugged and then turning, threw the word "Come!" back at his provoker, and stalked whence he had come.

John followed him into the ante-room between the audience-chamber and the royal private quarters, where the guard on duty was curtly dismissed and the door closed behind them.

"You insolent fool!" Steenie jerked. "You shall pay for this, I promise you. What do you want with me?"

"Some small satisfaction—only that! To tell you to your pretty face that you are a cheat, a mountebank and a whoremonger! And to ensure that you pay for what you have done. If you have the courage . . ."

"What a God's name are you at, damn you? More of this and I will have that guard back and you off to the Tower, you wretched Scotch ape! I . . ."

"Did you get your cloak back from my wife's bedchamber this morning?" John had to raise his voice to overbear what was almost a shout.

The other's open mouth opened wider, and then shut again, wary suddenly.

"You ran, Villiers—you ran, curse you! From her bed. Like the craven you are. When you heard me at the door. I was just too late to catch you."

339

Steenie cleared his throat. "I do not know of what you speak," he declared. "This of your wife. You rave . . . !"

"You lie, man! So you are a liar as well as the rest. You were in Margaret's bed last night. In your Wallingford House. When I came. Behind a locked door. You bolted—but left your cloak. The cloak the King gave you."

"You have no proof of that. Save the cloak. And I deny it."

"My wife did not deny it, hot from your arms!"

"Meg does not need to deny it. Since I do!"

"So she is Meg to you? What was your cloak doing in her chamber, then?"

"Some other must have taken it there. If there it was."

"Some other?"

"To be sure, some other. Think you Meg's bed is reserved for you?"

"Damn you, you dastard! You poltroon! Can you not at least admit your guilt like a man?"

"I admit nothing, Stewart. Now, go—before I call the guard."

"Call the guard—and I call others. Many others! Who would be interested to hear this! When you are to marry this Manners heiress in a month's time. I swear it should concern Rutland! And what of the King?"

"You would not dare, fool! I can silence you, never doubt it. And will. Silence you once and for all . . ."

"Ha—that is better! Now you talk sense. For that is why I am here. To give you opportunity to silence me—or me you! For good. I will meet you. Wherever you will. With swords, dirks or pistols. Name you the day and the place."

"Dizzard! Do you think that I, Buckingham, would demean myself to cross swords with you? And over Meg Hamilton? You must be crazed, with your cuckolding."

"Perhaps. But meet we will. Or else we will have this thing the talk of London . . ."

"You'll do nae such thing, neither o' you. And that's that!" They jerked round to find James standing in the further doorway, in night-shirt and hat. "You'll be done wi' this folly, the pair o' you, d'you hear? I'll hae nae mair o' it."

"But, Sire . . ."

"I've told you before, Johnnie Stewart—nae buts! This is the end o' it."

"It is my wife, Sire. I . . ."

"I ken, I ken—I heard it a'. Yon peep-hole and lug I made can be right convenient—as I told you, yon time. Your wife's no' a' she should be, maybe—but many's the wife's that way. Aye, and husbands. I dinna care whae's been in your Meg's bed—but you're no' going to turn a' here tapsalteerie because o' it, you are no'. Mind you that. And you, Steenie—the same to you. You've been a right fool, I can see that fine. But this is the end o' the folly, d'you hear? I'll no hae my court and plans cowped by any hot-rumpit wench! So—the twa o' you can forget it!"

"I cannot do that, Sire," John said levelly. "When it is a man's wife and honour . . ."

"Then you will leave my court and royal presence, John Stewart! Aye, leave it. I've been thinking for a whilie that it's about time you went back to Scotland. To bide. There's no' sufficient for you to dae here to keep you frae girning. You can serve me better up yonder. At Dumbarton, aye Dumbarton. I'll no' hae you hang-dog around here, wi' your grouch at my Steenie—fool as he is! So that's settled. You'll be awa', Johnnie—awa'. Forby, your faither aye says that you're never content but you're in Scotland—God kens why! So you'll no' break your heart, eh?"

John swallowed, scarcely believing his ears. "When . . . when do I go, Sire?"

"Just sae soon as you like, man. The sooner the better— for I dinna want you around wi' this wedding o' Steenie's coming up. You might forget yoursel' and my royal commands. You might talk. And there'll be *nae* talk, you hear? Nane. Noo—awa' wi' you, while I gie this Steenie a fleg in his ear! Ooh, aye—he'll get one, never fear. But, see you— come and see me before you go, Johnnie. I want to see you about ae thing or twa."

John bowed, and left them there.

He hurried out of Whitehall Palace, his heart singing— even though behind it there was the ache of lacerated pride and frustrated vengeance. He was going home. For good.

He wished that he could go right away, now, leave every-thing—in case James might change his mind. But George Villiers would work on the King *not* to change his mind, that could be relied on. He would want him away.

He went out into the London streets to walk again, tiredness forgotten, so very different from walking in the night.

James did not change his mind. He sent for John two evenings later, with the court moving next day to Hampton Court where the wedding was to take place, for rehearsals, decorations and the like. John found him in his bed, alone.

"Aye, weel, Johnnie—there you are," he greeted amiably. "You'll be off the morn, I've nae doubt—since you'll no' be joining us at Hampton, I'm thinking. Come, sit by me. You'll hae a cup o' wine?"

Clearing the usual litter of papers on the untidy bed, John sat, but warily.

"You're a thrawn, difficult crittur, Johnnie—you aye have been. But honest enough, I jalouse. I'll miss you, mind."

"Thank you, Sire."

"Aye. Noo—as to your Meg Hamilton. What do you aim to dae about her?"

John shook his head. "I, I do not know. Yet. I have not had time to fully consider it. But—my marriage to her is finished, that is sure. A divorce will be . . ."

"A divorce will *not* be!" the King interrupted flatly. "Nae divorce."

"But, Sire . . ."

"But naething! Nae divorce. I'll no' permit it. And dinna glower at me that way, Johnnie Stewart—or you'll be glowering at a cell door! Mind it." The monarch wagged a finger at him, but relaxed his severe expression. "Och, man—d'you no' see? You couldna sue for divorce without bringing in my Steenie. And that's no' to be considered. I've great plans for Steenie—for the guid o' this realm."

"I would not have considered that probable, Sire."

"You wouldna, would you no'? Which just goes to show how little you ken, my mannie. Steenie is the main rock on which I will wreck the Howards and a' their like. He may not aye be wiselike—but rocks dinna need to be, eh? To wreck ill craft!" James chuckled. "But, mind, he's no' aye foolish—any mair than you are! There's mair than folly behind yon bonnie face—there's the ability to survive, for ae thing! Ooh, aye—and that's a right precious commodity in statecraft, see you. There's no' that many have it. *You*, now—I wouldna just say that you have it."

"If I had to become like *him* to survive, then I do not think that I would wish it!"

"So—hoity-toity again! There you are, then—you'll never mak a statesman nor yet a courtier even, that's plain. But Steenie will. Given time. Once he's safe wed, I aim to send him to Spain, wi' Charlie, to tie up this Spanish match. Aye and contrive a treaty o' mutual aid wi' the Spanishers. That'll keep thae Frenchies looking ower their shoulders, to our greater comfort. The same way we in Scotland used the Auld Alliance wi' France hersel', to keep these English on their taes, eh? The same ploy. And right necessar. So—there's to be nae scandal aboot Steenie, before he's wed, or after. His Maist Catholic Majesty o' Spain doesna like scandal. Nor yet divorce."

John said nothing.

"I told you—tak the glower off your face, man. And dinna think that once you're safe back in Scotland you can jouk me ower divorce, behind my back, mind. You were wed in England, by an English bishop, and any divorce would hae to be contrived here. And *I'm* head o' the Church o' England! There'll be nae scandal." He paused. "What do you aim to do aboot your Meg, then? I dinna want her taken awa to Scotland. No' at this present, anyways."

"On *that* you need have no fears, Sire!"

"Is that so! I want her here, meantime. She's doing fine wi' that Manners lassie—who's a handfu', they tell me. A right strange bairn. But wi' a mint o' siller—mair than any mint o' mine! But she likes your Meg, who can handle her. Which is mair than yon woman I've had to make Countess o' Buckingham can dae! And, when Steenie goes to Spain, she's going to need handling. For she'll be Duchess o' Buckingham and it's fell important that she acts the part."

"*Duchess*, Sire . . . ?"

"Aye, Duchess. I'm going to mak Steenie a duke. To gie him the necessary authority to contrive this Spanish treaty. And to keep Charlie frae making a fool o' himsel'."

"Your Majesty knows best. But I would wonder that my wife is considered to be so good an influence on this future duchess. When she had been bedding with the bridegroom!"

"Och, weel—I hae a hold on your Meg noo, see you. I can see that she does as she's told. On Steenie likewise. Ae guid thing to come oot o' a' this. Hech, hech—there's aye guid in maist situations."

John gazed at his prince. "I see that Your Majesty has all worked out!"

"That's right, laddie. You canna rule twa kingdoms without using the wits the guid God gave you. Noo— enough o' this. On the matter o' Dumbarton you'll bring me the siller frae my rents and dues twice every year—bring it yoursel'. And if Johnnie Mar or his kin speir any questions at you, refer them to my royal self! Aye, and you'll keep an eye on the paper-making, forby. Thae Germans and Hollanders are a' right, but they need to be minded that they're no' on their ain! You'll see that the cargoes keep coming. And each half-year when you bring the siller frae Dumbarton, we'll decide on prices. Will Alexander will deal wi' Cockayne and the merchants at this end. Oh, aye—and there's another bit aboot Dumbarton. It's no' just best nor suitable that *you* should decide each time what you're going to deduct frae your collections for costs and expenses and the like. You might, by mischance, defraud yoursel', eh? Or me! So, I've decided on a better arrange. You'll get a pension each year—frae the Scots Treasury, mind. Paid on my express commands. That'll keep them off your back, see you, and nae argie-bargie. Eighteen hundred merks will dae you fine. You'll manage Dumbarton on that, easy—and what you dinna use you can put in your ain pouch! You have it—1,800 merks? Right generous. Aye, and you can continue to ca' yoursel' one o' my gentlemen— an *Extra* Gentleman o' the Bedchamber. That'll aye gie you entry here. How's that, Johnnie Stewart?"

John took a deep breath. "I, I do not know what to say, Sire! You leave me . . . without words."

"Aye, weel—when you dinna ken what to say, it's aye best to say naething! So—off wi' you, and gie a man some peace in his bed!"

"Yes, Sire." John rose and backed out, to be halted at the door.

"A guid journey, lad. And dinna let yoursel' fret ower much. Life's for living, mind, no' for aye fretting. And you're a right fretter! Guidnight to you!"

19

John Stewart did something which he had never done in his life before—he avoided Methven and Mary Gray. Coming from the south, he crossed Earn at Ford o' Gask and turned westwards instead of north-east, directly for Dalpatrick— and felt guilty as he did so. It was already evening; and if he had gone home first he certainly would not have got over to Dalpatrick that night. He had ridden up from London all the way at almost break-neck speed, so eager was he to convey his tidings. He was not going to waste almost another day, now.

He reached Dalpatrick, to be told that the mistress was out, that she often went walking along the riverside of a summer evening. Would Sir John come in and wait? He said no, he would go seek her. Did she usually go upstream or down? Down, he was informed—she liked to visit the chapel. Nodding, he left his horse hitched, and, stiff as he was from long riding, strode off for the bank of the Earn. The chapel could only be that of Innerpeffray, where they had twice foregathered. Let this be a more positive occasion than either of those.

It was peaceful by the waterside, with the last of the day's sand-martins darting, the first of the dusk's bats flitting and the mallards quacking sleepily from the backwaters. As he walked, the man felt something of the evening's calm touch him, not exactly settle on him, too much at stake for that; but at least the tip of peace's wing brushed him as he went to temper the agitation he had lived with for so long, temper but not banish.

It was over a mile to the chapel, with the sluggish Pow Burn to cross on water-worn stepping-stones. With the gloaming settling on the land and the shadows welling out of all the corries and hollows of the hills, and still no sign of

Janet, he began to wonder whether perhaps he was on the wrong track and that she had turned upstream this night, not down. He would go as far as the chapel itself before retracing his steps.

At the graveyard, the dusk deepened by the dark yews, amongst the moss-grown stones he still saw no sign of her, and was making doubtfully for the grey building where the bats made the congregation when, out of a corner of his eye he thought that he glimpsed movement amongst the tombstones. Was he mistaken, a trick of the half-light? There was no further stirring. But he turned in that direction.

"Janet—is it you?" he called, but quietly, out of some constraint.

He distinctly heard a gasp.

"Janet—are you there? It is me—John."

"John! John!" From behind one of the tombstones she came hastening, part-laughing, part-sobbing, arms out. "You . . . ? Is it truly you? John? John Stewart? I feared . . ."

He ran to her. "None other!" he cried, and caught her, picked her up and held her high, burying his face between her breasts, there to mumble and pant incoherencies.

"My dear, my very dear!" she whispered into his hair. "I was thinking of you, aching for you . . ."

For long moments they held each other, inadequate words dispensed with, patting, stroking, while time at least stood still.

At length, breathless, they moved apart sufficiently to look at each other—but still to hold hands as though they could not risk loss of contact.

"John—what . . . ? How is it . . . ? Where have you come from? It is not two months . . ." Janet wondered.

"I have come home. Left London. For good. I am back. For good. Home, lass!"

"Home? You mean . . . ?"

"Yes. Come back to Scotland. To Strathearn. To *you*, my heart!"

"But . . . ?" She stared at him, emotions chasing each other across her face. "John—I do not understand. The King . . . ? Have you left him? His service?"

"Yes. Or, not wholly. But in the main, yes. I am still one

of his people—an *Extra* Gentleman. But here, in Scotland. I have left the court. Thank God!"

"Oh, my dear, my dearest! This is good, beyond words, beyond belief! And, and your wife?"

"She remains. In London. Janet—all is changed!"

Briefly and bitterly he told her of events since his last journey south.

Janet turned, loosening her hold on him, and began to walk away, slowly. "Where does that leave *us*, then?" she asked, unevenly.

Following, he took her arm. "Lass—it leaves us at least with a choice. Which we did not have before. We can do this—see each other, on occasion, secretly. Oftener than before. For the rest, keeping our distance. Or we can be bolder, braver, ourselves!"

"And that means . . ."

"You *know* what it would mean, my heart. Perhaps too much for you? It would mean caring not what others said and thought. Taking our lives into our own hands, at last! Living together as man and wife, in the sight of God if not of others. Loving each other, openly, and letting the world judge as it will . . . !"

"But *would* it be man and wife in the sight of God, John? You took vows before God, at your marriage—as did I. I have been released from mine, by death. You have not."

"In a court of the law, if a man is proved to have lied, on oath, to pervert justice, then judgment is set aside. Is God's justice so much less fair than man's? I was tricked into making those vows. Is God tricked also?"

"I do not know, John—I do not know. It is that which troubles me—not the other, what folk would say."

"Then consider this. *I* have had time to consider it well, all the way up from London. If I had gained a divorce, you would have come to me? Wed me?"

"Yes—oh, yes."

"But divorce is only a device of man, is it not? Did God institute divorce?"

"No–o–o. But His Church did. . ."

"The Church, yes. But the Church will not give me a divorce, for no reasons of God. But because the head of the

Church of England, King James, does not want it. He made that entirely clear. Were it not for the King, then, I could win a divorce. He needs Buckingham, whom he is going to make duke, untouched by scandal. For this wedding. And for a mission to Spain after. What has this to do with God?"

"Nothing, no. You must hate the King? I think that I do."

"No. I do not hate James. He is a strange man and not easy to serve. And I mislike his fondness for Villiers. But he is the King and sees matters differently from us. And he has much that is good to him. He has shown me kindness, as well as—this. I do not know for sure, but I think that he was telling me something, in his last words when I left him, his farewell. He said that I was not to let myself fret. That I was a fretter—although I had never thought of myself as that. He said that life was for living, not fretting. And we had just been speaking of this, of no divorce possible. He was telling me something, that I feel sure. I have thought much on it—and believe that he was advising me to live as though I *was* divorced, as though I did have the divorce which he would not allow. It was a strange thing to say—and said strangely."

"Strange, yes." They were at the riverside again, now. "Does he know about me, John? Of your love for me?"

"That I cannot say. I have never told him. But he is ever well-informed. He has a great thirst for knowledge, of great matters and small. A deep thinker and an auld wife both, ever surprising folk by what he knows about them, even unimportant folk. I suppose that he could have questioned my father."

"If he knew, and said that . . . ? To live your own life and not to fret—you think that he could mean that we should . . . ?"

"It could be, lass. I do not wish to make overmuch of it. But, even if not so, we can make up our own minds, surely."

"What would the Duke say? And your mother?"

"I have no fears there. They have lived together as man and wife all these years, although unwed, my father married to others. They of all folk will understand. It is *your* father and mother who will make the trouble, I think."

"They would be outraged, yes."

"And that would distress you? Greatly? Sufficiently to . . . ?"

"Although living so near, I see little of them now. Since they forced me to marry, we have not been close. My father is an ailing man, become old and . . ."

"Janet—are you saying that their anger, then, this outrage, would not stop you? That you are prepared to consider it?"

"Where would we live, John? Not here, I think, at Dalpatrick. For that is something that my father *could* do, I fear. He could prevail on his brother to take Dalpatrick from me. To spite *you*!"

"No, no, lass—I never thought of Dalpatrick. Methven is mine—it has always been in my name. I would not ask you to share house with my mother—and Methven is her home. But it is a large property. There are other houses. One deep in the hills perhaps—Keilour? Where we need care for none. And remember that I am Governor of Dumbarton. There is a Governor's House in the castle. We could live some of the time there. None could trouble you in Dumbarton. Janet—say that you will consider it!"

"I *am* considering it, my dear. It is a big step for a woman to take. Give me time . . ."

Arm in arm they walked on along by the murmurous Earn in silence for a while, the evening turning to night around them; and every now and again he drew her round to kiss and be kissed. He had enough of wisdom not to press the matter of their future further at the moment. And they had no lack of other things to say to each other.

He carried her in his arms across the stepping-stones of the Pow Burn, at the run, laughing. He had not laughed like that for long.

When they came to the house, she led him in; and, having discovered that he had not eaten since mid-day, insisted that he must have a meal. So presently they sat down together in the candle-light—and realised that this was in fact the first time that they had ever dined in each other's company, further occasion for celebration.

Before they were finished, the hour was late. Reluctantly John noted the fact. "Time, and past time, that I was on my way," he said. "Loth as I am to leave you."

"Must you go? At this hour?" she asked. "It is a dozen miles to Methven. Near two hours' riding, in darkness. All will be abed. Your mother does not know that you are coming?"

"No. But if I do not go, your servants will know. And talk."

"They will talk anyway."

"You do not mind, Janet? If I stay here tonight?"

"I am saying that you should do so."

He reached for her hand and pressed it.

They sat for a while longer by the small birch-log fire that she had lit. Presently she rose.

"I will go see to a bed for you," she announced.

"Do not put yourself to trouble, this late. Anything will serve . . ."

She was gone some little time. When she returned, she was differently clad, in a long belted bed-robe, her hair hanging loose to her shoulders. He caught his breath at the sight of her.

"Janet—you are beautiful, beautiful beyond all telling!" he exclaimed. "You, you shatter me!"

She smiled and held out her hands towards him. "Douse that candle, John—and come."

Hand in hand they climbed the twisting turnpike stair to the second floor. There were three doors to the landing, but only one stood open, the soft glow of lamplight issuing. As they paused in the doorway, he saw that it was her own room—at least, her clothes lay strewn therein.

She did not release his hand, indeed her grip tightened. "Come," she said again.

His breath caught in his throat, as she led him in and closed the door behind them.

"Oh, lass, lass!" he got out, and only that.

She turned to face him, there beside the bed, eyes urgently searching his face. "You asked me to consider," she said, low-voiced but tense. "I have considered, John. Here is your answer."

Loosening the cord at her waist, her robe fell open. She was wholly unclothed beneath it, and of rich and promising loveliness.

He went to her. "Now praise be to God!" he cried—and that was worship and thanksgiving if ever a man offered it.